This is a product of fiction. Names, characters, places, stories and incidents are either the product of the author's imagination or, are used fictitiously. All statements, dialogue, descriptions, and information of any other kind contained herein are included for entertainment purposes only and should not be relied upon for accuracy of faith, belief, languages, or culture.

Dark World

By Ahmer Bashir

Aiden Deen and the Lost

Series

Dedicated to all who are ill and all who serve others, and all who tend to the ill and all who are good to those who serve, words do not suffice for your kind souls and gentle minds. Hold tight. Shine your light. God bless you.

Thank you to my best storytellers MB and NB. Keep the stories going: AMA, DMA, AAA, IMDA, MHA, MIH, SA, & TMB and all who are young and old.

It's been a long journey to cross this moor, with lots of cups of tea! Thank you to the jolly wisers who crossed my path: Lucy Christopher, Steven Voake, Melvin Burgess, Julia Green, Sara Bailey, Trish Cooke, Michael Lynch, Irene Lofthouse, Richard Smyth, Shazia Ashraf, Sophie Joelle, Debbie Coope, Halima Mayat and Jackanory, Marc Blake and Sarah Singleton
:)

Dark World

By Ahmer Bashir

**Aiden Deen and the Lost
Book One**

One immortal carried the seed.
Three immortals ensured it sewn.
Djinns and humans ensured he was learned.
Evil was re-born.

Realm of Exiles

Ya-Allah Al-Raheem An-Noowr, I messed up. I should have thrown the holy water… I was thinking I am going to melt its face, then use the blade to chop its head off. I opened the door. He looked like my English teacher... I know, I have been trained for this. Can't hesitate. I won't. It was so fast... It's eyes... astaghfirullah. Astaghfirullah. Astaghfirullah.

'How do you know which way is Makkah, considering you are not on Earth?' a voice echoed.

She came with the face of his mother, and how beautiful those round cheeks were if he could not see past her illusion. Her wrinkles were kind to her face. The high crown suited her dress. He had only ever seen the emerald dress floating at her feet. She was both similar and different to the duchess in how she carried herself.

Aiden straightened on the prayer mat. His room had been swapped for high walls with murals and décor from the Emerald's historical victories. He guessed he was in the East Wing. The lush carpet was turquoise, reminding him she was of two worlds, like him.

'I recite an intention that I face Kaaba, for Allah,' he replied.

'Very good.' She turned to stare at a painting of a divine throne, being contested by a human child and a djinn, but her senses were upon him. She was expecting him to read her.

Aiden was relieved he hadn't.

'We are born of fire, or we are born of clay. That's what this artist is expressing. It's an old saying from a time when djinns needed reminding.'

'Djinns still hijack humans,' he replied.

'We also disguise ourselves. We must. To protect. Fireborns yield to God's chosen,' she said.

It was spoken from wisdom and kindness.

Aiden's eyes heated. 'The infected, we cull.'

'Your existence, dear child, is impossible. Yet, there you kneel by the grace of God.'

She deserved compliments even if a scolding was coming. But she had pulled him into her space without any warning. 'I've… seen your face,' he said.

'Yes.' She walked gracefully, tapping the staff on the floor, whilst dragging her gaze upwards to a mural, where a beast was ravaging an immortal queen to save a human baby. The owner of Hibernation Pod 0092 seemed rather agile considering she spent most of her time inside it. Maybe it was true that she once purged an entire royal family to kill one Hellsborn.

'Aren't you worried? All Father says when she finds me she will trace everyone through my past,' said Aiden.

'This moment will be isolated,' she said.

'It's not safe,' he said, looking down at his hands.

'Do not be concerned. There will come a time when you are at your lowest, you will need this memory.' She paused to lower her head to a portrait of an old Jade queen.

11

She didn't bring him here to scold him.

'Are you my firemother?' he asked quickly.

If she was surprised, she hid it well. 'I am not the mother of your djinn father,' she said.

'Did you know him?' he asked, watching her aura for change. He was aware she could detect when he used djinn vision, his hazel eyes became brighter, though not as bright as a full djinn.

'You know I can't tell you.' She was shielding herself too well. He didn't know why he was dismayed. It would be dangerous if he knew.

'Can I still call you Great Mai?' he asked.

'Of course. We are related.'

'Why will I need this memory?' he asked.

She turned. 'At the right place, with the right words, I will help you.'

'In the dark world?' he asked.

'In another.'

'How will I find you?' he asked.

'I will come to you,' she said, walking.

She could phase into any world even though she was an exile. It was forbidden.

'Are you... that powerful?' he asked.

She stopped to touch an old, battered shield. 'We cannot defeat her with powers. Just knowledge,' she said.

'Why?' he asked.

'We used to think an Emerald Sister could turn the curse to our favour. This one was our downfall,' she said.

Aiden thought about it. 'Can she absorb powers?'

'She used our powers against us. She has a thousand-fold my might. We must kill her before she gains her ninth sight,' she said.

'Are we sure she has returned?' he asked.

Both hands clasped her staff, she was studying him. 'There are signs. But you know that, don't you?'

'The Hellsborn had a memory of a ceremony,' he admitted. 'Where he saw the face of an Emerald Sister, she was shaking with infection.'

'Wars between men are permitted until the horn sounds. Wars between djinn are permitted until the horn sounds. When wars cross over, Lightborns are swift and precise. This is what this Hellsborn wants, an opportunity to inflict upon the angels, her hatred for all Creation. When I saw that memory in you, it gave me great horror. A sister willingly succumbed to this abomination. And humans were present,' she said, hotly.

'It was too brief,' he said, quietly.

'Tell me what you know about this creature,' she said.

'Novem exercitum daemoniorum re-learns the powers of her ancient self until she is a devourer of not only Earth, but all worlds,' he said. 'She ate immortals.'

'The first she devoured was Ereshkigal, did you read about Ereshkigal?'

'The Hell-keeper entrusted with her imprisonment,' he recalled.

'That's right. On taking her first host, she tricked the Spellmasters to let her dine with them.'

He pictured the old calligraphy. 'She drank their blood and seized their powers' he recited.

'When her infection spread to other cities, she charmed Rozinians into thinking she was trying to help them. They lowered their shields and let her walk right into their protected ground.'

Aiden nodded. 'That's why they call her the Vinx... the friendly helper.'

'You see this staff? The star these emeralds originate from was far greater than Earth's solar system. It takes but a few words, and each emerald can wield its intensity. Yet she becomes impervious. The Vinx can grow until her hair touches the vacuum of space and her fists pummel into a planet's core. A thousand of these will not suffice to bind her. She is the Ultimate Demon.' Her voice resonated, waking the art creatures to turn their glares upon him.

He inhaled quickly to stifle the sob, 'I am sorry. I failed.'

She sighed. 'Oh Child. Let that be the last we hear you apologising. We each weigh a nemesis to a rank we know, it's a guess at best.'

'I was careless, Great Mai,' he said, wiping tears with a hand.

'Close your eyes,' she commanded.

He felt her body lower to kneel beside him. She took his hand into her long soft fingers. 'Asmodeus used to be a gentle king. You killed his corruption. A vile entity has no place in the living world.'

'I couldn't control it… raiding my mind,' he said.

'Asmodeus had old knowledge. He was before even my time' she said.

'It wanted…' he whispered, 'I could have blocked it but…'

'You didn't.'

Aiden was surprised she was calm. 'It saw Archdjinn's nightmare. Through me.'

'You will have many encounters with Hellsborn. Always show your human self, never the slayer,' she said.

'It said things,' he whispered.

'We heard,' she said.

Aiden remembered the surprise and disappointment in their eyes and the silence that followed. 'They shouldn't know,' he stammered.

'What do we say about a Hellsborn trapped?' she asked.

'A demon does what a demon does,' he replied.

'Did you know my uncle was also a protégé of the Archdjinn?' she asked.

'No,' he said.

'Yes. My dai helped the Vatican. Exorcism. Upon his arrival, demons would capitulate. That was until he cornered a Child-eater in Bosnia. My uncle could not recall nine days of his encounter with Asmodeus, during which thousands were bled dry in Foča. You recovered in a hundred seconds. Then you killed it. I would say that was a good recovery.'

'But now he knows,' whispered Aiden.

'What have we prevented?'

'The Hellsborn could have tracked me here,' he said, scowling.

'And?'

'Hell would know our sanctuary,' he said, slowly.

'From today, you will not warp. We have given thyself the ability to stifle, so stifle!'

'Yes, Great Mai.'

'You will do as Eloyhin asks. Limit his need for recourse,' she said, less sternly.

'Yes, Great Mai.'

'Now then. It appears, you have an ability to keep secrets from us.' He felt her probe. She was careful to reach his heartbeat without giving him a shudder.

'I was going to tell you.' he said, swallowing the lump in his throat.

'When did you first sense it?' she asked, barely above a whisper.

'The night the Pixie Queen returned my ears,' he said.

'He is a rascal. Leading you into her forest. Of course, a pixie queen is going to teach a lesson. Never mind. Your ears look better on you,' she said.

'Yes they do,' said Aiden.

'What fanfare she brought into our halls. You were trembling.' She inhaled sharply, 'Your mind was replaying! Clever boy. We thought you were adjusting. This is when you learned to conceal. Do you hear it now?'

'In every beat of my heart,' he said.

'And how it beats. Tell me... how does it sound?'

'A horn seeking me,' he said.

'*How*... does it sound?' she asked again.

'Low at first, inside my neck. But then it fills my bones, and my heart feels like it will explode.'

'The Horn of God,' she whispered.

'I don't know.'

Her cold soft hand squeezed his. 'During the days of my early hibernation cycles, I learned the Eye of Ethyrus was created by a djinn who glimpsed the Horn of God for a mere second. How it changed him! He designed great things, magical weapons, pyramids, portals and places to hide. The Eye travels through the multiverse, but it sounds like it has found you.'

'I dream when I am awake,' he said, sadly.

'What do you see?'

'I don't know.'

'Describe it,' she commanded.

'Dirt is scalding to my feet... roots burning from Hellfire. Seven suns turn dark. Tardigrades wither and die,' he said, though words could never explain the stench.

'Your flame does not wilt,' she said. Then gasped, 'Allah have mercy. Does it not frighten you?'

'It used to.'

'You made peace with destiny.' She sounded pitiful.

He didn't bother to reply.

'Do you believe creation is coming to an end?' she asked.

That came from mischief.

'I saw Hellfire consume the Huon pine,' he said, quietly.

'Oh Child. You kept a lot from us.'

'I hid from you,' said Aiden.

'To hide from him?'

Aiden thought about it. 'To hide from her.'

He felt her twitch. Her hand tightened. The question crossed her mind, but she did not utter it. Instead, she laughed. 'Son of the Lost! He was right. I am glad I aligned. You are, indeed, a torchbearer.'

He hated that word. 'I am me.'

'When your powers reach hers, skin will not contain your fire. She will not contain hers,' she said.

'I am not alone,' he said.

'Into Hell you will go,' she said.

There was that word that Eloyhin denied. A world she left behind. No creatures survive to mind. All of their glorious past reduced to one tormenting syllable. 'Will there be angels?' he asked.

'Alas, we hide behind shields we did not create. Hellsborn outnumber all. Your task is impossible. Though my daughter and the Great Chainer have a deeper understanding.'

'I ask again, Great Mai... will there be angels?'

She snorted. 'Should we need the People of Light, yes.'

'What consequences would... meeting an angel have?' he said, carefully.

'If angels come in human skin, you may doubt. In their true form, that's something to behold. For a clayborn, eyes earn prophethood.'

'I will be blind.'

'Ears make a Messenger of God.'

'I will be deaf.'

'Do you wish all species to die?'

Aiden shrugged. 'If it is Allah's will, so be it. I am no one, but the life I have.'

'Oh Child. We think we learn, but one is never truly learned.'

'On this, I am,' he said, rising to his feet. He folded his prayer mat. 'Prophet Muhammad, may peace be upon him, is the Last Messenger of God. I am a Muslim.'

'Faith is the ultimate source of strength. But you have another. Fire. Don't forget, you are also a djinn.'

$$\frac{٣}{١٣}$$

It was the Beginning of The End. The crest of Delius sank below the horizon, leaving a green glow rising above the forest until it became purple. The crimson sun had also begun its descent, there would be daylight for a few hours more. The moons did not approve of his decision, hiding themselves behind clouds.

For the Exiles, the disappearance of their star marked the start of resting hours. Courtiers and housekeepers retired to their quarters. Oleena's Palace would fall silent. The lucky ones would sleep.

You would think killing a demon would allow you a night off. Or at least an hour to be yourself. Words from the Hellsborn had set things in motion. Elders closed all doors to their meeting. This did not sit well with the hoplite prince who was convinced he knew why Oleena's Hall had been sealed with magic. Aiden listened to his plan. He did not agree, but he uttered 'Okay.'

The cool breeze swirling down from the towers, lifted their hair and collars.

'Lord of the Light Flower and keeper of our sleeping queens, I ask that you bless this night for the feat that we must do,' whispered Prince Eloyhin, before lighting the candle. He shook the match. Then lifted the twirling flower and held it away from the balcony. The flower spun down to the bubbling brook.

Aiden didn't wait to see it get swept away.

His sandals slapped on stone as they climbed. He tried to keep his mind numb from all thoughts, even the errors she had made. He had failed to block Asmodeus. She had got that wrong. Hiding from her was his idea, but now it seemed spot on. She didn't trust him. Perhaps he shouldn't have told her. Could he save... No! No. She deserved to know.

The tall prince led him to where the palace greeted the great white tower with a grand colonnade of pillars. Stone warriors and queens invited him to take the bridge and walk among their chosen flowers, but long fingers yanked Aiden's collar and up he went again. Whispers seeped through the magic, Eloyhin ignored them. Or could not hear. His mind entirely focused on his plan.

It suddenly occurred to Aiden he had given permission for a wilful stepson to invade the most powerful djinn's mind.... surely that would make him angry. His sandals sank into the eleventh floor's emerald carpet. Eloyhin looked back at him with a grin, 'He's not going to be mad at you, you're my pledgee, remember?'

'This is insane,' he warned.

'Totally,' laughed Eloyhin.

Let the prince do what the prince does. Aiden followed him into the giant chamber and closed the door.

A long shadow stretched across the giant room as the red dwarf sank below a tower. The prince paced back and forth from a little boiling pot inside the fireplace. His comments did not help the beginning, nor the end of his reasoning. Time would nudge them through. Aiden laid out a prayer mat and recited the evening prayer.

Footsteps hurried below. The doors were unsealed. Whatever Elders had discussed would no doubt cause commotions on Earth. The hour was upon them. Three moons aligning. Treachery was assured.

Aiden folded the prayer mat. 'Is this going to work?' he whispered.

'You can change your mind,' said Eloyhin, watching the tarry concoction settle in the goblet. The rhythm of Eloyhin's heartbeat and the curl of his lip told him that was false. Only the outcome of this mischief could be controlled.

Minutes shrank to seconds as their frantic whispering altered the plan. When his neck tingled, Aiden knew the Archdjinn must have reached the top of the tower.

'Lie down,' urged Eloyhin. Aiden wanted assurances that words he had uttered after hearing the demon's curse would not break his family. Seven years he had carried this secret, it meant something.

The prince nodded.

Aiden lowered his head to the soft pillow and closed his eyes. He waited to be bound to the unconscionable will of a powerful being. It always started with laughter. Stone giants guarding humongous gates. Birds carried kings. Musicians played strings. Hoplite soldiers watched vigilantly to make sure no powerful mischief could disrupt the extravagance.

Archdjinn strode through that ancient courtyard where guests chatted or watched entertainers. Djinn Vision could not reach the top of the humongous pillars, for each one had lifts bringing cargo from orbiting ships. Over the humped landscape, bird-eating flowers occasionally snatched prey successfully. This was why birds gathered this way in a swarm ready to tear flesh off their faces. Yet it filled the djinn with heavenly warmth. Had this been the Archdjinn's home world?

They came to greet him, people in strange hats matching baggy pants, warriors wearing decorated armour on tribal coloured tunics, and powerful ladies in colourful dresses laden with planetary jewels. Their smiles hid despise. Aiden walked as Archdjinn walked. He talked as they talked. He drank that noxious mead, even danced with ladies and a mage to appease those tongues. The djinn who lived this memory clearly loved them. None of this mattered. Hell's evil would unfold.

Archdjinn laughed at the naughty antics of a guard, one of the first who would die.

He must not feel. This was not his memory.

Archdjinn had reached the vestibule leading to the emperor's court. Pillars decorated with fine artwork told tribal stories. The statues were smaller than those in the palace gardens, each with unique carved hieroglyphs.

'Eyodeen,' a whisper echoed. 'I am in your head… as you are in his.'

Aiden almost stopped breathing, 'How?' he whispered.

'You are the anomaly.'

Aiden whispered, 'He will know you were here. Please go.'

'We discussed this. Minutes before, remember? I plucked your brow and boiled it with an imp's eye. You gave me a lecture that good Muslims don't do spells. And your face filled with disdain as I drank it. We are bound for this night. I am watching my stepfather's nightmare through your mind.'

Okay. That sounded… plausible.

Cold rippled through his body, the stench of death invaded his lungs. Feet scraped gravel. Everyone was exhausted. They were on a mountain, looking across to another, where Nature's blessed perished to dust, as if they were meant to bear witness. The dread he felt was not his own. As the great djinn hurried to the top of a fortified wall, the warriors he passed hastened to boost their stockpile of weapons. He felt it, from all of them, it was stifling. Archdjinn could not ignore the sight of the valley filled with the litter of battles. They jolted when the dead bodies twitched.

Soldiers hacked them as swiftly as they could. There were too many. Archers got busy. And still they came, stronger than they were alive, growling for blood. Heroes wept. Fire bolts erupted from the Jades to give them time to retreat. They stripped their leathers to reinforce new defensive perimeters. They learned cold fire burned the bodies faster. It would not save them. The great djinn fought hard for every djinn, he and the survivors fled wearing nothing but blood-stained loin cloths. Losses would follow him to the city. The fateful gathering of queens. That friend of his. The sacrifice. Words from his stepfather would not be good to dwell upon. Some things, a prince did not need to see.

Aiden opened his eyes and sat up in bed.

Eloyhin was bent forward on his chair. His eyes slowly opened, filling with tears. It was his first time.

Trembling, Aiden stood up from the bed and put on his shoes. Strong hands pulled him into a hug, squeezing him as he whispered, 'Thank you.'

'For what?' he asked.

He was surprised by the kiss to his forehead.

23

'Come along, Half-kin,' said Eloyhin.

Aiden followed the prince to the stairs, where he sat down overlooking the first dawn of the day. The white sun would rise beyond the forest, seizing the sky from the moons. He'd never known the prince to cry. This was a good thing. This was exactly what he needed. A chance to let his real feelings surface.

'Are you okay?' he asked.

'I know who that was,' uttered the prince.

'Who?'

Eloyhin stood up. 'Stepfather's darkest secrets shed light on a puzzle I never knew I had. It was a generous thing you did for me, Pledgee. Don't you dare use your gift for anyone else.'

They ate breakfast. After breakfast, they drank Nineses. After Nineses, they ate morning tea, which consisted of caramel tarts, fresh berries, puff pastry and buffalo cream. After petting the saddled birds, they sat down for lunch with the duchess and the most respectful djinn alive.

The prince offered sandwiches to his stepfather. 'How refreshing it is to see we have all rested from a good night's sleep,' he said.

Archdjinn shot a glance.

Aiden kicked him under the table, 'That was careless,' he mimed.

'Eyodeen, someday I will do something about your lack of tease,' whispered Eloyhin.

Archdjinn departed with a visiting general. The duchess also got up to leave with her maid. Eloyhin's eyebrow lifted, which meant he was to hurry.

$$\frac{٤}{١٣}$$

It wasn't odd that the prince asked him to do something outlandishly crazy. Just silly of him to go along with it. He followed him to the third floor of the palace. This was the chamber of her Royal Kindness. Dancing swan candles that pixies had moulded from beeswax and flora added a musky tone to the sweet Darian trumpet flowers. Inside her bedroom, Aiden headed straight to the tiny chamber inside the bed's headrest. He lifted the key to a place he had no right to ever go in.

'Whatever the duchess is hiding, she is hiding for a reason. It's what mums do. Why don't you get that?' whispered Aiden.

Prince Eloyhin wasn't inside his own face. Who was he eavesdropping upon now?

Sighing, he placed the giant key with seven notches into his palm.

On the Western rooftop, Aiden waited. The palace staff were not meant to watch the duchess and the Archdjinn leave, but some of them spilled out onto the courtyard. To his relief, the elders didn't look up. This did not mean they didn't know he was there. He must keep his thoughts filled with trivial matters, like how this elegant giant daisy had managed to seed and grow at this altitude with so little water. Oh, how beautiful that six-winged bird!

The portal opened. The elders entered it one by one.

The portal disappeared.

He hurried for her study. The bed chamber was locked now, it was a good job they took it when they did. Aiden helped Eloyhin move the bookcase for the secret door. The prince put the key into the lock and twisted after he repeated the words he had heard from his mother. The smell of dank moss hit them.

Inside the secret passage with vine-covered walls, tiny white, green, and blue flowers glowed. There was enough light to show they were heading down to a great depth. The further they descended vines multiplied thickly. Aiden counted seventy-seven steps. He followed the prince along an underground stream and down another steep drop before they reached a cavern. From stone, great arches had been moulded to create inlets for storage. Was the cavern always here, he was not sure. Could it have grown from magic? That would explain the vines. The duchess could have tossed something into a closet, which could have turned into this… secret base. Science was variable when one applied magic.

Aiden followed the prince through the maze of tunnels and made a mental note that the prince seemed to know where he was going, which could only mean he had been here before.

'Did you know the first story my stepfather told me was about a beard,' said Eloyhin.

Aiden laughed. 'Why?'

'I was trying to stop their marriage, so I said I would never shave unless he left. He said, there was once a sartor who couldn't grow a beard. People made fun of him. It was a time when all djinns had beards, and this djinn only could mend what others had created. Sartor couldn't marry because no lady took him seriously, he couldn't have kids, so he looked after everyone else's. They taunted him too. A jade took pity and gave him a plant for looking after her sick daughter. The sartor smiled but prayed for death. A Lightborn struck him with a fever. When the sartor stopped breathing, no one realised. A customer found a body with a beard, so they mistook him for a relative. They threw his skinny body and a dead plant into a swamp and forgot. Years later, a tailor turned up at a royal ball and drove all the ladies mad. The dresses were spun from the finest silk and glistened in every dye. He sold all his collection each time he came.

'Archdjinn followed him back to the swamp and found a tree wrapped in hair. Hair trapped pollen, which grew flowers and attracted bugs that spun the hair into silk. The tailor told him he was tired. Archdjinn read a funeral prayer. The swamp dried up and no one ever saw the tailor or the tree again.'

'So let me guess what he isn't telling us, the Jade obviously cured the sartor but Jades being Jades, she didn't tell him, so his ignorance asked for death,' said Aiden.

'Ah but, was sartor truly dead? The Lightborn could have had a cruel sense of humour,' grinned Eloyhin.

'Angels don't have humour. They only deliver commands,' reminded Aiden.

'Very well. The Lightborn might not have fully deathed him, until the sartor was forced to get his life wishes, i.e., his beard on a lady,' said Eloyhin.

'That's disgusting,' said Aiden.

'Come on, it sounds like a curse,' laughed Eloyhin.

'Actually, yes. It does sound like he was cursed. At least a few times, not growing a beard, and then not being able to die,' admitted Aiden.

'We both know most Jades don't curse. Considering it was my new stepfather trying his best to win me over, it wouldn't surprise me if the Jade wasn't a Jade and the Lightborn wasn't a Lightborn,' shrugged Eloyhin.

'I love listening to his stories,' said Aiden.

They came to another set of steps, which led into a bigger cavern filled with scrolls and giant books. Green carpet held tables neatly with long chairs.

'This library is awesome,' said Aiden. 'Eliza is going to love this place!'

Eloyhin turned with surprise. 'You still believe your clayborns are going to join you here?'

'What's wrong with that?' said Aiden. 'This world is protected.'

'This realm is protected,' corrected Eloyhin. 'For humanity's sake. By divine decree. You can't save your loved ones by plucking them from Earth and dropping them here. No djinn can. Not even the Archdjinn. He has to seek permission from the Lightborns.'

It was strange that he never thought about it.

Aiden's heart sank.

Eloyhin's eyebrows lifted. 'You're meant to read us all!'

'I did,' said Aiden, frowning. 'I just thought you were hiding it from me.'

'Oh, we hide things. Just not that. Sorry,' said Eloyhin.

'Why did you bring me here?' asked Aiden.

'Grab a book. Any book,' said the prince.

Aiden walked to a bookcase recessed between pillars. His fingers passed through the books. He whispered a spell breaker to no avail.

'It's not any sanctum, Pledgee,' grinned the prince. 'Mother's knowledge is the envy of the Jades. Her magic unbroken. Those she trusts are meticulous. Stored here in Zasanctamerior's deepest library, there are things we could never imagine. These pillars are protected.'

'If the scrolls can't be touched, why did you bring me here?' asked Aiden.

'Listening to a scriber is another matter,' grinned Eloyhin. 'I know her code for this tiny box here.'

Aiden watched him key in a number.

A cylindrical mantle rose from the end of the table.

'In the years following the Chaining of the Fallen,' said a deep voice. The scribe's hologram was young, though he sounded old. 'Elijans worked tirelessly to round up the tainted. It was not enough.'

'Who are Elijans?' asked Aiden.

'The First Tribe,' said the prince.

Aiden sat down on a stone chair. The chair squeezed to his size, comforting his back. The prince sat on the chair beside him.

'Lightborns bound us to hibernation cycles. Knowledge of immortal freedoms were taken from us. Djinns were given a choice to have skin, like clayborns, or forever suffer with blight. We are no longer what we were, and we can never go back.'

'What's wrong with having a face?' asked Aiden.

'That whole section there has poems about the ferocious power of our original state. How energy mightier than a star coursed from our hearts into our palms. We are beings of smokeless fire, tamed with skin, unable to feel what we should feel, with that we have driven insane,' said the prince.

'Looked like your ancestors were having fun to me,' shrugged Aiden.

'You are a hundred Millennia off your mark. My stepfather's nightmare was long after the Fallen. Djinns took punishment. And we learned to celebrate,' said Eloyhin.

'Considering your stepfather chained the Fallen and there is nothing written about him hibernating, do you honestly think he's that old?' asked Aiden.

'There are two sides of me, Eyodeen. There is the before you and the after you. Before you, I would have laughed at the ludicrous suggestion. Then along you come, the half-breed we pined for. And anything about anything is a recurring disappointment,' said Eloyhin.

Aiden was sure there was a compliment in there. 'Can you press play?'

'Lightborns provided us with keys to the Corridors of Light. We jumped from galaxy to galaxy in a day. We hunted our tainted,' said the scribe. 'World to world, we found them, we bound them. Zabaaniya dragged them to the Punishment Realm. These angels appeared as scythers or powerful jailors,' said the scribe.

Aiden remembered the angel from the dream. 'Why were they scared? I mean, what is the big deal? We have free choice. Angels just do what they are commanded.'

Eloyhin rolled his eyes. 'Are we really related? Pay attention. This is Hulius Octavius, he was there when it happened. His testimony is the best we are ever going to get.'

'Why do you know his name?' asked Aiden.

Eloyhin ignored him.

'Curfews were imposed. Technologies… confiscated from people's homes. Fearing a recurrence of the Fallen, we forbade magic. This did not go well with younger immortals. They rebelled. We appeased them so they could benefit humankind. We sent them to Earths. On every Earth, our young created powerful thrones to rule as gods.'

'How many Earths are there?' asked Aiden, showing surprise.

'Now I know you're jesting. You've been reading the Encyclopaedia of Dark Blood. The many Earths are covered between books three to seven. They were on your bed. Hush now. Mother could zap in,' said Eloyhin. 'You want to explain why you are down here when she specifically told you not to go into her room?'

Aiden rolled his eyes. 'No. She barred you.'

The prince inhaled. 'We've got three hours to hear ten thousand years of supernatural cock ups.'

'During the birth of a Pegasus called Hephaestus, the Chainer of the Fallen received a Lightborn,' said the scribe. 'Archdjinn accepted a warning. Elijan Knights were dispatched upon the new empires to exact justice. Pharaohs were disrespectful. One we drowned. One we buried alive. One we erased. We chose a human to outrank us. Solomon, son of Bethsheba was crowned Supreme King over Djinn-kind. Our debt was fulfilled. Angels disappeared from our courts. In and out of Jerusalem, knights loyal to the divine code enforced his ruling, long after his death.'

'Did you bring me here to learn about King Solomon?' asked Aiden.

Wide green eyes turned on him. 'Are you even listening?'

'One such knight was Dryad,' said the scribe.

He'd heard that name. Aiden straightened in the chair.

'Dryad returned to the Old Universe. Lord of the White Star accepted a title from the Fiannehedrin to become Custodian Emperor of Djinnkind. We were not aware that Dryad had asked angels for permission to ascend on the Triple Moon. We are not clear when Dryad had become lonely and tired of immortality.' The scribe listened to something. The image flickered.

'Were they able to do that? Pause a recording?' asked Aiden.

'Ancients were able to harness stars, jump from galaxy to galaxy, do you think they honestly missed the invention of a smartphone?' Eloyhin said.

'There was a whole giant glossary on your mum's desk. I never got a chance to study it,' recalled Aiden.

'Remind me to hit you in the head with it,' grinned Eloyhin.

'During the birthing moon, seven Emerald Sisters witnessed a Lightborn confirm Dryad could ascend as soon as he named his successor,' continued the scribe. 'The ruby and emerald queens, and the Great Red Queen arrived in Keffi, to give their blessing. Emissary Soodian gathered the lords. Dryad asked them to approve his son, Princeps Civitatis Iyaad the Third, from the House of the Great Cygnus, Eighth Descendant from The Liberator, the right to his throne. Senators of the Fiannehedrin named a queen for Iyaad. Princess Shivus objected.'

'That must have been embarrassing,' whispered Aiden.

'Princess Shivus asked to be heard. It was revealed that, Iyaad had chosen another. Dryad and Iyaad retreated from the Fiannehedrin. Upon their return, the Lords objected. Dryad had the right to overrule the queens. He had the right to dismiss the Fiannehedrin. He had the right to give his blessing to his son's choice. Iyaad married Ilgra the Drooj, the ninth of nine daughters.'

'Nine is a Hellsborn power,' recalled Aiden.

'If they'd known that then,' said Eloyhin.

'Dryad, First Knight to Solomon, Seventh Blade on the Fallen, ascended knowing his son was happy. He did not see the emerald sister throw herself from the tower. We were not permitted an inquiry into her death. We asked the Jade Queen to investigate.'

'That's odd. Why would an emerald sister kill herself?' asked Aiden. 'Emerald sisters swear to dedicate their lives to others, they have no concept of self.'

'Precisely,' said Eloyhin.

'Nine suns had set when Taagrevus was discovered in the empress bedchamber,' said the scribe, sadly. 'If his eyes had not seen it, Custodian would not have believed it. Ilgra was moved into a secure chamber. Ilgra adorned ritual garments. On hearing her prayers, Custodian was remorseful.'

'Before you ask, he means Iyaad,' said Eloyhin.

Aiden leaned back, grinning.

'The lords petitioned for her absolution. Again, Taagrevus was found with Ilgra. Custodian summoned a court and asked Ilgra to make a choice. Ilgra mocked our custodian and her vile tongue dared anyone to dethrone her. We were not aware Ilgra was the ninth descendant from Flaviulyssa the Keffian and his clan of bandits. But we trust the Jade Queen. We are responsible.'

'How could they travel through space, but not do a background check?' asked Aiden.

'Hush,' urged the prince.

'Iyaad could not forget the day he walked in on Ilgra's treachery. Every word from Ilgra, sent him to wander the palace at night. Custodian took the death of Emerald sister as an omen of his own making. He headed for pilgrimage to the mountains, where the body of his father lay in a tomb. There he came upon an old djinn, Izazil, who needed assistance to free a serpent from a rock.'

'I haven't heard this before,' said Aiden.

'You've never been down here,' said Eloyhin.

'At first, they couldn't see it, it was camouflaged to the rock. The serpent became as white as snow, and its eyes as dark as the night. They had never seen one whose scales looked like prickly hair, nor one which had a jaw inside its jaw. It is noted by the guard Elshinaar, that Izazil extracted a venom then swallowed the serpent whole. A mage testified to Elshinaar's account that the Custodian wanted to stay. The mage was disturbed Elshinaar did not guide him away. Despite his magic, Custodian was not safe. Izazil split his mind with his tongue. Elshinaar and the mage could not reach the Custodian, their feet would not obey. They witnessed the Custodian kneel. Using an old Kish language, Izazil offered the serpent's poison. The mage took down the words and we relayed these to the Emerald Court. They translate that the snake was only one of its kind. Elshinaar did not relay this encounter to the hoplites. We found Taagrevus unconscious. Ilgra too. Iyaad had poisoned his wife's wine. Healers tried their best. We failed to notice

Custodian had drunk the rest of the wine. When our finest physicians tried to assess why Iyaad was convulsing, he bit them.'

Aiden's jaw dropped. 'The second outbreak.'

'Now do you get it?' asked the prince. 'This is the moment Hellsborn seeds began.'

'I should never have let you into your stepfather's mind,' said Aiden.

$$\frac{\Delta}{\mathsf{۱۳}}$$

Here comes the hour, when one may lay down his head and close his eyes and surrender to the Keepers of Sleep. And angels will gently lift his soul for the Alternate Place, where he will be shown what he missed. He hoped it was less than yesterday.

How wonderful it must be to not know what he knows. To only struggle to get to the car on time for school. Every hour in England was busy, from the moment you open your eyes to the moment your head touches the pillow. No one had time to see what might be preying upon them. They had no time for djinns.

Once, he tested what his family believed. Aroosa said djinns appear as smoke. Arif believed they could suck the soul from your body. Dad said djinns appeared as humans and you could not tell the difference. Mummyjaan replied, 'Like your sister,' to which everyone fell about laughing. Dad didn't say a word for the rest of that evening.

Aiden closed his eyes.

He must first relax. And drift through dreams of happier times.

The vendor placed the screwball on to the counter and plucked the cone from the stack. Aiden knew he would reach for the broken flake. He didn't mind. The vendor smiled when he told him how to swirl the raspberry syrup away from the chocolate. He was reaching for the 99 when the whispers reached him. He must not panic. He paid but left the vendor holding the cone. Mummyjaan was in danger. Weaving through shoppers, he wanted to reach her before it was too late.

The whispers found a way into their mouths. 'We know what you are. Abomination!'

This was powerful magic! He took Mummyjaan's warm soft hand to coax her through an opening into a department store filled with sweet perfumes. Shoppers turned. They matched his pace, cutting them off at the escalators. Surrounding him with empty eyes and echoing the same whisper. The perfume lady bent over the counter. He yelled for Mummyjaan to cover her ears.

'You are holding the hand of a dummy,' said the perfume lady.

And he was. Where was Mummyjaan? Then, Aiden remembered about mind talking. Mind-talkers changed dreams and controlled weak minds.

He whispered a spell-breaker. The mall twisted into a school classroom. A bully shouted into his face and spat in his eye. A fat fist jolted him awake.

The safety dream worked!

Aiden lay breathing in the cool air wafting from a palace vent. Marble reflected the three suns so well the tower almost disappeared. When David brought him for the first time, he had been holding a lollipop. He spent the entire day captivated by the giants who bent down to peer into his eyes. He was five when he sat on a bird for the first time, the Archdjinn carried him so high that he had to breathe through a mask attached to a saddle. He was seven when toads rained from the sky. A golden toad bit him. A guard carried him to the tower, where the duchess bathed his hand and made him drink something foul, whilst seated in the Archdjinn's chair. He never expected anyone from the Monster World to say he was family. She told him this was the only room he could talk to her about anything, which was odd, since she did ninety-nine point five per cent of the talking, without really explaining anything. He wondered why she cried. If the walls were shielded, why didn't she tell him what bothered her?

Boy-o-boy the things you store in your mind. Are human brains as cluttered as yours? Tell me, what do you listen to from your clayborn kin? Do they regurgitate your tedious charm over boring pleasantries, or do they dream of arousing sexual conquests to escape their ignorant lives?

Aiden scowled. 'My family are off limits to you if you are going to be nasty.'

Oh, come on, should I not be curious about my half-brother of my half-brother?

Aiden smiled. 'He is my full brother, 100 percent biological brother.'

Technically, you are only half human. We mask this out of pity and to protect our realm. At any given moment, mistakes could happen. I wonder what your family would think of you if they found out.

Aiden sighed. 'You still haven't told me who you recognised.'

I counted six seconds where your mind was vulnerable in your sleep.

'Only six?' asked Aiden.

Takes one to end a life. You do realise, you are outside his tower? Not inside his shield.

'The magic here is the strongest,' said Aiden.

Hah! Don't deceive yourself. You miss your clayborns. Betrayal, I sense. You know we drop you back at the exact second you left.

'Did you have to ruin my sleep?' yawned Aiden.

Mother wove that hammock before your great-grandmother was an egg. How you pine for that old rot, I have no idea. I should burn it to spite you.

Aiden grinned. 'You're never going to tell me, are you?'

Listen. I know what the meeting was about. Asmodeus. The Child-Eater's rant has thrown everyone. The Old Goat's friends are scared. I will be on Earth by the end of the week. You need to tell Mother you want out.

Aiden sat up, causing the hammock to sway. 'Why?'
No lips. Mind-talk.

I thought you said it was an empty threat, he said in his mind.

Silence.

'Wayne?'

The Jerusalem problem just invaded Windsor Castle.
Aiden frowned. How?

We know we killed him.

I stabbed its heart. Aiden remembered the crunch sound of the bones breaking.

He didn't die. He crawled to the roof and jumped by the pool.

Where you stabbed it again. It tried to reach the road. I stabbed its neck and pulled it back to the pool.

We completely severed his neck and drove your stake deep into the shell protecting his vile heart. He turned to ash. So how has his contagion spread?

Either there is deliberate contamination… or there's a hive?

Alas. If I had a minute more… Mother felt my presence. I was thrown into a memory of me drowning. Next I was on a horse to come hunting. This spell of hers I can't unravel. She wants me out of the way until they suck you into the Unsuckable. Old Goat has swayed the Unswayable. I can't reason with Mother. You will tell her, no.

'Am I hearing this correctly?' said Aiden, grinning. 'A son of Kronos asking for help?'

Don't get giddy.

'Gosh Prince Eloyhin. You're rattled.'

I am not rattled, Eyodeen. I am a god.

Aiden smiled. 'You care what happens to me.'

As much as I care about boots.

'I remember a hug. Tightly squeezed. You saw something in your stepfather's nightmare that showed you're a dick at the best of times,' said Aiden.

That must be it. I am a dick. The light of the torchbearer is truly a gift.

'Come on Wayne, who did you recognise?' asked Aiden.

I asked first.

'What do you expect me to tell her?' asked Aiden.

Send someone else.

'Has it occurred to you that if they think I'm ready, I must be ready?' said Aiden.

Stupid is a rank reserved for a human. You are only half.

'I'm ready for another mission,' said Aiden.

I recall you once begged me to rescue you.

'I was seven years old,' he said, rolling his eyes.

Djinns are born ready. Time kindles fire. With me, you rage.

'Yes. We do. So, tell me who you recognised… Brother,' said Aiden.

I would not! For any given temptation laden with jewels and precious metals give a second thought to leaving a halfkin in the jaws of the She-Devil-Queen.

'Why, thank you,' laughed Aiden.

Abaddon is locked on the world he infected. It took all our knights and best magic to seal him there.

'You know I could easily probe your mind,' he said.

Confident, are we?

'Yes,' said Aiden.

Even if you are what they say you become, I can purge your mind until all that is left is an eternity of having someone else wipe your ass.

'We're bonded, remember? By heart and fire. For eternity,' said Aiden.

Then listen: From his prison world, Abaddon destroyed another and sent demons to a Messenger of God. And yet, he is only a mite of what she'll become.

Aiden leapt off the hammock. And straightened under the three suns' heat. From this height, he could see servants doing chores on all levels of the royal garden. The duchess stopped feeding her horse to ask something of the master of arms.

It was foolish to think anyone could hide their minds from immortals. Aiden hurried down the mountain, towards the scent of peonies and a roar of the waterfall.

He sat down on the shiny rock plinth. And spoke softly, 'Prophet Solomon, peace be upon him, pointed at Leybo drawing everyone's attention, Leybo froze. You think your stepdad panicked because Asmodeus ranted about that day. And that he could undo all that the hoplites have done to keep Earth safe. Except the Hellsborn was wrong. Ilgra the Drooj wasn't even infected when this happened and Flaviulyssa the Fallen's pet, was already in Hell.'

Just because we haven't figured it out, doesn't mean there is nothing there.

'You need to give your stepdad a break,' said Aiden, scowling.

The prince laughed.

Let us just say, Archdjinn has never made any mistakes. And we are in our prime to take her on. Can we save the billions consuming Earth from a Hellsborn infestation? Earth... will be devoured. No sanctuary there. Even if the people of light came to our aid, this realm, she will tear with her claws. No sanctuary here.

The scent of the wild tipsy tuberose filled his nostrils. The prince must have reached the other end of the forest.

Were you born to shoulder dreams or poke matters we can never finish? There's a world out there we can hide. You and me. And his key.

Aiden was sure this was another test. 'I can't. Everyone will die.'

So what?

'I am born from mischief. I live for the fulfilment of good,' cited Aiden.

Like a muppet.

'My gifts remind me I'm not a whole human. I'm not anything,' said Aiden carefully.

She'll smell your need for pity before your feet touch the ground.

'Maybe.'

She'll have you drinking your kin before you register the size of her fangs.

'I am my fire. I see my fire when I close my eyes and the air is calm and stills my heart,' said Aiden.

You shouldn't need to close your eyes to feel your flame, you dimwit.

Aiden shrugged. 'That's how I see mine.'

Finally! Doesn't this tell you, you're not ready?

'Your parents say I'm just different.'

I am trying to save you. Just because they say you are a saviour doesn't mean you have to be. Let a warrior take his mission.

'The mural warns that no djinn or clayborn. That's why they made me,' said Aiden.

Fine. We'll step in when they fail.

'She's a higher demon.'

The prince sighed. Bind to me.

Aiden allowed his senses to merge with Eloyhin. The hunters had crossed the valley to reach Thunder Hill. The sight of the broken-antlers and bloodied spirit deer filled him with sadness.

Eloyhin pulled away from the hunters to sit down by a tree. From here, he could keep an eye on the hunters and the deer.

'I can't unsee that nightmare,' said Eloyhin.

'I did warn you,' said Aiden.

'Why you? Why is it only you who can tap into my stepfather's nightmares?' asked Eloyhin.

'You're a son of Kronos, you tell me?' he shrugged.

'My fault for not staying out of your head,' said Eloyhin.

'Yes.'

Eloyhin ran a hand through his golden locks. 'I wish to God the Old Goat had never clapped eyes on the human king descending from Heaven on a gold chariot pulled by a flying fat four-legged horse with a horn. No illustration in the library does justice for that dreadful sight. How any human could ever be given title above djinns beats me. Fortunately, he turned his attention. And we saw the blessings on that ancient world… and it was glorious.'

'You have a strange interpretation of your ancestors' mistakes,' said Aiden.

'Tut tut. Our ancestors,' said Prince Eloyhin, his eyes returning from the deer. 'Even if you deny the djinn-blood pumping through your clayborn heart, those families were the founders of every bloodline, from pharaohs to the King of England. Includes your Akbar ancestors. Nine hundred royal clans in all their rapturous splendour assembled to witness a divine king bless a new emperor.'

'It haunts the Archdjinn.'

'My stepfather's mind replays what he missed. I saw tonnes of joy. Sure, everyone perished. His dilemma, not yours. So, tell Old Goat to go shit on another mountain,' said Eloyhin.

One of the hunters turned his head.

How could anyone not respect the All Father? Aiden felt discomfort. He unhooked his senses. He almost marched away from the waterfall, but then sat down on a rock and returned to Eloyhin.

Aiden folded his arms. The biting of a lip could not melt his scowl.

'You know I have good reason,' said Wayne.

'Do I?'

'Think about it. King Solomon pointed to Leybo. Leybo's leathers were not half as shiny as those around him. How that tiny clayborn finger condemned us all.'

'First of all, he was a prophet so have some respect. If not because you are a deluded spoilt brat, then for me. Second, I don't think you are that naive to be emotional about a human pointing to your stepdad's friend. You're hiding something,' said Aiden.

'Are you kidding? General Leybo is the reason we are alive! There would be no Earth and no sanctuary of Jades if Leybo hadn't stopped the Second Great Calamity. He saw people gasp. We saw Leybo's confusion through the Old Goat's eyes. We felt their blood turn cold. The fact that he was watching Leybo, is guilt as clear as day. Leybo's eyes wandered the entire day before the penny dropped. But my stepfather... had seen everything before. He would have known what that tiny finger meant. Did he warn anyone that hell was going to unfold?'

'Wayne, would it have made any difference?' he asked, frowning.

'We shall never know,' said Eloyhin, red-faced.

'Why are we doing this?' groaned Aiden. 'I was asleep. You could have let me have a few hours before dumping your gloom.'

'You're the prophecy. The past is your valuable lesson,' said Eloyhin.

'I haven't made my mind up about anything,' said Aiden.

Eloyhin straightened from the tree, 'Is that so?'

'Yes. All this about the calamity, is just a distraction from me guessing who you saw. You know what, don't tell me. I'll just wait for the next time your stepdad conks out,' said Aiden.

'Shall I punch you in the face?' replied Eloyhin.

'There's never a good reason to be rude,' he replied.

Aiden returned to his body and made his way back to the courtyard, where a table of refreshments had been prepared for tribal leaders.

$$\frac{\text{٦}}{\text{١٣}}$$

Eloyhin was connected to his mind when the white sun was setting, and the royal cocks crowed. Dumplings were served delightfully spongy in a goose stew. He ate with manners to denote appreciation, slurping the garnish slowly, breaking the dumplings into small bites and then spooning the stew quickly. The Archdjinn departed from the table first. Aiden was careful to ignore the prince. The gentle prayer given to the buck in its final moment was deeply stirring. He felt its heart shudder.

'I take it our chef replicated the meal from your first compliment quite successfully?' asked the duchess.

Aiden lifted his head, to see the elegant lady pouring herself a glass of wine. No amount of ageing could ever dim her beauty. He wiped the tears rolling from his eyes. 'Yes Mal,' he said, forcing a smile.

'My questions may come as a surprise since we had our talk. I made you a promise. I gave you teachers, none more important than those from the Scimitaff of Elders. Tell me what you learned from Imam Shafi,' she asked.

'Gölgeden, Tanrı'nın Meşalesi taşıyıcısı cehennem kraliçesini öldürmeli,' replied Aiden softly. He reached for a glass of water.

'Spare me your recitations, what did you learn?' asked the duchess.

Aiden drank it quickly and put down the glass. 'After each host is killed, her next host will be stronger. I must slay the vinx without being discovered.'

'It fills me with dread that I cannot protect you with magic,' said the duchess, sadly.

'I know,' he said.

'Do what you must to survive her ninth. She must not seize your power. If she takes ours, not even Gog Magogs are safe,' whispered the duchess.

'I will not feel,' he said.

'No face is true, no words she cannot feed. Trust no one.'

'Not even Wayne?' he asked.

'No friend. No kin. Not even me,' she said, fiercely.

'My mission is my own,' he said, carefully.

'Very good. Tell me, what did you learn from the Rabbi?' said the duchess.

'Everyone and everything become her weapon. And so, it must be mine,' replied Aiden, carefully.

'Are you satisfied with the family you have here in Zasanctemerior?' she asked, putting down her glass.

Aiden straightened. 'Yes, Mai.'

'No. Your conscience is happy with all you have there, and all you have here. But your subconscious mind is connected to djinnkind, linking with powers without recollection. It thirsts if it is not fed. Your powers have been surging at night, to fill this hole in your soul. It has wedged a door into the Archdjinn's dreams, keeping the Keepers of Sleep in disarray.'

Aiden leaned back with shock. 'I am sorry, Mai,' he said, hoarsely.

She sighed. 'Lucky for us, it did no harm. The water you drank contained our incantations. I have done what I can to keep you safe. Eventually, she will unravel all we have done.'

'Eloyhin said I am not ready,' he said.

'Eloyhin does not know what we know,' she said.

'Yes Mai.'

'Of course, you want to know your father's name. It is imperative that the vinx does not. She would use it.'

'I understand,' he said, masking disappointment.

'Be patient,' she said, her eyes glistening. 'I will tell you myself when this is over.'

'Yes Mai.'

'We are joined from heart,' she said.

'We are fire from fire, we are blood of blood,' he replied.

'That is our truth,' she said. 'When you reach the Elders, do not venture further than the stones. Giants will not take kindly to your trespassing. The stones are protected by Lightborn laws, no magic can overturn.'

'Yes Mai,' he said.

'Eat your cake,' she said softly. 'Etienne will bring you a coat.'

'Yes, Mai.'

$$\frac{\text{٧}}{\text{١٣}}$$

The duchess withdrew to hold a meeting with tribal leaders. Aiden accepted the coat given to him by the royal usher, just in time for the landing.

Giant claws tore up the courtyard's cobbles. Missing pink feathers confirmed it was the bird he had saved from a predator. Flythin's four wings flapped quickly as she came in to land a second time. Beady eyes acknowledged him.

'Come along,' said the Archdjinn, climbing onto a saddle.

Flythin soared over the valley where the Five Forests merged. Delia, the green sun, was turning purple when the carved rock floating from a mountain came into view. On landing on Angel's Wing, Flythin squawked and tossed them off.

Unhurt, Aiden turned to smile for the bird. Then followed the Archdjinn into the territory of the protected. From hidden homes inside the trunks of the Grandfather Elders, long heads appeared. Then tiny spears. Of course, imps were troubled by their arrival. Slanted eyes glowed, but they weren't red. When eyes turn red, he should worry.

Everyone should worry, whispered Eloyhin.

Aiden stopped. Underneath his feet, he felt the Elders opening their capillaries to give nourishment to tiny arthropods and fungi.

Elders give sanctuary to friend and foe.

It was comforting to know he wanted to keep watch over him. But this was an important mission. What could he do if things went pear-shaped?

Why do you dishonour fruit with failure?

'Get out of my head,' he whispered.

I can't believe you told her you're ready.

Aiden stopped again. 'It was the truth,' he whispered.

Are you afraid?

'No.'

You should.

'No, I shouldn't. Because I figured it out. You said you knew who that was, you were crying but that joy, you could not hide. You pulled away, ever so gradually, and turned to hide something that you suddenly realised. You were afraid. The person you recognised has something to do with my father, doesn't it?'

The connection severed.

Aiden hoped he hadn't made a mistake.

Nearby, a jungle cat fought desperately to defend itself from a giant eagle, sending the kingfisher and macaws to flee their nests. Aiden hurried to catch up. As they reached the clearing, the abnormal sight was more weird than creepy. The Giants of Elfrynn sat on branches, spying on monkey-eating raptors.

Archdjinn headed for the centre of the clearing. Aiden remembered to stop on the green rock with intricate markings. Sweet scent from ninety thousand flowers was gifted by Old Beroe's mistress. It wasn't strong enough to smother the fermenting leaves and giant's poo, but it was comforting to know the spirit of the forest approved of his arrival into the ring of stones.

The great djinn's gold helmet dipped. It was the moment to pay respect to Deelya's last light.

Aiden offered the dusk prayer. A blue nightjar landed by his knees and hopped across the ancient inscription, turning its head regularly. 'Assalaam alaikum wa rahmatullah,' he said to each shoulder. He must heed the warning. 'I am my fire, as cold as ice… as still as rock,' he whispered.

Aiden closed his eyes until his neck was cold. A war owl's hoot drowned the green tail's song. The sky was deep red. With djinn-vision, he could see clearly through the darkened trees. Suddenly, the forest was filled by shrieks and squawks. Tiger imps, peri, thriae queens, bee eagles, chamrosh, squirrel birds and monkeys thundered past him for the valley depths. Branches cracked as giants leapt with speed.

The red sun was descending when the forest fell silent by three heavy thuds. The hunters remained hidden. An angry giant, who once threatened to eat Earth's mightiest army, sat down on the trunk of a fallen elder, unashamed of the carnage his tribe caused. He chewed on the raptor's beak, while it still writhed in his arms. His creased eyes warned he could stamp anyone to death just for speaking.

Archdjinn marched into the giant's inner circle. 'Good evening, Chief of the Ninth Nephilim, Great Gilliobad son of Great King Ichshibad.' All Father softened his voice, 'May the Season of the Beak Powder be kind to you this winter.'

'Have you come to do us a favour – and die?' growled the giant beside the chief.

Gilliobad chortled, a beak piece slipped from his teeth. Surprisingly, the raptor was not shaking any less than when it had a beak longer than his arm.

'Balathor. What I want is a moment with your chief,' said the All Father.

'Malachi. Is that a half-breed to save you? Should we all prostrate to the Hellsborn now?' sneered Balathor.

Aiden felt his stomach tighten. He'd called him by his old name.

'This half-breed… may be your salvation,' said All Father.

Gilliobad bellowed with laughter. Laughter came from the trees.

Archdjinn spoke kindly, but when Gilliobad swung both feet to the other side of the elder's trunk, all went quiet. They shook the ground, dropping from branches.

Aiden almost lifted a heel, then remembered to remain as taught. Watching as they circled him, dragging their blades, axes, and scythes. Words could never hurt him.

One spat.

Oh dear. Why did they always believe they could intimidate the chainer of the devil?

Archdjinn grew and grew and grew. His toe pinned a giant's head to the ground. Gilliobad was terrified that the toenail would poke into his eyeball.

What is the lesson? All Father whispered into his mind.

There's always someone bigger, he replied.

And?

Hold thy ground, he recalled.

He felt the warmth spread from his neck.

'Nearly time,' whispered David.

Magic sewn by the People of Light ensured whenever a human returned to Earth, memories of Zasanctemerior would delete themselves. He was not a whole human, so he remembered. That also gave him discomfort inside his stomach. Why would he leave Oleena's Palace for that? These snow-capped mountains with endless creatures... lots of friends.

'There was a time when you refused to come to Zasanctemerior,' whispered David.

Back then, the palace scared him. Pixies had stolen his clothes and shoes. Then they stole his ears. Werewolves and shape shifters followed him if he left holy ground. The mountains had too many shadows. Even the wondrous sky, with the ever turning of the three suns and the enchanting moons couldn't stop his panic attacks.

Archdjinn pushed him to be better. And he pushed back, by running to the Sacred Ground to find the door back to Earth. Archdjinn always found him there. One night, the immortal prince trapped him. His words lured him to the Pixie Queen, where he negotiated the return of his ears. Inside Oleena's Palace, he watched the three moons join with his new friend, then explored the tunnels all the way to Outcast City.

On every visit, djinn masters taught him something new. Some he didn't like, but he memorised spells for those who gave him their time. The duchess was known to all from her days of being a Jade Warrior, protecting Earth from the Insidious. She taught him how to hold back so an enemy would perceive him to be weak. Wayne's family were his family, and none could say it wasn't so.

Archdjinn returned in his human form, walking briskly. He stopped outside the stones, then his eyes glazed white.

Aiden knew immediately he was inside a shield that no mind could penetrate.

'What is your opinion of Great Mai when you told her?' asked David.

'It was a split second. Her hands tightened on her staff when I asked her if she was sure. She knew that I knew about her nightmare, she tried to hide it,' said Aiden, carefully.

'Very unfortunate,' said David, sadly.

'Is it true?' asked Aiden, stepping off the magic stone. 'Did he confirm it?'

Archdjinn's eyes slid back to his normal green. 'Head back to Oleena's Palace. I have something I need to attend to,' he said.

Sighing, Aiden walked through the hills, keeping the chamrosh herd at a distance, to ensure he was well clear of the Naga, the serpent lady who almost ate him one time. Archdjinn didn't return that day.

$$\frac{\text{٨}}{\text{١٣}}$$

Aiden kneeled on the bloodstained grass to lay flowers where the buck died. He had half a mind to take the path to join the hunters, when he heard the tat peeler talking to Lwyin, the Alkonost. Her words sent him back down the mountain path. Before taking the bridge, he pulled the sammensprog grass from where the nut milk flowed. Then went straight to the high pavilion, where he could see all five valleys. He chewed on the sammensprog and watched the spirit deer lock horns. Treehorn was gentle today.

The long emerald dress floated over the old stone cobbles. The duchess was wearing the official colour. Guards marched down the steps to take their place to greet a djinn's return.

They bowed as he passed through the gates. Seven Scimitaff senators and their warriors followed sombrely up the long path.

Aiden hurried down.

The Archdjinn climbed the thirty-three steps without taking his eyes off the duchess. For every child djinn, telepathy was the first skill taught. It used to be funny plucking thoughts before adults spoke. Today, he only wanted to hear words wrapped in kindness for the duchess. She led them to a table in the courtyard. The servants had laid goblets and bottles of Dragon's Legend, it was the only drink Wayne had been forbidden. It was clear, the warriors were not staying. They sat down only as a courtesy.

Aiden listened to their news from around the world, they were talking with their mouths, but another conversation was happening with their minds.

'Wait! The pope is infected?' he asked suddenly. 'That means the apostolic successor kneels to Hellsborn. It's part of the prophecy, isn't it?'

The warrior with the green helmet straightened in alarm.

'Gentledjinn, my godchild is from your world,' said the duchess.

David filled his goblet. 'Very good. So… what did you not hear?'

Aiden's heart pounded. 'The soul of Ethyrus is coming.'

'What does it mean?' asked David.

'The Queen of Hell has taken form,' he replied, respectfully.

'So begins war,' said a warrior.

'War is the eternal shape shifter besting all gods, Lightbearer,' said the duchess, tiredly. 'She retreats after she has sewn and returns with fury. We must be captains of treachery or ruined by folly.'

Eloyhin was still in the mountains, three valleys North, with the best of Earth's defenders enjoying a hunt. 'War will spill on all worlds,' Eloyhin had warned.

'He learns like the child king Zimredda of Siduna. Are you ready kid?' asked David.

David had referenced the Phoenician city. Someday, he would work out why. What was a vinx even like up front? Asmodeus could have apprised anything from him. And he was just a lower Hellsborn.

David's eyebrows were waiting for an honest reply.

'Do I need to answer this now?' he asked.

The duchess laughed.

'On his final quest, the Torchbearer will uncover the answer to his inner peace,' said David.

Aiden stopped sipping the fiery drink. 'What answer?'

'Oh, I think you know,' said David. 'Do you remember, you were bothered by one answer I wouldn't give you.'

'I asked who my djinn father was?' he said.

'There you go,' smiled David. 'You are blessed with two fathers. One human. And one who will give you inner peace.'

Mai waited until he announced he was going to sleep, before despatching the servants. But he couldn't sleep. He took the path with the least creaking floorboards. And spent much of the night sat cross-legged on an old stool, gazing at parietal artwork in the hall below the cellars.

What did these Nephilim know? It was a wonder how they could let him face a higher demon knowing he knew the location of this realm. Shouldn't they have wiped that memory from his mind? Not that he was even scared, he was sure he would try his best to keep their secrets safe. But she was a world eater, that's what it said in the book. How could he be sure he could protect his mind from a world eater? He could back out. Doing nothing was an option. Go back to Earth, fit into his life. Repeating chores that boring people do. If her demons were coming, he would die in ignorance. Never find out who his second father was. Was this why he came down here? The artwork was a warning. All life depended on action. The giants had taken no action for their addiction.

The mural was a copy. The original wall was on the world Archdjinn left behind. The art caught his attention when he tried to hide. Eloyhin said the art had been commissioned by King Solomon's most trusted general. It showed Elian Nephilim with long foreheads, wearing noble armour, with faces of mystery. The kind faces had the same wide nose and raised supraorbital bone as the giants who carved crowns out of sticks to hide flat skulls.

'How could builders of the old pyramids sink so low from one addiction?' Eloyhin had whispered.

'They pissed off God,' he'd replied.

Eloyhin had laughed so hard he fell off a stool in the library.

Aiden smiled.

In the palace kitchen, he helped himself to a glass of deer milk. Reaching the rooftop next to the duchess's quarters, he sat on the old woven hammock and was about to slide deeper into the curve, when he caught sight of something blink in the dark night. Red eyes. They were gone before he was on his feet. Was it possible for the contagion to reach here? It couldn't be... No. Zasanctemerior was protected by magic. Earth wasn't.

The white sun dawned without any incident. The palace stirred as the servants went about their duties. Aiden put on the clothes he arrived in, the same black jeans and green T-shirt.

They waited in the courtyard. The Duchess hugged him for a long while. Her parting words were strong enough for gods to tremble. Aiden told her what he saw, she didn't even blink to the horror. She guarded her thoughts, though he knew she was speaking to someone.

Aiden turned to the forest. 'Goodbye Brother,' he whispered.

David sliced the air with his eagle staff and the portal opened.

Instantly, he was filled with memories of a holiday in Florence, his family had invited their neighbours to their holiday. For a moment, he wondered if these feelings were his own, but then his love grew stronger. He felt relief of returning to the simplicity of being an ordinary Muslim boy. Cool crisp air blew faster through the portal. He ran into it quickly, for every world door was unpredictable.

EARTH:

The room stopped spinning. His stomach churned. Aiden reached for the jug on the mantelpiece and drank quickly. The water was good for his throat. It felt odd to have carpet under his shoes again. He hurried to the window and looked out for the familiar view of the Shipley hills. It was getting dark, but he could see the green and how blessed he was for this moment!

Voices from the dining area drew his attention. He wiped his eyes quickly.

Aroosa was wearing the polka dot dress she bought in Florence and had turned part of it into a headscarf. Matthew and Arif must have come back from the gym without showering. Eliza had her I told you so face, whilst listening to their story. Luckily, no one caught sight of the portal to Zasanctemerior before it closed.

'Why is a boy with a devil tattoo in my living room?' bellowed Dad. The conservatory door closed behind him. Dad's glare fell on the space beside him.

Everything worth remembering washed away by this new dilemma.

It didn't matter that Prince Eloyhin Áine - descendant of the super-goddess Gaia — had long glorious curls, eyes filled with galactic miracles and could leap eleven flights of stairs in a split second to stop a vampire from killing his half-brother. Dad only noticed the image of Kronos with horns. Which to be fair, was Wayne's fault, breaking his own rules of being inconspicuous. And stupid enough to follow him through the Worlds Door without following protocol. Not even Kronos could end this matter!

Wayne marched quickly to sit down at the table, in Dad's chair, causing a series of shocked glances.

'Amore mio! Smells divine! Hmm spicy! Goodness, Aiden, how spoiled you are at supper. Just look at this feast. Is this lamb?' said Wayne, scoffing the biryani straight from the serving ladle, which shocked Dad into a one-word answer.

Dad placed his mosque hat on the dresser and sat down opposite.

Aiden breathed relief. Dad signalled with his eyebrows for him to sit down.

'Would you like curry with that?' said Aroosa, disguising her amusement. Mummyjaan hurried back to the kitchen.

Despite Matthew dropping hints he wanted to visit his mum in hospital, Eliza slid in the chair beside him. It was clear Wayne had everyone's attention. Arif decided to be a comedian by airing everything he knew about mishaps from their childhood.

'What are we having for pudding?' asked Wayne. He took a giant spoon of creamy fruit crumble and shoved it into his mouth. Then from the bowl of halva. 'I am guessing this is semolina in molasses. Dried grapes. Almonds. This is divine.' Before Dad could think of what to say to the uninvited guest who enthralled and appalled him, Wayne wolfed two slices of Mummyjaan's Victoria sponge, even picking up the pistachio crumble topping with his fingers.

Aiden's face of displeasure could not balance all the staring.

'Dear chap, do your parents not feed you?' asked Arif, leaning forward.

Eliza laughed.

'I am blessed. Signoria Sophia, may I say your fusion of many cultures brings delight into my tummy,' said Wayne.

'Why thank you,' said Mummyjaan, blushing. 'Aiden never told me he had an Italian friend. Would you like me to pack cartons to take home?'

'No!' said Aiden quickly, pushing back his chair. 'Ami, Wayne is leaving, I will show him out.' When they entered the hall, he pulled the door closed. 'What is your game?' he hissed.

Wayne leaned against a wall.

'Did you not go hunting?' he scolded. 'I bet you ate that poor reindeer.'

'Delightfully he was,' grinned Wayne. 'I would have cooked you a steak had you not put on your big head. There I was, stepping off my trusted Tristan, when I saw my dear stepfather open a portal. I thought to myself, no he wouldn't. And you did.'

'I need time with my family… before… what's coming,' he said calmly.

'Should we celebrate I tasted your mother's cooking?' asked Wayne.

Aiden scowled. 'You created a story for every Eid.'

Wayne grinned, 'I did, didn't I.'

'Why are you here?' he asked.

'Why does a godchild turn halfwit?' said Wayne.

Aiden realised he needed to shield this conversation. He closed his eyes. 'He said when I kill her, I'll meet my djinn dad. Since you can't be bothered to tell me who you saw, I have to find out for myself, don't I?'

'You should have waited,' said Wayne, quietly.

'I need to see him before she finds me,' he said.

'What's wrong with the father in there?' hissed Wayne.

'I love him. But he can't give me answers,' said Aiden.

'Answers?'

'I just want to know who he is before I die.'

Aiden could tell he was pulling the twisted face. 'I'm sorry,' he said.

'If he's dead, he's dead. If he's alive, he's a scumbag,' said Wayne. 'For killing the few brain cells, you have!'

'You know what I find so odd? Humans trace ancestry with one drop of blood. Djinns know their blood by the feel of their gut. And I'm expected to magically detect who my father is, in all the billions scattered through the vastness of space and time? I tried to put this out of my mind, but I can't. You reeled me in. I said no, not listening and then… I lost my ears. So, I am doing... without you.'

'You were going to slay the she-devils all by yourself until you found your da'?' scoffed Eloyhin.

'Yes,' he admitted.

'Confident, are we?'

Aiden's heart thumped. He lifted the necklace from under his shirt. 'I accepted his sigil.'

'Malachi's protection and anything Mother has given you will not withstand the Hell Queen, and you know it,' scolded Eloyhin.

'I do,' said Aiden. 'But I also have duas from the Quran.'

'Kronos was a killer of gods and he himself fled from her,' said Eloyhin.

That must have been difficult to admit. Aiden swallowed for his dry throat. 'Are you really here to change my mind?'

'You stand on Earth with the Archdjinn's sigil,' said Eloyhin.

'One minute, you're dropping stories from the ancients. Next, you're telling me we should run a million miles. Which is it?' asked Aiden.

'The one that's too late.'

Aiden sighed. 'I have to stop her.'

'We! We must stop her. You allowed the crones to reel you in too fast,' scolded Eloyhin.

'Are you saying I set the prophecy in motion?' he asked.

'Who knows? I should have locked you in her library but here we are. A stake might work once. Not twice. Do you get how hard it will be to break into that evil chest and stab that demon heart? We couldn't even crack Asmodeus, she's Asmodeus times who knows,' said Wayne.

'Shut up,' said Aiden.

'Your eyes are closed. She can't tap this memory. So, listen to me, use others. Don't run to put yourself in her jaws,' said Wayne, tenderly.

'It's my responsibility,' he said.

'It's our responsibility. We're bound to jig this infernal path. Steer others to kill this demon. You kill her ninth. That's what it says in the prophecy, right? Be the torchbearer.'

It made sense.

Aiden frowned. 'Dad cannot remember what just happened, I mean it.'

It was good to hear his laugh. 'Anything else?'

'What about -Do I fake my death?' he asked. 'He never told me.'

'Relax Halfkin. You will… remember your cautions.'

Aiden opened his eyes to see Wayne biting his lip. 'Training is over,' he said.

'On the contrary, a learning journey is never over. Did you check to make sure I was your friend?' asked Eloyhin.

Aiden grinned, 'I probed.'

'Strength not power once it comes,' said Eloyhin. 'We remain hidden.'

'Yes.'

'Torchbearers slay from shadows. Slayers slay on many worlds to save unworthy lives. Friends though... caution from precious hearts. Look at me,' said Wayne, pulling away from the wall.

Aiden stepped back. 'Hah. I remember that one. Not going to trick…'

Too late, his eyes stopped on Wayne's arm. When the tattoo turned, he remembered there were many ways to be ensnared by a djinn.

'I thought we were brothers,' he gasped.

'I could ask the same.'

Aiden struggled to breathe, 'We are.'

'I told you to sit this out. My dearest Claykin, your first mistake was dropping the hint. You let yourself feel. Didn't we teach you not to feel?'

Aiden couldn't move.

'You sensed why I was here, yet you did not act. You did not trust your instincts... you could have thrown me back. His name you cannot utter. His face you must not remember.'

Aiden's heart pumped faster. 'I don't know what you're talking about.'

'You saw me recognise him. You... put it together. How hard you hide it,' hissed Eloyhin.

'Wayne,' said Aiden, glaring, 'let me go!'

'He cannot be found.'

Aiden tried to turn, but the immense force would snap his bones. 'Stop... Wayne.'

'Love... is your undoing,' growled Kronos.

'You wouldn't dare,' he gasped.

Kronos grew until the hall filled with Hellflame, swirling and raging, eating through plaster and wood. It was not real... the magic was too strong, Aiden choked in the hot hand of Kronos until he could no longer avoid the power inside his eyes. 'I dare for Zasanctemerior. I take from you what you hold dear. For she is cunning. And she is demon,' howled Kronos.

Hellfire raged upon angel shields. Aiden's strength failed.

'Don't!' he gasped.

'Water in clay, memories betray. I am fire. Fire bakes clay,' whispered Eloyhin.

$$\frac{\text{١٠}}{\text{١٣}}$$

Aiden woke up in bed, tucked incredibly neat for a good night's sleep. The cotton was not warm nor sweaty, which was odd. Had he slept late? Sitting up, he caught sight of the mat folded on the floor, which was odd, he could not remember reading the morning prayer. If he could not remember reading the morning prayer, he should read it again as if he had not.

Entering his ensuite, he made an ablution quickly. He reached for the towel and paused at his reflection in the large mirror. Had the mirror slipped? Or was it always that low? He was wearing a necklace. It had an etched design with a flame inside a star. Blasphemy! He almost lifted it off, but his neck was tingling. This was a ward of some sort. It felt important to be wearing it. Dad won't see it if he buttoned his shirt to his neck.

After performing the morning salah, he sat on the window seat staring at the blue sky, trying to remember where he was yesterday. David's old books had all returned to their hiding places. His fingers stroked velvet. The sun was golden. It was cooler than the holiday in Florence, but decent for a walk on the moors.

Neighbours were spilling out of their home, into their pretty garden. The absence of clouds would fill this family with joy. And yet... everything seemed so... slow.

He heard the creak of Aroosa's door. Whispers from her bedroom. Did this mean Eliza had stayed overnight?

Aiden rubbed the cold etched carving in his fingertips, watching neighbours pile into their shiny white SUV. The family were heading to their caravan with kindness in their voices. Filey may not be as hot as Florence, but their seaside trip will be memorable.

The garden seemed pleasantly inviting. Sod the books. He should be sunning on their hammock. Having a normal day, like any normal person.

KNOCK. KNOCK.

He was tempted to open the window and fly.

'Eddie?'

Aiden crossed the room to turn the key.

The door swung open.

The muscled figure surprised him. 'She came to rescue you,' said Matthew, warning too late.

She seemed taller than he remembered. Hairs from the bob slid over her eyes as she grabbed his face in her sweaty palms. 'Crackerjackers! Look at you. That awful Arif, saying horrid things. And all my duckie wanted to do was feed his starving friend.'

Sweet sandalwood invaded the back of his throat.

'I don't know what you're talking about,' said Aiden, trying not to cough in her face.

Aroosa entered, pausing by the door. 'You've been sulking all day. And we know why.'

'D'you need a hug?' asked Eliza.

'Why would I need a hug?'

'That's right. You don't need people to hug you to know you're special. Though I'll hug you anytime, any day. I'll squeeze you so tight, you'll die of fright,' said Eliza.

Aiden laughed. 'I have no idea what brought this on.'

Matthew ruffed his hair strongly. 'They were awful, Eddie. Arif wants to tell you he was a dick. He was, by the way. I told him to stay downstairs. God your room is clean.' He paused to marvel at the painting of a giant Spitfire on his wall.

'It wasn't fair what Dad said to you,' said Aroosa from the doorway.

'What did Dad -'

'In all the years we've known you,' said Eliza, plonking herself on his neat duvet. She yanked his wrist to sit beside her, 'we have never seen your dad hug you. I mentioned it to Rose, and she can't recall either. Your dad comes in and squeezes Arif. Gives him a hundred quid and the keys to a new car. And you got a scolding just for feeding a starving friend. So, it's okay. I know why you're quiet. I see you, my delicate duckie.'

'Feed who?' he asked.

'What was that charmer's name?' teased Eliza.

'Walter,' said Matthew.

'Wayne,' grinned Aroosa.

'Wayne! Wa-a-ayne! Your mum said he can come anytime,' sang Eliza.

'Eddie, he's alright. We'll take him for a curry. How come you don't bring your friends around?' said Matthew.

'You know you can talk to us about everything. Absolutely anything,' said Aroosa, crossing the room to plonk down on his curved velvet chair.

What on Earth…

Oh.

Was Wayne on a mission? Hang on. Is this why he can't remember? What demon would cause temporary amnesia? A siren! Wow. David must have carried him upstairs, while Wayne distracted everyone downstairs. That must be it.

Reveal nothing. Conquer all feelings, David would say. Today be the best of me. Until tomorrow. Aiden exhaled, 'Thank you.'

'Why are we hiding in your room?' asked Eliza.

'Meant to be reading,' he said.

'What book?' asked Aroosa, sliding her things through her hair. The last time she sat there, it took an hour with tweezers to remove hair from the chair.

He couldn't remember. 'A book,' he said, shrugging.

'Come downstairs. Arif will apologise,' said Aroosa.

'I don't need anyone to apologise for being themselves,' said Aiden.

'What's up?' asked Aroosa.

'He'll talk to us when he's ready,' said Eliza, stretching a big wide smile that warned anyone. 'Eddie, my adopted aunt is frying. And you know I love your mum's samosas. We'll scoff in the garden. Kick a ball. You know we like kicking a ball! Then we're going to Trinity Mall. You're coming with.'

'She means it,' said Matthew.

Aroosa waited for Matthew to head out of the door. 'Just… come and kick the football,' she said.

'Okay Baji,' he said.

Wayne had eaten supper. In this house? How did he miss that?

Aiden put on a nice shirt, then followed them into the garden. Mummyjaan had fried three baskets of samosas. Aiden chose one of each filling, then watched them kick the ball as he ate.

He ate the vegetable one first, to please Mummyjaan, who kept bringing   more samosas. He had just finished the mung bean and chickpea samosa when the ball bounced off Eliza's knee and rolled. Eliza moved to listen to Matthew's story, forcing Arif to do the same.

 Aiden bit into the chicken samosa and was quite content watching them when the horn filled both his ears.

He felt its weight drop with every bone in his body. He could have waited to catch his breath, he could have poured himself a glass of Ribena, he could have let his mind catch up, but he saw them look. And he saw her move.

Aiden hurried to get it.

١١
١٣

HALLWAY OF WORLDS:

Aiden felt the intense vibrations ripple through his bones. He staggered until it lessened enough for his senses to grasp there was indeed a solid glass surface underneath his feet. He stood, frozen, averting his eyes from underneath, waiting for acrophobia to pass.

The hollow star eating the cosmic cloud was spellbindingly close.

He touched the crystal.

The moment he bent down to squeeze underneath the bush left him feeling dismayed. How could he be so stupid? Why did he always end up ruining a good day? He was sat on the patio, eating samosas, the chunky chicken kind. All he had to do was nothing. But no, he had to get it. He assumed they heard it drop. But that wasn't possible! Stupid. Stupid. Stupid. Why didn't he just leave the crystal a few hours? Wait for everyone to go inside, then call his training slayer.

Wayne…

…didn't touch it.

No.

No.

Oh.

Was this a test? Like the one Imam Shafi talked about? Was it bigger than when Wayne saved an American audience from a Hellsborn hiding in the artist's voice box? A big mission. Bigger. A mother of all missions. It had to be. But whose M.O.A.M?

Focus.

He had felt each pulse shatter the statues. Ancient light magic… protection magic… allowing him entry to this magnificent place. Dust and shards shifted back to their natural places. The ball of light that came with him was now repairing. Not a crack left to notice. A giant statue of King Hammurabi stared contemptuously at the Hellenics. Spotless.

Soles screeched on the hard surface. 'Crackerjackers!'

Aiden turned.

Eliza and Arif were gawping at the cosmic surroundings. 'Woah,' they kept saying.

Do not feel.

Observe.

The floor and windows showed they were in space… no… there wouldn't be that many stars and a black hole together without interference upon each other. This was a dimensional intersection.

Arif wanted to explore the statues of 'gods that time forgot'. Eliza grabbed his hand and dragged him from one wide window to another, yelling at live images of cosmic catastrophes.

It would take them a while to grasp it was endless. They entered a new wing called Djinnus. The statues here were frightening.

Like the book!

Oh wow. Yes. Oh crap.

Crap.

So crap.

First Mistake: The crystal landed inside the evergreen bush, no one knew. Eliza saw it because he brought attention to it. Second mistake: The picture in the book showed the lady and the knight holding it at the same time. Two persons activate the crystal for teleportation. When Arif and Eliza reached for it, why didn't yanking it out of their reach occur to him?

Eliza squealed. She yelled for Arif to climb onto a three-headed dog with fanged teeth.

Sparks flew. Aiden ran to grab Eliza's sleeve and pulled her behind a pillar. Energy pulses flooded the chambers with bright sparks and deep humming.

Aroosa materialised with Matthew, both holding the shard.

Eliza and Arif yelled in delight.

Aiden was going through events in his mind. Did they know David? That would mean… no! They were 100% human. Their thoughts were filled with each other. Exhilaration. And wonder. They knew jack squat. This could not be their M.O.A.M. This could only be his… Mother of All Missions.

The Hell Queen.

Oh.

Why were they here? What did David not tell him? David was a powerful telepath. He had a brigade watching over everyone. All telepaths.

Oh God, this was one big cock up.

The shard glowed. Pulsating, like it belonged in a machine.

'Arif,' said Matthew, 'You carry it.'

'The throbbing is getting to me,' gasped Aroosa.

'Let's climb up!' shouted Eliza.

Pathways going up the high pillars were a criss-crossing of stone and monstrous bone, wide enough to hold gods and angels, as colourful and dramatic as Michelangelo's artwork.

Aiden looked again at the pre-Earth cuneiform scribing. 'Shield thy head or lose thy head. Allah's Breath... no... cosmic currents. Don't climb!' he shouted.

'Don't wet your pants!' Vibrations drowned his brother's words. 'We're gods now.'

That was it!

Aiden shouted over the heavy thrum, 'God is glorified in countless worlds and countless suns, not in a single universe, but infinites!'

The vibrations stopped. Bone paths, stone structures and rare minerals dimmed out of transparency. The only light came from burning torches.

They stared at the darkness, then they stared at him.

'I feel dizzy,' said Aroosa, sliding down the giant bone. She sat on the foot of a goddess.

'Feel sick,' said Eliza, jumping down. She vomited on the statue of a naked king.

Arif helped her sit down. 'Does anybody have a bottle of water?' he asked.

Matthew shook his head.

Aiden exhaled, feeling sick too. 'I'll look.'

Arif comforted Eliza, handing her a gold-potted plant that he found beneath a purple queen called Hathor. Eliza said it reminded her of her darling brother, Tom.

No washrooms. 'The writing mentions a fountain of youth. It might be further on. I haven't found it,' said Aiden.

Eliza's cheeks lifted with a grin. 'You are funny.'

She meant weird. He was being weird. Of course, they don't know what he knows. He needed to play it cool. Anyway, how did he know for sure that they were not invaded? Was that even real vomit? A demon could be inside her body. All their bodies. Oh God. Could he slay them?

Aiden turned. 'I am my fire. And my fire is mine,' he whispered.

Their excitement made him smile. Matthew said it was the best spaceship he'd ever seen. Arif didn't think a spaceship could be this big. Eliza questioned whether what they were experiencing was even real. Arif liked this idea, were they in a Virtual World?

'I'm starving,' said Matthew, suddenly.

'I should have grabbed more of your mum's samosas,' groaned Eliza.

'I wish I was tucking into a cheeseburger, right now,' said Arif.

A wrapped bundle rolled to his feet.

'It came from the plant,' gasped Aroosa. She pointed, 'I saw it!'

١٢ / ١٣

Aiden stared at the giant statue of a scowling queen, quite puzzled. Had he not sat yards from this section with Arif and Eliza? He turned slightly. There, by the green knight, just outside this area secluded by eight pillars, they had tried to work out where the crystal brought them. Arif had led them through the triple arches to the hexagonal junction, and Eliza insisted they return to the green knight's junction where they tapped Hathor's Tree and thanked the benevolent goddess in jest for the fast food it dropped. He had a full view of this area while they talked. How come he never noticed the gold torches? How did Aroosa see it the second she teleported in?

The queen's poise was beautiful and majestic, almost familiar... She looked powerful. The writing said she was the Jade Queen of Darius, killed in battle on Ethyrus.

'She's just a character,' said Asif, before urging them to move.

She looked real.

Aiden spied a little nook, where he could pray away from the statues. At peace with the fresh scent of Rozina horn flowers, butter roses and Elyssian lilies, Aiden was quite happy staying. Aroosa was convinced she smelled peonies and wanted everyone to follow their noses. Finding a garden in deep space was 'the most brilliant thing anyone could ever experience,' she said.

'If it is written, it can be found,' said Arif, quoting Mum.

Aiden took a skullcap from his pocket and read the evening salah. When he had finished, he noticed their voices were fading. He got up to hurry, but she caught his eye.

Queen of Jades. There was danger in her confrontation. It was like her eyes were asking him to notice. Aiden circled around her stride. Her shield showed she was a fierce queen in a defending poise. What was her palm doing? Furrowed eyebrows showed she was not at the mercy of the attacker, they warned. Her mouth was petite. If she was alive, he might have liked her... had she not been a stupid queen! What kind of queen has no shoes?

'I spy a Judah. Has the goddess Inanna delivered me fortuity?'

Aiden's heart skipped a beat.

A boy with a square jaw grinned by a satyr statue. He couldn't be much older than Arif, but he was taller. David didn't mention anything about a religious boy. Or was he? A pilgrim's ihram is normally made from two white sheets. The sheet covering his shoulder was green. His arm was covered in gold and emeralds.

Pilgrims don't wear jewels. 'Wa qur rabbi a'oozu bika min hamazaatish Shayateen,' whispered Aiden quickly. He hoped the protection worked.

'Salvē Judah!'

'I'm not Jewish,' replied Aiden.

'Did you not prostrate to nothing? Is that not what Judah do?'

'I am a Muslim,' said Aiden. 'Christians came after Jews. Muslims came after Christians. Now we just argue with each other.'

'By Delius. Shalomalom Muz-zlim mage,' said the boy, joyfully.

Always be your humble self, never the slayer.

'Wa-alaikum salaam,' he said.

'What Judah leaves the sanctity of Earth to help us?' the boy asked.

The others were out of sight. Aiden swallowed, 'Pardon?'

His chin tilted. 'Which hand touched the Eye?'

'What eye?' asked Aiden.

The boy laughed. 'Eye found you. No use hiding it.'

State what is known, give nothing, Wayne would say.

Aiden straightened. 'It teleported us.'

'Wa.' The boy walked from pillar to pillar, in sandals with leather straps that wrapped his calves. 'Magic flows through all of us, but not like you… Elahi Mage.'

He was fishing.

'Are you the caretaker?' asked Aiden.

The boy jumped from statue to statue. 'Depends on what you mean by caretaker.'

Aiden wasn't sure if he was moving to spring a trap. 'I mean you no harm. Why don't you sit down, and tell me what you want?'

The boy paused on the head of a lion. 'Diadromos Tou Kosmos… a place for gods to rest… mortal minds must explore. Those who pass through have their memories fade like a retreating tide. What one learns is embedded for life. You know this Elahi, you were trained by a master djinn… you read what is written on these elegant walls. Is that not why you were able to meditate with such peace?'

Aiden swallowed. 'When you say…'

'A torchbearer must let the heart decide what to borrow,' said the boy.

Aiden glanced again down the corridor.

So quiet.

'What's your name?'

The boy paused near a throne. 'You know.'

'I don't.'

The boy swept closer. 'Who am I?' he asked, with marvel and expectation. The colour of his eyes matched his emerald. The aura around him was like the holograms used in banks and on station platforms. Yet the air around him was cold.

Aiden stepped back. 'A ghost?'

The boy blinked. 'One is always a ghost to somebody.'

'Is this a riddle?'

'Master forged you. Sharpened… we shall see. All djinns are ready, so must you be.' The boy moved to the shiny stone table jutting out of the pillar. 'This is yours. Pick it up.'

Aiden was sure the table wasn't there moments ago. An emerald heart was the kind of thing Aroosa would have loved to place in the front room's glass cabinet. It was beautifully bevelled, fitting neatly in his hand. Would it give him new powers?

It was heavy.

Nothing.

'What is it for?'

Ghostboy's eyes glazed. 'Crafted by the strongest magic djinns have ever spun.'

'What?'

'You freed me from this wretched place. I will haunt you until you stop breathing,' said Ghostboy.

'That's the stupidest thing I ever heard,' laughed Aiden.

The boy crouched on the lion. 'Take my hand.'

'Yeah… not happening.'

'Pray Elahi.'

'I don't talk to strangers,' said Aiden.

'Sirens are treacherous, more than you were led to believe. I need you alive, as long as can be. Take heed, we will profit. Desperate souls are our customers,' said Ghostboy.

'What are you talking about?'

'Once the eye is touched, war is afoot,' said Ghostboy.

You will not carry it… you must carry its weight.

Had he read that somewhere? David gave him books. Which book?

The boy was staring.

Aiden inhaled, 'I get it. But I don't have it. My brother Arif has it. He's big. And strong. And Matthew isn't scared of anything. Eliza and Aroosa have stronger fists than me. I'm nobody really. I have nothing to offer you.'

'You are Nobody?'

'Nobody. Truly nobody.'

'Nothing to offer?'

'Truly nothing.'

Ghostboy stretched his ethereal palm again.

Expecting to sweep air, Aiden obliged. The hot grip that yanked him set his veins on fire. Glowing green eyes multiplied. Memories raced into his mind from a distant time. A man lay sweating from fever on a bed, his eyes were familiar blue. Swords clashed, gates closed, good witches took to the sky, a giant dark devil kicked fortress walls. The man wore armour now, fighting zombies with all of his strength focused into a sword. Everyone shouted for a general. Those poor djinns, their sobs, their cries. Aiden wanted it to stop. His lungs were wrung of air. When the boy let go, Aiden wretched on the clean marble.

The vomit passed through the floor.

Aiden whispered, 'Oh my God. I've just vomited in space. People haven't even set foot in a rocket, and I've emptied my stomach to swirl around the big nothing. So, it's… true, this isn't an illusion… we're actually walking through another galaxy?'

'Always better not to have seen a secret,' said Ghostboy.

Aiden dropped on his bum. 'That was transference, wasn't it? You don't have access to all your memories unless you connect to a living brain. Was that the djinn war?'

'Hah. Magic flows through you, Nobody Nothing Nihilominous,' said Ghostboy.

'That's where you're wrong,' said Aiden. 'There was a moment back there with the humming and the shaking, I should have sensed why it was happening and… something isn't right. It's like I can feel the weight of my body which I haven't felt before. I'm not accusing anyone of anything, but it feels like if I had powers, someone has confiscated them. I wouldn't put it past them. They can do that, you know. Which means, I'm out of my depth. Thrown into the deep treacherous sea and sinking to the bottom. I mean, ghosts... zombie worlds... no. No!'

'You came like a boy caught in a song from the daughters of Potamoi,' said Ghostboy, his eyes widening.

'Can we go back to the haunting bit. What do you mean?' demanded Aiden.

''Tis just a curse before mortals. Unbreakable,' grinned Ghostboy.

'Not for me,' said Aiden.

'What has your master taught you... about the curse of Ethyrus?'

Aiden bit his lip. He was sure he was allowed to answer this one. 'No torchbearer can restore the Ethyrus Heart.'

'Wa.'

'What is your point?' asked Aiden.

'Good citizens do what good citizens do, let the goddess Tyche dance with Moirai,' said Ghostboy.

He thought about it. 'You're asking me to lead them through the door to Ethyrus. Ethyrus is... so flippin' dangerous. No way!'

'Too late. You touched the Eye, speeding the curse on Terra. Infinite die. No matter to me. Not my world, not my time, not my people. See. Their souls have no weight upon me,' said Ghostboy, twirling. 'Hide here, plenty to see. You will not die. I will not wither.'

Aiden swallowed the lump in his throat. 'So... how do you fulfil your Death Life purpose?'

Ghostboy straightened. 'Return my emerald heart to my nephew. I will hide you in the Holy City. The Holy City has many holes to hide.'

Aiden gasped. 'No! I can't do this right now.'

Ghostboy laughed. 'Such a delightful proumnon has never beholden. And I own you for eternity.'

Aiden stepped back. 'Do you though? You-oo tricked me. Surely, that's not fair.'

'A djinn does what a djinn does!' said Ghostboy, skipping back to the lion.

Aiden folded his arms. 'Is there a rulebook on hauntings I can check?'

'An uncle I am. A fadder you seek. I depend on you. And you depend on me.'

'You win the King's Award for being downright annoying,' said Aiden.

'Why thank you. It is always good to annoy a king. Royalty are the highest fools.'

'There are djinns more powerful than you,' said Aiden.

Ghostboy returned. 'Where is your master djinn? How come you are here, and he is not? Has he deceived you, Mikmok? Could he be watching his little bundle of errors?'

That wouldn't surprise him one bit. David had all manners of gadgets for every mission. And the spells he knew of, no one was as gifted.

How was he going to explain this catalogue of stupidity? Aiden felt faint, 'I'm not saying I... just don't haunt me. That... freaks me out.'

Ghostboy climbed onto a four-horned mammoth and lay on his stomach. 'Alas! Handor Moloch harnessed a comet to free his betrothed from a ghost. His magic repelled, turning him and his castle into rocks.'

Aiden snorted. 'Did you just make that up?'

'I believe he is here among Fool's Trinkets. It may take you 6000 years to find it, there are so many,' smiled Ghostboy.

'You'd say anything,' said Aiden.

Ghostboy frowned. 'I haunt in two ways, with or without misfortune. Resist, I dare.'

'If I could punch you I would,' said Aiden, scowling.

Ghostboy laughed. 'I am no Caesar, alas do not test a ghost.'

'No one owns me,' insisted Aiden.

'Hah! Will they not hate you… for what you hide?' sneered Ghostboy.

Aiden stopped himself fidgeting with his necklace. He ran his hand through his hair. 'Mrs Banks has cancer. Send Matthew home. Then I'll think. And we'll talk.'

Ghostboy swept closer. 'By Solomon's beard, you speak not what you desire. Had your friend come here, would all be well, I fear?'

'Yes, it would,' said Aiden.

'You own nothing to negotiate.'

'Please.'

'I do not know that word,' said Ghostboy.

'It means, I beseech thee,' said Aiden.

'Alas, I have no power to send you back to Terra,' grinned Ghostboy.

Aiden glared. 'You're lying.'

'Hear me, we tried our best to stop it. Closing this gate, we gave our cost. Fool you, picked it up. Solomon's Eye, so begins the End of Time,' said Ghostboy.

Aiden unhooked his arms. 'What?'

'Apocalypse.'

'Which one?'

'This is not a mission to save a relic, Torchbearer,' said Ghostboy.

'I know that.'

'Ayla made us special. We were foolish to think we were precious. Angels delivered demise. Arrogance invited the curse. We shared with humankind. Chains from the Fallen rattle closer with time. How easy do you think this monster is, this Queen of Hell? She brings Quod autem omnes Hermagedon. All good things die. By stars and holes. Everywhere.'

Aiden laughed. 'That's stupid.'

The boy's hot palms gripped his face.

Suddenly, he was home. Striped wallpaper glistened silver under light from the street. Purple flowered bedspread? This was his parent's room.

Bang!

Aiden spun round. In her silk nightgown, Mum gripped Dad's elbow, shouting that she was calling the police. Dad whispered 999 wasn't working. Mum grabbed her mobile from her dresser. An automated error message filled them with confusion.

Wood splintered. The door flew off the hinges.

It moved so fast, splattering blood, hurling Dad through glass.

Aiden ran down the stairs and through the door-less front into a night filled with screams. On the road lay a dead dog and a beheaded cat. Mum's eye sockets were empty. Rapid breaths made him turn. Perched on the wall, the thing held a body in its teeth, feeding glands had ripped into Dad's chest. Dad shook involuntarily. The night was filled with a hollow haunting call.

The ghost let go.

Aiden vomited bile, then reached for the queen's leg to steady his balance. 'Mum… died?'

'The road of do nothing leads to darkness,' said the boy.

'So… it… hasn't happened?' wheezed Aiden.

Ghostboy shrugged. 'Torchbearers are blessed by those with power. Such a dilemma, I want you alive, they want you to die. I say fight small! Save only he who saves none.'

'Wait a minute. No Hellsborn nor djinn can pass through the regions of Heaven or Earth, unless God permits it. She can't come to Earth,' said Aiden.

'Hellsborn were already on Earth long before both our times,' said Ghostboy.

'Even her?'

'Let me see. It would be watered down considerably for clayborn minds. Many succumbed to Hellsborn infections may have been scribed as forbidden desires and evil ways. Was an ark built? Was there a great flood?'

Aiden felt surprised. 'Maybe.'

'Angels watch upon you. But Hellsborn can still inflict carnage. It's a shame that your species has a short memory span. There have been many extinction events,' said Ghostboy.

'That's true. Okay. I saw the crystal in your mind-meld. The same one. Okay. If it is the Eye of Ethyrus, a hell queen has risen. Okay. That's if those were memories. But then you're a djinn. It's your nature to lie,' said Aiden.

The boy swept closer. 'A ghost.'

'A dead djinn,' he said.

'I deceive when I see fit, I do not lie.' Ghostboy walked back to the mammoth. 'How you hide what you recognised from my life... the father of your friend.'

Aiden didn't flinch.

The boy was smug, lying on his stomach. 'Pray Elahi. I felt you tense.'

'She's just... a vampire. Okay... a powerful one,' he said. 'I have staked a few vampires.'

'The vinx is the Ultimate Hellsborn Destroyer. Two worlds destroyed in her first incarnation earning her a reputation as the devil's daughter. They sent you to extinguish her dark demon flame. Bravo. Queens and angels foretold this day. Alas, you may deny your friend his father,' yawned Ghostboy.

Aiden folded his arms. 'As a matter of fact, I deny nothing. Mr Banks died in Syria,' he said.

Ghostboy laughed, 'Sweet Fiori, how you try not to show wheels turned inside your clayborn head. A single life concerns you when Armageddon does not.'

'In a car bomb,' insisted Aiden.

'Alas. Richard the Bold is stuck in time,' said Ghostboy.

'Wh-are you serious?' said Aiden, frowning. 'He's alive?'

'By a thread. Neither here nor there,' said Ghostboy.

Aiden picked up the emerald heart from the queen's toe and put it in his top pocket. And fastened the button. Then sat down on hard polished stone. 'Help me understand.'

$$\frac{\text{١٣}}{\text{١٣}}$$

Aiden didn't know how long he'd walked trying to forget Ghostboy's words! He wasn't even sure he was heading towards them, since there were so many junctions. Beyond the giant archway, the colour of stone was lighter and the windows smaller. He was leaving sections holding history of djinn civilisations. And entering Adamah, where there were relics of lost human civilisations.

Voices carried.

How could they not know he'd been left behind? Arif and Eliza teased Matthew.

It was nice to watch them fool around with treasures.

Aiden backed towards the fountain to sit down. The statue with the bow caught his attention. He stroked the smoothness of stone with awe. It didn't feel like it had been shaped by instruments.

The piece was titled, 'Breaker of Hellstone, New Archdjinn of Terra, Capturer and Chainer of Iblis the Corruptor.' The warrior held chains on the other hand. Filled with youth and vitality, he could have been a Hollywood stud. The narrowness of his nose and dimple was familiar. There was no denying it. This was him. Standing between two species, like the protector he was.

There could be no memory. No sight. No sound.

Aiden shut his eyes. 'Hear me,' he whispered. 'I found the ghost. Then I jeopardised the mission by triggering a curse. And screwed my entire family. When I think about it, you said lots of things, without telling me anything. Wayne... isn't... here.'

'This is not your first mission alone.'

Aiden felt his neck warming. 'He wants me to take them to the planet.'

'Inevitable.'

'Was this foreseen?' he asked.

'You're making progress.'

'I am?' Aiden was careful how to word it. 'I don't remember anything about taking... family on the craziest mission in the entire Multiverse.'

'They are... assigned.' The voice was hollow.

'They are?'

'Avoid the vinx.'

Aiden felt relief. 'Wait! What changed? Who kills her? How will I learn who my djinn father is?'

'Open your eyes.' Stone rumbled as the head turned, coming alive with the Archdjinn's face using ancient technology. 'Restore... Heart... Expose... search...'

Right. That made a lot of sense!

Stone rumbled again. The hand lifted his wrist. The bow changed from stone to steel and slid all the way to his elbow.

All was quiet.

Repeatedly carved into the bow, were tiny buffalos with giant antlers, surrounding a warrior's face, who seemed to be shouting a battle cry. In the centre of the bow, his growling mouth surrounded a hole. Aiden lifted the bow, as light as a feather. The buffalos faded.

Aiden wasn't impressed by the magic. 'Could you not tell me, just a little bit more? Like where's Wayne? Why are you not here? God I am talk-ing… to… a statue.'

He marched fast.

'The blessed find their parents seeping from heart and soul,' Imam Shafi once said, when David gave him his third book.

Aiden drank from the fountain with his cupped hand.

'Love from a father brings one to better decisions, fairer ideals and the zeal to build a safer world,' the Rabbi had stated, the day after Dad had punished him for something someone else did.

The bow surprised him. The buffalos had been replaced by calligraphy, declaring there was One God and Mohammad was the last Messenger of God. The Archdjinn had sent him a gift. A bow that bonded to him. Who made it? What stories did it have? Goodness! The calligraphy cut deep and twisted around the bow. He couldn't help it.

Aiden returned to kneel on the hard stone floor. And closed his eyes. 'I am my fire. My fire is mine,' he whispered.

Under the statue of a prehistoric bear called Ometecuhtli, he half-listened to the howling of air currents whizzing through the arches. The others were chatting. Why did David ask him to open his eyes? Didn't it matter if his mind could get hacked by Hellsborn?

He jolted awake.

The window had moved to a red sun. Eliza had her knees wrapped in her arms, watching eruptions from the photosphere. 'You slept like a rock Eddy. Gosh, I'm not tired in the slightest. Red suns are meant to be only half as hot. This one is magnanimous. Isn't it amazing to witness plasma colliding from so close?'

That brought a smile to his face. 'Each of those eruptions could burn a world to the ground,' he said.

'So, flippin' awesome,' she grinned.

'We can barely feel it, there must be shields around this place,' he said, looking above the window.

'Yo dickhead!' yelled Arif. 'Next time you want to go AWOL, tell someone.'

'Eddie, how did you manage to sleep on the floor?' asked Aroosa. She was missing her king-sized bed.

'I don't know,' he said.

'Is anyone hungry?' asked Arif. 'Shall we sit on the gods?'

'Lead the way,' said Matthew.

When she least expected, Aiden hugged Aroosa. She teased him. Matthew laughed. They were all teasing each other when they sat down on stone feet and knees.

'French toast with honey and berries,' said Arif, handing Aiden the wrapped bundle.

'Thank you,' said Aiden, though he wasn't hungry.

'How did they paint all that up there?' asked Aroosa.

The artwork on the ceiling was one he'd seen before, here it looked sad.

'Is he a Caesar? He seems important,' said Arif.

'I like the ones cornering him better,' said Matthew.

'The artist wants us to like them,' said Arif. 'See how the light is used around them?'

'Are they chucking acid on his face? Are we admiring cruelty?' asked Eliza.

'He was an emperor who poisoned the empress with Devil's blood. This caused hell's plague to spread across an empire. They're chucking Ayla's Tears on his face, whatever that is,' said Aiden.

'Like you'd know, dipshit,' said Arif.

'He reads books, Arry. What book is that from then Eddie?' asked Eliza.

'It's written there,' said Aiden, pointing at the white stone. Sumerian-like scribing was a little faded, but he could read it.

'Like that gobbledygook makes any sense, you little shit. You don't need to lie, just say it's great art,' scolded Arif.

To his relief, Eliza broke the awkward silence. 'Why is one smaller than the others?'

Ghostboy appeared by the eagle and disappeared through a giant archway, making his heart thump. Aiden felt the need to stand up. He grabbed his bow.

'What? Why do we have to tiptoe around his feelings? Why?'

Aiden hadn't realised he was walking until he reached the archway. He turned his head, ignoring Aroosa scowling. 'Are we going?' he asked.

They followed him, stopping only to study gleaming treasures that lay on tables, on the floor, inside alcoves, or hanging upside down. Aiden ignored the whispering and the looks from Eliza.

Aroosa tried to tell him that Arif didn't mean what he said.

He touched her elbow, 'I'm okay' he said.

Arif was being Arif. There were two things that always ended his irritability, one was talking about friends, the other was allowing him to pity.

An arrow pointed to a new library to learn from, Aiden continued walking. The mission was a priority.

They passed a window that overlooked a green sun. Aiden stopped at the Fountain of Youth and drank water with his cupped palms. The others drank too.

'I've washed them, there's no soap and I can't stop thinking I touched something creepy back there,' said Aroosa, studying her hands.

Aiden searched the alcoves and found a vessel made of light gold for his sister. Aroosa dipped it into the fountain and drank until she burped. She passed it back to him. Aiden closed the lid. The spouted vessel was suddenly heavy.

Was it magic from the fountain or the flask? He'd seen this… in Ghostboy's memory. The Jade queen had given a flask like this to Uncle Richard. And Uncle Richard had carried it into an elegant stone hall, filled with angry soldiers guarding three evil djinn lords. Ghostboy had thrown the water onto the emperor. What did that memory mean?

It was awful what he must do.

'He must never know,' Ghostboy had said.

Poor Matthew…

This was bigger than he thought. Everything is at stake. 'How does one quantify? His everything is not the same as our everything,' Wayne would say.

Aiden smiled, then strapped the vessel to his belt. And grabbed four more.

Each of them took their water vessel with curiosity. Aiden demonstrated to Arif, by pouring water onto a statue, then closed the lid. Arif gaped inside, making everyone giggle. Then Eliza was hungry, so they sat down beside Hercules and Andarta. The intertwined gods sent everyone into another fit of laughter. After they had eaten, Arif picked up Hathor's Tree and handed it to Aiden.

'I am unapologetically sorry,' said Arif, looking at him with his head bent.

Aiden laughed.

'Try again,' said Eliza.

'He's not even bothered, for God's sake,' protested Arif.

Ghostboy appeared and disappeared by a crumbling stone serpent.

Aiden moved to stand by the serpent.

They hung the water vessels over their shoulders and stopped talking. Eliza walked past him, straight through the arch. The others followed. Walls were covered in old drawings of birds and pink waterfalls. They moved slowly towards the grey door at the far side of the square. The door was clearly rotten.

Why didn't the crystal transport them back when Matthew passed it to Arif, both hands were on the crystal at the same time. Had it stopped working? What triggered it to transport?

He read the scribing, 'Heed travellers, where traitors dwell, dead hearts feed. Bringeth the light. Waketh the night. With Allah's tears, fight the blight. Cometh the son. Cometh the right. Hail Daraan. Hail the queens. Hail the general. Look. Can we turn around...'

Eliza twisted the old green demon-headed handle. She shoved the grey door. It shuddered open.

He froze.

The four of them slipped from safety into the night.

Aiden blinked hard. He inhaled air to fill his lungs. Then fastened the water carrier, straightened the Silver Bow on his back, picked up Hathor's Tree and followed.

The door swung so fast. Creak. Clang. It was gone.
He was trapped.

Dark World

1

Aiden:

Aiden couldn't move for the invisible wall. His ears popped and his vision bloodied. The gold pot tore from his hand, narrowly missing his foot. Strange ripples seemed to make his bones heavier, his heart pumped faster. An intense squeeze held him, protecting him from crushing planetary forces. He wasn't sure if it was spells… or something else.

Peace be upon you blighted Ethyrus, I ask you to be good to me and my kin. And I will pray that the Most Merciful is good to you. Most surely your Lord is watching.

A sudden ease lurched him forward. His hand flew out to steady his balance, the stone was too slippery, grass caught his knees.

Air came suddenly, forcing him to cough. He wretched to expel the repugnant taste of cindering flesh, except there was no fire he could see. Tremors rippled through him.

Hot soft dirt caught him.

The safety of the Diadromos was gone. What had he done? On his back, he recited an Ayat to calm his breathing, for his heart to stop pounding and the ringing in his ears. And another for protection, 'O Allah protect me from my front, behind me, from my right and my left, and from above me, and I seek refuge in Your Magnificence from being taken unaware from beneath me. Please bestow mercy upon this world. Ameen.'

Grass cushioned his head. Why was it so dark? No stars. Not even a moon. Intense gravity could only mean he was on a bigger planet. Right? How nasty would creepy crawlies be on a bigger planet? Bigger planets meant magic... much more powerful. Is that why the air felt so heavy? He should be dead. Perhaps he was blind? It was probable. Very probable. Shit. He moved his finger closer to his eye and could just make out the nail. Thank God! Aiden suddenly felt a déjà vu. Had he been here before? No. It was just one of those moments when a phone was really needed for a torch. Magic killed their batteries, and this upset Arif the most. Aiden wouldn't blame him if he started moaning again.

The outer edges of the leaves in Hathor's Tree glowed. Aiden got to his feet, picked up the gold pot and clutched it tightly. He drank from his carrier, waiting to hear a sound from the four. Any sound. He couldn't even see Arif's white shirt. He didn't know how long he was stood waiting. He could only feel his own breathing. At least he was alive. They would be too. He wasn't sure what salah to read on an alien world. But Asr felt right, besides, it would be afternoon somewhere on Earth. As he finished, the sound returned like the coming of water.

'She's scared.'

'...will be going mental.'

'No. Only you'd think Mum and Dad would say you're being sold online.'

'Shut up Arif!'

He felt relieved. If they treated him like he was ten, he deserved it. He wasn't ready to answer. Ghostboy's taunting face made his eyes burn. 'Magic protects the travellers,' he whispered, it had been inscribed on the floor.

His sister's voice drifted. 'Our Food Tree will be on the news everywhere, even on Snapfam.'

'Well with your Snapfam -definitely!'

'Shut up. People will want to buy it. The government is bound to ask the police to take it from us. Even if Uncle Shukker's army stopped them, powerful people will hound us. The crystal is like a rare painting... like magic beans. Everyone knows that story. If you think the MI5 are not going to sit us all in fancy chairs, sweating the secrets out of us, you're out of your mind. So, we might as well hire an agent, get rich people to pay loads of dosh for us to take them to the Hallway of Worlds!'

Aiden found it fascinating how his sister could think all of this at such speed. She did have a point. A bad one. Treasures get stolen.

Just like he stole everyone's water carriers. And this. Mum would not be happy he took Hathor's Tree. The thought had never occurred to him.

Crack.

No. The ghost had stared at the bow and given him that same look with the funny eyebrows, so he was borrowing. That's all. As long as Arif didn't lose the Core Crystal and didn't open his big gob. He didn't need to tell Mum anything. End of. They would all forget about all of this. Simple.

Crumble.

Aiden turned to face the direction of the sound. As soon as he saw the statue, he knew magic was at work, it was the same green glow when they picked up the treasures. Had he triggered a spell? Did he touch the statue when he fell? Maybe. What did it mean? The smooth stone was breaking, bits fell off. Then another. Something moved underneath the rubble. Hind legs lifted. Debris slid off freeing a head, horn and hide at the same time. It was an odd, beautiful creature, as dainty as a Great Dane, but taller than a donkey. Aiden stepped back, with fear.

For a moment, all was quiet.

The eyelids lifted slowly. Glowing sea blue eyes with green and purple rings looked at him for the first time. Aiden inhaled with his mouth ajar.

'Kill it.'

Aiden turned, aghast.

Ghostboy offered him a blade. 'When helpless and hopeless, let there be mercy.'

Aiden stepped back.

'Heroes have many burdens, Elahi Mage,' said Ghostboy, sadly.

'I've known you five minutes. I don't trust you,' said Aiden.

Ghostboy glared. 'Would you leave a baby deer on a world filled with starving wolves?'

'Get lost. Leave!' snapped Aiden.

Ghostboy laughed as if he'd gone mad.

The creature took one step towards him and faltered, lowering its horn.

Ghostboy faded away.

It looked at him.

'He's my secret,' whispered Aiden.

It trotted slowly towards him. The neck lowered again. It snorted hot air.

'What's that sound?' called Matthew.

'What sound?' called Arif.

'They're my family… I'm Aiden. What's yours?' he whispered. A long-wet tongue slopped his face. 'They must never know.'

The creature stepped back one leg after the other, gentle eyes never left him.

Aiden raised a hand and stopped, waiting until the head dipped. Aiden stroked the soft silky mane. 'I don't want to think about it,' he whispered.

The creature moved sideways then backwards, like it was testing each leg for bone movement.

'Eddie!'

'Aiden?' said a familiar voice softly.

'I'm here,' croaked Aiden.

'Shit. You scared the crap out of us,' laughed Matthew. He sounded far away.

'Where are you, bro?' gasped Aroosa.

'Why does it smell of poo?' shouted Eliza.

'More like rotten eggs,' said Matthew.

'I think it's sulphur,' said Arif.

'Like in a volcano?' shouted Eliza.

Aiden looked around; he didn't think it was a volcano. But how would he know? He could only see as far as the magical glow of his new friend.

Dirt rolled.

He turned. 'Eliza?'

'Yes, it's me. Where are you, Squirrel?'

'I don't know,' he said.

Eliza laughed, 'It's freaky dark. I'm scared I might take a step and fall down the volcano.'

'There's grass under my trainers,' said Aroosa.

'Grass grows on volcanoes,' grinned Aiden.

'He's right.'

'Are you saying we're actually on a volcano?' shrieked Aroosa.

'We're inside it. Or at least underground. It's too dark to tell,' said Arif.

'It's too cold for an active volcano, Silly,' said Eliza.

'There are volcanoes in Iceland,' mused Aiden.

'Shut up Eddie! I'm trying to stop her freaking out,' shouted Arif.

Aiden smiled, watching the white beast watch his family make their way towards him quite blindly. He was sure the green glow around the creature was a shield of some sort.

'Did anyone bring a torch?' asked Eliza.

'Aiden, did you grab a torch?'

Aiden rolled his eyes. 'No Arif. Did you?'

Why did he need a torch? He had a new friend, who could always light the way for him. The creature turned and trotted. It was a nice feeling to know only he could see him.

Aroosa screamed. 'Allah Jee! Something licked my hand.'

'Don't be silly,' said Arif. He sounded scared.

'I think it's coming to me,' shouted Matthew, with panic in his voice. Gravel shifted.

Eliza screamed. 'Something's licked my neck. I've seen that movie. The monster is cute, then it licks you and then it sticks you and lays eggs!'

Aiden giggled.

Five glowing fingers appeared, holding a super-fluorescent crystal shard. The scruffy hair definitely belonged to him. The weight of the shard didn't seem to bother Arif, who glanced at Eliza, then at his free hand, Aiden never understood why he always did that. Some things about Arif will always be a mystery!

They shifted together when they saw the horse-like creature with eight legs and a horn in front of them. The unicorn's tail lifted and both wings gently lifted from the back, it was spellbound to the crystal.

Aiden stepped forward. 'Herionus won't harm you. He's not glowing, which means he thinks you're harmless. He's the son of Perak, it's important he said. I think he's related to Pegasus from Mount Helicon.'

His brother pulled a funny look. 'What're you on about?'

'He told me.'

'Eddie talks to animals now. Got it,' said Arif, putting on the voice he does to ridicule.

Aiden forced a smile. 'Herionus whispers inside my head. He's telepathic.'

Eliza was captivated.

'It's… beautiful,' gasped Aroosa.

'I think we should all move away from it,' said Eliza.

'Yes. We don't know anything about where we are,' said Matthew.

'Best do what David Attenborough does, keep your distance and observe,' said Arif.

'He's harmless,' shrugged Aiden.

'Did he tell you that dipshit?'

'Yes.'

'Vampires say they're harmless too,' said Matthew.

Matthew had heard him!

Aiden inhaled. 'Mr Smith always says we must try to understand a poem in which context it is written. Herionus is a survivor. He's gentle. He eats Kishelberries and grass. But I think he meant blueberries because the picture he showed me looked like blueberries.'

'When you look at it from here, it's so damn beautiful. When you look at it...' Aroosa walked sideways, 'from here, isn't it weird it's got eight legs?'

'Crackerjacks. Like a real life My Little Pony monster,' laughed Eliza.

'Herionus is not an it. And he likes you, even though you're being mean,' said Aiden.

They took turns stroking the magnificent eight-legged animal's fur. Herionus suddenly jerked and neighed.

'Herionus says darkness is coming,' said Aiden, frowning.

'He's not very bright then, is he?' said Arif.

'Ask him how we get back,' said Matthew.

'He said we should run,' said Aiden.

Arif walked, holding the crystal higher. Aiden followed him around the edges of the hill, noting where the slope was steepest. The silver grass tilted towards the crystal.

'It doesn't look dangerous,' said Arif. 'What're you doing?'

Matthew stopped swiping the air. 'This is where the door was. I thought it was just camouflaged. It's gone.'

'Duh,' laughed Eliza.

'Are we really accepting all this happened... because of magic?' said Aroosa.

'There must be a way back,' said Matthew.

'Magic reveals itself when we're ready,' said Aiden, feeling sorry for Matthew.

'Oy dumbo. Magic doesn't think, it's science that we don't understand yet. Anyway, what the hell? Minutes ago, we were in the most amazing place with treasures from lost civilizations. And you picked up a plant?' scoffed Arif. 'Look at us, we've even got blinging jewels. How is that meant to help you get rich?'

Aiden tightened his arms around Hathor's Tree.

'He's got a bow.'

'Not treasure.'

'Arif, your brain cells are worse than my gran's. That plant he's holding gave you a cheeseburger,' said Eliza.

'Eliza, I find it extraordinary that I have to remind you what century we live in. A food tree is useless when we order cheeseburgers from an app.'

Eliza rolled her eyes.

Matthew laughed. 'Let's just say you're right. If we are back, how far is this volcano from home? How far do we have to walk for bloody streetlights?'

'He's got a point. Got no Wotzat or Snapfam. I want to know what's latest at the Salts Hill Manor,' said Eliza.

Aiden turned at the mention of the neighbours. 'Why?'

'The attempted murder. They arrested him,' said Eliza.

Aiden stopped. 'Who got arrested?'

'Where's he been?' said Eliza, cocking her head with disbelief.

'Book Land,' said Arif.

They laughed.

'Come on Eddie, you had to have noticed all the cop cars last week?' said Matthew.

There were?

Aiden wondered if he should risk reading his mind.

'And forensics,' said Eliza. 'Mum's friends went all over his house. Said he's a hoarder.'

Maybe all of them? No. He cannot fail in the first hour of arriving.

'Eddie?'

'What?'

'Arif's talking to you,' his sister said.

'Yes I know. House at the end of our street. I'm listening,' he said.

'Do you remember old Mr Khagan?' asked Arif.

'Yes.'

'What was he like?'

'He didn't like me,' said Aiden.

'He didn't like anyone,' said Matthew.

'Scrooge was a glass of milk compared to Mr Khagan. Frightened his daughter to run away. Hiring tradesmen and then cheating them out of their hard-earned hours. The guy who built his extension - Mr Thatchwood - was owed 30k, but Mr Khagan refused to pay his balance over a technicality,' said Eliza.

The shoots of grass behind her suddenly opened into long red flowers.

'Khagan got Thatchwood sent to prison for threatening his life,' said Arif.

'Thatchwood waited two years until he was released,' said his sister.

'He went to collect his money. Found Mr Khagan hiding in a panic room,' said Matthew.

The grass was straightening around them.

'Khagan laughed at him. Thatchwood saw the shelf with all of his money. He went bonkers!' said Eliza.

'Thatchwood beat him so much,' said Aroosa.

'In a change of heart Thatchwood called an ambulance. Then took his money and ran. Last week, police took Mr Khagan to the station. And it was back on news,' said Eliza.

'Turns out, the panic room was not a panic room. And Khagan wasn't laughing his head off, he was just happy to see someone. He thought he was being rescued. Thatchwood had beaten the wrong guy, Mr Khagan had kidnapped his brother over a property dispute in Pakistan, and nobody knew,' said Arif.

'No way,' gasped Aiden.

'How come you don't know this Eddie? All of Nabwood's gobbing about it,' said Eliza.

'I must have been reading,' he said, shrugging.

'Oh my God. Look at the ground!' gasped Aroosa.

Surrounding Arif, plants were growing and coming into their colours. Dirt shifted for new grass. Rock sticks shed dust for gold and green stems. Shoots emerged for dazzling flowers. Arif took steps back and life followed. 'Flippinora!'

'You're bringing life to dead dirt,' mumbled Aroosa.

'It's the crystal,' said Aiden.

Stems stretched towards him.

'Could be,' said Matthew.

'Or a warning... because you repulse them?' suggested Eliza.

'Ha-ha,' said Arif. 'We'd have to be deep underground for a plant to do that. Or... there might be a tiny possibility we've flipped to a future after the sun died and the world got screwed. On the bright side, this arm-ache must belong here.' He waved the crystal.

It was quite satisfying to see the veins of light feed colourful petals. Reds, whites, blues, and gold defined the curves of the hill.

Herionus looked at him and trotted to the edge.

Eliza followed.

To Aiden's surprise, Arif handed the crystal to him. He took it in both hands and walked slowly, feeling the magic in each stride.

'Wow!'

'Woah!'

'Go Eddie!

Aiden laughed, hopping from one rock to the next. The longer he stayed in one place, the stronger the beauty from the flowers. When he spun, light and colours cascaded in every direction. Herionus neighed and jumped with delight.

Aiden handed the crystal back to his dumbstruck brother.

The air was dry. Eliza thought it was wise if they replenished their thirst before setting off, they sat by a rock and drank from their treasures.

As they began walking, Aiden bent down to look closer at the glowing grass. 'It's so different!' he whispered to Herionus. Aiden closed his finger and thumb onto the blade of grass and pressed gently.

It burned hot.

So hot.

Aiden gasped, rubbing his hand on his clothes. Then spitting on his fingers. Herionus blew on it, making it better.

From the deep pit of darkness, something rumbled.

Crack. Roll. Boom.

Vibrant plants bent ever so slightly, then the distant hills were snuffed out.

Arif stopped.

Rumble. Boom. BOOM!

They drew together, facing the darkness from all directions.

The ground shook.

All was quiet.

'What was it?' whispered Aroosa.

'Probably an earthquake,' guessed Matthew.

'Earthquakes mean landslides and falling debris. I don't want to be buried alive,' said Aroosa.

'If we're in a cavern that has lasted millions of years, it's highly unlikely it will fall down from a tiny tremor,' said Eliza.

'How come there's no dangling bits then?' asked Aroosa. 'Don't caverns have dangling bits?'

'If you mean stalactites and speleothem, you're right. It depends on geo-history. We might be so underground that nature is different here,' said Eliza.

'Nature evolves to fit the extreme environment,' said Arif.

'Arif, the new talent for the Discovery Channel,' said Aroosa.

Eliza laughed.

'This doesn't feel like a volcano,' said Matthew.

The tone of his voice caused Aiden to look. Matthew was back to himself. These last few months were horrible.

'Have you ever been in one?' scoffed Arif.

'Doesn't feel like we're inside anything,' said Matthew.

Contain the situation, David would say.

'Come on! It stinks. We're clearly not breathing just air,' said Arif.

Matthew stared at him. 'There's no... toxicity.'

'Yes! And we prefer to keep it that way. Even if we are at a safe distance from dangerous areas, we have to be careful.'

'I miss the violent conversion of hydrogen to helium,' sighed Eliza. 'Give me daylight.'

'I wouldn't be surprised if there was nothing over our heads but an empty sky,' said Matthew. 'We're on an alien planet.'

This was too soon. Aiden tried to recall if Matthew had seen the ghost in the Diadromos. He couldn't have, surely?

'Now you're being silly,' said Arif.

'Where's the lava?' asked Matthew. 'Not even a spark.'

He was speculating. Good. It would be bad for all if Matthew saw the ghost.

'I smell a volcano. I agree with Arif,' said Eliza. 'We're sticking to his idea, until we find evidence.'

'Herionus is nothing like on Earth,' said Aiden.

'Your pet is nothing more than a freak,' said Arif. Then took bigger strides down the hill, shouting, 'If one of us was sensible enough to have picked up that damn compass, maybe we could've worked out how far we are from England. But we didn't. So... Let's stumble to Albion.'

'Staying close to the crystal,' Eliza said, hurrying to follow Arif.

'I miss the internet,' sighed Matthew, pocketing his dead phone.

'Hold that thought. I've got my bank card. Gonna get the best room in a hotel. Warm bath, room service,' sighed Aroosa.

Herionus neighed softly. Aiden quickened his pace to catch up.

As they descended, the grass got taller and the luminance more colourful. The flowers were reds, whites and purples, blues and the odd yellow. The sheer drop made them steer right for a gentler slope curving down the hill.

Aiden stopped. The others gasped. A green glow lit the horizon. A city of skyscrapers hidden behind a giant wall. To its far left, the silhouette of another fortified city glowed red.

'Did we just prove Arif's post-apocalypse?' asked Eliza.

'Doesn't fit our timeline,' mumbled Arif.

'They've got lights… can't wait to charge my phone,' said Aroosa, sighing.

'They look weird,' said Eliza.

'Different technology,' said Arif.

'Shut up!' said Aroosa, mortified. 'We might not be on Hawaii, but Underground Hawaii is still in Hawaii.'

'Oh, come on!'

'Why is he laughing?' shouted Aroosa. 'Are we not going home?'

Eliza laughed.

'You shouldn't have walked through the door,' said Aiden, heading to Herionus.

'We're going home,' reassured Matthew.

Herionus ate grass. Aiden let his fingers slide on his silky mane, comforted by the heat of his long body. He remembered how quickly he knew Ghostboy was telling him the truth. 'I didn't want to believe him. In his memories, Uncle Richard trusted him.'

Herionus paused chewing.

'I can't. It's my secret,' Aiden drew a long breath. 'They're going to take their time being bigheads.'

'Don't walk away from me!'

'You need to calm down, Sis,' said Arif, lifting his eyebrows.

'Is this the way home?' she hollered.

'I don't know. Do you?'

'Why aren't we going that way? Or that way? Or that-?'

'You're welcome to take the lead,' sneered Arif.

'I'm just saying what you all should be saying,' yelled Aroosa.

'Let's just recap what we know,' said Arif, louder. 'And that is... nada.'

'When Eddie found the crystal-'

'Yes. Eddie was holding it. Eliza and I reached for it. Bang. Three of us teleported. The crystal did not. It teleported when you and Matthew touched it.'

'Why did it happen?' she asked.

'You tell me. You said it was five minutes. For us, it was a day at least. What does that tell you?' said Arif.

'Have we died?' gasped Aroosa.

'Don't you dare cry,' he said.

'This thing is hurting my arm, so I can't be, can I?' she said.

'I haven't got a clue,' said Arif. 'We explored the most mind-blowing place with stories of magical beings. We drank from the Fountain of Youth and thanked Hathor for bestowing her benevolence in providing a food tree, treasures that followed us, quite creepily by floating in the

115

air. In a place that could quite possibly be, as long as infinity. Who knows? It was too much for us to process. That's why Eliza picked the grey rot of all rots to walk through because an old door always looks familiar.'

Aiden looked away.

'Are you saying the crystal brought us here?' asked Aroosa.

Arif sighed. 'Let's stick to facts.'

'We stole scientific wonders, but we don't know shit about it,' said Eliza.

'Freaking me out,' said Aroosa.

'Come on. Positive signs of civilization. Proper beds,' said Matthew, grinning.

'Which one?' asked Arif.

'Which one looks homely?' said Matthew.

'Green one,' said Aroosa.

'Are you nuts? Red one is closest. Second… it's still the closest. Third, what kind of nutcases would light a whole city green?' scoffed Eliza.

'It feels wrong,' said Aroosa.

'Says the one pointing to the walled city,' laughed Arif.

He should be feeling something by now. Did the Ghostboy lead him into a trap? How would he know? Aiden lifted his head tiredly from Herionus. 'He said he'll haunt me the rest of my life.'

Herionus neighed.

Aiden scowled. 'Time to go,' he whispered.

They had paused for him to catch up. 'People head to cities to get help,' continued Arif, 'make a home or learn how to get home.'

'All I'm saying is… I have a feeling that's creeping me out. Something… bad,' said Aroosa.

'You're not in any danger,' groaned Arif. 'There's five of us. And a unicorn.'

'Why can't we just find the way out of this cavern? So far, you've not given me any evidence we're not safer staying here,' said Aroosa.

Arif laughed. 'I get it there is no sky, but I agree with Matthew. Over there, people know where we are!'

'Don't try to copy Dad's voice because you're not Dad. They'll be wondering where we are, you know. Mum will have all of Shipley combing the moors. Including Uncle Shukker and his entire Yorkshire army. You know it's true Arif!'

Arif marched so fast, he overtook Aiden and Herionus.

'We're on a creepy alien planet,' shouted Eliza, hurrying to catch up.

Matthew sighed. 'All I know is the crystal brought us here. If we head to a city, we'll learn why. Solve the problem. Get home.'

'Why do you have to agree with everything he says?' asked Aroosa.

'Stay-' shouted Arif, turning. 'We're going this way. Hurry up, Matthew.'

Herionus chewed on grass.

Matthew hurried.

'You believe me, don't you Eddie?'

The chill he felt, he should not ignore. Aiden bit his lip. 'Baji, you stopped us getting on that boat in Italy. And saved everyone from a leaking boat. But you also stopped us getting in that taxi, which could have got us to the airport faster. It's dark and God-knows-how dangerous, but we're in it. We need to stay together.'

'They're waltzing blindly.'

'If we're under Hawaii, lava should have burned those cities,' said Aiden. 'If this is a different planet, with a different rotational orbit, one night may be years on Earth. If you want to sit here and wait for daylight, I can ask them in the city to send you a taxi?'

Herionus neighed.

'Alright!' screamed Aroosa, making a run for Eliza.

Herionus came to a standstill.

'You talk in riddles,' whispered Aiden.

Herionus snorted. The glowing eyes looked stern.

'My sister. Not yours. If you're that bothered, why don't you let her sit on you?' said Aiden.

Herionus shuddered.

'Thought so.'

They passed three clumps of elephant-sized tulips.

'What if they're not friendly?' asked Eliza.

'They could eat us,' said Aiden.

'Eddie!'

'No – Eliza and Sis are right,' Arif said, faltering, with one boot on a rock. His finger stroked a glowing daisy, 'We need to be on our guard.'

They walked past jutting rocks, through sifting dirt and white grass. Arif led them onto an old path of flat stones. They ran downhill and climbed. Aiden was certain the path had been laid to go around the hills. The tiny canyons were steep. His sister pointed at giant glowing mushrooms. Matthew seemed content. It was nice to see him like this for a change.

'Think Aroosa's right,' said Eliza. 'Why do those cities have towers and walls? Why aren't the people out here, living with cattle? Why isn't there a squeak of an animal? Not a cat, not a cow, not a dog. Not even a slimy slug. Something's not right.'

Aroosa glanced at Arif. Aiden could tell she was glad to have the crystal. Light was truly precious in this world.

Herionus jolted.

Thud. THUD. The ground shook. Flowers on a distant hill snuffed out. A disturbance was moving, bringing death with it.

Herionus backed away.

It roared.

They ran.

2

THUD. THUD. BA-DOOM.

It was fast, snuffing out plant life wherever it landed. Arif called to him to take a hard right. A deep crevice was there too.

The noise stopped.

Arif held the crystal higher, it shone brighter.

Crack. Crack.

Red eyes grew from darkness, each one ghastlier than a giant raptor, staring at Aiden.

'Shit that's huge,' gasped Eliza.

'What is it?' screamed Aroosa.

Aiden's eyebrows furrowed, 'It's a ghul!'

'That's no ghoul,' gasped Arif.

Aiden couldn't care to reply. He searched for Herionus and could not see him.

'Run!' shouted Arif.

Down the hill, the rumble of the beast followed. They ran through the boulders of rock. The land was treacherous now. They hopped over crevice after crevice, sometimes slipping but never stopping.

'Hurry Eddie!' yelled Arif.

Aiden's throat was sore from gasping, 'Can't see my unicorn.'

A strong hand grabbed his. 'Keep running!' said Matthew.

Past giant rocks, five pairs of feet pounded dried alien grass. Straight land gave way to a steep hillside. Aiden pulled his hand free when his trainers landed on soft dirt. He needed a drink. The beast thudded close. Rocks tumbled into a crevice. He glanced at the others, they were pacing, their minds focused on getting across the deep dry riverbed. When they thought they had finally found a path, it landed, shaking the rocks. Aroosa fell off balance. Arif helped her up. Giant claws tossed dirt towards them.

'It's toying with us,' groaned Eliza.

Light from the crystal dimmed.

Eliza reached for Arif's hand.

All went dark.

A blood-curdling growl came from all directions. Aiden felt Matthew's back touch his own. Aroosa's hand grabbed his. The growl was so loud now, Aiden couldn't hear what Eliza shouted. Where was Arif and the crystal?

Thud. THUD.

Bright light.

The growl turned into a blood curdling shriek.

Heavens!

Wings wide as a shield, Herionus emitted light like a sun.

The beast staggered. Back to the darkness it fled.

Light returned to their crystal. Plants glowed again. Aiden was relieved. Had he listened to George…

He went to stroke Herionus and hugged his soft silky head instead.

Arif got up off the floor, his head had scratches.

'Are you alright?' gasped Aroosa.

'Knocked me for a six. But yeah… That unicorn!'

'Herionus saved us,' said Aiden, tearfully.

'Can it fly?' asked Aroosa. 'Can it take us to the city?'

'No,' said Aiden, recoiling. 'He's delicate.'

'Yeah? Delicate is my new friend,' said Matthew, stroking Herionus.

Smiling, caused dry lips to stretch painfully. Aiden's throat was parched. He unscrewed the flask's cap.

'No time to drink. We need to put walls and towers between us and that thing,' said Eliza.

The land was unforgiving. Deep crevices and soft earth forced them to slow down. At Matthew's suggestion, they kept to the rocks, where their soft rubber soles could bounce easily. The monster thudded occasionally behind them.

'Predators follow prey until they're worn out,' shouted Arif.

'Arif, shut up!' shouted Aroosa.

His sister was terrified, her shoulders kept bumping into Matthew's.

The beast roared again.

Herionus ignored Aiden's call.

The crystal dimmed.

They stopped.

Aroosa fell to her knees in a fit of sobs.

Dark shoots erupted from the ground, knocking the crystal from Arif's hand. Aiden went to it. He caught Arif looking at him, with remorse in his eyes. There was nothing either of them could do.

'Herionus!' he called.

Nothing.

Roar.

'Come on then, show yourself!' shouted Matthew. He picked up the crystal and it shone again, so bright, Matthew had to hide his eyes behind an elbow.

'I don't know what you're doing, but I think you scared the beast,' shouted Eliza.

'Dammit.'

'What?'

'My feet are sinking,' said Arif.

Each stride took effort, like wading through snowfall. Matthew led them to clumps of glowing stems which they could hold for support to haul themselves back onto the stones. 'I think we're off course, but if we climb the next hill, we should see the Red City.'

After the next hill. It was just dark.

Thud. Thud.

'Look,' said Arif. 'Dark stalks grow whenever it is near. Keep an eye for them.'

Aiden wanted to ease his dry throat, but Eliza urged him to match her pace.

They stopped at the edge of another canyon.

'The gap is narrower down there,' said Eliza, pointing.

Rumbling filled the air.

Arif shouted, 'It could have caught us ages ago. It's toying with us. We have to kill it!'

Matthew drew his sword. 'Let me do it,' he shouted. 'Take the others over there.' Matthew pointed to the other side of the canyon, where white flowers glowed. An obelisk-shaped rock made a bridge.

'No. It's you and me,' shouted Arif.

Aiden ran across the obelisk and leapt onto a ledge, catching Eliza's hand, who yanked him to safety. They climbed the steep slope to hide behind rocks. The loud thuds stopped.

I know you.

Startled, Aiden took a step back and fell. His back hit soft gravel, causing him to slide. A plume of dust covered him. He coughed. Eliza reached for him.

Herionus appeared again, wings wide, his horn shining like a sun. A battle of light and dark! Each one pulsed, the other grew weaker. The beast roared so loud, they had to cover their ears. Matthew and Arif hurried across the obelisk. A giant grotesque claw appeared from the dark, slamming into the unicorn. Herionus rolled and slid with a shrieking neigh. And tried to flee.

The beast cut him off.

Light dimmed.

Aiden felt for the necklace and held his breath.

One hoof after the other, Herionus retreated. As the dark crystal grew, so did the beast. The white hide of the gentle friend turned grey.

Aiden gasped.

Aroosa paled.

All went dark.

Silence.

'Everybody, come to me.' With Arif's words, the crystal shone brighter.

Aiden watched for a change in Herionus, but the unicorn remained lifeless.

The ghul watched them with red eyes.

'We're screwed,' said Arif.

'It turned the unicorn to stone. What do you think it's going to do to us?' gasped Aroosa.

'Turning to stone may be a defence mechanism for Herionus, like a fish changing colours at the sight of a predator,' said Eliza.

'He's not dead?' exhaled Aiden.

'Plants around him, Eddie. They're glowing,' said Matthew.

'Yeah, but why?' said Eliza. 'Why does that thing let a few flowers glow?'

'It wants us to see it,' said Arif.

'Why?'

'It hasn't swallowed Herionus... or us because it might not want to. Or it can't. Yet it grows... when we're scared,' said Eliza.

Matthew held the crystal outwards and abruptly drew in a deep breath.

The silhouette of the beast was even bigger than before, its claws longer and sharper.

'Swords are toothpicks to that thing,' gasped Aroosa.

Grass shrivelled and died.

Embedded within the bones of its jaws, was a corrupted crystal throbbing darkness. The red in the eyes had shrunk like a solar eclipse.

'We're going to kill it,' said Matthew. He sounded tired.

'It's draining us,' gasped Arif.

'I don't want to die,' sobbed Eliza. 'Cuz, I'm never going to see our Tom!'

Her words gave renewed strength to Matthew, but each time he got up, he fell to the ground. 'Aiden,' gasped Matthew. 'Your turn.'

Of course! The crystal had shone brighter every time it changed hands. Aiden closed his fist around it. His strength returned. The crystal grew, gaining weight. He held it up.

Aiden stepped forward. The dark crystal shrunk into the beast's flesh. Arif by his side, sword drawn. Matthew too. The beast backtracked.

They charged.

When they saw its drool scorch the ground, his brothers stopped. With the cracking of bones, the beast thickened, dark fur split for scales and molten blood. The dark crystal hung from its flesh. All eight legs shifted wide, like a giant predator poised to eat dinner. Moving with the beast, they kept turning. A horny tail hit the ground.

Matthew struck it, breaking spikes.

A scream!

Aiden looked sharply. Aroosa was in the air, flailing her arms, the emeralds in her bracelets had been activated, they were glowing. Eliza jumped up to catch her leg.

The ghul turned.

'What do you want?' he whispered.

A growl resonated inside his bones.

Devil eyes flitted to him. You will fail.

Arif and Matthew tried fervently to stab it.

The dark crystal grew, scales kept lifting and fur kept extending from hellskin.

The new horned tail struck the ground.

The girls were astonished they had dodged it. They rolled as it struck again.

Devil eyes followed.

Matthew stabbed repeatedly to climb onto the furry neck.

The beast stomped.

Matthew tumbled off.

Eliza ran, stopping abruptly to avoid falling down a crevice. Aiden grabbed her hand and pulled her back.

Aroosa screamed.

'No!' cried Matthew.

The beast shook her violently. She went limp.

Aiden remembered his bow. Exhaling, he unclipped it off his back. The ancient steel was cold in his hands. Drawing the string slowly, he waited for the magical arrow to appear. And fired.

Ice spread across the head. Aroosa was thrown. The dark crystal shrank. Then grew. The growl was angrier.

Aiden pulled on the bowstring, but it was knocked from his hand. A claw pinned his arms. The rush of air tossed his head. Chill seemed to spread from the beast to his body.

The flask tapped his leg.

He would die thirsty.

The rush of air carried their voices.

'...crystal I'm telling you,' Matthew shouted.

The chill made his brain throb. The dark crystal was pulsing now... draining them.

You have no fire.

Twisting, Aiden wriggled an arm free. And unbuckled the water carrier from his belt.

'I'm not afraid of you,' he said.

Devil eyes turned. The cold claw crushed his back.

'You're so worthless that nothing is more than what you are!' yelled Aiden.

Red eyes grew. Giant fangs ascended, bringing rancid stench of hell.

Aiden tilted his hand. Water poured from the flask...

... into darkness.

Fiahra!

Red eyes expanded. The monster choked. And cracked. Molten lava leaked from its scales. The claw broke.

Aiden landed on grass painfully. The howl was deafening. Knowing what was at stake, Aiden scrambled for his bow. He marched quickly to fire at its heart, adjusting his aim at the last second to the throbbing sound. The ice arrow shattered the black crystal.

Now it shrieked.

They covered their ears. Eliza hunched over Aroosa.

The jaw fell off. As it disintegrated, Aiden guessed that each horn and tooth was grown from a victim. An image of a general clambering over a hill of dead bodies flashed in his mind.

The beast was dead.

Herionus was stone.

Eliza wailed.

His sister was lifeless.

3

Matthew:

Matthew's head felt like that day when Govinda tackled him in rugby, his ears were ringing, and for a moment he felt he was back in the school's tournament.

'Mum,' he whispered. Except he knew she wouldn't be standing with the parents. He blinked twice to block the image of her sleeping on her hospital bed. She'd want him to live in the present. 'We protect those we love,' Mum had said. Her eyes held him, until he nodded. The darkness was here now.

He rolled onto his front and spat to expel the bitter salty taste from his mouth. The beast had tossed him over a mound. The light from the crystal was nearby. This was the third time he had tried climbing onto it. It was all going to plan and then it wasn't. The beast was turning…

Arif yanked Elly just in time. A claw landed.

Rose.

Rose.

Rose!

Claws scooped the ground, dirt and rocks were pelted at him. Every time the legs adjusted, the beast moaned, as its shape metamorphosed into another ungodly threat.

'It's guarding its prize,' shouted Elly.

'I'm going to kill it,' shouted Matthew.

'Wait,' said Arif, breathlessly, with one hand on his knee as he stood up. 'Captains solve problems.'

It felt like a déjà vu. Except this time, Arif didn't sound all there.

'That is not a problem. That's hell on legs!' said Matthew.

'We need to work out a way to draw it away from Aroosa,' said Arif.

'I'd kick it in the balls if I knew where they were,' shouted Matthew.

Arif looked sharply. 'That's it! The black crystal is feeding off us! Matthew, you found the monster's balls.'

The eight-legged dragon-bear kept turning.

Matthew groaned, 'They're all the way into its jaw. I'm not swinging from its horns.'

'If we don't, we're dead.' Arif gasped.

The tail came so fast, they only had time to flatten on dirt. Matthew seethed, 'You draw it, I'll chop it.'

Running, he leaped onto its tail and climbed. Matthew thrust his blade through the fur. It sank under the tough scales, squelching into flesh. Beast jolted.

He fell.

Gravel cut his hand. He got up sharply.

Arif and Elly were frozen. The kid was in its claw!

Matthew's blood ran cold. He didn't realise he had climbed back onto the beast, until the softness of his rubber soles stopped on its shoulder. Thing had to die!

He hacked monstrous flesh until a horn fell off, but the beast's neck only grew longer. Dragon-eyes ascended away from him. Matthew stabbed the scaly neck. Blood spatter missed his face. The jaw widened. Matthew struck bone, he pushed his sword with all his might and felt something snap. The beast wobbled, ready to crash.

Matthew jumped onto soft dead grass.

Thud. Thud. The hind legs narrowly missed him.

The beast had recovered. Arif waved the crystal to draw it.

The claw still held the kid, the kid was twisting to break free. That poor kid.

No!

Matthew saw his sword. Hobbling, then running, he picked it up. It was making an awful racket. Matthew struck at the horned tail and was stunned when it fell off. Ice arrows hit the beast in quick succession. The black crystal shattered.

He gasped. The whole ten storey nightmare was crumbling.

He backed away.

Faster.

The kid staggered to Elly. Large chunks of cindered flesh tumbled. Matthew ran to him and yanked him away just in time.

The hills shook, throwing everyone off balance. The rumbling stopped. Someone cried. Plants started to glow brighter.

Elly-?

The wail made him turn 180.

He ran.

The sight of dear Rose left him speechless. Blood-soaked blue dress. Limbs distorted. A hole in her chest. His stomach muscles tightened like before.

'Arry! You're okay. Right?' Elly propped Aroosa's head on her knee. Tears rolled down her cheeks.

He should do something.

Assess the victim.

Matthew knelt. When her brothers called her name, his eyes misted with tears.

She was cold.

He'd failed.

No.

No.

He waited. 'I've got a pulse, she's alive' he said, choking.

'Thank God,' said Arif.

Too much blood.

'What do we do?' asked Elly.

So far away were the double doors and the dim lit ward where the best person to help him lay on her bed.

'Matthew?'

'I'm not a… surgeon. She needs a hospital,' he croaked sorely.

'You said you were trained by the Yorkshire Ambulance Service,' said the kid.

'I handed leaflets,' he said.

'You spend a lot of time in the hospital,' said Arif.

Matthew glared. 'Are you saying I'm a qualified doctor because I visit my cancer-sick mother?'

Elly touched his arm, 'Matt, Hun, we just need to keep her comfortable, right? Arry and Eddie will run to the city and ask for help.'

Just keep her alive, his cousin's eyes were telling him. Did she think he could perform miracles?

He yanked the cloak from Elly's hands and balled it up. The gashes looked deep, but he had to start from somewhere. He pressed down. Warm blood seeped over his hands. 'In a hospital,' he said calmly, 'she'd have X-Rays and MRI-'

'Yeah... not happening. What can you do right now?' asked Elly.

'If... it was an artery, Rose would be dead. Her pulse is steady, she's struggling to breathe, which means there's something...'

'Lungs?'

'Don't know. I've only ever watched this on Amazon Prime,' said Matthew. 'I need to put a tube below her ribs to release the pressure. Does anyone have a pen?'

'Aiden, have you got a pen?' asked Arif.

'In my pocket.'

'Will it help her breathing?' asked Elly.

'It did on TV.'

'Where are the fangs?' asked Arif.

'They disintegrated when it died,' said the kid.

'Inside her?' said Arif.

Matthew tried to think. 'Even if it did, foreign bodies can be removed by surgery.'

'Surgery?' gasped Arif.

'O-kay. How far is it to the hill where we arrived?' asked Elly. 'We'll look for a door. It might just be hidden like an illusion.'

'We can't move her,' Matthew said, quickly.

'How far to the city?' demanded Elly.

'Back there, I would have guessed ten miles. But we covered a lot of ground. And we went off course. Who knows?' said Arif.

'Her bracelet is glowing,' said Matthew.

'Everything glows here,' said Arif.

A leg moved. Crack. Then the arm. Crack.

'What's happening?' yelled Elly.

Rose drew a long breath, inflating her chest. She opened her eyes, blinking twice.

'Oh my God!' cried Elly.

Matthew was stunned. 'Rose? Are you in pain?'

'Every-pissing-where,' groaned Rose.

The kid laughed.

'On the scale of one to ten, is the pain-'

'Don't tell me… are we still on the sodding planet?' groaned Rose.

'Ere. Take it easy. If you hadn't opened your eyes, Matthew was going to stab you with a pen,' said Elly.

Rose sat up sharply. 'You what?'

Matthew gawped.

'What?' she said. 'What is it?'

'Your… holes,' said Matthew.

'No-no-no. Not my dress!' wailed Aroosa.

Elly's eyes narrowed. It was the look she used when she first heard the news about his mum. Elly had followed Tom and interrogated the doctor, which he meant to do, but never found his voice to.

He felt the huge weight lift off him.

'Swear to God, you were chewed like a melon,' said Elly, twisting a hairpin to close the ripped dress.

'She's okay,' he laughed.

'You had us worried, sis,' said Arif.

The kid took his flask and opened it, Matthew washed his hands. When he closed it, Matthew hooked it onto his belt. The ground hissed, steam was rising where water landed.

'That thing had you... in its jaw,' said Elly, sounding confused.

'Something exploded in my head,' whispered Rose. 'My life was flashing, everything I'd done. I thought this is it. I'm dead, you know.'

'Gosh. So close,' said Arif.

Matthew grinned.

'D'you feel you have special powers?' asked Elly.

'Might explain the tingling,' said Rose, glancing.

Matthew's cheeks burned.

'Your emeralds were glowing,' recalled Arif.

'That's not all that's glowing,' said Elly.

'We shouldn't have left Diadromos,' said the kid, hoarsely.

'I'm just gonna lie here for a minute, if you don't mind,' Rose said, lowering her head onto his knee. Matthew watched Arif for a reaction, but he had already turned his attention to Elly pursuing the kid.

The glowing plants were growing! White veins turned red or blue. Mum would love to see these man-sized orchids. She would probably hop around, field to field, taking selfies to share to her friends at work. Not caring if there were deadly insects or snakes. She would go on and on about picturing carnivals and music festivals, ringing all her friends to ask which performer was available. She would laugh whether there was good news or bad. He should be in the hospital. Why did he walk through the door before checking it was Earth? It had been only a minute's difference between all of them touching the crystal, yet hours between them arriving in the Diadromos. Time worked differently they said, he had to believe it was true. He will go back to the exact day he left. And take the cloak. It healed Rose. It will heal Mum.

'There's something wrong with him!' yelled Elly.

Matthew straightened. Rose stood up, flicking her dress free of dirt.

'You're bleeding,' said Arif.

The kid shrugged his brother off. No surprise.

'You're not alright, until I say you are,' said Matthew. He took Aiden by the elbow and led him back to the crystal. 'Lift your shirt... Need to look, that's all.'

'Eddy!' gasped Arif.

Skin was torn in two parallel gashes front and back where the beast's claws had gripped. Matthew exhaled, 'That's... got to hurt.'

'Oh, hunny bunny! We'll pay for a doctor in the city. Whatever it takes. Vaccinate you from all diseases that thing gave you,' said Elly.

'Do we have antiseptic?' asked Arif.

Matthew snorted scornfully.

'What did they use before medicine?' croaked the kid.

'Alcohol,' said Matthew.

'And piss,' said Arif.

Elly laughed. Then gasped, 'God, he's looking pale.'

Matthew yanked the elbow to steady Aiden's balance.

'What's the matter with Aiden?' Rose hurried.

'I'm okay,' croaked the kid.

'Oh, my little Yoyo-eating brother. What did that monster do to you?' wailed Rose.

Matthew smiled when she tried to hug him. This is what Mum meant. They all needed protecting, every one of them.

'Sis, you were at death's door… and now you're not,' said Arif. 'Can we use the cloak on Aiden?'

'No,' she said. Then quite surprised, 'I mean… I don't know.'

'Why are we even talking about it?' said Matthew, retrieving the cloak. He wrapped it round Aiden tightly. Arif took over, pushing the kid down to sit on a rounded rock.

'I could have sworn this cloak was covered in blood,' said Arif.

The kid was quiet.

How did the cloak get rid of the blood? It was spotless. Not even a crease from when he rolled it up. How did it do that?

'Is it working?' asked Elly.

Matthew caught the kid's glance. Kid was missing his unicorn.

'I'm okay,' croaked Aiden, blushing with the sudden attention. He drew his knees upwards and crossed his arms.

Movement hadn't made him wince; Matthew could tell he was better. 'Who was it that chose the cloak? Because it healed Rose. And now Eddie.'

'I don't think it is a question of who, we touched objects out of curiosity,' said Arif. 'Eddie, you're stupid and brave. You'll have a great future with the army.'

Ellie straightened. 'Jealous, are you Arry?'

'Am I heck.'

137

Matthew laughed with Rose. The bullish colonel had recently taken a special interest in his youngest nephew. But not Arif.

'Who did the cloak belong to?' asked Elly, sitting down on a rock.

'Everything in the Diadromos was owned by legends,' said the kid.

'The treasures belong to us until we return them,' said Arif.

Matthew was relieved to hear him say that. He sat down by the kid.

'That thing could have eaten you, dipshit,' said Arif. 'This place is dangerous. Stay well out of trouble. We can't do jack if you fall down a pothole!'

Elly looked sharply. 'Eddy! How did you know water would kill it?'

Arif glanced.

'Water killed it?' said Rose, her forehead creasing.

'I saw him pouring water. Next, the Devil went poof – like -like in some kind of game.'

Matthew straightened. 'Game? Yes! Course. We're in a game world.'

'Don't be silly,' said Arif, pulling a face, like he did when he knew Elly was right about Kamaldeep having a crush on the maths teacher, but just didn't want to admit it.

'Okay. So how do you explain that thing?' dared Matthew.

'I don't flippin' know.!'

'Just think about it. If we're in a game, we've got to reach the end goal, then we've won. But who's Player One? I can't remember sitting down for it,' said Matthew.

'The one collecting rewards and winning levels,' said Elly, turning her head.

'Heroes killing beasts. Finding a unicorn,' grinned Rose.

Matthew smiled.

'It's not me,' said Aiden, blushing.

'Well, if we did enter a game world, then the cloak and the tree make sense. But not all heroes make it to the end,' said Arif.

Damn shame. The cloak would have been the best thing for Mum, if it worked in the real world.

'Let's eat,' said Arif.

'We need to get home,' said Elly.

'Where is my Food Tree?' asked the kid, getting up sharply.

Matthew folded the cloak. Everyone headed in different directions to look for the tree. The kid cut sharply towards the steep crevice. Matthew knew where he was heading.

The stone creature was surrounded by new flowers. Light flowed from roots to petals, every flower a different colour. Giant flowers had trumpets he had never seen.

'Isn't he dead?' whispered Matthew, hoping the kid wouldn't cry.

'Sometimes we don't know how we know what we know,' whispered the kid, 'but we know that we know. And, we have to try. Do you know who said that to me, Matthew?'

'Who?'

'Your mum,' said the kid. He touched the stone creature.

Stone cracked.

Matthew gasped.

Herionus lifted himself from the rubble to lick the kid's face.

They laughed.

He edged slowly to stroke its silky head. Herionus snorted.

'Found it,' shouted Arif. 'Oh. Hello Herionus. How the-you know what, I don't care. Here, I think a flower's broken off, it's lost soil. No real damage.' He passed it to his brother and came to stroke the unicorn.

'Heri! My friend!' squealed Elly.

'Not feeling well,' said Rose, sitting back down. 'I'm glad it's all right, Eddie. Just keep it away from me.'

'Sure.'

Everyone joined Rose to sit down on the rocks. 'Tell me it works,' said the kid, placing the tree before Arif.

Arif moved closer to the tree, blatantly ignoring the gesture of kindness from his brother. 'Tuna salad baguette, please,' he said, tapping it.

A wrapped sandwich appeared before him.

Rose insisted she wasn't hungry. Instead, she stared at the illuminating landscape as they ate sandwiches, then fruits and cakes. Some flowers were as tall as lampposts, but she wasn't filled with wonder. She seemed worried. Matthew chewed his turkey slowly, wondering if he should ask something.

Elly picked a daisy and tucked it behind Rose's ear. Rose barely flinched. Mum would get annoyed if anyone picked a flower. 'The life of a flower should always live and die in the wild,' Mum liked to say. Rose liked flowers, right? Or is that only the ones in his garden, not the amazing glowing kind?

'Where's my water?' asked Elly, gulping down the kebab.

The kid closed her water carrier and shook it. Then passed it to Elly.

'Bloody hell,' she said. Her eyes lit up, causing Matthew to laugh.

Matthew drank his flask empty. Rose hadn't even opened hers, she had to vomit by a ditch. Her body was still dealing with trauma.

'Aiden tell us what you know,' Arif said, wiping crumbs off his jeans.

Matthew picked up his apple and bit into it, crunching quietly.

The kid shook his head, 'Nowt.'

But his eyes had twitched.

Matthew swallowed. 'Eddie. We'll just sit here until you remember.'

'What?'

'You know summat,' said Matthew, gently. 'Tell. Because if you don't, and we face another one of those things, none of us will be this lucky.'

The kid's jaw parted, horrified.

Matthew tapped the tree and caught a bunch of grapes. He passed it to the kid.

Aiden unfroze to take it. 'I-I was thirsty... for... for a while. I thought if I'm going to die, I should at least have a drink. It was an accident, really. I opened the flask... and it spilt. One of the arches that me and Eliza looked at before you two arrived, said Heroes of Clay. Then we moved under the arch that said Heroes of Fire. So, when it died, it clicked,' he paused to swallow the terrifying memory. 'We... are in a world for djinns.'

'What?'

'Okay, I'm not a hundred percent. But my ice arrows hurt it more than your swords.'

'Screamed like effin crazy,' said Elly.

'He's right,' said Matthew.

'Djinns - aren't they made of fire?' said Arif.

'We're in hell. Is that what you're saying?' said Elly.

'You're scaring me,' said Rose.

'Let me get this right… exactly what are we talking about?' asked Matthew.

'We may be on a demon world,' said Elly, laughing.

'Stop it Liz! Aiden, stop this nonsense. Matthew said we're in a game,' said Rose.

'Mintukka Lyanta Jenn means People of Fire,' said the kid quietly. 'I poured water into its throat. It died.'

Rose deflated.

'Things in our world are generally made with a high percentage of water,' said Arif, thoughtfully. 'What if, their meaning of water is not H2O. That would mean, we can't drink theirs. We can't eat alien food. It also means, the most precious things we have right now are our water vessels and Hathor's Tree. We need to guard them with our lives.'

The kid smiled with relief.

It was odd to see Arif agree with his brother.

'It doesn't make sense, Arry. If water is scarce and everything here is made of different chemistry, why haven't we barbecued,' asked Elly. 'You know since we're made of water.'

'Magic protects us,' said Aiden.

'Magic,' laughed Elly.

'We don't know the science of this universe,' frowned Arif. 'Everything is… extraordinary. With all we've been through, I'm not even that tired.'

'I'm not tired either,' said Elly shrugging. 'And I normally sleep a lot. You know that don't ya, Matthew. Isn't that odd? Very odd!'

Matthew nodded his head. Uncle Pete called Eliza Sleepy Head.

Gravel tumbled. Something scraped.

'Someone's coming!' whispered Arif.

Elly grabbed a rock. Matthew stood up and drew his sword facing the glowing rustling reeds. Aiden pulled slowly on his bowstring until an ice arrow appeared.

He was ready this time.

4

Two cloaked figures ascended the slope with long strides. Almost human, but their eyes glowed, like emeralds in heavenly light. On their jackets, they wore an emblem of a green star. Their hair was green too.

'Stop where you are!' shouted Matthew, taking a step back so he could keep them in sight. He wasn't buying their alarmed faces, not when they were armed. 'You're trespassing.'

The aliens stopped.

'Toss your weapons to the ground,' he ordered.

'Matthew, we don't want trouble,' said Arif.

'We're neck deep in it. Swords and boots say soldiers to me,' he said louder.

'Afli Ayla szhin,' exclaimed the monobrow alien.

'To the ground,' said Matthew sternly.

She stepped back, then glanced at him, 'Wera.'

'Ehud tooshta?' said the monobrow alien.

'They're speaking alien,' gasped Arif.

She pointed past them. 'Narthrin!'

Matthew turned to glance near the dusty remains on the hill. Herionus was chewing grass. Herionus lifted his head to stare back.

'We don't speak alien,' stammered Arif.

'Identify yourselves,' said Elly.

'Arla Daraan,' said the lady alien, her stance once again cocky.

Monobrow dipped his head. 'Arla oshri Daraan kildana lyanta metava vastariva. Daffariff leeyan kinda Kand Ehud!' He glanced at him.

Then something strange happened. The aliens lowered with a knee on the ground.

Matthew was sure it was a trick. 'Stay back,' he warned, grabbing the kid's arm.

'He wouldn't be saying blessings be with you children of the clayborn, slayers of an evil lord, if he wanted to harm us,' said the kid.

The monobrow lifted as if surprised. 'You speak Jenn?'

'We prefer English,' said the kid.

'What is English?'

Elly laughed. 'We take our language to foreign places and expect others to speak like us. That's English. Lovely to meet you.'

'Eliza wants to shake hands because we shake hands' laughed the kid.

Matthew watched with unease as the aliens greeted Elly, the kid, then Arif. The big guy came to him next, his smile disappearing, 'You are hiding from something.'

'No, we had to run from it,' said Matthew. He returned his sword to its sheath and shook his giant hand equally hard.

'I am Teiaar,' said the lady alien, 'He is Feios. We are scouts from the Emerald Order of Jades and Daraan. These are treacherous lands.'

'We get that,' said Arif.

'Come, hasten to Jade City.'

'Why should we follow you?' asked Matthew.

She turned slowly.

'When we don't know who you are,' said Matthew, ignoring Elly's glare.

Lady Alien spoke tenderly, 'Astonishing to see what we see. Our heads we must obey. Kildana, when we say these are treacherous lands, we mean the dead. They smell you. And you just killed their lord.'

No one breathed.

'What?' he said.

'I believe in your world… you say… vrykolakas?' said Lady Alien.

The kid rolled his eyes. 'That's Greek. We say vampire.'

'Vampiyur?'

There was a flurry of questions. Matthew could tell his cousin was annoyed the most. She gave him that look, which signalled she was angry with someone, but he wasn't sure who.

Aroosa yelled, 'Don't touch me!'

Lady Alien straightened, stepping back. 'You have nothing to fear from us.'

'What?'

Lady Alien pointed at her bracelet. 'Sister.'

Aroosa hid her arm behind her back.

'Your eyes… look at me,' commanded the lady alien. 'Begone!'

That sounded strange.

'Rose?' Elly went to her.

'Oh, for heaven's sake,' groaned Arif. 'Sis, you heard her. We should get going.'

Rose's head turned 180, jaws stretched with giant fangs.

Matthew froze.

Arif recoiled.

She growled.

Matthew couldn't believe what he'd seen. That was biologically impossible, right?

'Leave me!' growled a voice so monstrous.

'Rose?'

'Jesus.'

'Mena baarda!' yelled Lady Alien. Both aliens drew their swords.

Matthew moved quickly to block them. 'Stop!' The aliens were a lot taller, but he was not afraid to use his sword. 'Arif, you tell them. If they take one more step, I will cut them down.'

'I will too,' said Arif, drawing his sword slowly to show he meant it.

'Little boys, she is baarda.'

'Who is she calling little?' he yelled.

'What do you mean damned?' asked the kid, joining him.

'This one…' Lady Alien pointed her sword at Rose, 'is coming baarda. We must chop off her head. Or she will take yours.'

Rose growled like an animal. Her eyes rolled. Her jaws kept stretching and snapping.

'Granted, she's acting weird. She's my sister,' said Arif.

'Back off!' snapped Matthew, raising the sword to the lady's eye.

'It is an achievement to survive a kand ehud,' said Feios. 'Now he lives inside her.'

Lady Alien pointed her sword at Rose. 'The Ethyrian Daraan have sworn to protect. Clayborns, I serve notice unto you that she will die! It will be my honour to do it for you.'

Matthew felt his blood boil. 'Our cloak healed her. That thing is dead! So, screw you!'

'I repeat, my honour!' said Lady Alien.

'Die will you!' Rose spat at the alien but missed her short. Her eyes bulged. She growled. 'Darr yee Koonta... yee farr san toosh.'

'Baji threatened to kill every one of us,' said the kid.

What the hell?

'Rose?' Matthew grabbed her elbow and steered her towards a rock to sit down.

'Wha'jussht'appen'?' Her eyes returned to their sockets.

He touched her forehead. 'You've got alien flu.'

'There must be another way,' Arif said, fearfully.

'Can the cloak heal her?' asked Elly.

'Magic has no effect on the curse,' said Lady Alien, stepping closer.

'She's just exhausted,' said Matthew. But her body was on fire. She needed IV antibiotics. What was it they gave mum? Teicoplanin and Vancomycin. No, she would need antivirals. Christ. All of them. How much would they cost on an alien planet?

'Keep her jaws from your neck,' said Feios.

'Her bracelet is glowing,' he said. 'It's healing her!'

Lady Alien sheathed her sword. 'It buys her time. There is a chance our elders can help her. It is a possibility and not a certainty? Ten thousand strides lie ahead. And the damned fly.'

'Let's go!' he said.

'Are you rushing to help her or are you running from something?' asked the lady alien.

What was she on about?

He spoke with his hair prickling, 'Tay-aar, that's your name, isn't it? Fay-oss and Tay-aar, I'm Matthew. We will be ever so grateful… Please. Just help her.'

'We will stop at Leybo's Cavern. It is holy land. It will protect us,' said Feios.

'Can Aiden's unicorn carry us?' asked Elly. 'I mean, just Rose?'

'It is a crime to place gentle creatures near the infected. Baarda are driven by hunger,' warned Teiaar.

'Her proximity will weaken it. We need its light if we are attacked,' said Feios.

'Let's hurry,' urged Arif.

'The damned are silent, but they see everything. They will hunt us,' said Feios, sliding his sword. 'Though we pray Ayla protects us, we must fight when it is time to fight.'

'Always,' said Arif.

'Let's go!' yelled Matthew.

5

Eliza:

Crackerjackers. Me and Cuz, Arry and Arry. And Eddie. We are walking with aliens.

This wasn't the way she imagined it would be walking on an alien world. No special space suit, no majestic landscapes, so much dirt, everywhere, what would it look like under a microscope? Hello Mother, you keep cutting up those bodies, I'm doing real science right here. I bet you wished you were here.

Eliza's shoes made gentle crosses in the dirt as they crossed a dusty riverbed. When they reached the other side, fields of aquamarine daisies gave way to giant red poppies. The new glow was sublime, but this was not the time to be comfortable. There was something not right about Rose. And how in this sodding world have they come to trust aliens in less than five minutes?

It bugged her. Every now and then, she thought the aliens turned their heads ever so slightly, as if they heard what whizzed through her thoughts. She wouldn't be shocked in the slightest. She had grown up with a Doctor Who-loving brother. Compared to that, these aliens weren't even that alien. No. Ever since she had stepped through the doorway, she had this eerie feeling she wasn't alone. She didn't like it. Not one bit.

The cold clammy feeling at the back of her neck was just her nerves, she had thought. But then that horrible monster came along. And now Eddie was talking to someone she couldn't see. It couldn't be Herionus. That sweet animal was nothing to be ashamed of. Poor Eddie, slowing down so no one would know. He tried to sneak off, trying to hide his bleeding too. It wasn't normal for him to hide anything from her, he always told her, right? All those times he would sneak off to the library, to see his special friend, he would plan it with her. 'Elizabeth, you're my bestie,' he would say. One time, he said he didn't want to go to a gig, but he really enjoyed it. She knew him better than his own sister.

But there was something else, a bad feeling in her stomach that had to mean something was not right. Not right at all.

In fact, she felt the chill in her bones before she even saw the beast. How was that even possible? She was meant to hide, but the rubies got hot, and she was frozen on the spot. Of all the magical things she could have chosen, she had to choose jewellery that heated up like therapeutic patches Grandpa Derek used to put on his saggy skin back. The voice inside her head kept repeating courage. Was that the peak of its abilities? Why didn't she pick up a shield? For heaven's sake, she chose the door. She walked through it. How could she tell their sick aunt, if anything happened to Matthew?

… And Eddie.

… And Arry.

… And Arry.

Jesus.

Arry was very quiet. Just a few hours ago, she'd have been dancing on the hillside laughing as the grass came alive with colours.

Eddie came closer.

'Why don't you ride your unicorn. If that was my pet, I'd be on that thing every second of this journey,' Eliza said, smiling.

'Because' he said quietly.

'Because?'

They passed tall white grass turning luminous green. Eddie kicked dirt.

'How can you understand what they say?' she asked quickly. Eddie had become one of those boys that talked less and less as he got older. She expected him to argue with Aroosa that day, but he just smiled. It was one of his sad half-smiles, so she barely knew what to say to him. A boy like him should be playing footie, watching Youtube or playing video games. Not tagging along with a sister and brother, getting clawed by monsters! Poor thing will end up like Uncle Leo, not fitting in anywhere except the bunk bed at a youth hostel.

Halfway down a rocky slope, the scouts turned, leading them away from the canyons. The land was waking up to an alien nightly spring. Old, shrivelled stones had changed to wide leafed plants, shimmering alien daffodils. The plants had larger leaves here, plants that cast shimmering colours on their path. Illuminated veins of emerald, lighter greens, a spectrum of blue, or leaves shaped like reindeer horns glimmering white to hold back the darkness. Eliza couldn't help pausing to marvel. They were nearing the bottom of the steep hills and straight land stretched outwards for some distance. Feios led the way now.

Eddie seemed to be enjoying sliding his feet and crunching gravel. 'I don't know. It started in the Diadromos. I was looking at the writing. It meant nothing to me and the next - I understood it all.'

What on Earth was Cuz doing walking beside her? That thing growing inside Arry should creep him out. Surely Cuz could tell the difference between a girl to quicken his heart and one that would eat it raw? Eliza turned her head to whisper, 'Why are we following them two? We don't know owt about them. What if they want your sister to be a full-on vampire and are leading us into a trap?'

Blue veins reflecting on his face were from the glowing vegetation. 'Teiaar said they can help her. We should trust them,' said Aiden.

Eliza stopped to look closely at a trunk. Red veins ran up and scattered along the branches feeding tiny, cupped flowers. 'What makes everything glow? We should take samples and study these plants. Do you think there's any real wood in this tree? We need wood to kill vampires.' Elizabeth Hughes stop talking! 'Mind you, isn't it all just so wonderful? Old me would never have thought I'd be walking with aliens. Especially, carrying this plant,' she jolted Hathor's Tree, 'it gives us food... like the no animals were harmed vegan-friendly kind. If we didn't have it, would we be able to eat anything on this whole-wide-world? If it didn't give us food, could we even carve the wood? It's tiny. Makes you think, dunnit, everything is... just short?'

Did she just see her ruby in the bracelet glow? It wasn't. She could have sworn that it glowed.

'Huh?' Eddie kicked a small stone and it tumbled, causing a landslide of dirt.

'What I'd do now for a Cola Max!' she said. 'I put a can in the fridge before coming to your house. I bet Tom drank it.'

Matthew turned his head closer. 'Rose-?'

BFF hadn't answered in the last four times Cousin had called her name. Eliza grinded her teeth. Pathetic!

'I think I took us to the wrong door. But if we get out of here, I know it is because you're here. You're the strongest and cleverest.'

Eliza turned and saw his smile. 'Aww. That's sweet. But you're right. I am the cleverest. So, you better stay close.'

'Do you think they've missed us?' asked Eddie, walking in rhythm to Herionus' hooves.

'Don't you think its weird none of us are even sleepy?' she said.

'We're not sure time on this world flows the same as Earth,' he said.

She giggled at the thought. 'If it did, Mum will have gone ape! We'd be on news. Hayley Donnelly will be on Victoria Derbyshire telling the whole wide world how she knew us. Silly sow.'

Her shoe kicked a stone.

'Tom 'll be worried,' said Eddie.

'Serves him right,' she said, rolling her eyes. 'I am so thirsty. Let's have a gob.'

Eddie removed her water carrier from his shoulder and handed it back. The water was soft and gulped down a treat! She wiped her mouth with the back of her hand and gave it back. Eddie closed the cap and shook it. It was full again!

'You lot,' barked Big Arry, scowling, 'walk faster.'

Eddie placed it back on her shoulder.

'God, isn't Arry a bossy pants?'

Arry and Arry, that's how she knew them. 'Are you alright, Arry?' Though she didn't care if BFF replied. Aroosa's face was grey and sullen. Wood. That's what everyone needed. Good strong oak sharpened to smash through any chest. She couldn't believe she was thinking about it. A strong stake was worth all of these treasures. Gosh, if only she had worn her Shelley Knight shoes, those heels could stab every vampire. BFF or not!

Eliza hadn't walked very far when her friend's voice croaked. 'Leave me alone. Please Matthew… just stay away from me.'

She speaks.

She spoke.

Exactly how much of Arry was left?

'Just want to… to see if you're alright,' said Cuz.

Arry was silent.

Was she crying? Vampires cry, don't they?

'Rose?'

'I'm alright. Honest,' she said faintly.

Eliza tugged at his strap. 'Matthew. Would you like a drink?' Though it wasn't a question.

Matthew drank slowly. Eliza wanted to say a lot of things but wasn't certain if anything could be said without being heard. She knew what Matthew wanted, even before the tilt of his head. She took the flask Eddie was holding for his sister and offered it to BFF.

BFF recoiled.

Turning to Matthew, Eliza shrugged her shoulders.

Arif was in a world of his own. 'Why has it gone so dark?' he asked, clearly not for Eliza to answer.

The alien lady was captivated by the dimming flowers. 'We know songs about the forests and fields of flowers and read scrolls in the library, but this is the first time I have seen such elegance,' Teiaar said.

An alien lady, on an alien world, saying she had never seen an alien plant? And he was buying it. What an idiot! He hurried to her, like he was intoxicated by her smell. Maybe she had glands secreting to entrap him, who knows? She needs dissecting. A proper post-mortem by Mum. God she would have loved to be here.

Eliza drank water thirstily from her vessel. She closed the cap. Then loosened it to drink again. The water was soothing her throat, but her stomach barely registered it.

To think, she used to boast about Big Arry being her boyfriend.

'You have killed Kand Ehud. Hellsborn will compete with savagery until a winner is found. Dark Lords make no hunt until heads stop falling.'

Yaadeyadeeya, yawned Eliza.

The air was getting lighter. The glow from the plants was getting stronger, like as if God had increased the wattage Tom would say. That brought a smile to her face.

Suddenly, Feios raised a hand for silence. The crunching of their feet on gravel came to a stop. His nose moved to his left as if listening and feeling for something in that direction. He whispered something to Teiaar. Her chin tilted and she glared towards the hills before turning her head South-West. 'Riders. We must move quickly. What comes with them is deadly.'

So much for her heads not falling speech.

'I'm sick of running,' moaned Big Arry.

'Can we not make a stand and fight?' asked Matthew. 'We killed the beast. Running got us nowhere.'

Eliza agreed, but the excitement building inside her wasn't her own. She pulled again at the jewelled band on each wrist.

'We are too exposed at this location. We run for a cavern at the foot of that hill. It is not far. There we can make a stand. There is also a possibility we may be seen by our sentries.' There was urgency in the alien lady's voice.

Arry turned his head, noticing BFF's head was cocked as if listening for birds.

In another world, Eliza would have snogged him just for that look. But her rubies were glowing. Her arms were still sore from the last time they burned. If Arry was right, and they were just tools of some kind, surely, she could turn them off? She rubbed the biggest one and watched with horror as a glow spread up the veins in each arm. She dug her fingers underneath the gold. All the rubies heated up. She closed her eyes and slowed her breathing just like the voice inside her told her. The rubies cooled. The glow still spread up her veins.

Mum, where are you when I need you?

She was cursing under her breath when Matthew called ahead, 'Arif!'

Big Arry turned.

Eliza moved closer to the boulder and a cluster of blue flora with white veins.

She saw nothing in the sky. Her rubies were glowing. All of them. What did this mean? Eliza closed her eyes and immediately felt shadows circling above.

Dark fluid passed over Aroosa's eyes. They all saw it.

'Rose? Tell me what's happening.'

She pushed him back. 'Aa-aarta!' she screamed at the pitch-black sky, 'Aarta!'

'Don't go near her!' shouted the alien lady, terrified.

Too late. BFF grabbed Matthew's arm, twisting it near breaking point and flung him far. 'Aarta!' came a monstrous growl.

It was all quiet. Then screams replied. And again. Third time closer.

Numpty dusted his trousers.

'Sirens are gaining control of her mind. I sense she is resisting, though for how long, I cannot determine. We must make haste,' said Teiaar.

Numpty walked.

Eliza blocked him. 'Let experts be experts. Everyone else keeps their distance, or I'll belt them all the way back to the first place they took a piss. Does everyone hear me?'

Matthew's jaw parted, 'I wasn't-' then he straightened his shirt 'Yes.'

Teiaar raised her palm towards the lost cause. 'Bismillah liffa yee nozlur diffa kin kildaan.'

In God's name, we evoke you to leave this child? Eliza was astonished she understood a shielding spell. Her rubies weren't glowing as much as they did before. Did the magic go inside her?

Rose snarled like a trapped animal. Dark blood flooded her eyes.

This was her best… friend! Eliza was out of breath resisting the powerful urge to snatch Arif's sword.

BFF swayed and collapsed.

Eliza swallowed relief.

Teiaar stopped chanting.

Matthew bent down quickly startling even Big Arry. He rolled her over and she opened her eyes. Colour returned to her face. 'It's inside me,' gasped Arry, sobbing. 'It's so evil. I can't... I can't!'

They were way out of their depth.

'We need to be honest,' said Eliza, her neck tingling. 'We've all seen Dracula. We cannot be certain if Rose is Rose. And if she is, at the very least the filth inside her is waiting to trick us. We have to do Teiaar's plan. Chop off her head. Clean off. From the back of her neck should do it.' She was shocked at her own words, but it was like she was a spectator now in her own body. 'We cannot want any of us to be a Hellsfilth! Least of all the young boy. A merciful end is what Arry would want.'

Stop it. Stop it!

They looked at her, their brains still processing what she said.

'You're saying Aroosa wants us to chop her head off?' asked Big Arry.

'Thing inside her wants to drink your blood and plant its seed inside you, where it will slowly eat your soul for eternity. There's no cure,' she said, straightening.

'No,' said Eddie. 'That's my sister.'

'What the hell's wrong with you,' yelled Matthew, disgusted.

Her voice was strangely deep, 'Bind her. Seek the Oakenstone. Break the woodstone and sharpen.'

Stretching their necks, the aliens watched her.

A tremor passed through her. Eliza stepped back, then turned to yank off the bracelet. It tightened more into her skin. The rubies burned her so fast she almost cried out.

Feios used a knife to cut off his sleeves. He cut them into long pieces. 'When we get to Aran Daran, we will cleanse the girl,' said Feios, handing her a long piece of cloth. 'I will urge everyone to cover their mouths, the damned will try to infect you.'

'Why have charrelles not attacked?' asked Teiaar. 'They have opportunity. Darkness overwhelmed the child.'

Feios thought about it. 'They've never seen so many akhwidein-vegetation before. They may think it is magic. And don't know what effects it will have on them.'

'Light is not an effective defence against the undead,' said Teiaar, fastening the cloth into a facemask on Aiden.

Eliza missed the crystal as soon as Arif shoved it into his trousers. She pulled the cloth over his mouth and nose and tied it at the back of his head. Then did Matthew.

'Nevertheless, it has bought us time. It's likely they know where we are heading, but we must head there all the same,' said Feios.

'Sirens are the most cunning,' agreed Teiaar.

Eliza agreed with every word that they uttered, even though she didn't know why. It felt like the rubies were telling her to be impressed by these aliens. The cloth was softer than silk but stronger than nylon. If only Tom could see her now. He would have found a way to remove these awful superhero-like bracelets, probably would have stopped her going through the door.

For a moment, her rubies glowed. Suddenly, her head cocked with alarm. 'Vampires!' she cried.

Hooves approached from a distance.

They ran. Moving directly into the cluster of tall glowing plants, they followed Feios over a broken bridge and a dried riverbed. The plants were bigger here. A forest of stone trees, with white glowing veins. From above the glowing forest, came a deathly shriek.

The screams shifted left to the right.

Eliza broke a stone branch and snapped it, passing one piece to her cousin. She was a fast runner. She always had been. At school, she always took part in the one hundred metre and relay circuits. She won most of the time. Other times it had been Denise Duffy or Farah, whoever had more practice for that day. Last week she raced a neighbour from Moorhead to Stoney Ridge and down to Cottingley roundabout. She always won. These aliens would not best her! But she couldn't help glancing at Aiden. A voice told her she needed to protect him at all costs. Why was he important? What did he know?

Herionus stomped the ground with his hind legs and Aiden puffed harder to run faster, but they were far behind with the alien lady. Teiaar kept stopping to fire her arrows at the darkness.

Another scream.

Doubling back, Eliza grabbed Aiden by the waist and threw him on Herionus, slapping Herionus to urge it to gallop. It was a small creature, but capable of one rider. If only Aiden could hold the mane in his hands, she watched him wobble from side to side.

'Fly!' yelled Teiaar, racing towards her.

She heard the thuds closing in from behind.

Eliza turned and ran.

She could see they were hurtling towards a large mouth of darkness ahead. Feios tapped Arif and signalled to draw his sword. Matthew drew his too.

We are ready, the voice inside her head said. She ran side by side with Herionus, until she saw the pathway curved, she took the shortcut for the oakenstone and kicked a branch to snap it. Aiden passed her on Herionus, holding his bow.

Eliza turned her head to look for Aroosa but could not see her. She frowned.

'Run,' shouted Teiaar. 'Keep your eyes alert. They are coming!'

As she ran from behind, Teiaar drew her bow and prepped an arrow so fast that if she had blinked, Eliza would have missed it. For a moment, she didn't want to follow. Her heart was pumping. She wanted to be back in her home and sat on her sofa, playing a game with Tom. Oh, sweet darling Tom. What will happen to him?

Feios led the boys into the giant dark hole. They disappeared. Her heart slowed when the burning throb reached the back of her neck. The rubies were pulsing so hard, she felt it deep in her chest. Her veins were like volcanic flows. She closed her eyes and immediately felt the presence of the amassing enemy heading for the clearing ahead.

'Charrelle!' she screamed.

Eliza ran.

'Eee-fa...nozlur...yeee-aa...too-oom!' she heard Teiaar chant as they flew together out of the forest. They ran faster, seeing how the boys were exposed to danger. Swords clashed with demons. Stonewood slammed into beasts. Ice arrows seared into the air!

6

ARIF:

There were days when Arif wished he wasn't the eldest. He didn't have a big brother to show him how to survive his exams, get his first job or make it last with girls. Firstborns are expected to drop everything and do 'kind' things. He never liked it. No way. Dumping chores on wallies was worth it. Mum didn't mind. And watching Aroosa scream and stomp around the house filled him with satisfaction.

The sulker was another story. Teasing Aiden was like winding up an old alarm clock, you wind and wind until he cried his eyes out. Year before last he stopped talking. To everyone. Dad gave him 'the talk' about being a better brother. Like as if it was his fault Eddie was born socially inept. Like as if he had time with all the work he had to do for college and getting Eliza to forgive him for snogging Julie, and Julie to forgive him for texting Callie, and Callie to forgive him for breaking her taillight and getting dumped by all at the party. Yep. Yep. So, of course he was going to ask the idiot if he was getting bullied. That's being a big brother, isn't it? Okay, so what if the entire neighbourhood was in the house, it wasn't his fault. Come on. Flippineck. Aroosa shouldn't have stuck up for sulker and maybe he wouldn't have said what he said.

If sisters didn't ask questions they wouldn't be humiliated would they? If adults didn't yell, he wouldn't have yelled back, would he? The conversation went the wrong way, it's not like… those… topics were news. Okay, maybe to Dad. It was Aiden's fault, all of it.

One, for being the topic in the wrong place at the wrong time. Two, for listening to that crap talk and being so quiet. Three, being clueless how to deal with problem people, means he lacked assertive skills and needed a crash course on having a real life. That's his fault and that's their fault and her fault for trying to make it his fault. She should not butt in and make it all about herself. So why would they want him to feel bad about telling the truth?

Of course, he was sorry.

Big brothers are always sorry. Just can't show it, that's all.

Okay. Sometimes.

Eliza came up with a brilliant idea to use Matthew's… situation… to coax Aiden out of his room. They gathered everyone in the garden to 'cheer Matthew up'. Then dipshit had to go near the bush and pick up an alien crystal and land everyone in this sad awful place.

Aiden was different now. He wasn't just ignoring him… it was like nothing really fazed him. Like he knew what was about to happen. Confidence, Eliza called it. Aiden knew exactly where to go in the Diadromos. He knew how to read those alien pictograms and calligraphies. And he looked at peace with that… birth defected unicorn. Even smiling. Why didn't he smile at home? What is his problem? Maybe having shit dumped on you by older brothers makes you confident someday.

He pulled off the cloth mask to get air, it was wet from his breath.

'Shit's happening!' yelled Eliza.

He turned. Teiaar was running like the devil was after her. Herionus galloped with Aiden trying his best to hold on.

Running, he saw Feios touch Matthew's cheek. The thing slid to cover his face. It was a mask! He was so busy watching that he nearly crashed into a large rock. Feios yanked him by his sleeve. 'Touch it to your face,' he said.

It was a tiny green butterfly. Arif tapped it to his chin, it unfolded fast to cover his mouth and nose. There was no time to marvel on this military grade technology.

He reached the clearing where no plants glowed. Herionus galloped ahead with his brother. For a moment he was going to yell for him to stop, they should check first before running into pitch black without a plan. Matthew flew past. Then Eliza.

Arif checked the mask, it felt like leather, but smelled metallic. It was definitely stuck to his face. It was better than the rag, he could breathe properly.

'Eefa nozlur yeea toom!' cried Teiaar.

God almighty, isn't she? Under all that gown, she has a stunning figure.

Feios and Matthew drew their swords.

Teiaar's arrow lit the sky like a rocket.

Holding the heavy steel blade, Arif watched the burning torches spill down the hill, where a beast-riding vampire commander took position. His heartbeat echoed in his ear when he saw they kept coming. Eyes to your left, she had said. How did he understand that?

Charging towards them were giant-fanged soldiers with blood red eyes. Rotted faces! Claws dived from above, forcing his friend to duck. Herionus shrieked and lifted on hind legs, the pulse of light forced vampires to cower and zombies to divert their path. Aiden fell off, but he had fired an arrow before he could call his name.

And he kept firing.

How was he this fast? And how come every arrow hit a target? It wasn't possible. Right? The zombies were crumbling faster than he could set eyes on them.

Arif heard his name being called.

Hurtling rotten flesh flew past him. Steel struck again. Feios was quick and agile, severing winged vampires to protect him. A zombie lunged from his side. A large steel blade caught it, Matthew pushed the creature down and struck its throat.

'Arif!' came a muffled cry.

Arif turned swiftly and stabbed the axe-wielding zombie, the sword went in easier than he thought, the creature's guts squelched out when he pulled back his arm. Dead blood spilled, plants withered and died. The zombie's head still growled.

'Get back' he shouted, trying to keep it at bay with his sword. He heard his name being called again.

'Aaa!' Matthew crashed into his zombie, delivering a severe blow to its throat. He pulled back his mask to say, 'Don't you just love it?'

What the hell?

Arif tightened his grip on his sword. He would not be outdone by the boy who learned everything about Fortnite from him. An axe-wielding zombie attacked, Arif stepped aside and struck a killer blow. Well almost. Blood gushed from its neck, but large talons kept reaching for him. Using all his might, he struck at the elbows. It left him breathless. How did Matthew have so much stamina? The zombie kept reaching. He closed his eyes and pushed his sword into its mouth, twisting until it stopped wriggling.

He took quick breaths again. Wow. Wasn't so hard... right? Who was he kidding?

They came growling. Arif backed inwards towards Feios and Matthew. It was important to defend his friends.

The thing pressing against his jeans was everything he needed. His mouth was so dry, he could risk being bitten for a mouthful of water.

No.

Matthew used his whole body to deliver deathly blows and he was so swift, he even swung at those that attacked him.

Arif.

Arif turned. Aiden was firing arrows without tiring.

You chose your sword. Let it protect you.

What-? How the hell did he do that? What the hell is this place?

He loosened the grip. The sword swung to impale a zombie's throat. It swung again, beheading another. Suckin' Nora. His sword was alive! It found zombies before his eyes and ears caught up. Some were too tall, he had to raise his shield over his head to deflect their blows, but the sword knew where to dismember. He was winning! How the hell was he winning?

He caught the red flash from the corner of his eye.

A scream erupted from above.

It was frightening, though now he was getting to expect worse. Two floating ladies were struggling to put out red flames on their bodies with their claws. When the next round of fireballs killed them, every zombie faltered.

Arif turned to see where the fireball came from.

It was Eliza. He'd never seen her so angry. Flares discharged from her rubies so fast if he'd blinked, he would have missed them. Explosions tore the hill, scattering zombies into body parts.

Eliza was a weapon!

'Every army in the world is going to pay a trillion quid for that,' he said, laughing.

'You almost got it,' she snapped.

'Yeah?' He knew what she really meant. She still cared…

Another burst of light from Herionus. He caught sight of Aiden standing back-to-back with Teiaar, his arrow aimed at the horde, while she faced the stone trees. Vampires were blinded by Herionus and struck by Aiden's arrows. She must have coached him on how to do that.

Arif was tugged. He turned to face a growling zombie with the sword in its throat. Arif yanked it out, but the sword struck its throat again, and the zombie fell. Feios appeared behind him, to face off the next attack. What made his sword kill so effectively? When the zombie's fell, they didn't get back up. Who made it? Did it only work on deadhearts?

A dark figure struck Herionus from the sky, Aiden warded it off with a burst of ice arrows. One of them almost got him. As luck would have it, Aiden tripped onto his back, missing her giant claw by inches. Teiaar helped him back up. Herionus sat down, causing both to falter. Eliza turned her head too, but Herionus just looked tired, he began to chew grass.

All that bursting of light must drain him, thought Arif. He started towards Aiden but found himself quickly surrounded. Feios fought to reach him. 'Stay close, Kildaan. I cannot protect you if you wander.'

He needed protecting. Was it that obvious?

Aiden was alert and firing again. He barely blinked when a siren floated towards him. Her cries seemed mournful at first, then she hurtled towards him screaming, her talons ready to rip. Aiden turned and fired at the zombie charging Matthew, leaving Teiaar to fire frantically at the siren until it was killed.

Arif was gobsmacked. Why would Eddie do that? Damn it, where was Aroosa? She had better stay safe and out of sight. An army of zombies appeared on the hill with six vampires. How was he meant to protect them both? In this?

Eddie is vulnerable right now. He's acting crazy because he doesn't care. And you caused it.

FFS.

Arif marched quickly. Teiaar killed a vampire commander. She pulled back on the bowstring and another arrow appeared by magic. Arif reached his brother and fixed his mask. 'Aiden, stay close.'

Aiden fired at a vampire, it fell backwards and rolled down the hill.

Rumbling came from the darkness.

Not again.

Teiaar primed her bow in the direction of the noise.

On the hill, vegetation light snuffed out. Zombies and vampire numbers swelled with burning torches. They parted and the dark giant emerged, this one was shaped like a boar, with nine lidless eyes. Hundreds of fangs deformed its face.

Eliza had a fireball ready, but she was frozen with fear, her chest rising quickly.

'Retreat,' ordered Teiaar.

Arif turned to his brother. 'Eddie, remember you've already killed one. And that was bigger. We'll take care of the rest.'

A shrill cry forced them to look sharply. A snarling dead soldier ran towards them, Arif adjusted his mask, stepped aside, and spun quickly for his sword to sever.

Protected by face guards, Matthew and Feios were fighting hard to deflect the assault from North-West, zombies kept losing their heads. Arif moved with his sword, which fought faster. He felt the zombies' shudder when the beast made a ghastly noise. Between each kill, Arif kept watch over his brother. Aiden drew back his bow, he dipped the appearing silver arrowhead into the water flask and straightened.

The beast roared again. Three vampire ladies leapt into the air. Eliza's fireball was intercepted by one of them trying to protect the middle one. She tumbled. The air was shattered by siren screams and a roar from the beast.

Aiden had a clear shot. The neck of the beast was stretched, exposing all nine edges of its protruding dark crystal.

'Kill it Eddie!' yelled Arif.

To his disbelief, Aiden adjusted his aim and fired at another siren. The arrow struck her chest, throwing her to the ground. The beast roared mournfully over the siren's scream.

'The zombies,' said Teiaar, looking astonished. Arif didn't understand the rest of what Teiaar uttered, other than 'She was a vinx.'

What was a vinx? Why did it matter?

Oh wow!

The army of zombies had just become bodies lying all the way to the slopes.

The vampires retreated behind the beast. The thick trunked claws of the beast adjusted widely and closely, until it faced the stone forest. The jaws parted again, the roar was louder and stronger.

From the giant stone vegetation, leapt a thin figure into flight. Emeralds glowing green, a green aura flooded her whole body as she caught the vampire lady and tore off her head. Then she spun faster towards the enemy's mass, the aura growing ever more intense, until a burst of green light was so bright the vampires and the beast burst into flames. The giant beast stood its ground, trying to resist the green inferno, launching dark spikes towards her. Two of them were caught by red fireballs, the rest returned to his body with a vengeance.

The head of the beast tried to shield the dark crystal embedded in its neck, giant trunk legs retreated.

The green inferno adjusted.

The dark crystal exploded.

Vampires scattered.

The burning beast staggered with breathless pants, then stood still. It crumbled.

Arif laughed, he ran to his sister and threw his arms around her, laughing. 'I don't know how you did it, but well done!'

'I thought I was dying, but this bracelet was warming me against the cold. Then I felt a shudder. Everything went quiet. And the green heat spread up my arm, I could feel the energy racing inside. It was awesome. I was infected. Now I'm not.'

'Yay!'

They laughed with jubilation.

Then he saw Eliza inhale horror.

Aroosa's hand went to her mouth.

The gentle sob from behind. His brother was kneeling, holding its head. 'Turn to stone,' pleaded Aiden, repeatedly.

Arif moved swiftly to reach him.

'Look at me. Turn to stone. Please... Herionus.'

Herionus was breathing with a strange throaty guttural noise, his eyes half closed. The poor creature shuddered.

'Eddie,' said Eliza, crouching down.

'Why won't he listen to me?' sobbed Aiden.

Herionus shuddered again. It neighed pitifully.

Tears welled in his hot eyes. He placed a hand on his shoulder.

'Maybe he can't,' said Matthew, softly.

'Herionus please turn to stone,' sobbed Aiden.

'He's infected,' said Feios. 'It is merciful to use a sword.'

'No!' yelled Aiden.

Everyone glared. Feios got the message and sheathed his sword.

'There is a time spell that we once used to cure a mithrin, until we could gather enough aylarhiyssa to bathe it,' said Teiaar.

'So Herionus can get better?' asked Arif.

'Theoretically speaking,' said Teiaar.

'What d'you mean, theoretically. You said you cured your mithrin,' said Arif.

'The mithrin died,' said Feios.

'A mithrin is three times the body mass of this pet,' said Teiaar.

'So… can we do that?' asked Matthew, his eyes glistening.

'I strongly sense it will work,' said Teiaar.

'We need to try,' said Arif, feeling for the gentle creature.

Feios asked for them to form a circle around Herionus. Teiaar instructed what they must recite. Arif joined hands with Teiaar and Aiden. 'We beseech the spirits of the past who met the People of Light,' he chanted, with them. 'Take our might, hear this creature, bind its blight, grant us grace to cleanse it with light.'

A heptagonal shape of light appeared binding them to each other. A cascade of light drifted down to cover the unicorn. It went green. Herionus hardened to stone and disappeared.

7

ARIF:

Arif was glad when he felt the air change, he had reached a wider space, where the cave was naturally lit by hanging stalactites. The crystal was giving him a shoulder-ache.

The others were still walking slowly. 'How did you do that back there?' he asked, turning to his brother.

Aiden stopped drinking from his flask. 'What?'

'Put words in my head when I was fighting? Are you like telepathic now?'

Aiden's eyebrows creased together, then his neck lifted, like it did when he expected a punch, 'What?'

'You said something to me when we were fighting,' Arif said.

Aiden clipped his carrier to his belt. 'I… don't know what you are talking about.'

'Well, if you didn't put those words in my head, then who did?' he asked.

'Er-what words?' his brother asked.

'Forget it,' sighed Arif. 'Is this a base of some kind?'

As he stared, something popped, and a pillar was lit up in bright light. Sequentially, white flames popped alive inside torches hanging from the high carved ceiling. Moss covered stone tables, the hard floor, abandoned pots and spoons and broken chairs. Yet it wasn't damp, the air was dry and clean. Grand pillars decorated with etchings and djinn scribing held up the ceiling.

At the far side, tables were joined near an old, dried fountain.

'Now this is a cavern,' said Arif, pointing at the giant stalactites.

The others had stopped to marvel at a romanticised battle, involving a beast, a demonic queen, two saintly queens and a saintly knight. The painting was rich in colours and seemed to have taken a lot of artists a lot of time and effort.

'It is a montage to Leybo's war after the traitorous Day of Abaddon,' said Teiaar.

Arif took a sip from his water carrier. 'What's the Traitorous Day of Abaddon?'

'The day Leybo - may he rest in peace - discovered his best friend, the Emperor of the Nine Djinn Worlds had drunk blood of the devil and condemned all djinn kind. Blessed were those by Leybo's side,' said Teiaar.

'Protective magic is strong here. It will give us reprieve,' said Feios.

Eliza marched to a table and plonked the plant. 'I'm eating here, not on some grubby rock.'

Aiden sat down beside Eliza looking like the day he lost his journal. Okay, that was a weird day. Mum and Dad had gone to Birmingham. He'd hoped he could have fun reading his darkest secrets and teasing him until he was blue in the face. But the pages had been empty.

You'd have thought the way Eddie cried that he'd put his heart and soul into it.

Teiaar glanced with disdain, 'We will refuel.'

What was that? Did she..?

That was the old me. The new me cares… well, I will.

'Fish and chips,' sighed Aiden.

'Just what I was thinking,' laughed Eliza.

'Water carriers were placed in the middle to make room for the meals.

'Carbs and protein,' said Aroosa, who normally ate little.

'Okay, well here goes. Fish and chips with salt and curry sauce,' said Eliza closing her eyes. She touched Hathor's Tree. A bundle rolled towards her.

Arif watched her eyes widen as she unwrapped it. 'God Almighty! I mean just look at size of mine, it's like it was just caught and fried,' she said.

'They're just like us,' said Aiden. 'All that fighting! So glad we have food.'

Arif grinned when she passed the plant to him. 'I'm going to offer our friends some fish and chips,' he said.

'No, you eat. I'll do it,' said Matthew.

Surprised, Arif sat back down.

Teiaar shook her head when Matthew offered food.

'What are they eating?' asked Eliza quietly.

'Looked like dried bread,' said Matthew, sitting down.

'Why can't they eat our food?' she asked.

'I dunno. They didn't want it,' said Matthew, taking a bite of battered fish.

'Perfectly okay. We don't know if aliens can eat our food, their biology might be different. They might only eat gluten,' said Arif.

'Might not like it. I saw him smell it,' Aroosa said, scoffing chips.

'They're nice people,' said Arif, looking down at his fish.

'Hey up, he's not hungry,' said Eliza. 'Have you ever heard of Arif Not Hungry?'

'No way!' said Aroosa, laughing.

'He's falling for her,' laughed Eliza.

'Arif, she's huge. How are you going to reach up to kiss her?' laughed Matthew.

'I don't know what you're talking about,' he said, feeling his face heat up. 'But come on, Teiaar is hot pretty.'

They fell against each other in fits of giggles.

He caught her stare, almost smiling, she turned her head.

Arif ate fish and drank his water. When he'd finished, he noticed the others had left the table. Aiden was studying engravings in pillars and tables, which were barely visible through moss and dust. Arif wanted to ask why, but his brother seemed less miserable.

Best not rock that boat.

'Do you think the general 'd mind if we looked around?' Eliza said. She waltzed to the far side of the cavern.

'Look at this!' cried Aiden.

Arif hurried to look. Behind the longest stone table was an angel faucet. The water glowed and did not seem to dampen the moss, it flowed down the gully to a hole.

He moved his hand slowly to touch it. It didn't burn. The water was silky and tepid. He tasted a few drops from his finger. It was tongue-tingling and sweet.

Immediately, he felt a warming sensation sweep through his body.

He felt alive. 'Wow!' he laughed.

Aiden cupped his hands to drink.

'You're drinking water that could be contaminated?' asked Matthew.

'Yes Arif. Why would you do that?' asked Eliza.

'I swear to God, you want this!' said Arif.

'Ilfa!' came a cry from behind them. Teiaar glared past him. 'Feios!'

'Uh-oh. What have you done, you two?' asked Aroosa.

'Feios! Feios! Ilfa fiara!' sobbed Teiaar.

'You don't think it's a shrine… What does an alien holy shrine look like? Oh crap. Have we violated their culture?' he said.

'Let's be clear, you violated their culture,' laughed Eliza.

'She said it's water from fire,' said Aiden.

'How does water come from fire?' asked Matthew.

Feios laughed loudly. Then hugged Teiaar. 'Ilfa fiara wen Shaara!' he shouted, shoving his face and arms into it.

Teiaar laughed too, drinking with her palms.

'I don't get it. I thought we weren't meant to do that,' he said.

'Arif, they're aliens,' said Matthew.

'You'd think we'd stumbled on a well of vodka, the way they're carrying on,' said Eliza.

'The rivers flow again,' said Teiaar, wide-eyed and joyful.

She hugged him very hard. Arif watched with astonishment as she hugged the others.

'It is true. This is aylarhiyssa… God's tears outside a city… must be flowing from the Shaara -' Feios paused, captivated by what he saw.

'Aylarhiyssa?' repeated Aiden.

Eliza took another sip. 'Doesn't taste like vodka. And I'm not choking to death, so that's a bonus. Christ that's hot!'

'Teiaar said she could cure Herionus with aylarhiyssa. Let's do that,' said Aiden.

'No Shava,' said Feios. 'It only takes one Jade to cast a spell, but many Jades for healing spells. We need to carry your friend to a bathing place.'

'Not until we can verify you killed the vinx,' said Teiaar.

Aiden looked about to cry.

'What's a vinx?' asked Arif, quickly.

'We do not know that the siren was a vinx,' scoffed Feios.

Teiaar turned her head. 'Mage of Jade, I know what I saw. A silver arrow struck her. And spirits departed from the dead. A dark lord was shaken. No siren does that. It is written, the death of a vinx will deplete the devil's might. Accept that it might be true, Feios.'

For a moment, his eyes dimmed. Then he said, 'Emeralds will verify. We must hurry.'

8

Aroosa:

They had taken the fifth tunnel where the draught was the strongest, Feios said it felt right. Aroosa watched Matthew stay close to Aiden, probably giving her space. Arif was ignoring her, and Eliza was evading her question with a story about prehistoric cave paintings. Aroosa listened, while her finger slid underneath the emerald sleeve to free a hair. It was odd that she couldn't remember how she first put it on. Did she even? There were no signs of any clasps to unhook. The gold lifted around the shape of her finger and when removed, the gold returned back to her arm.

'Are you even listening, Rose? I'm saying the aliens are not from the dark ages, they're erudite.'

Aroosa shrugged. 'I can't help feeling that everyone and everything is not making any sense.'

'We're getting left behind,' said Eliza, sounding disappointed.

Aroosa took a sip of water from her vessel, then picked up speed. 'So, you want to stay on this world with the clever aliens?'

'I didn't say that' said Eliza.

'I get it. You're interested in aliens. Voila, you've got aliens. Back there though, you changed the subject,' said Aroosa.

Eliza hopped over a root. 'Tom would go mad if he learned I didn't learn as much as I could in what could be the biggest and most exciting exploration in the history of humankind.'

'Are we not going to talk about what we both want to talk about, because it might freak you out?' whispered Aroosa.

'Freak you out. Not me,' whispered Eliza.

'No?'

'I kind of like her,' said Eliza.

Aroosa sidestepped a fossilised root. 'I do too. But her questions are odd... maybe perfectly normal for an alien. A fast fighter... okay you weren't talking about Teiaar, were you?'

'No.'

'What are we talking about?'

'Dear Rose, have you not met yours?' laughed Eliza.

Aroosa exhaled. 'I am asking about... what happened to both of us back there?'

'Now who's changing the subject.'

Aroosa faltered. 'I'm not really sure what happened.'

'Look,' said Eliza, lifting her ruby arm. 'Our sleeves are some... kind of technology. How do they function? Why do they exist? What is the significance of having different jewels?'

Aroosa frowned. 'You're planning on taking them apart?'

'Not yet. We activated them when we put them on. Best to learn more. Don't want it blowing me up,' said Eliza.

'Eliza, we stole weapons. People on Earth will want them. Dangerous people. And dangerous things here,' said Aroosa. 'We should take them off. When we find a way back to the Diadromos, we'll come back for them. And return them.'

'You do that.'

'What?'

'My rubies are mine,' said Eliza.

'That's not you Eliza,' gasped Aroosa.

'Yes, Rose, you know me so well,' said Eliza.

'What's that supposed to mean? You hate celebrities. You're always going on about the one percent. You give money to beggars all the time.'

Eliza stopped. 'I want it for what it is.'

Aroosa gasped, 'Why?'

Eliza's rubies were glowing. 'Do you know what I felt back there? I felt the power of these rubies tap into the gravity of this world and the molten core underneath our feet. Yes, that's right. The molten core. I saw it bubbling and quickening and I smelt the noxious gases. It was exhilarating.'

'You think your fireballs came from the planet's core?' scoffed Aroosa.

'Standing on an alien world should fascinate you to your core. Don't be the old you, that runs a million miles from wonders that come your way. Embrace the change, Rose.' Eliza caught up with Matthew.

Aroosa walked in silence. Alone.

Eliza's water vessel looked nicer being flat, hers was curvy. It was odd hers had a red top and she had a green one, matching her emerald bracelet. What a coincidence! It was nice of Aiden to bring everyone a vessel back there. Very thoughtful. If only they had time to look around, who knows what else they could have found.

She stepped over fallen rocks, into another opening. Matthew was talking, Eliza had her cousin all to herself. Where old roots could not reach, the Whitestone was held in place by obelisk pillars, carved from chrysoprase and greenstone. The floor had tiled illustrations of knights hunting a half-breed, but the ceiling had circular illustrations of happier times.

'Are you scared?' she asked her brother.

'With you Baji? No,' he said.

'Aren't you at least a little creeped out?' she asked. 'There were zombies, dead soldier aliens - flying zombie aliens, trying to eat us. And they stank worse than any gutter that I have smelled. Yet we just ate fish and chips and filled our stomachs, like… I don't know. I can't believe we're acting normal.'

He seemed confused. 'We're going to go home.'

'We are.' She wanted to believe it.

'We are,' he said strongly.

'Course we are,' she said, wondering if she should shut her mouth.

'You were brilliant back there,' he said.

'I was?'

'Yeah. You killed that monster devil. That was you. All by yourself,' he said.

'It was this thing on my arm,' she said.

'A weapon is just a tool, Baji. At school, we learned a tool is only as good as the person using it. I reckon, the weapon has bonded to you, and you healed yourself and killed that thing. You're very lucky, you know.'

183

She laughed. 'I hope so.'

Teiaar dropped back to ask questions about her childhood, which made Eliza shoot a warning glance. Aroosa ignored it and answered politely. This cavern didn't seem to have an end.

Arif and Matthew had stopped to examine a stone statue of a warrior, forcing Feios to backtrack. Aroosa seized the moment and sat down on a stone seat and closed her eyes. She focused on her lungs rising and the ache in her back. Teiaar was asking questions about the voice, but she wasn't listening. Juices and dust particles from dead people made her feel dirty. Trust Arif and his big gob to mention that.

Aroosa flexed her fingers, savouring the muscles stretching. She could feel dryness in her eyes and the aching in her feet. It was good to have feeling of her body without any numbness. But her gut was tight, like something bad was coming.

'Your eyes turn green when your emeralds glow. If you were infected, it would not happen,' said Teiaar.

That statement felt creepy.

It was odd that she didn't remember the beast chewing her body. Matthew said she might have amnesia from trauma. Teiaar said saliva had changed her blood into Hellsblood. Hellsblood. Hell had been inside her body. That evil... evil voice... would do all that to their parents to serve an abaddon? WTF was an abaddon? Of course, she had rinsed her head and arms in the fountain. But white stuff wasn't real water. She would have to open and close her water carrier twenty times to fill one of their buckets. She needed a real shower. If only she had shampoo. And conditioner.

Teiaar watched her brothers with fascination.

'This place is impressive,' said Arif.

'You'd think giants made this cavern,' said Eliza.

The place felt safe. She wasn't going to say it, she hardly deserved their ear. Yes, it was important to keep going until they discovered a way home. But why the hurry to leave this place?

'How did they bring stones of that size inside here?' asked Matthew.

'There's no tracks or scrapes. Can't see any signs of machinery,' said Aiden.

'People often assume ancient civilisations were illiterate, but it is a misconception,' said Eliza. 'I think these designs are from Teiaar's people.'

She was right. Aroosa first saw monoliths when they cast the spell for Eddie's unicorn. They were each meant to think of a moment of peace. Teiaar's memories had crossed into them. Her memory of peace was a moment when she followed a long line of Jade Warriors to a natural underground pool. Whitestone held the cavern's ceiling, as Teiaar walked through a wide opening, stone pillars gave space for thousands to seek shelter underneath her city. Teiaar's peers had been filled with sadness when they saw how much aylarhiyssa the pool had lost. Gracefully, the mages dropped their robes, then each sister. Teiaar kept hers, as she followed them onto the dried pool bed, ignoring the ridges pressing into her feet. She reached the Emerald Mother, who poured glowing water from a wine jug onto her head and down her back. Her sister had taken the jug, and the mother's soft fingers had wiped her face. Then they watched the Jades in emerald robes descend from their pavilions to form a circle with them. The Emerald Mother asked that they close their eyes and focus on the flame inside them.

The sense of love that Teiaar felt sent a warm tremor through her body. Aroosa asked if this was her religion, but Eliza scolded her to stay quiet in fear of jeopardising the spell.

'Why do you feel remorse about how your father spoke to your brother?' asked Teiaar.

Arif stopped.

Eliza said, 'Eddie, go tell her to mind her own business,' which echoed loud enough for Teiaar to hear and anyone else in the cavern.

Eliza's peace memory had been sitting in the car with her brother Tom on the way to a canoeing trip. But the first memory that spilled into her was when she walked through the stone woods and wanted to stab her best friend's heart with a piece of alien wood. Why would that surprise anyone? Eliza was logical. Eliza would have expected the same from her if she had become infected. But there was something different about her tone now. Eliza had changed. Would she not be her best friend anymore?

Aroosa groaned. 'Anyone that survived a possession and had powers they didn't understand might find this a little overwhelming. Throw in real magic and demons from old stories that aunties tell you when they visit.'

'They're djinns, not demons,' said Aiden.

'Who cares?' she shouted.

Her voice echoed in the cavern.

Aiden laughed. The cavern echoed that too.

It was nice to hear him laugh.

'I hear you sis,' said Arif, setting off with Feios.

Eliza and Aiden followed.

Matthew waited.

Aroosa accepted the squeeze of her hand by thick warm fingers, but Matthew's mind was with his mum.

They walked in silence.

'Given time, Hellsblood would still your heart and turn you into a siren. You would have been trapped inside your body until your soul would have been spent by the Hellspawn, as it infected more to release an army from Hell,' Teiaar had told her by the Aylarhiyssa Fountain.

It sounded bonkers.

It wasn't.

The old lady by the ghost tree had saved her. How did she do it? And who was she? The Hellspawn didn't see the lady, like she was there but not there. It had been filled with rage seeing Teiaar fighting two vampire ladies. Aroosa had wanted to stop. The Hellspawn ran to kill Teiaar. She didn't know how she managed to flip her hand. Only that she did. The old lady grabbed it and yanked her body. She heard the curdling growl, and a whimper when it couldn't see who was holding its throat. The lady's long face was old and then young, as skin unstretched an eon. She was breathtakingly beautiful when green fire grew inside her eyes. 'We are one,' the lady said. Then the emeralds shone brightly on both their arms.

Then she understood. These were powers from the dawn of time surging through her veins. Aroosa had leaned on the ghost tree to catch her breath. She was aware of the urgency as she emptied her stomach of a stinking black mess. Teiaar made her drink something metallic. She had never felt so good. Then they were both killing vampires.

Was it gone?

Didn't Matthew say that during an infection, lymphocytes cells adapt to detect an invader returning? Antibodies are made to prevent the invader from harming cells again. But doesn't that mean her body has been changed by Hell? Hell. Inside her body. Forever. If relatives found out, they would never look at her the same.

Matthew let go of her hand to catch up with Arif.

Would God cut her off? A good Muslim girl who earned her place in Heaven. Okay, to be honest, she could've worn hijabs as strictly as Fazana, and maybe not started dating Matthew in secret. But she did tell Dad. Eventually. Okay, Arif said it first. Then Mum admitted she knew. Dad only asked her to slow down, he didn't blow his lid like Arif said he would. And she fasted every Ramadan. She prayed when someone was ill. Like Matthew's mum… poor Stephanie, surviving cancer all alone.

Mum will be there for her favourite friend. And Dad. Course they would. And Aunties Haleema and Naseem. And Eliza's brother Tom. There was no apocalypse. Things are normal in Shipley. Everyone was safe. That Hellspawn… was telling lies.

Side-stepping a statue of an old king, Arif turned to glance. Then Feios.

Aiden too. The pressing of his lip on one side, meant he was worried.

Matthew was clearly walking at a safe distance.

Crap. Are they going to treat her like she is always infected? Will they whisper when she passes by? Slam doors in her face? It would be so typical of Arif to do that. 'No offence sis, you had Hellsblood inside you, who's to say you're cured? Best be safe than sorry. You know how it is.' She'd be an outcast in her own home until the day she died. And what about the Afterlife? In the eternity of all things, how do angels treat ex-possessed girls?

'Sorry love, this is Heaven for the Untainted. You belong with the tainted.'

In Shipley, she would have yelled at everyone. Not Arif. He got embarrassed too easily to yell. Maybe that's why Teiaar didn't tell him she ran to kill the vampire sneaking up on him. Maybe she realised what a prince he liked to be.

Teiaar saved Arif and he didn't even know it. Teiaar was saving everyone while still trying to work out who they all were and why the hell they were here on her world.

They were coming to the end of the burning white torches. She rubbed her bracelet. It glowed again. How odd. For the first time, she noticed an owl's head. An eight-legged horse encircled the emeralds and diamonds, with hooves pressing down on the neck of a dragon. Dad would never let her wear anything like this, he'd say, 'No idols or beasts allowed.'

She had touched it in the Diadromos because it was beautiful, but she couldn't remember seeing any creatures on it. Were the dragon and the horse always there?

Aroosa watched as Matthew slowed. He was clearly depressed being away from his mum. Her hand was glad for his.

She smiled to make him feel better.

His eyes lifted when he smiled.

A chilly breeze introduced the end of the cave.

They stopped beside Teiaar to marvel. On every hill, plants glowed in bright colours. Far away, emerald beams swept in sequence from huge towers. A sign of hope. A fortress against darkness.

The others had turned. The second she set eyes on the red dome the beats entered her skull. It swept her towards the path, a powerful magic woven into every beat.

Dum dum dum. Boom boom boom.

How it lifted her!

Dum dum dum. Boom boom boom.

She heard her name, but her feet sped over the dirt and rocks. Through giant open gates, a stone orchard, a winding path, a long corridor. The beat resonated in every bone. Flames rushed down from a giant red dome. She spun with the dancers, rubies and stars spun too. She could not stop. Round a hall they went.

Welcome to the city! The whisper was hot inside her head. Hands reached through the dancers. She giggled as she was carried like a mannequin. They stopped by a pillar to lift her head. A hand brought a cold vessel to her lips. The drink smelled foul, but she could not move. It rolled into her mouth like wine. She gulped. Her heartbeat quickened, heavier like it was being crushed.

Betrothed you are...

To the Dark King,

His pawn, his vinx,

His blood you drink...

Aroosa screamed. Cold hands grabbed her head, parted her jaw, and poured the foulness into her throat. She spluttered, gasping. Her mouth stung. They carried her towards a chilly draught. With all the strength in her body she kicked and pushed until she landed on the ground. Panting, she stood up.

They were gone. All of them. A dark figure floated forward. 'You will surrender your mind and your soul!'

Filled with absolute terror, Aroosa's legs buckled. She hit her head hard.

9

Eliza:

Eliza stepped away from Aiden, feeling her senses recover from the hypnotic spell. Her breathing was increasing at seeing a great mass of elegantly dressed people dancing and revolving under a giant red sun, painted on the ceiling of a giant dome. Aroosa was swirling with the crowd, tilting her head as they did.

'Eee-liizz-aa! Eee-liizz-aa!'

Welcome.

A hole in the crowd appeared, allowing her to slip through. The mass closed in around her. Two nuns dressed in burgundy came from either side of her and took her arms in theirs. 'You are safe with us,' they said. Brown-leathered soldiers escorted them through the dancers.

The voice inside her wanted to see everything, the dome, the thousands that danced beneath it, but Eliza felt heavily exhausted. If it wasn't for them holding her, she would have laid down on hard stone. They floated her to a room decorated in white and red stars. Red crystals hung from the ceiling. The beat of the drum was distant now, how she missed it inside her chest.

They sat her down in a tall chair, her fingers stroked the soft suede. She tried to remember how much alcohol she had, but it was all a blur. Here she was among strange, elegant people, bringing her silk and velvet dresses, placing them before her. Red, her favourite colour. It must be a dream. Oh… weren't they lovely? Ever so.

'Bless you child,' said the many women.

'It is an honour to serve thee,' said an old man, draping another silk dress on the pile.

'Hello… very much,' she said, trying not to slur. She lifted the dress and let go because it was heavy.

More nuns walked in gracefully. 'This is the child?'

One gasped, 'She is tiny.'

'Clayborns are pitiful creatures,' said a wrinkly man in robes.

'We should abort,' said the youngest.

'She wears it,' said the podgy one, her eyes looking aghast.

'Be respectful of our Gracious One. The City of Ithfir will test her return to us,' a tall man dressed in white robes said. His eyes shone red as he looked upon her. Like the people she'd seen in this city, ashen hair fell to his shoulders with streaks of red. He was a man of importance.

'Huh-ah-hello?' said Eliza.

'You wear the rubies of our city,' said a soldier softly, leaning in with glowing red eyes. 'As per the prophecy, you are a descendant of Adam. Did you not take part in the demise of the dark lords on your way here?' He had a thick red crystal on his helmet. His leathers were lighter with refined stitching.

Eliza stared at his prickly face, feeling a sudden urge to push her hand through his burgundy hair. She stopped her hand mid-air. 'Who-yes!' Her heart pounded. Of course, Aiden and Aroosa killed them, but it wasn't a lie, she had taken part.

'We saw flares from our towers. Crimson fire can only come from these stones,' his hot fingers touched her arm. 'To wear these jewels, we know she permits it. She led you here.'

'Who?'

'Mother.'

Eliza laughed. 'You are funny.'

'Is this not a breach of our treaty?' asked the white-robed bald one.

'A treaty we have not signed,' said the general, turning.

'Aren't we bringing our sword before we know where we stand, General?' said the white-robed bald one, glaring.

'No lord has fallen in a thousand years,' said the general. 'Not by Ithfirian, Lemothinian or even the Jades. Yet this Clayborn killed two. Do your duty, Lord Thallas. The people demand it. Or are you afraid?'

Lord Thallas reddened. 'What nonsense!'

'Complete the ceremony,' said the podgy nun.

'Wait a…' gasped Eliza.

10

Aiden:

Aiden arrived at the foot of the cave. Two cloaked figures emerged from the darkness. Feios brought a steel canister to his lips, he took a sip. Then more. Whitewater magic rushed to his head and toes. He felt so much better.

He sat down on a rock. 'What is that place?'

'Ithfir has a reputation for deceit and dishonour,' said Feios. 'It claims to be neutral, but they are traitors. Nevertheless, you found your way back.'

Teiaar sat down beside him.

'I heard your whisper,' said Aiden.

'A counter-spell,' said Teiaar, placing a folded robe on the ground. She made him lie down. 'We need more aylarhiyssa, if we are to save your friends. Rest with Feios.'

'I'm going to pray first,' he said.

It felt odd praying Maghrib in pitch black night, but Isha didn't feel right. When he finished, he lay down near the rock and closed his eyes to drift into sleep, but their whispers reached him.

They sounded scared. How is it that these djinns were so different to David? David was never scared, he always felt safe with David. Did he know the ghost would tell him everything? Were all the memories genuine? How much did David hide?

'One should not assume a djinn has met all djinns.'

The ghost was sitting cross-legged on a rock. The wreath on the ghost's forehead reminded Aiden of the scolding. The ghost had worn it when he marched out of his father's home and crossed hills to get away from his parent's farm. A friend had followed, the memory seemed important.

Aiden squeezed his eyes shut. 'Go away. They're telepathic.'

'Masters of mind are Jades, yet they fail to read you. Like the help you gave your brother. You cannot allow them access to your mind, but you cannot let them believe you have power, so you select what they can hear and what they cannot. You are an anomalía, the Elahi Mage.'

Aiden turned his head. 'They can't see you?'

'I am hidden from all eyes except thine, a curse none can unbind, except I.'

'They can't hear you?'

'Alas.'

'Where were you?' whispered Aiden.

'One lost is found by mercy,' said the boy.

Aiden grinned.

'You asked for her to be good to you and your kin. How did you know Ethyrus was sentient?' asked the ghost boy.

'I am not sure I share your meaning of sentient,' Aiden replied.

'Oh come, God commands the Earth, and the Earth obeys. Ethyrus too is a living rock that obeys,' said the ghost boy.

'Were you eavesdropping my thoughts?' he asked, scowling.

'I haunt you for eternity,' grinned the ghost boy. 'How did you know?'

'Just a feeling,' he said, quietly.

'She held you. As she did your kin. Asking Ethyrus saved you all.'

'Allah saved us. The rest is politeness,' he replied.

'Rare is the torchbearer, rarer still is the one to sense feelings from a rock. In the old days, the highest gifted Jades would have earned that connection with Old Lady Ethyrus. Through years of kindling their flames. And yet you established it within seconds,' said the ghost boy.

'Don't know what you mean,' he said, yawning.

'You are gifted, Torchbearer,' said the ghost boy.

'I'm going to ignore you unless you tell me your name,' whispered Aiden.

'I glimpsed your memories too, darling Fioha. Your master showed you one vampire, weak from despair. It is the nature of dead-heart humans to seek solitude. However, dead-heart djinns seek power. A vinx weaves chaos. Many dead hearts behave as locusts.'

Aiden rolled on his side. 'Ignoring you.'

'After death, one no longer has a designation,' said Ghostboy.

'You died,' whispered Aiden, 'but I hear you and I see you... so either you are an earlier version of you, or this is your Deathlife. Either way, you exist. What's your name?'

Silence.

Aiden knew he could never sleep with questions on his mind. He rolled back.

Ghostboy was staring tearfully.

Aiden's heart sank. 'I'm guessing you're not allowed. I'm going to call you George,' he whispered.

'We are what we repeatedly do,' said George, quietly. 'Excellence, then, is not an act, but a habit.'

Aiden sat up. 'You stole that from a human. I remember it was carved on Aristotle's statue. You don't need riddles to talk. Be yourself George.'

'I cannot,' said George, sadly.

Aiden watched him. 'This world is home, isn't it? That world with three suns?'

'I pledged to haunt, but I prefer my other place.'

Aiden thought about it. 'Are you scared?'

'Very.'

'But you're already dead,' whispered Aiden.

'You have no idea what waits in the dark,' whispered George.

'I do. We killed two,' said Aiden, feeling gratified.

George looked down.

'Fine. I'll find your nephew. I promise,' whispered Aiden.

'Seek your friend, Elahi,' said George, fading away.

It was all too quiet under a starless sky.

How on Earth did it happen so fast? Okay, David had been telling him for so long, but how did anyone know the End of the World really was the End of the World?

He never had any intention of being in the garden. He wanted to read Phillip Pullman's book when they all barged into his room. How come the neighbours were going in the same car? Like one big happy family after the divorce last year? Didn't that lady have a restraining order?

And Dad let Matthew stay the night? Okay, they were planning an engagement… not yet though. Dad lectures everyone about what is Islamically appropriate. Matthew's mum was back in hospital, yet he hadn't mentioned it once. Arif said sorry for being an arsehole. Last week he took his TV off his wall and invited his friends to play a game, then made fun of him, but he never apologised for that. He doesn't apologise unless Mum was standing over his head. Damn it. The signs were there! 'The universe was upside down and you totally ignored it', David would say.

His mind had been filled with how David had hugged him, with a hand at the back of his head. All for memorising a story. Did David do it to let the whispering djinn slip away? Why was he hidden? He never would've given it a second thought if Eliza and Matthew hadn't mentioned that his dad treated him differently.

Why doesn't Dad hug him? How come he never noticed? 'Your dad doesn't hug you and it's not fair,' Matthew had said. Matthew assumed that's why he was upset. The ball went to the bottom of the garden. The Core landed. He wasn't thinking when he reached down to pick up the crystal from the bed of roses. Everything David had taught him had led to that moment, and yet his brain wasn't in gear.

David.

A grandfather would be like David.

Was the whisperer a high member of the Megalo Fianehedrin? A Mycenaean or Akkadian? It felt wrong that he never saw his face.

Gravel shifted.

He closed his eyes.

'We shouldn't go,' whispered Teiaar.

'We must.'

'Kildana were overcome from mouth of the cave. It reached them from such a distance. Five minds. I've not seen it happen,' said Teiaar.

They wanted him to hear.

'I am aware,' said Feios.

'Dark magic weaved by Ithfir! If Lemoff gets word of this, the authority of the Jade Council will be questioned.'

'Yet, there is that we have not yet considered,' said Feios, looking up.

Teiaar whispered, 'Sirens!'

Aiden stared at the red glow of the city until Feios tapped him.

The cobbles grew larger the further they went into the city. Occasionally, Teiaar turned her head to glance. It wasn't because his legs were smaller that they kept having to wait for him. He kept turning to look at the cavern. Beyond, was his sleeping friend, the friend he dared not picture in his mind in case charrelles overheard what he was thinking. Deadheart females have telepathic abilities, Teiaar had said, pointing at the pitch-black sky.

He shuddered. In all the worlds - surely there was someone stronger, more gifted, who wanted to do whatever they needed to do? Why did it have to be him?

He missed his glow walking beside him. George said he haunted him for life, which he seriously doubted. It wasn't allowed, surely? Where was he? What was this Afterlife that he liked?

Herionus.

His eyes heated. The streets were too quiet.

The two storey shops used to have large windows, but they were now sealed with glowing crimson stone. Some neat, some built with untamed stones. Feios turned right, to follow a cobbled alley to the domed building. No illuminating plants here, just rocks.   After a steep climb, the road straightened and became smoother. The palace was enormous. Giant glowing red stones must have been laid by giants. The dome was bigger than St Paul's Basilica. The windows were decorated with coloured glass. Steel shutters were probably a defence against vampire attacks. Carved stone guards shielded the giant arched doors, but one was ajar.

'The fact that she screamed, tells us that your sister was no longer under a spell,' said Teiaar, entering a wide passageway lit by white torches and the occasional red crystal. 'We will retrieve her quickly.'

Faded wall paintings showed diners and dancers, all gazing at a red-haired queen.

Boom. Boom.

Aiden froze.

Teiaar yanked his sleeve, pulling him sideways down an exposed corridor. Enormous pillars held an elegant high domed ceiling. Dancers were densely packed. Their glowing red eyes were abnormally wide, reminding him of the mischievous thief Wayne tracked in Cairo, perhaps the thief originated from this city? Heads tilted in sync to the beating drums.   This was no concert. This was creepy.

Feios' hand landed softly on his shoulder. His eyebrows lifted. It was a warning to remain by the pillar before he slid between two ladies and disappeared. Teiaar was gone too. The Jades had a plan, but they hadn't told him anything.

Aiden sighed. Djinns were like parents, big-headed and secretive! After David, he should be used to this.

Eyes to your right.

The hair on his neck prickled.

Are you in my head?

Focus.

The light changed. In the split second it did, he caught sight of a shadow of chandeliers behind silver mesh on the upper pavilion. Two soldiers stood on guard. Of course, he should know about this room! It was a music room in George's memories. Happy memories. And sad. Maybe that's why he wasn't around?

Aiden lifted the bow from his back. As soon as he pulled on the string, an ice arrow appeared. His hand quivered just slightly. He closed his eyes as he had seen the ghost's sister do. A crimson pulse filled his eyelids. In every pulse, the people inside the room appeared as shadows, one pounded a giant drum. Sight of the chanter confirmed why his skin crawled.

He let go. He fired again at the drum. The pulsing stopped. All went dark. He opened his eyes.

They weren't moving. Their eyes were different… they turned in confusion.

Ice coated a gaping hole in the mesh. A shattered drum splattered with black blood. A wail caused everyone to look up. And then at him. Murmurs from the crowd.

A hand reached out and grabbed his collar.

11

Aiden:

'The spell is broken. The citizens of the Red City have glowing red eyes. Those that don't will head this way to go home,' said Teiaar.

Djinns passed them in increasing numbers, some of them stumbling, some of them rushing. Teiaar's hand drew Aiden closer. Aiden wanted to help those that were confused and lost. A few were that skinny, he felt they could have been drained of their blood or not fed for some time. Teiaar yanked him again.

'If they want help, they could ask,' she said. 'And even then, we may not.'

'Why?' he asked.

'We are outnumbered. And in unfriendly territory.'

'Can you sense the others?' he asked.

'Be patient.'

They waited for the numbers to thin. The sheer size of the space under the dome was becoming clearer. What were the upper levels used for? The red eyed people wore symbols of a crimson sun. They gathered with their loved ones, as if waiting for something.

Feios emerged with Matthew and Arif in tow.

Whoosh.

An arrow narrowly missed Arif's head, it skidded off the ground and bounced off a pillar. Feios drew his sword. Teiaar primed her bow. 'It came from above,' she said, aiming at the room where the drummer had been.

The balcony was swarming with soldiers.

Aiden inhaled.

'We can't go without our girls,' said Matthew.

'Jades don't abandon. But we must leave,' said Teiaar.

Her hand grabbed Aiden's and then he was running. They kept to the outer edges of the exposed corridor, running faster between the columns.

A second arrow hit the pillar in front of Aiden. Teiaar turned to fire. He slid on his knees. Another arrow hit the wall missing his head. They were targeting him!

Teiaar fired back.

Aiden fired as a warning, the wall behind the archers exploded in ice.

An echo of boots alarmed them all.

A battalion of guards were running across the balcony. More soldiers spilled from underneath the arches. Arrows sliced the air. This time from down their corridor.

They took cover behind three pillars.

Teiaar returned fire. Someone cried in the distance.

'There are too many,' said Feios. 'It is inevitable there will be a confrontation. It might as well be outside where we stand a better chance.'

An arrow landed upright on the floor not far from their position.

They hurried down a passageway, keeping close to the walls. As the huge doors came into view, they saw with disappointment that a wall of red eyes blocked them. Shields tapped the hard floor. Left of them, more shields were propped to block them. Behind them, six archers took aim. Swords drawn, the line of guards advanced on their position. There was no chance of an escape.

Matthew and Arif shouted with their swords pointed. Aiden knew who they wanted.

'We should surrender,' he said.

'Kildana, under no circumstances will we make any admissions. Do you understand?' said Teiaar.

Aiden inhaled.

'Lay down your weapons,' barked the commander. The soldiers parted to let him through. The commander's gold gleaming armour didn't seem to have any scratches, whereas the young officer beside him had dents in many places.

'You lay down yours and we'll lay down ours,' yelled Arif.

The commander laughed, then sneered, 'You're hardly in a position to negotiate.'

'No chance of us laying down our weapons. Grant us safe passage and we will leave,' replied Teiaar, she gripped her bow tightly.

'You have no options. Surrender!' said the commander.

'On the contrary, we have many options. One of which would be to kill as many of you as possible,' said Feios.

'Watch your tongue, Darian!' growled the commander.

'You were trying to kill us!' shouted Matthew.

'Dark magic luring children. Is that the value of the red city these days?' asked Feios.

'If we wanted to kill them, they would already be... dead,' sneered the commander.

'Enough!' The one in the dented armour straightened and took a step back. Then he turned his head to look at the Jades, 'My apologies. I have no doubt that you are all competent fighters, however no one needs to die - the children especially! Lower your weapons. You will come to no harm. I am General Ithrandir, First General to the City of Ithfir. I have orders to bring you before the Queen.'

The Jades froze.

'Queen - what queen?' Teiaar asked quickly.

'Queen of Ithfir?' Feios said, puzzled, though he lowered his sword.

'Yes.'

Teiaar lowered her bow. 'There has been no queen since the fall of the High Council. When was this position filled?'

Ithrandir spread his arm and the soldiers parted. 'Follow me,' he said.

'Why was this position filled?' she insisted.

'That is not for me to answer. You may ask your questions in the presence of the Royal Counsel. Now please surrender your weapons.'

'Not a chance!' yelled Arif.

'No offence General, an Ithfirian promise is regarded as an insult. Though we gave your city magic, Daraan and Lemothinians have had poor misfortunes at the hands of your people,' said Teiaar.

Aiden watched as Ithrandir's shoulders slowly sagged. He stared at the ground.

'Yet you stand there, surrounded on all sides, insulting a descendant of Centurion Ferosh, from the battle of the Three Points,' said the commander.

Ithrandir sighed, 'I can honestly say true to my heart, I know of no dishonesty from my kin. If the word of a Feroshan carries no weight, I offer my sword.' He turned his sword and offered it with both hands to Feios.

Feios stepped back, looking gobsmacked.

'Give them your weapons,' said Teiaar, hoarsely.

12

Aiden:

'Eliza!' gasped Aiden.

She smiled when she saw him. One of the servants leaned forward with a bowl of giant red fruit. There were berries, grapes and fruit resembling bananas and mangoes, except they were different shades of brown, orange, burgundy and red. She took a small branch of brown cherries and ate hungrily.

A djinn in a white robe addressed them, 'Strangers to the City of Ithfir, you enter the Royal Court. You will bow before the Queen and bestow upon her your grace.'

They bowed. The crowd behind also bowed.

'Elly, you okay?' asked Matthew

Two guards stepped forward, drawing their swords to his chin.

'You dare address our queen?' snapped the white robed djinn.

Teiaar placed a hand on his shoulder. 'Our apologies to the Ithfirian Court. Perhaps we should be dignified as to introduce ourselves?'

'Ah but you have no need to introduce yourself, Teiaar the Jade and Feios the Protector of the Silent Moors. Welcome clayborns... Arif, Aiden and Matthew. I am Lord Thallas,' he said, nodding to the guards who withdrew. He walked closer, 'Queen's Counsellor, Former Keeper of the Great Red City.'

'Where's Aroosa?' asked his brother.

'Is she not your sister?' sneered Thallas.

'Enlighten us Lord Thallas, when was it that a servant of a city became First Hand to a queen?' asked Teiaar.

'No sooner than when you arrived to attack my citizens, Teiaar the Jade. Be blessed you weren't arrested.'

Matthew wanted to get to his cousin, but Feios stopped him with a strong hand on his shoulder.

I will not feel. Aiden edged closer to Matthew.

'We are aware the sister is not here presently, but she came here hexed to the dark magic that your servant spun,' Teiaar said strongly.

Thallas' face darkened. Then he smiled, 'I assure you I have no knowledge.'

Ithrandir shot a look of surprise.

'She arrived here. This Imperial residence - is it not fortified by soldiers who do your bidding?' said Feios, glaring.

'Perhaps... she left you?' said Thallas, tilting an eyebrow.

Eliza stopped eating and a servant wiped the fruit juice from her mouth. She waved him away.

'Eliza - Queen of It-fyor, can we address you directly?' said Arif respectfully softly.

Eliza ignored him. 'Cousin, sorry to hear Rose is missing. But she did get infected. Perhaps her infection wasn't really cured?'

Matthew straightened. 'Are you for real?'

'If Lord Thallas says he does not know, then he does not,' she said, flashing a smile.

'Come on!' said Matthew.

'I hear Eddie managed to leave the city. Perhaps Rose went looking for Wi-Fi?' The deep voice alarmed all of them.

'What if she's kidnapped somewhere?' said Arif.

'Yeah,' said Matthew. 'You've been here five minutes and you trust dipshit over there?'

'WATCH YOUR TONE!' Eliza stood up, growing to a giant. Her fiery eyes grew, red flames twisted around her from head to toe. 'I AM QUEEN OF ITHFIRIA. POWER OF MY PEOPLE!'

Aiden's eardrums felt like they were about to pop.

Rubies on her bracelet dimmed. As the rumbling subsided, dust fell from the dome. Her shoulders shook, then she shrank to Eliza. The glowing eyes remained.

Aiden knew he'd seen this happen before.

'Forgive us, Great Red Queen,' said Teiaar breaking the silence. 'If you should be so kind as to permit our leave.'

'Of course, Teiaar. You may,' she said, in her usual way. She lifted her hand to flick her wrist. A servant brought forward Hathor's Tree.

'You will be pleased to know we have adapted very well. Take it before I change my mind,' said the foreign voice from Eliza.

13

Aiden:

The old road to Aran Daran was surrounded by glowing colours of shrubs and giant flowers, the ones with smaller leaves had tiny spikes which Teiaar said were good for medicinal purposes. He was barely listening. Images kept popping into his mind. Aiden was struggling not to feel. He stared closer at the delicate veined flower, the ancient petals that had seen more than he wanted to, trying to block another image in his mind. Feel only what is in front of you, not what is inside. Devils be devils. They always listen. He should be crying right now. Arif had been.

'That's not Eliza. I know Eliza and that's not Eliza!' he said, stopping on the climb.

'Her veins were literally glowing,' said Matthew.

'How could she grow like that? And her eyes!' said Arif.

'It's that thing on her arm,' said Matthew. 'It's poisoned her. I mean, what do we know about anything in Diadromos?'

'She's possessed, mate. Our sweet Eliza,' said Arif, tearfully.

'We're going to get them back,' said Matthew, kicking a stone.

'I don't understand how we could lose both so quickly!' said Arif.

A green arrow landed with a thud by Arif's foot.

Holding the bow, Teiaar glared from the sandy hill.

'Clayborns, are you inviting the dead to dinner?' said Feios, glaring.

Matthew turned to glance, 'Eddie, keep up.'

Picking up their pace, Aiden didn't say another word until the Red City was hidden behind the sloping moors. He didn't intend on speaking at all, but George appeared walking beside him, wearing a leather tunic covering his stomach to his knees. His strange boots seemed to be held together with steel studs. 'The boy Matius turns his head again. Extraordinary that your own blood is not as watchful.'

Aiden adjusted his path to avoid a rock.

'Their ignorance reminds me of the story of Dolus,' said George. 'Dolus betrayed his master to breathe life into the statue of his lover.'

Aiden rolled his eyes. 'He's my brother.'

'They feel responsible for dragging you into hell,' said George. 'You are not innocent.'

'Why?' whispered Aiden.

'I saw your memories too, darling Fiori. Having to lie to friends, teachers, and your parents. Guilt is lock and key to your life of secrets, yet you have none from David. Extraordinary,' said George.

Memories of his first day at school popped into his head. Aiden stopped walking. Hair on his neck prickled.

He turned, scanning past the white stalks, the rolling hills of illuminated flowers, to make sure no vampires had picked up his thoughts.

'Hypothetically, for a task of this magnitude, a master would ensnare the senses of a disciple at birth,' said George.

'Shut up,' seethed Aiden, glaring.

George sat down on a rock, folding his arms over his knees. 'A master shapes where the enemy cannot sink their claws. Angel laws prohibit a disciple under the age of three, thus he would have had to gain blessings from a Fianehedrin senator. He needs to hide his disciple, so he took you to a djinn dimension, where he had ultimate control over the pace at which you learned. Eleven Terra years he and his disciple journeyed through supernatural gates to other worlds, with all their godly splendours and time distortions. Your body is aged fourteen, your mind and soul are not.'

'I'm ignoring you,' said Aiden, his heart beating fast.

'A blessing you broke my curse, yet I cannot be certain how I feel, since you are the first, I haunt. Why did you hold your tongue in Ithfir?' asked George.

'I didn't.'

'Pray Elahi, you like Matius and the girl. You wanted to tell her everything. I felt it.'

Aiden left him. He was conscious of not letting his trainers make a sound as he hurried over the dirt to return to the ancient road, where the others were walking in pairs. Arif and Matthew were keeping their distance to talk discreetly.

George floated back to his side.

'I know who I am, you're wrong. I have a brother and sister, and I have a brother and a sister,' whispered

Aiden. 'Not like - I don't like anyone saying like- it either is or it isn't. Two brothers, two sisters. End of. I need all of them to leave this hell safe and sound.'

'Blood is born, then tried and tested. A heart is forged through trials and heartbreak,' said George, staring ahead.

'Only the learned thrive,' whispered Aiden.

'Elahi, be careful what you recite in treacherous lands,' said George. 'Hellfire might be listening.'

Aiden stopped to glare. 'Oh, you care now, do you? You know what I've been thinking? How you found me. It was like you rehearsed it. What was it, two thousand years you were there? Two thousand years of exploring. Two thousand years to plot a con!'

'Five. Add a trillion more to reach one end,' laughed George.

'A ghost keeps the haunted alive to feed off torment, that's why you haven't told me yet. Isn't it?' said Aiden, folding his arms.

'Torment? Pray Elahi, not I.'

'Where's Aroosa? Tell me, what did you see?' demanded Aiden.

'Are you asking or commanding me, Elahi?'

Aiden remembered how George had left before. 'I was born on Earth, I have human blood, so when I command, a djinn must obey.'

George was silent.

Aiden folded his arms. 'I command you.'

George exhaled. 'The devil's lair.'

'What?'

'Deadbrains carried her to the city's gates where she was placed onto a beast with a siren,' said George.

Aiden's heart sank. 'Why didn't you tell me?'

'I have just.'

Aiden inhaled, 'Is she infected?'

'She drank nefarious wine. And she liked it,' said George, grinning.

The soles of his trainers made hardly any sound on the soft dirt. Aiden didn't know how far he'd run, until he caught sight of a crimson glow behind a dark hill. A vampire djinn would have heard him miles away. Why hadn't they come? He ran faster. George appeared in the path ahead. 'Elahi. I warn you. My Afterlife Induction was very clear. Should a torchbearer rush like a fool, toss a shoe to his head, the Boat Lady said. I have gold heels. Clobbering is tempting!'

Aiden leapt onto the rocks to cut around him. And found himself running up supernatural steps, which suddenly yanked away from the hilly moors. It was a jewelled staircase leading to a dazzling light in the sky. Aiden grabbed hold of the railing. The gold turned into a hand that closed onto his wrist.

'Keep climbing, darling Fioha,' said George, whose staircase appeared beside his.

'Let me down. I have to save her,' shouted Aiden.

George frowned with sympathy. 'Look around Elahi. Do they need your help?'

Below, the hills suddenly plummeted. Hanging from super bright arteries in the cerulean sky were millions of staircases. Some staircases were crafted with the most beautiful mouldings, some glowed bright and some held owners resigned to sit for eternity.

A gentle frail woman with a round tired face stepped up and smiled. Her wrinkles faded, she grew tall, and her curls grew until it reached her shoulders again, dark, and lush. Then she looked up with surrender. Hands from a beam of light lifted her and her staircase disappeared.

'That was Elizabeth Regina. It's the Steps of Destiny,' gasped Aiden. 'I've read about this. Every sentient being will either ascend or descend from the choices they make. How are you showing me this?'

'I break no covenant. You are a torchbearer. It is your right to be shown the Stairs of Ascension and the Descent of Fools.'

Below, the scarlet abyss was frightening. Anything he could see vampires will surely see. 'Stop it George,' yelled Aiden, squeezing his eyes shut.

'Hellborns cannot probe this moment,' said George.

'What?'

'Not a second will remain in your memories, aside from a cognitive turn of this lesson,' laughed George.

Aiden opened his eyes slowly. 'What lesson?'

George stretched his eyebrows. 'Truly. What lesson?'

'Learning is many steps,' whispered Aiden, gobsmacked by the supernatural view. A hand-painted book in David's library was one of the earliest books he had to memorise. 'Strive for discovery and see the light of Heaven,' he recalled. 'Strive with mercy and strong steps bear your weight. Embrace enlightenment for the Golden Gates, records of labour guarantee light way. Beware, hate rots fate.'

A crumbling staircase floated by. George pointed to a man trying to hang on to the banister. 'Even now he could ask for help. But his heart is sealed with arrogance.' The man plummeted into the scarlet abyss.

People in formal attire were not moving on their stairs. The closest stairs were black. An old lady in a suit clutched a cross on her neck then tore it off. Her skin grew pale, her wrinkled eyes emptied to darkness. A dark stone grew in her throat.

'It's our prime minister. Is she a vampire?' asked Aiden.

'Wait,' said George.

A wooden stake tore through her chest. The prime minister exhaled, then stepped out of her body. Her face glowed and she shot upwards to the light in the sky. Her staircase and body plummeted. Stakes tore through more, but there were too many infected to count.

To his relief, the jewelled staircase turned away from the masses, taking him closer to a staircase of light. Dad was ascending, his frown transfixed on the stairs in front. Mum held his school jersey to her chest. Aiden wanted to stay, but his jewelled staircase floated by a ruby staircase. Eliza took a powerful step. She was regal and elegant.

'She's the G.R.Q.,' gasped Aiden.

'Big red shoes to fill,' said George.

On blue stairs, Arif took one step, then sat down to think.

The next staircase was deep green.

'Does she need your help?' whispered George, as they reached Aroosa. The skin around her red-veined eyes was dark and grey.

'She's infected,' said Aiden.

'Where is she looking?' asked George.

She was staring at the emerald pulsing in the banister.

'But she's infected,' said Aiden. 'I should help her.'

'See how it glows,' said George.

The viridescent glow ran through veins in her staircase… no! Veins were thinner and more entangled as they got closer to his sister.

'They're roots,' gasped Aiden. 'From her feet. The emeralds have tapped into the planet. I could have missed it if you hadn't asked me to look.'

'Pray Elahi, what have you learned?'

'There's still time,' said Aiden, feeling relieved.

From a vibrant staircase shrouded by mist, Matthew turned his head and looked straight at him. Shocked, Aiden closed his eyes hard.

When he opened them, he toppled down a dirt bank and onto the road. The sky was pitch dark again. High-pitch ringing filled his ears.

Aiden ran to catch up with George, whose feet floated through rocks.

'Let me tell you about a rhyme from my mother,' said George. 'She brings light into night, she holds it high, she holds it tight. All souls save their own. You are a torchbearer, not a warrior and not a saviour.'

For a moment, it felt like David himself had spoken. Could George and David be related? George's forehead was more like Wayne's, not David's.

Wayne.

Aiden sighed. He shouldn't be remembering.

'How far are the others?' he asked, feeling exhausted.

He side-stepped away from two potholes. The silence caused him to glance.

George had disappeared.

He was in the middle of nowhere. In the dark. With hairs prickling, Aiden ran until the road turned. Two figures emerged, causing him to step back.

'Thank God,' said Matthew.

'Yo. Where y' been?' Arif grabbed his elbow and nudged him forward. 'Stay close!'

They climbed the peak silently. Feios waited with Teiaar. To his dismay, more hills stretched ahead, and the huge emerald towers still seemed far. Incandescent plants showed a dry riverbed, passing alongside their road.

'Behold, our holy grounds,' said Feios, smiling.

'Can we stop, please,' panted Aiden, slumping his bum on a rock. Exhaustion washed over him.

'Yes. Replenish,' said Feios. He sat on the rock beside him, facing the way they came. And offered an aylarhiyssa pouch.

'Are the vampires watching us?' asked Matthew. He sat opposite Arif, closing their circle.

Muscles in Jade's face tensed and untensed, as if he was probing the night. Telepaths. How much did they know?

Teiaar glanced sharply.

Aiden gulped the White Fire Water. Aches and exhaustion left him.

Matthew ate a tortilla wrap. Arif tapped twice so he could give one to Teiaar, then placed the food plant before him. Aiden offered a hot cheeseburger to Feios, who studied it as he ate. Suddenly, Feios froze.

They listened.

Panting.

Slow hooves grew louder on a slope.

'Riders!' whispered Teiaar.

They stood up.

Matthew drew his sword.

Arif held the crystal high to illuminate the slope.

A long creature's head appeared in the distance with glowing green eyes and pointed ears. As it sauntered closer, it looked less frightening. White mane parted, showing strands of purple or green. The creature had eight legs, as if two giant horses had been stuck together. The saddle was big enough to carry three people. Another appeared behind it with another rider.

'They are Darian,' said Teiaar.

Matthew re-sheathed his sword.

The first rider wore leather armour. The epaulettes and sashes had been matched to his smaragdine coloured eyes. The second disembarked with ease. Both had an assortment of weapons.

'Aya Teiaar,' called the first rider. 'Aya Feios.'

'Aya Teiaar! Aya Feios!' echoed the second.

'Murffa!' said Feios grinning.

'Ana multana yee etteh?' said Teiaar. She gave each of the riders a quick hug.

The first rider grinned, 'Ef soman a nozlur …'

The four lowered their voices.

'What're they saying?' whispered his brother, glancing.

'Hello and what brings you here. That one is called Liyoot and the other is Loosh.' Aiden paused. 'Doesn't matter what they're saying. The fact that they're here means we're safe. We can get to Jade City faster. And find Aroosa.'

Matthew stared at him. 'You think they took her there?'

Aiden was taken aback. 'No-don't know.'

'We'll make them help us get her back,' said Arif.

Matthew frowned. 'Everyone's got weird names.'

'They're not human,' said Arif.

14

Aiden:

Aiden stirred with the smell of cherries, spices, molasses, and apples and thought his dad was baking in the kitchen. But Dad wouldn't burn pans. He opened his eyes to find Liyoot's arms pinning him to a saddle. A giant wall passed over them, the long tunnel showed the wall was thick. Green lasers scanned them at each of the seven gates. The guards wore strange green armour. They trotted through, heading for the city of anti-vampire skyscrapers. Body bits trailed off spikes under emerald windows, surprising Aiden that it wasn't safe, even inside the great Jade City.

There was no shortage of illumination. Stones, plants, and cobbles glowed. Veins of light fed chalky-skinned fruit that hung from turquoise buildings. Incandescent petals spiralled downwards, whipping upwards to circle around them.

Darian traders paused with their customers. Perched felines and canines jolted with alarm at the sight of them. They had long ears with extraordinary vibrant eyes, just like the mithrin.

Liyoot noticed Arif's awe. 'We can't see the suns for the veil, but our city grows. Jade magic makes harvest possible.'

'It's awesome!' whispered Aiden, turning his head to Matthew, who watched without holding onto anything.

The road became a path, smooth and shiny. They passed pillared gates at a steady trot, marvelling at the rocks that turned out to be houses with tiny green windows and steel doors. A song whipped up around them. It was a live performance inside a provincial building. It was beautiful.

'Somebody must have died,' he mumbled.

Soldiers were gathered on the cobbled square. As they approached, they fell quiet. And bowed on their knees.

Liyoot whispered to his mithrin. They halted by the entrance to the Oval Hall and disembarked. Guards came down the steep stone steps of the Oval Hall.

Matthew grabbed Arif' sleeve. 'People thriving on a world deprived of a sun, filled with vampires. I don't buy it,' he whispered.

'Be on your guard,' whispered Arif.

Neither of them trusted friends? Aiden didn't like the gut-sinking feeling.

'Hurry,' said Teiaar. 'The Jade council is in session. Wyfzira has heard of our arrival.'

Arif ran up the steps.

Wyfzira-? The name was familiar. Aiden tried to recall in which memory had the ghost known him?

'Eddie, keep up,' urged Matthew.

He was obviously worried about them separating. Aiden hoped they were not in any danger in this city. And didn't have to flee in a hurry. Where would they go exactly?

Matthew faltered at the top. Three guards on either side had to push each steel door.

The white inscription above the doorway was decorated with jade stones.

Ffyada nozlur Kiyafa. Daffi kiyaf.

'Enter to inspire. Leave inspired,' Aiden said, passing him.

'You must seek Euthalia in the room of learning before you seek the counsel of Wyfzira,' said a captain. He matched Teiaar's pace as they entered the hall. 'He has ordered that he will send for you.'

The hall was grand, decorated in precious metals and decorative glass. Leaves, three suns, a moon and some of the plant species they had seen on entering the city. Hanging from the ceiling on silver threads were crystal horn-shaped flowers with small birds hovering as if a reminder of a world they had lost.

'This way,' said Teiaar.

At the end of the passageway lit by green-flamed torches, they entered a large library with shelves storing old scrolls. An elegant lady in a long green gown, floated towards them. In her right hand she gripped a white staff, with a giant glowing emerald. 'Sirens took him' she wailed.

The Jades hugged her.

'I am sorry for your loss,' said Teiaar, holding her shoulders until their eyes met. 'Feenash was a good man.'

The lady dabbed her cheek, her eyes met Aiden's. She straightened. 'Salomalom. Aya kildana. I am Euthalia, Advisor to Lord Wyfzira.'

'Hello. I'm Arif, this is Aiden and Matthew.'

'Welcome to the last sanctuary for the people of Daraan,' said Euthalia.

Feios appeared at the door. The ladies turned, looking startled.

Euthalia spoke quietly, 'Take them to my old quarters. Ensure they suit well. Despite my reservations, the Llianehedrin have insisted on an occasion of celebration.'

'Did you see that?' whispered Arif when they were in the corridor. 'Both of them were horrified when Feios came in.'

'His mouth didn't move,' said Matthew.

'They're telepathic,' whispered Aiden.

'All this time?' whispered Matthew.

He wanted to tell them. He had to. Somehow. How could he be certain George and David were telling the truth anyway?

Euthalia's old quarters had spiked windowsills and metal shutters. On each bed was a pair of dark green trousers and jackets, which Teiaar insisted they wear. Each item stretched neatly onto their bodies, as if tailored to their size. In the washroom, the silver mithrin headed spouts blasted steam not water. Aiden didn't know what to make of it, but Matthew came along and inserted his shirt. The grime from his journey disappeared.

Matthew and Arif slipped out to explore, while Aiden lay on his bed, thinking about freeing Herionus from his hibernation. Teiaar said aylarhiyssa could cure him, he knew where he could get it now. From the cavern. It wasn't a question of how, it was a question of when he could go back to save Herionus.

Matthew closed the door. 'Rose... we need to find Rose, Arif.'

Arif turned. 'I was thinking... we slip out and see if we can find her in the streets. Without them lot.'

'Are we even sure she came here? Wouldn't she have been waiting for us? Half the city was staring. Shady as hell.'

'Or she might not be here,' said Arif, 'I heard a guard say an emissary had arrived. An emissary from where? We saw people in blue uniforms leaving the Red City, they weren't Ithfirian. And they don't belong here, this city is OTT with green, making my eyes hurt. If Thallas was telling the truth and we don't know for sure that he was, which city took Aroosa? And who do we trust to help us find her?'

'She didn't run away,' said Matthew.

Aiden didn't like that they were worried.

'Empty heads are better left empty. Telling empty heads is a fool,' said George. He walked to the window nearest his bed and looked out on the city.

Aiden scowled. He would love to punch George, if only he knew how to contact his annoying face!

'Let's eat,' said Arif, lifting Hathor's Tree.

Aiden watched them whisper Greggs' pastries and baguettes. Arif placed Hathor's Tree on his bed. 'I'm not hungry,' he said.

'If you want to join us looking for Aroosa, you're going to have to,' said Arif.

'It's my fault,' said Aiden.

George turned quickly.

'You remember in the Diadromos, we saw statues of immortal kings and queens. And titans... who came together to defeat The Fallen,' said Aiden. 'Iblis got revenge by poisoning their descendants with his blood. He promised to fill Hell with God's chosen and scatter his seed into the living. That painting should have told us to go home. We shouldn't be here.'

'It doesn't change the fact that we're here,' said Matthew.

'How many stories did the Greeks tell, were any of them even true?' said Arif.

Aiden's eyes burned. 'I picked up the crystal. Now my sister is missing.'

'We're gonna find her,' said Matthew, rubbing his shoulder.

'If she isn't already a vampire,' sobbed Aiden.

'She's cured,' said Matthew.

'Yeah, stop balling. Aroosa's gone to find a working phone,' said Arif.

'I heard a scream,' said Aiden, hoarsely.

'Yo. Did you see her?' demanded Arif.

'No.'

'We don't know what you heard, dipshit. What you thought you heard is neither here nor there because you talk to yourself. Now choose a burger, tap the tree, and shut your mouth,' said Arif.

The door swung open. A Darian lady barged in. She fussed over them like a nineteenth century mistress, repeating 'Ufufuf'. To their jackets, she pinned an assortment of Darian jewels. Matthew refused. But she succeeded in placing a long green crystal hung by a silver chain around his neck. After inspecting them, she disappeared just as fast.

A soldier in brown leathers entered, keeping by the side of the door. His helmet supported a band of short green feathers and a large green crystal. 'Your presence is requested, my lords,' he said.

'Okay – er – lead the way,' said Arif gesturing his hand. The moment passed to a feeling of awkwardness as the soldier didn't budge, so they walked out.

The soldier closed the door gracefully. And led them through corridors and halls lit by green torches. His green cloak floated as they walked around the edges of the dome, to a double doorway concealed by pillars.

Inside, was yet another grand hall. Crystal daffodils hung from the main dome. In shades of green attire, Darian folk gave a rapturous applause on their arrival.

A tall man with an emerald coat of arms on a white suit came towards them, smiling and bowing. 'Salomalom. Aya Kildana. Em ichyara Osimion - my name is Osimion. Follow please.'

He turned, leading them through the hall to another corridor with marble stairs. As they passed, people fell silent, bending to their knees or bowing their heads. In another hall, soldiers and officials stood listening to a giant djinn giving a speech in the Jenn language. Osimion turned to whisper softly, 'You have to give a speech, Kildana.'

Aiden's heart skipped a beat. Arif and Matthew looked at each other.

'What do I say?' whispered Arif.

Aiden felt relief. Of course, Arif can do the talking. 'This is our chance to ask them if they can help us find Aroosa,' he said.

Osimion gestured to continue ahead of him and stepped aside.

'People of Daraan...' said the white robed giant, a green crystal dangled from his neck, '... I present to you, Chosen Ones!'

227

An applause arose followed by a loud cheer. The anticipation of hundreds of Darians watching him made his neck warm. Aiden followed them reluctantly up the stairs, where the giant held his arm out, expecting them to approach his side.

Even though he was on a high stage, Arif was barely eye level with the Darians. He seemed to have stopped breathing, his hands fidgeting like the times Mum confronted him. 'Hi. Erm – we're here by accident.'

Some laughed.

'We met your neighbours.'

Silence.

'I can't take the credit for it,' Arif looked at him, gesturing to move closer by his side. 'We fought to defend each other. My brother here... killed a beast with his arrows.'

What the hell was he doing?

They murmured.

Aiden scowled.

Arif suddenly cocked his head. 'Has anyone seen my sister?'

'Why do you lie to us?' said a smartly dressed djinn, with a goat beard.

'Pardon?'

'You say you kill baarda. You are tiny!' laughed the djinn.

'He's not lying!' snapped Matthew.

A murmur grew. The white robed giant raised his arm to quieten them down, 'Perhaps this celebration is a little premature. The children have travelled far.' He spoke in Jenn, telling Darians to eat their meals and not keep them from a well-earned rest.

Osimion led them to the back, where Darian soldiers were enjoying their drinks at a round stone table.

'Wey-yy,' they cheered.

Aiden found the chair to be huge, even though it looked too small for the soldiers to sit on. He had to sit at the tip, so his knees could bend. The soldiers offered them a bowl of strange fruit, to which they each declined. Not that they were full, from their Food Tree meals, but because they knew their bodies had different physiology. Best be cautious than be ill, whispered Arif.

One of them poured drink into goblets from his jug and passed one to each of them.

'Drink Kildana,' he gestured to them before they could decline, 'it is an honour you grace us – drink!'

The din of the bustling hall made everyone speak louder.

'What is it?' asked Arif, peering in the glass.

'Krill Juice,' replied one of the commanders.

'What's Krill Juice?' asked Matthew sniffing at the drink.

Aiden sniffed too. It smelled fruity.

His friend leaned forward, 'Juice of Krill.' Then looked at his companions who burst out laughing.

'Wise guy!' chortled Matthew. He raised his goblet in salute and took a mouthful. The goblet dropped, his hand pressed his forehead, 'It's burning,' he croaked, swallowing for air.

Both Aiden and Arif banged his back.

'Is all etara?' asked Osimion, appearing suddenly. He grabbed another goblet and brought it to Matthew's lips, 'Drink to fofo. Quickly now.'

Matthew took small sips. 'It's actually not bad,' he said, finding his voice, albeit wheezy. He half-smiled.

Then his head tilted, like when he wanted to upstage someone.

'Don't Matthew,' said Aiden.

Matthew drank slowly, his eyes never leaving the djinns. When he finished, he slammed the goblet down on the table.

Aiden was astonished.

Osimion grinned. The soldiers cheered, raising their goblets to drink in his honour.

'Fofo,' said Matthew, showing a thumbs-up. 'I swear to God, it's awesome. You can feel it surging through your veins. Ramping up muscles. Try it, Arif!'

Arif looked down at the goblet.

'Look, don't do what I did. Drink it all,' said Matthew. 'To fofo. Feels great.'

Slowly, Arif emptied the goblet and leaned back on his chair, groaning ecstatically.

'Great innit?' said Matthew, holding out his goblet for the soldier to refill.

'Fantastic!' cried Arif.

Aiden decided if it was good for them; it would be good for him. He took a small sip. Burning engulfed his mouth, then fire swept through his body. His lungs tightened. His head felt like it was exploding.

The goblet fell.

'Eddie?'

'He's going a funny colour,' said Matthew.

Osimion shouted something.

A soldier placed his arm around him, bringing a goblet to his mouth. 'Drink kildana. First sip is fire, second is for heavenly peace.'

The burning turned cold as soon as he had taken the sip.

'Thank you,' he croaked.

The soldier withdrew back to his chair.

Osimion crouched to place a small sweet in his mouth. It melted immediately. 'Etara?' he asked.

'Etara,' whispered Aiden.

'You want some more?' asked Matthew. 'He said Krill is Fire and Ice. Feels like WOW!'

'Don't,' said Arif.

'Yes, I will,' said Aiden.

He took the goblet and drank slowly, pausing to reassure all eyes that watched him. 'Tastes fruity now,' he said, trying to sound his normal self.

'Your presence is required,' said Osimion.

Aiden and Matthew followed, but Osimion blocked their way. 'Just Lord Arif. Lady Euthalia requests your presence,' he said, glancing behind them.

Aiden turned, the guard from their room waited at the doors. They followed him. In the library, Feios stood as if bad news was about to be spilled. The elegant lady exhaled twice, then spoke quickly, 'I have grave news. Before the light of my life died from his wounds, he gave word to Dereen - son of Marvia, that a human wearing the stones of the Jade council was seen carried.'

It hadn't registered with Matthew.

'Feenash said the Grim carried her through the gates of Dozukh Fort. He followed in the hope of rescuing her. They carried the girl inside the South Tower. Feenash was fatally wounded bringing us this news.'

'Rose?' said Matthew.

'We are sorry for your loss, Lady Euthalia. We are indebted to your husband,' said Aiden.

'It is our duty,' she said, sadly.

'I'll go,' said Matthew.

'Wyfzira will never agree,' said Euthalia, 'Demon lords are powerful in their own territory. Kidnapping the girl was an ingenious move.'

'Why do vampires want my sister?' asked Aiden.

Euthalia opened a book and placed it on a table for them to see the picture. 'These are power stones, like the ones your sister is wearing. This is a like-for-like of an image documented historically in our scroll library. From a time before our troubles started. If your sister is wearing true Darian stones, from which our defences are built from, corrupting them will allow the dark lords to not just overturn the curse that keeps the vampire armies to sleep, but it will also render our magic from here to the White City useless. Our shields will fail.'

Damn George. He must have known.

'So, it is in our interest that we get my sister back,' said Aiden.

'Indeed,' said Euthalia.

'Old Greva has set the trap. He knows we will attempt a rescue,' said Feios.

'Greva is the new High Lord of the Damned,' said Euthalia. 'His past may even make him more powerful than Yandraago.'

'I'll go alone,' said Aiden.

They jolted with surprise.

'You must go to Wyfzira,' Euthalia said softly, 'He has a task for you which no one else can do. Feios will accompany Matthew.'

Euthalia thought Matthew was the only one able to rescue Aroosa. 'You'll need this.' Aiden split his necklace and placed one half around Matthew's neck.

'What is it?' asked Matthew.

'It keeps the wearer safe. Don't take it off,' he whispered.

Matthew hugged him and left.

15

Aiden:

It was a long climb up the winding steps, and even longer walking through the corridors overlooking the square. The city's lights created shadows onto the wall. Arif had lots of questions to ask Teiaar. Aiden slowed to create distance from her when he saw George leaping from windowsill to windowsill.

'Is this home?' he asked.

'I am home with you,' said George, leaping down.

'Not for long,' he whispered, walking briskly again.

'We are eternity,' laughed George. He appeared in his path. 'Speak your mind.'

Aiden whispered, 'A djinn guarding an emerald heart would know the magic his people use. You knew Eliza and Aroosa were wearing power stones.'

'The proumnon does glow,' grinned George.

'You didn't warn me,' whispered Aiden. 'And now Matthew is going God-knows-where to save her. How am I meant to keep them safe if you keep things from me?'

'You're not,' said George, floating closer.

Aiden's face was on fire. 'No! I told you, they are my family.'

George leaned to his ear. 'Careful. Best of djinns may fail to read you, dark minds are always listening. A slip of your tongue will undo all spells your master spun for you.'

Stifle emotions. Be still inside, even when you feel like a boat tilting in stormy waters.

Aiden exhaled.

'The Llianehedrin was once a big pompous meeting of idle folk,' said George. 'In the Year of the Devil, the Jades hijacked it.'

Inside the giant chamber, Aiden understood right away when he saw the boots. A second pair was seated opposite. Both owners were hidden, preferring to remain where scrolls overflowed the alcoves and light could not reach. There were many angel statues, some dangling from the ceiling, presumably to protect the inhabitants of the room, but they were old and creepy. He followed Arif, past a row of benches.

From his throne, a giant moved quickly to walk around the table and caused Arif to flinch. He had a long white braided beard. And he walked straight through George.

'Salomalom, peace be upon you and upon me. As we say in old Darian, Arla Daraan, hail you! Kildana, murffa,' said the giant.

'Salomalom,' said Arif.

'Arla Daraan,' said Aiden, surprised that he'd dropped to his knees. A djinn of his size should not have to bow to anyone.

'Oh, but I must,' said the giant, turning his emerald eyes upon him. 'Odds are against humans leaving our world alive. It's a miracle you even survive.'

'You're a telepath,' said Aiden, feigning surprise.

The giant smiled warmly. 'I am Wyfzira. Keeper of Aran Daraan. I offer sanctuary. You must surely be surprised that anyone can exist in a world of eternal darkness? It wasn't always this way. A long time ago, Ethyrus was-'

'Can you lend me Jades to rescue Herionus?' said Aiden quickly.

'Herionus is the name of our unicorn,' said Arif, but he needn't have bothered. The dip of their heads and the dimming of their eyes showed they were conversing telepathically.

'A narthrin!' exhaled the kneeling giant. Giant fingers squeezed together. 'Narthrins were rare even before the Year of Our Downfall. For a delicate creature to arrive here... in the long treacherous night? Remarkable.' Wyfzira stood up, narrowly missing an angel with his head. His hand swept the air invitingly to the benches. 'We need to discuss the danger spilling from Dozukh Fort. Greva seeks unification with Draje and the lords of the North.'

Arif sat first.

'- with Draje?' scoffed Teiaar. 'The baarda are sworn enemies.'

'We followed a deadheart-,' came a whisper from the right. 'It was received by the Krull. They are joining.'

Aiden wondered if he should ask again. Everyone seemed to be studying Wyfzira for clues.

'Has this been confirmed?' asked Teiaar.

'Do you doubt our efforts, Teiaar?' asked the husky voice on the left.

She sounded old.

'Do you doubt the prophecy?' said the djinn on the right.

'I leave talk of prophecies to my aunt and the market square,' said Teiaar.

'Abaddon's lords failed to breach our defences,' whispered the seated djinn. 'If they wake up his armies, we are doomed.'

George paused by a reading angel, glancing in his direction. Aiden walked quietly to examine her. The dainty nose, the high cheeks, it was a younger version of the Jade queen in the Diadromos. Her hand was positioned as if waiting for a child to take it, but the child was in her arms. Who was it for?

He touched it.

It buzzed.

Aiden stepped back. Like clouds fading, the stone changed to glass. The eyes were emerald colour, just like the giant.

They were quiet.

He turned. 'Sorry' he croaked.

The giant threw a dust sheet over the statue and looked to Teiaar.

'If your source was my late cousin, I do not doubt it,' continued Teiaar. 'They will require a vinx to complete their awakening. And I saw her die. The kildana killed her. She crumbled.'

'You saw what they wanted you to see,' said the one on the right.

Aiden returned to the bench.

'It is possible.' Teiaar slumped down on a bench.

'If there is one vinx, there may be five more. Ilgra the Drooj infected five powerful queens, who destroyed three worlds, before devouring them,' said the husky.

Aiden felt a deep dread fill him from within.

'We are not there yet,' said Wyfzira, resolutely. 'If they forge an alliance, the Dead Army will be resurrected. They will flood all valleys, affecting the magic within our walls, depleting any hope we have of ending the curse. The Lemothinian Army is heading to the Jaw of the North. The generals will meet us at the Valley of Three.'

'Our magic and our city defences combined, will not withstand bloodthirsty barons commanding an army five times our number,' said Teiaar.

'What about Ithfirians?' asked Arif.

'Ithfirians?' scoffed Wyfzira.

It didn't surprise Aiden that his brother was missing Eliza. They went to school together in the same car for years. But how could he forget what Eliza had done? Maybe Arif wanted to learn more, Aiden knew what that felt like.

'The Ithfirians have crowned a clayborn girl as their queen,' said Teiaar.

Wyfzira returned to his throne. 'Pray tell me, Teiaar the Jade. Why were the kildana at the Red City of all places?'

Teiaar looked down. 'At Leybo's cave, a spell took us by surprise. I have not encountered powerful magic from Ithfirians before.'

George moved from the scrolls to study the map on the table. Aiden resisted the urge to join him. Why did George want him to study the queen? It was clear she wasn't reaching for a child but protecting someone. Who was she protecting? From whom? The Jades seemed friendly, what did George mean?

'A spell?' scoffed Wyfzira. His wrists dangled from the arm rest.

'It was powerful,' said Arif.

Then again, one of them seemed to be trying too hard. And the angels seemed to be warning him with wide eyes that he was in a room of telepaths… ones that faked ignorance.

Wyfzira glanced sharply.

'Very powerful,' said Aiden quickly.

'When I countered the spell, I got this pain – I have not encountered before,' said Teiaar.

Wyfzira stood up. 'An Ithfirian spell resisting a third level Jade? By Ayla's breath! Preposterous, one would say…' He turned to stare out of the window. The green glow from the high towers felt safe.

'If sirens are in the Red City, Ithfirians are beyond approach,' said the husky voice.

'One must be allowed to investigate,' said the shadow on the right.

Wyfzira faced her. 'I have come to know the name of a Feroshan general. Teiaar, you made his acquaintance.'

'Ithrandir is a true Feroshan, honourable to his ancestry,' replied Teiaar.

'Ithrandir does not sway the queen's court,' said the left shadow.

'Thallas is not to be trusted,' said the right shadow.

Wyfzira sighed. 'General Leybo himself had difficulty negotiating with the Great Red Queen. To be a queen is to sacrifice the self for a people that seldom deserve it.'

Arif stood up. 'Eliza is family. She'll listen to me.'

'She has to,' said Wyfzira. 'Persuade the Red Queen to provide her army. After all, it is not just to our benefit, but theirs too. If Greva succeeds in waking the Dead

Army, he tilts the status quo. Ethyrus will forever be lost to Hell.'

16

Matthew:

The man with the black hat was outside Mum's hospital room. Where had he been all this time? Were there other relatives? Matthew stepped round him to enter.

'Easy, Matthew,' said the old man, blocking him with an arm. His blue eyes looked less wrinkly today. He smelled of tobacco, coffee, and Arabian scent. It brought back a memory of him watching the old man comforting Mum in their living room. How come they never talked about him?

'You're... er-David,' said Matthew, questioningly.

'Did she have flu-like symptoms a few weeks before she was diagnosed?' he asked.

Matthew thought about it, 'Yes. Why?'

'Your father is alive,' said David.

'What-?'

'You must not tell her I was here. Let me look into it,' said David.

'Why-what makes you say-?'

David nodded to his mother, sleeping on the hospital bed. 'She's sick. That's how we know.'

'What?'

'Love is an odd power. No literature, holy doctrine or science can fully contain what it is and how it works. But it's great for protection. The protection we devised on your family was never broken,' said David.

Matthew looked around for a bodyguard. 'I don't see any protection.'

'Nor should you. It is tiny.'

Matthew laughed, 'What… are we talking about?'

'Stephanie has tumours created by a particular virus, which should not be happening. The virus is harmless. But when a person is enlarged with a certain spell, the virus goes into a frenzy. And creates anomalies. Your mother has not been enlarged to a giant, has she?'

'No.'

'So, it leaves a possibility, improbable though it might sound, it is not impossible. Stephanie has anomalies. Therefore, your father is alive. In a place I used to know,' said David.

Strange that he didn't think David was crazy. 'Are we related?' asked Matthew.

The old man laughed.

Matthew jolted. The animal had stopped and lowered its belly to the ground. The others were already hiding.

Matthew crouched behind a pile of rocks with his heart beating. What an odd dream!

Below them, torches flickered. The Grim looked the same type of soldiers he fought near the cave. If he wasn't seeing it with his own eyes, he would never have believed they were there, not even the careful tread on gravel could be heard.

He waited.

Are you running to help her or running from something?

He wasn't running. The opportunity to get back just hadn't cropped up. Right. Oh crap. Why hadn't he tried to find a way to get home? He had just followed the others through that door. Just like that. How could Teiaar have known so quickly? Had she read his mind? Had he been thinking about Mum in that moment? How did telepathy work? Jades, they call themselves. Telepathic elite of Daraan. How could they be sure Rose could be rescued, what did they not tell him? Why would vampires keep anyone alive? She must be scared out of her mind. Poor Rose. What did they all want from her?

Feios turned to glance. Liyoot lowered his hand. They wanted silence. Wasn't he already? Matthew slowed his breathing. How do Jades survive on this dark world? And why do vampires need an army of zombies?

Feios unfurled his arms from the animal's neck. Tefaan snorted approval.

'I'm going to place this on your ear,' whispered Feios, showing a tiny dot on his finger. 'It will dampen your thoughts. You are too noisy.'

Matthew waited for him to inspect his ear, then he climbed back onto the middle saddle. Feios flipped onto the front saddle. The animal rose like the camel he once rode in Dubai. They were again the fast riders with air slamming into his body. Liyoot wrapped an arm round his stomach, as if afraid he might fall off.

The land dipped suddenly. Tefaan slowed to a halt. Ahead the shadow of nine dark monolithic structures protruded from a giant grotesque rock. For a moment it looked terrifying. Then Matthew wondered why he could see it.

'Why do vampires need light?' he whispered.

Feios disembarked smoothly. 'We used to think it was to strike fear. But we now know torchlight is for their lords. Lords have normal vision until they transform.'

Matthew unhooked his shield from the leather and slid down. Liyoot led Tefaan into a ditch. Just in time!

Four gates swung wide. The Grim stood motionless. A horn sounded. Thousands of feet marched through the gates like one giant orderly serpent. Matthew squeezed the cold leathered handle of his sword. The Grim were heading to the flatlands.

'Far tower,' whispered Feios. 'Be silent. Lords are always listening.'

Feios leaped softly from rock to rock. Matthew followed, trying not to set the dust rolling, conscientiously breathing slowly, preserving the silence of the wretched night.

The ground lifted steeply to cover half the size of the jagged death wall. Feios showed him where to place his fingers as he climbed the remaining wall. Matthew slid down the other side until two hands helped him touch ground silently.

Feios touched his hand. He followed him along the wall towards the far jagged tower. Behind them, a cry erupted.

Matthew froze.

It sounded like a long wail coming from ahead. Were they discovered? Feios beckoned him forward.

There were more torches in the West side of the fort. A large rocky structure joined on to the main tower, with a jagged opening for a doorway. It was at least nine storeys high, which made Matthew wonder how tall the main tower was. It was too dark to see the very top, even though the burning torches lit every window. Feios pulled him to cover underneath the steps, keeping hold as they waited. Suddenly, zombie legs marched down the steps. A guard shouted at a pile of bones. Beyond, from the darkness something moved which made Matthew's heart jump.

Feios gripped his arm tighter.

It was gigantic! With no neck. The skin was scaly and grey, it's teeth jagged and black. Large bulky arms flopped side to side as it hobbled forward. The guard cracked it with his whip. The creature moaned. It was a terrible din. Matthew covered his ears.

Two more hideous giants emerged from the darkness, hobbling towards the gates. The damned turned and marched slowly behind the creatures.

'What are they?' whispered Matthew.

'Draconi,' whispered Feios. 'They were once Eli. From the City of Rosh. Only Draje is known to use Draconi. Draje was an enemy of Greva. This confirms their alliance. We must move quickly.'

Matthew followed. Feios led them away from the piles of bones and out of the torchlight until they reached the smallest side of the jagged building. The sides of the building were very sharp. Feios went to investigate how they would get in.

Suddenly, the air changed. Hair on his neck prickled. He looked up to see a burning torch was gone.

Thud.

Matthew turned.

She held the torch so he could see every monstrous tooth that could rip him apart.

Matthew ran.

As he reached the slope, the shrill scream filled his eardrums.

Talons dug into his shoulders and lifted him clear off the ground.

17

Aiden:

White towers built from glowing stones with emerald windows. If humans could make stones glow, Dad 'd be happy with the bills.

After praying for everyone's safety, Aiden sat on a balcony overlooking the fortified Western gates, eating his meal from Hathor's Tree. The drink was pleasant, but he craved the Krill Juice. The guard didn't allow him any, even though he said he drank it before.

The Darians were taller than humans and carried weapons. It was clear danger was always on their minds. When he walked through the town, he didn't see many children, which probably explained why he found himself the centre of attention. They offered him their hand-crafted stoned necklaces, leather sandals and a leather waistcoat.

'For slaying Yandraago,' Loosh told him. Loosh had been quite content promoting things he never realised he had done, and the gifts kept coming.

'You have them,' said Aiden.

'N'my Lord. These are from their hearts. Hearts we must always respect,' said Loosh, directing servants where to place them in his room.

Loosh was very likable.

Unlike George, who seemed to be in a world of his own, staring at the people streaming through the gates, sometimes in dozens and sometimes in hundreds. From their clothing and glowing blue eyes, Aiden guessed they were from the City of Lemoff. A different colony. It was nice to see how joyful the Darians welcomed them. These were refugees hiding the cruel reality that they had left in fear of their existence.

George probably remembered this moment from his past. Those happy friends. He'd known many cities and many towns and many villages, all gone now.

A hand on his shoulder startled him. Teiaar smiled, 'Why do I sense my Lord is not admiring the view?'

'I am... kind of. Your boss ignored my request.' When and how did she pass through his room without him hearing her? He really needed to be more alert if he was going to be fighting vampires.

The parting of her jaw showed puzzlement. He wasn't afraid now. George said they could speak telepathically, but they could not probe his mind. It probably bothered her.

'Pressing tasks come first,' she said.

'What tasks?'

'The Jade army needs to be led through the valley of the Three Points.'

Aiden straightened. 'I'm listening.'

'There is a more difficult task for my lord.'

'Don't do that.'

'Do what my Lord?' she asked.

'That! My name is Aiden. Just Aiden.'

She laughed. 'Come. It is time.'

Teiaar led him through the old fort back to Wyfzira's chambers.

'Blessings upon you, Aiden,' said Wyfzira, parting from the giant window, as they entered.

The room was brightly lit. No sign of the djinns in the shadows.

Wyfzira chewed something, then knelt to place a giant hand that touched his shoulder to elbow. 'I have a very difficult task for which one may not succeed. Try we must.'

Aiden waited.

Wyfzira's smile was the shape of a crescent moon dipped in tar. His breath stank worse than Arif's. The giant moved back to his throne. 'If we are to succeed in defeating the Army of Dead, then we need to mobilise every Jenn to war. Including Eli. Three Stars guard the White City, they will let you in. Eli are more powerful, but they have turned their backs upon us. They strive for redemption from an entity, that shunned all living things on this world.'

Aiden felt dismayed. 'I can't imagine what horrors one experiences to lose faith, Lord Wyfzira. Mercy is there when I feel I need it.'

'Here lies the difficulty, the Eli are stubborn,' said Wyfzira.

'The old fool wants your word,' said George. 'Be warned Elahi, do not make promises to strangers. His demons are not yours.'

'I will try my best to persuade them,' promised Aiden.

George sighed.

'You will be rejected,' said Wyfzira.

'I shall try again.'

Wyfzira locked his fingers. 'You must not do that. Put your case forward. Then walk away. Otherwise, you may never leave that confounding city. If Greva has resurrected the Army of Dead, we will be overwhelmed, magic or no magic. We need all hands. A mithrin rider is waiting.'

Aiden was glad to leave the tower.

'I have to admit that was a clever deal, Elahi. Heading East will take us away from the fighting. Dead Army will no doubt lay siege to Aran Daran. All protection spells will be undone. Except for the White City, it doesn't need spells.   When we arrive at the White City, I know of a place we can hide,' said George.

Aiden ignored him. 'Arla Daraan,' he said, smiling.

'Salomalom, Lord Aiden, it is a pleasure to serve you. I be Nethrin. This be Feena,' said the armed rider in the courtyard, greeting him with a quick bow. He helped him climb onto a mithrin with a purple mane. He clipped the leather seatbelt from the metal bar for safety. 'Gellana!' said Nethrin, lifting the reins.

Feena trotted down a wide street, heading for a different exit. They passed through a neighbourhood filled with blacksmiths, to a square. The sight surprised him. Tethered to stone wheels, giant hairy beasts with wide jaws, looked like a cross between hippos and mammoths. The hybrids moved in a circle, grinding the rocks.

'They are making power stones,' said George.

Of course. Djinns needed jewels to enhance their weapons… Aiden blocked the memory by smiling at a stone-smith.

'They cannot read your thoughts,' George said.

Aiden found this hard to believe.

On leaving the gate, Feena galloped until her hooves no longer touched the ground. They passed over dangerous moors, magic cushioning them from sound. Air pressed into his body.

'You need not worry,' said Nethrin, inside his mind. 'The Damned will not enter this territory without dark lords. Our magic is strong here.'

Aiden hoped George was right.

18

Aiden:

Plants whizzed by, deserving all glances. Aiden couldn't lift or turn his head. Strong winds forced into his body despite the spell Nethrin had chanted, ripping seams of his shirt. Nethrin had taken the time to make him safe, yet at this speed, he was sure there was risk to his neck. He cursed George for not warning him about the animals.

Oh crap. Aiden squeezed his eyes shut. He shouldn't remember David.

Feel the present.

Wind howled in his ears. It had no edge. Why wasn't it chilly? A world without a sun should be colder than the North Pole. Eliza would have a lot to say about that. He missed them arguing. Why wasn't she upset she was missing? What did his sister do to piss Eliza off?

Will Matthew have reached her by now? What if he couldn't rescue her? What could they do if both got turned into vampires? Would Eliza be able to get a cure? Would she even listen to Arif? He cheated on her. Yes, they were good friends. But she always had that look in her eyes when his back was turned, that she was remembering Arif had cheated.

Arif was different. He seemed more serious now. Eliza's change must have shaken him. And Aroosa snatched. Maybe he felt responsible.

He hoped he was okay.

All of them.

The wind eased, releasing his body. The mithrin was slowing to a trot as it crossed the stone bridge to another hill. His neck and back ached from stiffness. Bright and wide, high trunks with branches must have been trees in the old non-glowing world. They seem to be guarding the little flowers scattered between their stone feet. Darkness was defeated on this hill where nature itself gave life.

The formation of the white city's towers and buildings looked like a lady sat on rocks, sunning herself. But there was no sign of an ocean, just a wide dusty canyon. Feena crossed another bridge taking them to another side of the fortified city. It was definitely built on a cliff. The closer Feena trotted to the gates, the more eery and deserted it felt.

A bugle sounded. Someone shouted. Boots ran along the inside of the wall. The gates were smaller than those at Aran Daran, the Jade City.

'Eyana Gelada!' came a loud cry from the sentry post above the gates.

Feena stopped.

'Am fi Nethrin nata ama multana kinda metava,' shouted Nethrin upwards to the sentry position.

'Ana?' shouted someone.

Aiden smiled. The guard clearly hadn't heard Nethrin.

'Nethrin!' he hollered.

'Aya Nethrin! Sabre!' came the responding cry from the guard.

A lever clanged. Iron moaned as the gates swung outwards. Within the walls, the weight of the gates caused something to shudder, then stone and steel screeched. Nethrin lifted the reins gently. Feena trotted forward.

Wide glowing eyes of the five djinn tribes stared as they passed by. Those with glowing blue eyes had darker skin than the Darian soldiers they had been paired up with.

The city was deserted, save for the occasional guard who bowed as they walked by. At the head of the winding path, two soldiers blocked their path to the white domed building.

'Aya Nethrin!' said the Lemothinian tiredly, 'Ana multana yee etteh?'

'Our business is our own,' replied Nethrin.

They moved aside and Feena trotted forward.

'Hallowed are the Eli!' yelled the Darian.

'Hallowed the lazybones,' exhaled Nethrin.

Feena reached the oval courtyard and Nethrin disembarked quickly. 'Though we hope there are only friends in this city, keep a distance. Sirens turn Jenn against Jenn.'

'Right!' said Aiden, jolting for his benefit.

'The Eli never mingle,' Nethrin said, as if he heard his thoughts. 'They believe Ayla will wake up one day and lift the calamity that plagues our world.'

The mithrin came to a stop by the entrance steps of a white domed building. The guards joined their spears together to block entry. Nethrin untied the strap bounding Aiden and lifted him to the ground.

'We are here at the most prestigious of the domes,' Nethrin said quietly. 'This is where we receive the seldom ear of the Eli. If anywhere, this is where we may be heard for our cause. Come follow me.'

Aiden turned towards the building and ascended the seven high stairs to the entrance.

'Halt!' cried the two guards placing their palm upwards. The one on the left was Lemothinian and the one on the right was Darian.

'Eyana Gelada!' said the Lemothinian with piercing blue eyes.

'I come with business from Lord Wyfzira himself for the Eli Council.'

The Lemothinian guard moved aside, the Darian opened the doors.

19

Matthew:

The pain in his shoulders was real. The wind was real. The foul taste in his mouth from her smell was real. This was no game, surely! He was rising too fast. His body jolted, then hurtled sideways. The charrelle had turned course. A stone jaw passed him. They flew close to the fire channels, molten lava gushing down one of the giant megaliths gave him enough light to see his hands. A tower hurtled towards him. Spikes and jagged edges swept outwards as if to impale a swarm of airborne attackers.

The windows looked eerily silent. The charrelle turned sharply, the centripetal force pulled his legs, her grip tightened, sending painful shockwaves through his chest. Another tower lit by torches. On a rooftop, deformed creatures were being tortured by giants with sunken heads.

The charrelle dived through an archway, travelling at speed through a dusty tunnel. The air currents were chilly. The ceiling pulled away. The grip loosened. His head narrowly missed a pillar, he tumbled on a stone floor.

Matthew opened his eyes. What he saw did no favours to the air filling his lungs. Dangling from the joists were heads. Dried and flaky with their eyes open. Some with fangs. Trophies... they had to be.

He got to his feet, his head pounding. Blood oozed from the punctures in his shirt.

'Yoo-oo-man... I smell... you...'

Matthew retreated backwards to a pillar. His hands worked quickly to draw his blade.

She moved so fast.

Matthew staggered sideways from the kick. The sword clattered feet away.

The creature could hear his heart thumping. Why wasn't he dead already? Crouching on all fours, she spied him from the high ceiling rafters.

Think. Matthew, think! Torches... of course. Fire!

The charrelle clucked, 'In my sleep I heard you, in my yard I saw you. Brave yooman. Deliss-i-yuss yooman.'

'What's your name?' he asked.

The glee disappeared from her face. She straightened. 'Whaii-y Ma-a-ffyoo... don't you recognise me?'

Scales melted away. From grey to pink, her skin was supple and healthy. Roots straightened to her shoulders, golden and bouncy. The polka dot dress was just like he remembered. She smiled like the day she got her job at the college.

'Mum?' he gasped.

'Matthew.'

'I.... how-?'

'Come here. I missed you. Did you bring your charger?' she said.

It was a memory.

257

Matthew inhaled. 'I'm… sorry.'

'Hug your mum?' she asked softly.

From the depths of Dozukh Tower, something shrieked. Then came the blowing of a horn. A chorus of shrieks followed.

The creature lost her camouflage when she turned her head to the dark. 'He's mine!'

She leapt onto a rafter and scurried along the joists.

Matthew ran for the sword. The walls were shaking. A booming sound echoed up the tower. Over the din, he knew by the hair prickling on his neck that she was going to attack. He picked it up and threw it with all the strength he could muster from his bleeding shoulder.

Her leap fell short. She staggered. The charrelle lashed with her talons, narrowly missing his neck. He struck to kill, turning his face away to avoid the blood splatter.

She fell.

Still.

The chorus of shrieks was mournful this time. A deep roar shook the walls. The shrieks stopped.

All was quiet.

Then he heard it.

Patter. Patter. Patter.

Matthew turned too late. He was shocked to find himself so quickly surrounded. Their limbs were long, some as oddly as the tibia metatarsus of a spider. Torchlight reflected on dark eyes. Inside extended jaws, they snarled.

They hissed.

Too many circled him. Too many fangs.

A horned beast appeared from where torchlight failed to reach. One thudding hoof after the other, the furry devil came towards him with eyes of raging Hellfire. 'Yeesan fiarr-r-rtushsh!'

Matthew's heart thumped rapidly. Fear! They feed on fear. 'You talk. Yandraago didn't. He was bigger.'

It growled, blowing ghastly air.

Matthew waited, twirling his sword.

Steel tapped onto stone.

The beast froze. All of them.

'Minakh Vee!' came a hoarse snarl.

The creatures scattered.

The beast's roar blasted, forcing Matthew to take steps back.

A gaunt figure drew closer, clutching a gold staff, serpent heads held a black crystal with their jaws. 'His blood I smelled first. Not you. Not any! Do I make myself clear?'

The beast roared again.

The staff made a heavy clang on the ground. 'He's MINE!' The gaunt figure moved between them. It was clear in his red-veined eyes, that he knew how to control the beast.

It was fascinating to see the beast lower its head and shoulders. Under the watchful eye of the gaunt deathly figure, the beast shrunk. Fur retreated into rags which repaired into colourful clothing. 'All I ask for is a morsel to taste. I've never had a clayborn before,' it whispered.

'And you will,' snarled Gaunty.

The round-faced vampire arose and dusted himself. He was suddenly impeccably dressed in velvets and silks.

Gaunty turned. 'Bow Clayborn.'

'Why don't you kiss the sharpness of my blade?' dared Matthew.

Gaunty scoffed, 'Unlike Yandraago, I do not feed on fear. Sleep!'

The room wobbled. The floor seemed to be rising. His head felt heavy, but Matthew forced his eyes to widen. And took steps backwards. 'Where is she?'

'You're losing your touch Lord Greva. It came for love,' laughed Roundface.

Matthew tried to picture how he could slay them. In every scenario, he lost. 'How d'you know I was a clayborn,' he asked, 'if you've never seen one?'

Gaunty almost smiled. 'Who says we haven't?'

'Are there humans... on... this djinn world?' he asked.

'Would there be, should there be, lose your head for less. I have eternal hunger,' growled Gaunty.

'And you smell so... sweet,' growled Roundface, sniffing around him. 'He's protected.'

Gaunty stretched his staff to push away Roundface, glaring disdainfully. 'You're afraid of a sigil?'

'It's not any sigil,' hissed Roundface. 'It's Malachi!'

Gaunty looked sharply.

'Malachi sent him,' sneered Roundface. 'He must know. And if he knows, the Scentaff knows.'

'You've lost me,' said Matthew.

'No doubt they expunged your small mind of the memory,' said Gaunty, glaring. 'Malachi's tribe installed themselves as gods on your world, long before Annunaki took the Sumerian throne.'

'Annunaki the God-maker. We ate him too,' said Roundface.

'They rule your world. And your people are unaware. Malachi is not here, because he is old and afraid. Investing his time on a pathetic species. You will return to Terra and instrument the fall of the Scentaff at my side. Hunger overpowers all the mighty can throw at us,' said Gaunty.

'Are you sure? This clayborn endangered three to save one,' said Roundface.

Matthew inhaled, 'Three?'

'Jade spells are not all they make them to be,' sneered Roundface.

'You're waiting...' said Matthew, 'You need me to surrender.'

'I can take your body by force,' said Gaunty. 'The hellsborn will be obedient. But brainless. Save your brain for your immortal self. Become my sensa, a knight to Iblis. We will visit all we despise. Earth will be our throne.'

'I'll still kill you,' warned Matthew.

Roundface laughed.

Gaunty grabbed the tip of his sword and pushed his body into it. The acrid stench of death and skull-tearing fangs came inches from his face. 'Sleep your mind.'

The dark crystal grew.

A long black nail had pierced him.

His heart shuddered. He felt cold and numb. The sword fell. When Gaunty spat on the cut, air sucked out of his lungs. The chill sent shockwaves throughout his body.

Matthew dropped.

'From hell to your shell,' growled Gaunty, 'and all to plunge. Blood drinks blood, masters eat masters. We keep our promise to Iblis.'

Matthew tried reaching for the sword, but it was kicked away. He rolled on his back.

The creatures pattered back. One yelped.

Roundface growled.

The dark crystal kept it at bay.

'Begone!' shouted Gaunty.

'Let me have my thirst,' roared Roundface.

A shadow moved on the rafters.

Matthew trembled with cold stabbing pain.

'Your persistence is trying my patience, Grakh. He is to be turned as it is written!'

'Just a morsel I beg, Greva,' howled Grakh.

'Lord Supreme,' snarled Greva.

'Before your spawn takes hold, bleed him for me,' whimpered Grakh.

'I do not see you at my feet,' said Greva.

Grakh roared, 'You are NOT THE KING!'

Torches flickered. The hall shook each time the beasts collided. A shadow moved again on the rafters. Matthew fought to stay awake, but his vision obscured with darkness.

20

Aiden:

Underneath the large dome, Aiden crossed the long wide passageway with Nethrin quickly.

The guard paused. 'Hallowed are the Eli!' he said.

'Hallowed the lazybones,' said Nethrin, unapologetically.

The guard grinned, moving aside to let them pass.

Yet another passageway.

Aiden followed Nethrin, who seemed to know where he was going. The outside of the building had been deceptive, he only saw one dome. After the sixth, Aiden wondered if there was any end to the endless passageways and halls. The seventh dome was different, it was wider. A green metal railing ran the entire length of the balcony. Below, slim giants sat motionless with their eyes closed and their palms resting on their knees Were they sleeping?

'Are they praying,' asked Aiden.

'The Eli seek mercy,' said Nethrin, placing a hand on his shoulder. 'Praying is all they do.'

Aiden caught sight of George passing the statue of a giant warrior. George headed down the emerald staircase.

'Why did we come here?' asked Aiden, suddenly unnerved that he'd never find George if he waded among giants.

'They are Children of the White Star. Everything we know about clayborns has been scribed by them. It will be a blessing for them to see you,' said Nethrin, gesturing to the staircase.

There was no metal to support the emerald staircase, not even a pillar underneath. Glass just seemed to be fixed to air. 'I-What if I fall?' he asked.

'I am right behind you.'

That did nothing for his nerves. But George was reaching the bottom. Aiden took his first step onto the glass. It didn't wobble, his trainers gripped it. George faded. Aiden took long steps down. Every now and then, he caught sight of him. There were eighty-one stairs he counted.

Underneath the balcony, crystal pillars and arches stretched towards a glass gate, marking the entrance to an underground city. To his right, there were reading places with soft cushions and scroll shelves. Aiden marvelled at the space above him, the dome had an intricate etching of stars glistening in silver. The gowned giants were still and silent with their eyes closed, facing a giant chair, seated in rows, with a sizeable gap down the middle.

Empty throne?

The abandoned throne! What was it David had said... no... he read it, when? 'Eternity oath... The king of the first tribe swore an oath never to meddle again... meddle in what?' said Aiden, glancing at George.

'Children of the White Star are descendants of the divine ones who defended creation from the revolt of the Fallen,' said Nethrin.

'Do you mean Abaddon or Iblis?' asked Aiden.

'My Lord!' gasped Nethrin. 'We don't ever mention the Fallen by name, not even whisper. Especially on holy ground.'

George knelt beside the frailest Eli, who seemed asleep.

'So, the Eli are the First Tribe?' asked Aiden.

'Their forefathers and foremothers weaved magic to help the People of Light imprison the Fallen,' said Nethrin.

'What the fool didn't say was that the Fallen are also from their tribe,' said George.

'So, are they more powerful than Jades?' asked Aiden.

'Every thread of magic, including Jade magic, originates from the Spinmasters,' said George, staring sadly. 'Alas. Those who live the longest think they know it all.'

Spinmasters... where had he heard that name?

Aiden made the intention and offered an evening prayer. He closed his eyes and recited an old prayer for Aroosa and Matthew's safe return. His neck tingled. He opened his eyes to their stares. Their eyes glowed like pearls on white. Metava vastari they whispered. They stood up in a wave.

'Abomination!' one said.

'Abomination,' echoed another.

Aiden stepped back.

'Don't let them intimidate you,' said George. 'No matter how big they are in size or numbers, your ultimate power is you.'

A bearded Eli, stepped closer, his shoulders hunched. His eyebrows squeezed together over his fierce eyes, 'Abomination!' he hissed.

'Stand your ground,' said George, 'You are Clayborn. You outrank them.'

Aiden's heart thumped all the way to his ears. What exactly did he mean? He could ask, but then what if it becomes a catalyst? Even the frail Eli seemed capable of striking him dead.

He suddenly remembered why he was here. He turned away from the longbeard. 'Peace be with you Children of the White Star. I came to greet the Spinmasters. Do not fear this title, it is your greatest gift. I am Aiden. We brought the Eye of Ethyrus. It led my brothers and my sisters to this world... so help us.'

The Eli straightened their backs. Feet shifted. They spoke as one voice, loud and hollow: 'Eli welcome Iodin of the blessed, sing thy sin, sing thy best. We hear not. We see not. We care not. We tether redemption. Rest abomination.'

There was that word again.

Aiden watched them turn away.

The frail Eli stared at the ground.

'Gosh… it's a wonder they aren't extinct. Do they always insult?' asked Aiden.

'I am with shame for bringing you here,' said Nethrin.

'Ignore him. We are safe here,' said George.

'What just happened?' asked Aiden.

'They've dismissed us,' said Nethrin, quietly.

'They've chosen to forget,' said George, smiling. 'We have sanctuary!'

Aiden's jaw closed slowly. He was meant to leave now. This was the moment Wyfzira had talked about. But he was facing the people David showed him books about.

'I will have you know - I came for the sake of coming. I wanted to rescue Herionus. But you've upset my ghost. George remembers when you were better. This seat here, this throne, shouldn't be empty. Is it not true that the walking dead have good souls trapped inside their bodies? Yeah. My unicorn told me. My sweet friend who doesn't deserve being infected. Imagine, being trapped in a rotting body, watching how it kills, unable to stop your soul from being eaten for eternity. I don't want that for Herionus. I don't want that for my brothers and sisters. I don't want that for any person that is alive today. Not even you! Kindness that we give to each other is our only true value. I ask you for your kindness.'

The Eli didn't budge.

'Quite a speech, Elahi,' said George, frowning. 'For a fool's court!'

'Narthrins are solitude creatures with the ability to escape a world when threatened. They congregate with their own kind on the seventh plane where the People of Light offer protection. That one should find you is remarkable. That one should arrive here, on this wretched world, is inconceivable.'

Aiden turned to find the deep old voice. 'I'm not lying. Herionus is in trouble,' he said.

'You are haunted?' asked the frail Eli, without turning his head.

Nethrin's jaw parted. He looked concerned and mortified at the same time.

'George is harmless,' reassured Aiden.

'Tell me about your ghost,' said the frail Eli. His voice was remarkably deep and steady without vocal tremors.

'Do not,' gasped George.

'What do you want to know?' asked Aiden.

'How long has he haunted you?'

'That's none of your business,' said Aiden.

'Elahi, when one is tasked to be a torchbearer, light is currency. This is a place where your light must reach,' said George. 'Bestow what he needs to hear.'

Aiden was taken aback. In a second, George had sold himself. Why did he want to stay here? Could anyone trust these djinns? Think logically, Arif would say. When Matthew returned, the others were bound to talk about the Diadromos. Arif and Aroosa were bound to yell at each other. It was inevitable djinns would learn things. 'Okay. The crystal landed us in a giant... cosmic... museum before Eliza opened the door to this nightmare... world. George called it the Artery of the Multiverse,' he said, carefully.

'Is he Clayborn or Fireborn?' asked the dark-skinned Eli.

Aiden folded his arms. 'Why? A person is a person.'

'My Lord, it is a blessing that they are talking,' said Nethrin.

'No. It's not,' said Aiden, scowling. 'Why do you even put up with this nonsense? They're telepaths. Don't they have mouths too? Do you hear any chatter? Why aren't they talking about their problems, they've chosen silence. Silence does nothing to help someone in need, or in this case, an entire civilisation. It's selfish arrogance. They should be ashamed.'

'It matters to them,' said George, his eyebrows lifting.

'Well, it shouldn't,' said Aiden.

'Elahi!' scolded George.

Aiden groaned. 'Crackerjacks! Okay. George was a Fireborn.'

The Eli turned slowly, their eyes glowing kind now, their bodies no longer hunched.

It was troubling and fascinating that they only cared he was haunted by a djinn.

The frail Eli beckoned with his hand. 'Do not be troubled by our treatment. The arrival of the Eye has clouded our senses. We have tried to read each of you, we see voids. This is unsettling to us.'

'I'm here to help so we can go home,' said Aiden.

'He is named George?' said the bearded Eli. The shifting of wrinkles made him look gentler now.

Aiden shrugged. 'He is my ghost. I can call him what I want. Are you going to help?'

The frail Eli rose to his feet without use of his hands. 'We will pray,' he said.

The Eli dispersed for the glass gate.

Bewilderment quickly turned to dismay. With his eyes burning, Aiden said, trembling. 'This was a complete waste of time, Nethrin. Let's go!'

'Elahi! This is the safest place on Ethyrus. One should stay!' protested George.

Aiden hurried up the stairs and left the white domed building. It was a relief these telepaths couldn't read him. Yet if they refused to help, how on Hell could they win? Nethrin helped him onto Feena, and they rode out of the White City.

21

Matthew:

'Mathew...' came a whisper echoing upwards from the depth of the tower.

From the great arched windows, the breeze grew warmer. Torches flickered, bending shadows across the giant hall.

'... wake up!'

'Dad?' whispered Matthew.

A sudden gust blew towards him, his collar turned, his hair lifted gently.

'Take the crystal.'

Matthew stirred. 'Don't go,' he sobbed.

Something howled.

Matthew opened his eyes. The realization that his father was not there churned his stomach. Dad's funeral happened all those years ago. He couldn't even picture him.

To his relief the stabbing pain was gone. His body was cold and heavy. Greva had poisoned him with saliva. Saliva shouldn't be poisonous, but then again these were aliens. Something moved inside his rib cage. A parasite? Could he cut it out? What if Greva's saliva had lots of little bloodsucking baby parasites taking over his body. He needed to get back to the cloak pronto. He could not be a vampire!

He calmed his breathing.

Not a sound could be heard inside the tower.

They were still there, he knew it.

We are blood of Iblis.

What the heck?

Spawn from Abaddon.

Was it speaking to him?

Forge with us. Or die.

'Who 's Abaddon?' he asked.

We replace you.

An image of his hands ripping into Mum's neck flashed before him. Another of beheading Arif. Shocked, Matthew dug his nails into his palm. The images kept coming. It was using his memories to learn who to kill. He should get up now. His arms and legs were numb. Was he paralysed? His whole body was getting colder.

We are blood of Iblis.

Rose.

Rose needed him.

How could he save her if he could not save himself? He couldn't give up now. Clenching his teeth, he willed his hand to move. The elbow jumped. Cold spread inside his skull.

'You know if ever you need me, you only need to look in your heart and you'll find me.' Mum had tears in her eyes when she spoke those words. The morning sun caught her golden hair, as she lay exhausted on cotton sheets.

'Oh mum,' he sobbed. He missed helping Mum sit up to sip water, the chemo always made her mouth dry.

'Wherever you'll be Matthew, you'll always do the right thing,' Mum said.

His hand slid to the leather belt holding two pouches which Feios had given him. The cave's water! Of course! His fingers moved. Good. He undid the tie, and his teeth undid the stopper. He blew the stopper onto the ground.

We claim your body.

He couldn't move. He felt the chill enter his chest. The parasite had won. All it had to do was keep his limbs rigid. In minutes, he would be one of them.

'You know Matthew, the problem with you is you need to believe things work out,' When he saw her on the hospital bench outside his mother's ward, his heart had raced for the first time. His head had been all over the place. Rose missed school that whole week to keep him company. 'You love your mum, so hope for her. Hope and faith are superpowers.' He loved listening to her voice.

We claim your beloved.

No!

He had to find her. He had to. And escape this hell hole.

His hand jolted, aylarhiyssa landed on his face and on his tongue. Heat erupted inside his mouth. He felt a sharp tug to his cervical vertebrae, the parasites had shifted. Pins and needles travelled down his arm. He rocked, tilting his neck to catch droplets from his nose. Heat made his heart shudder and unlocked both his hands. He took three gulps. Shocks of ice and fire swept through his body.

Tar escaped his wound. He wasn't sure it was blood. Aylarhiyssa caused him to gasp, but his wound was clean now. He lunged forward as vomit forced its way out, tar spattered the pillar. The cold vice inside his head was gone. No voices. He took another mouthful just in case. A hot shiver ran through him.

The sword lay close. Careful not to scrape the ground, his fingers closed on the leathered handle. Holding it under his armpit, he opened the water carrier and drank until he felt better. Earth's water was the best. He splashed the sword to wash Greva's blood away.

The rafters creaked.

Hair prickled.

A growl came from behind him. He spun around, swiping his sword widely.

Nothing but pools of light from the burning torches. And darkness.

Scratch.

It came from above. He followed the noise. He passed a pillar and froze. And controlled the sound of his breathing to listen.

The burning torches allowed him to just make out something hanging from the ceiling. Too big to be a bat. It moved. Then again. It scurried so fast, that he lost it.

'Show yourself...whoever you are!' Matthew shouted.

No sound above the flickering flames of the torches could be heard.

Matthew waited.

Snarl.

It scampered on all fours.

He spun quickly and felt bone through his sword. As it slid on the ground, he ran to hack the neck. The vampire clawed the dirt. Then wailed. He thrust his sword and twisted until something snapped, this time it went still. The body crumbled.

Matthew sighed relief.

Scratch.

His nape hair prickled.

It came from the far end of the room.

How many were there?

Which was the best escape route? The corridors could help him check out what lay inside the tower? The window… Falling to his death had to be better than turning into one of them.

The scratching was drawing closer.

He backed to the window.

The creature scuppered quickly to his right.

He survived Gaunty.

It snarled.

His heart raced.

It was above him.

The growl became louder. A head appeared with pitch black eyes. Matthew flung his sword, catching it just as it leaped. He ran quickly to push the sword deeper. Monstrous hands tried to seize the sword. It wriggled, gurgling dark blood.

He'd done it. Jesus. Twice on target.

He should chop the neck.

'Matthew!' it whispered. The eyebrows tilted.

He stopped.

Colour returned to its cheeks.

'No -' he choked.

It wasn't her. He had to kill it.

It swiped to cut him. Limbs pushed the body into a spider-like position. The jaw stretched hideously; each fang capable of severing his neck with sabre-tooth ferocity.

Matthew kicked the head. The creature fell sideways. He kicked the arm to stop it getting up. Then placed his boot heavily on the neck.

His hand ached from gripping the sword. 'I'm sorry,' he sobbed.

It said his name again.

He froze.

'Golden hair… poorly hair… we kiss it better. Oh, how she waits you.'

He didn't come all this way to not try.

Loosening the tie and stopper quickly, he dropped aylarhiyssa slowly into the abomination's mouth. It stiffened. The emeralds glowed, then faded. The fangs snapped at him. But the growl sounded softer. A tentacle inside her neck U-Turned. Matthew grabbed her cheeks and pressed hard until the jaws parted. He poured the remaining contents of the pouch. And pressed her jaw closed. She choked. Her whole body shook violently from the fire sweeping inside her.

The scaly skin` crumbled, leaving soft hands. Inhuman eyes gave way to blood shot veins and the familiar brown pupils of the person he loved.

Rose leaned sideways and vomited black tar.

'Drink quickly,' he said, unscrewing his water carrier. He lifted it to her mouth.

She took long gulps. Paused. And drank again. Then her sunken cheeks turned to him. 'You came,' she whispered.

'Course.'

She sobbed against his chest. He wanted to say it wasn't worth thinking about what had transpired, but the lump in his throat stopped him. Who knew what horrors she had experienced? There'd be so much counselling afterwards. Lifting her chin, he kissed her lips gently.

She pressed against him.

He wrapped his arms around her.

The tower shook. Pillars cracked.

'Roundface,' he whispered.

She turned her head to look around. 'We should go.'

'Yeah.'

'Matthew,' she whispered, 'They took me before we even arrived. Snatched me from a city that's meant to be safe.'

'We'll talk later.'

'They knew where we'd be. They laid a trap. For me. They want me. For a prophesy. Some kind of gate he needs opening.'

'I've met Gaunty,' said Matthew.

'Him not being here can't be an accident. Promise me -' she whispered.

'I'll kill him,' he said, holding her face.

'It's happened twice. You've got to save yourself. And Lisa. And Aiden. Definitely Arif.'

'Whatever.'

'You have to kill me,' she said.

He laughed, 'What?'

'It's the only way.'

He couldn't believe what he was hearing. 'No.'

'Evil was inside me... his parasite. She knew everything... and everyone I care about. Greva wants Earth. What if he gets me again? We won't be this lucky. No one is safe.'

It made sense. 'We'll talk about it,' he said.

He kissed her dry lips. Placing his sword back in its sheath he picked her up. She was lighter than he expected. 'Fill your thoughts with the next Halloumi burger courtesy of Hathor.'

She noticed the way he was walking.

'You're bleeding!' gasped Rose. 'Put me down. The cloak-We need my cloak.'

Matthew followed her from pillar to pillar, until they found it crumpled near a pile of dust and remains, with her flask. 'Don't ask me what I did here,' she said, looking guilty.

'Technically, it wasn't you,' he said, shuddering.

With a sweep of her arm, she floated the cloak to his shoulders and tightened it. 'Hold it there. Greva says you're the chosen one…' she whispered, 'We have to keep you well.'

The wound was closing. Matthew was glad the stinging pain was gone. His body felt calm again. Matthew wanted to stroke her hair into place, but her hold on him was tight and she seemed to need it.

It came from the tunnel.

Matthew slid Rose behind him.

'I told you I'd be back,' growled Roundface.

22

Eliza:

She missed the log heater Tom bought for their garden, but Bodysnatcher was thrilled by the cold. The tent looked out on the Southern side of the Valley of the Three Points. The bodysnatcher made sure the soldiers were happy setting camp, which Eliza didn't mind, until she saw the inside of the tent. The tent was huge and sparse. The royal chair looked dainty and uncomfortable. And then the chill became non-stop shivering real. Eliza never liked camping. She hated it, Tom knew that. Tom would always make sure she left the house with her coat or cardigan. Could she ask them for one of their furs, what would they think of their mighty queen needing a fur? Would that lose her respect?

Someone entered the tent.

She was relieved that the shivering ended.

'The Darians arrive, My Queen,' General Izan said. He bowed with his right knee touching the ground.

Servants entered with food.

'The clayborn host would like a coat,' the Bodysnatcher said.

'Yes, My Queen,' said Izan.

Why did she say that? Didn't she realise that others might now see her as two persons?

The bodysnatcher spoke more gently, after sitting down on the small red throne, 'Son of Ithfir, welcome Lord Arif when he arrives. Bring him to me.'

Why was she watching Ithrandir like a hawk?

A soldier nodded and left the room.

Ithrandir returned and bowed.

Her heart quickened.

The tent was getting crowded. Five commanders and the two generals waited for three servants to finish preparing her table. Would she eat in front of them, without offering them any food?

'How have we survived two millennia in darkness?' she asked.

'The Alliance formed. Jade magic saved our city walls. From there on, we had no more infiltrations,' said Izan.

'Infiltration?' she snapped. The bodysnatcher felt disgusted.

'Sirens. The scrolls say we used your personal possessions to create shields. But they did not suffice. Our fathers had to seek help,' said Izan.

She was watching Ithrandir's silence. What was she expecting him to say?

'How long did this help last?' she said.

'Until the Siren Chokurra was killed,' said Izan.

'Tell me General, how is it that half of Ilchond is boarded? How is it that the Great Red City of Ithfir is empty of its infamous traders? Should I guess our Alliance of Honourable Defenders ended shortly after my departure? Ithfir set on a path to rot. And the best traders left, am I correct?' she asked.

Now Izan was quiet.

She took the red banana from the tray and bite into the skin, tearing off a chunk. She chewed with her mouth closed, surprising Eliza this time.

'We have news that they are on their way. We should reposition our troops for battle,' said Izan.

'So be it,' said the bodysnatcher. 'What news from our allies General Ithrandir?'

'Greva was seen with Draje. They have parted. It will only be a matter of time before we will have to engage,' said Ithrandir, quietly.

'This Greva... feels like the Half-Born. If he has survived to this night, then his treachery has no bounds. How many archers in total, Izan?'

She took another bite.

'We have seven thousand archers. And fifty thousand fighters,' replied General Izan.

That sounded like a lot to Eliza, but the poor guy's shoulders had sunk, like he was disappointed.

She swallowed the fruit. 'How many Daraan?'

'Tenfold our estimates. A quarter will arrive in the valley. A quarter to Lemoff. The rest will take position in the mountains.'

'Curse the day I hunted the Dark One. This valley is long and deep!' the bodysnatcher said, putting down her fruit. She saw the tent parting. She stood up graciously and walked again to the cold, to stare into the night. The bodysnatcher was incredibly gifted with her sight, she could see the soldier on the next hill laughing with his friend, and the one who was taking something from his satchel that didn't belong to him. 'Many will die here,' she said. 'We stand a better chance if commanders have strong discipline, and our djinn knowing the consequences of not doing duty without diligence. See that they are reminded why we fight. The damned swarm like locusts. We are either a shield or we are nothing.'

'Great Red Queen, I hear you. You speak my thoughts exactly,' replied General Izan, looking pleased when he straightened. He left confidently.

She returned inside and faced the Feroshan, who held a long fur coat, as dark as the night with ties of red silk. Her voice wasn't kind, 'Kin of Tenwa, dark lords do not want to obliterate, they would have done so already. No. Something else is at play here. The long game. Which, thanks to our sloppy fathers, we know nothing about. This danger we must identify. Feroshan you are, Feroshan has no meaning unless he is war-ready! I want scouts, even where allies nest. We must be informed to know the Hellsborn strategy. The Dead Army outnumber us by far.'

'Very well, Great Red Queen,' said Ithrandir. He placed the coat on her shoulders and gently fed each arm, then bowed and left the tent.

The rubies stopped glowing. Eliza was allowed control. She slopped down on the throne, totally exhausted. Oh, how brittle was that woman! How utterly tiresome.

A servant poured her a glass of wine. This was her life now. Lucid only to drink more wine. It was sweet before it burned.

A lower ranking soldier returned and bowed. 'Jades have arrived, the clayborn says he is Lord Arif, my Queen.'

At last! Sanity.

Eliza beamed, 'Thank you, what is your name?'

The servant looked startled. 'Sisi-Zemme, my queen.'

'Sizemme, I would like aylarhiyssa brought in for our guests. Is that possible?' she asked, gently.

'Yes, my queen,' he said.

'Crackerjackers,' she said, smiling.

The rubies glowed and the body snatcher returned, lifting her to a great height and snatching all the air in her lungs. 'Quickly now! Bring them forth!'

Eliza was disappointed that he looked relieved by her transformation. 'Clayborn is accompanied by five Daraan and one Lemothinian Officer,' he said, more graciously.

The body snatcher turned her head to the General.

'Double the guard outside the Royal Tent. Send for General Ithrandir,' ordered General Izan.

The soldier nodded and left hastily.

'Where is General Ingoliff?' asked the Queen suddenly aware of his absence.

'He was seen leaving with Thallas, for what business or purpose, I know not.'

The Queen waited for Ithrandir to enter and bow. He was weighed by the world, and she did not like it. She returned to the throne. 'Bring forth our visiting friends.'

Ithrandir nodded and left. He reappeared holding back the tent entrance to seven people, one of them carried large scrolls under his arm. Eliza's heart leaped to see Arif and Teiaar. It was odd seeing them bow to her.

'General Daash at your service,' said the one carrying scrolls. He bowed and took his position beside Arif and Ithrandir. He was stout with long green hair, wearing leather armour from the Jade City.

'General Serosh at your service,' said another, similarly dressed but the leather seemed not from a mithrin.

'General Icra at your service, Great Red Queen and this is General Vendriff from the city of Lemoff,' said the man with the shortest hair gesturing to the Lemothinian by his side.

'General Turc at your service,' said the last Darian.

'Welcome to my Royal Tent, my newfound allies. Clayborns are most welcome to Ithfir anytime, Lord Arif.'

'Thank you.'

Eliza could feel the fire in her eyes. 'The Dead Army have awakened with the death of Yandraago, I am told. This message scribed personally by Wyfzira, Lord Keeper of the Aran Daran and the Jade City, the bastions of Ethyrus Daraan. Now I will not pour scorn upon your beliefs, but the Dead Army do not march for low-ranking demons. Neither do they march for vengeance. They are vessels for a Hellsborn army, serving a grand master. No doubt, they are coming. I feel it in this wretched air and these feeble bones. If the Dead Army are marching, where is the treacherous serpent? You have no idea whom I refer, but this one does. I see it in her eyes. Teiaar the Jade, you are quite sharp for a humble ranger. Gentledjinn, let us go over the schematics of your strategy,' she said, moving further from the throne.

Arif watched General Daash unfold the largest of the scrolls. They came closer to study its markings. Izan to her left, and Ithrandir to her right. It was a map of the valley and surrounding areas.

'Old Greva has been spotted here, making his way eastwards along the valley depths. He travels with one of the Northern Lords and Bussa. We have reports that suggests Garva was the one killed at Leybo's cave,' the Darian general called Serosh said.

'From what we have determined from our queen's recollection, we concur. Is it confirmed... that Lord Garva is the one who died?' asked General Ithrandir.

'Nothing is certain, as yet' replied the Lemothinian general.

'It is certain, if we concur,' said the Bodysnatcher.

Vendriff froze, looking startled.

Serosh continued: 'Venn Varda Mountains stretch all the way to the North Pole. The Azurans tell us one of Draje's columns has been spotted moving West out of the Venn Varda. One million heading to join Greva. They will emerge on this side of the valley.'

'His other?' asked the Queen.

'The Lemothinian army and seven battalions of Daraan wait at the Vedaffy Pass, to block passage to the City of Lemoff. Eleven dozen Jades will work with the Azura defending from the heights,' said Daash, pointing on the map.

'You cannot stop an army of dead by positioning yourselves in its path,' said Ithrandir, alarmed.

'We have fine shields. Blocking is the best strategy considering numbers,' said Turc.

'Assuming no one gets infected,' said Teiaar. 'Who signed off on this?'

'It is madness!' said Izan. 'Mage of Lemoff, surely you see sense in taking position in the inner pass?'

'Sending mage further into the Venn Varda, means stretching them to cover too large an area,' said Vendriff.

'To divert the Dead Army into Dead End Gully,' said Izan.

'This did not work for Leybo,' said Vendriff.

'It will limit those that pass through. The Azurans can pick them off from the caves,' asserted Izan.

'The caves are out of reach for now,' said Turc, pointing to several Vs. 'We believe a den of sirens has taken position. I will not risk a single djinn to a siren bloodbath.'

Eliza felt the Bodysnatcher's dismay. 'Teiaar the Jade, the Jades I knew, would never let this pass. It is not a task for mage. It is a task for sisters!'

Teiaar's head dipped, and her eyes dimmed. When she looked up, Eliza and the Bodysnatcher both knew she had spoken to her superiors. 'We are aware.'

'Azurans are in agreement with the Great Red Queen. Mage of Lemoff and Daraan too, will be easy game for sirens,' said Vendriff. 'The width of the pass does not work in Lemoff's favour.'

'Tell me Lord Arif, how many commanders are required for this valley?' asked the Bodysnatcher, looking at him.

Arif was shocked he'd been asked anything. 'I-?'

'Here we are, with the Jade army and yourself, at the mouth of this valley, ready to defend these hills when it seems our greatest weakness lies North,' said Bodysnatcher. 'Is it not naive to assume that the enormity of the conflict will occur in one place? Can a large column of Hellsborn be stopped by the Lemothinian Army placing themselves in its path?'

'No,' said Arif, thoughtfully.

Eliza wondered if he really knew what he'd just said.

'A reduction in our defence of these hills will be catastrophic. Everyone depends on the Jade City,' protested General Turc.

'We will not risk this valley!' said Teiaar, looking sharply.

'Stopping the Dead Army from leaving the Venn Varda is our primary goal. We can't allow the Hellsborn lords to reach the Flatlands,' said General Icra, strongly.

The Bodysnatcher straightened. 'Do you really believe any inch of these cursed lands is safe? Are we not allies here? Are we not here to defend each other? The City of Lemoff hangs by a thread. It is not the hellsborn that threaten its walls, it is a tide of stupidity from its mage that will uproot Lady Olocon's foundations. Oh, would she not shake in her shoes if she heard you today? Did it occur to any of you the Shaara used to flow underneath Angel's Breath? Will it not be dry now, leaving tunnels to bypass your best?'

Daash straightened, glancing at Vendriff.

Eliza wondered which part had caused them to feel ashamed.

'Arrogance. This is what you present to me. You believe you live with the night and know where she comes, you expose your families to her wretchedness. You are children pretending to be soldiers. The plan for Vedaffy Pass is not a plan,' said the Queen hotly.

'I take responsibility. I will ensure the tunnels are protected,' said Vendriff.

'We can't leave the Blue City exposed,' agreed Teiaar.

'I'll go,' Arif said, surprising everyone. 'I'll need archers. We'll take position further up the Vedaffy.'

'Lord Arif, you will meet me here,' said Daash, pointing to II next to a pile of rocks. 'I will bring 2000 Daraan. We will have clear view of the valley and the caves.'

'Then it is settled!' said the Queen, satisfied. 'Vendriff will assign a battalion at the tunnels. Lord Arif and General Daash will realign with the Lemothinian Army. My armies will defend the southern side of this valley and I trust, Teiaar's sisters will command the Daraan to seal the valley?'

'Yes,' said Teiaar.

While listening to Teiaar, the Bodysnatcher allowed her eyes to see through the opening of the tent, where Daash and Arif paused by their mithrin. But then Eliza realised, the queen was watching their lips. Teiaar's voice could be heard talking, but his words were there.

'We must take care,' Daash seemed to be saying, 'that we do not underestimate our new friends.'

'Yes. Something is off.'

Eliza felt hurt and wasn't sure it wasn't hers.

23

Arif:

Eliza is still Eliza. He wanted to believe that. He had to. But who was in her body?

Oh God! The speed at which these creatures could travel made him feel like he was back in Alton Towers, on one of them lesser popular rollercoasters, which travelled faster than the big ones, and knotted his stomach. It felt like it was never ending. But then the mithrin reached the peak of a hill. Ahead, white towers lit up the night like beacons to lost travellers, to come within its walls where they might find safety. It seemed odd that anyone could defend a city as large as a county from evil, but there it stood. Green light meant good magic, good people. It wasn't the sight of the Jade City. which made Liyoot pull on the reins. It was the mass of soldiers marching from the gates of Aran Daran, battalion after battalion. 'Wow!' said Arif.

Tefaan descended the slope slowly.

The sea of soldiers moved steadily westward. Green torches were carried by the Jades, white torches were carried by soldiers. They lit up the flatlands as they passed. Though their tall bodies moved silently. If he did not have his eyes open, he would not have sensed their movement.

Most of the soldiers wore leathers and armour in the traditional Jade colours - brown, turquoise and greens. Large banners flew over each section of the army in emerald, Jade green and the traditional apple green seen on the clothing and jewellery of the Daraan.

The gates opened wide. Darian soldiers directed mithrin to heave giant catapults out of the city. Bug-like armoured vehicles towed big cylinders on wheels, Arif wasn't sure if they were guns, they looked odd. One passed by, it had many narrow shafts. As Tefaan moved over ridges, giant wheels tied to mithrin rolled past them.

As the last of the machinery left the city, city guards pulled at something to get the gates to shut. Lady soldiers marched through the closing entrance, gracefully holding their emerald star banners and each wearing a shining white crystal around their necks as they followed the departing column. They each held white staffs with large green crystals at the top.

'Are they archers?' asked Arif, after noticing identical long bows on their backs.

'They are Jade Sisters,' said Teiaar.

'Are you one of them?' he asked, noticing the same green star on her grey robed arms. Her hair was the same colour and style.

'Yes,' said Teiaar proudly, 'I am a Jade.'

Her scent was intoxicating. 'Er-sisters?'

'A school of learning from the Jade Council. We learn and practice together.'

He couldn't see her face, but he was sure she knew what was going through his mind. 'There seems to be a lot leaving the city. Who will defend Aran Daran if it is attacked?'

'Mage and Aarta will be woken from hibernation. Soldiers will remain to ensure this happens. Civilians can also be counted on to serve and protect the city.'

'You hibernate. Wow,' he laughed.

'You are not alone in regarding Aran Daran and the Jade City as one. There are three cities inside our walls. Aran Daran is the older city that lies at the foot and centre, uniting the new and old Jade Cities. Built by Daraan, occupied by all who seek shelter,' said Teiaar.

'It does look massive,' said Arif.

Liyoot said something. Tefaan increased speed across the dirt ground through the throng of soldiers and up the slope where the gates of the city lay. Then slowed, as Wyfzira appeared before them. He signalled them to stop.

Arif was amazed that Wyfzira was at able to look down on him, despite the fact he was on a mithrin, three times the size of a horse. 'Back so soon and at the right moment needed, Lord Maaz,' said the Keeper of the City. 'A million Grim have been sighted. They will be at the valley in a few hours. What say you?'

'The Queen sends her regards, Lord Wyfzira. She will meet us before battle.'

Wyfzira's gaze turned over the mountains. 'Greva will attack from the West. Draje will stay on the valley heights to keep an eye for his prize possession – the Blue City. Beware the poisoned arrows. Kildaan, lead with an open mind and you will see that which calls upon you.'

As if that made any sense. 'Thank you,' he said, 'Has there been any news from Matthew?'

'Not as yet.'

'How is Aiden?'

'Your brother is in good hands. He will join you soon.'

'If you'll excuse me Lord Arif, this is where I must get my own ride,' Teiaar disembarked from Tefaan as another rider pulled up by their side.

'You're leaving?' he uttered.

'Aya Mereen!' she called and leaped on to his mithrin. 'Fay ra nozlur kinda feraana!' she said firmly asking him to head to the frontline.

They rode towards the departing soldiers.

'Go now, Lord Arif. The enemy draws near,' said Lord Wyfzira.

'We're going to win,' said Arif.

Wyfzira laughed, 'I should hope so!' Then he drew breath, frowning with graveness, 'Everything is at stake. Our world. Your world. We cannot fail.'

Liyoot signalled Tefaan to leave.

Arif felt the keeper was staring at them. When he looked back, he was gone. The city guards drew the gates together. Giant bars of reinforced steel drove into place sealing the city.

He was out here. Exposed.

24

Aiden:

The first sight of the Damned in the valley was made by Diyafa the Third, the son of Gisthenia the Learned One of the Jade Sisters Fellowship. Like all Daraan from the Jade City, Diyafa was born with Nightsight and trained to master pitch black. He was inspecting his bow which was a gift from his mother, when he felt the sharp chill on his neck and caught the movement creeping insidiously up the far hill.

When he arrived, he was pleased to see plants coming to life with bright colours, he had never seen this happen in the Wildlands. It gave him comfort to know that Yandraago was dead, and the tide was turning. The outpost was the sum of a boulder and some grassy patches for him to sit down alone, not like the steel tank that his friend, Rhiffa was allowed to bunker. Diyafa was careful to choose a spot where he could see the enemy approach, and build a kemmy, a pile of kindle slabs which he could set on fire at first sign of trouble. Diyafa was always commended by his friends in the battalion as being the sharpest and most alert in all their combat training. 'It'll save your life one day, my friend Rhiffa said.'

Aiden smiled to show he was listening. The accent didn't seem to suit the young attractive white-haired archer sat before him, whose eyes glowed in green rings.

'They came down the slope. Ey bodies didn't hobble like I was led to believe. I set fire to e kemmy and blew my horn. It was a hollow note, not enough to reach Rhiffa, so I blew again. I am grateful mi bow was made by Mai. Blessed was e bright arrow zipping through e air and hitting e baarda, before ey rot reached my nostrils. Mai's devotion found e darkness and smited it. Blessed were her hands that crafted my bow to re-arm itself, blessed her soul eternal. I thanked her, I thanked her again. I heard e Ithfirian battle cry and e sound of ey boots and e stone rollers thundering into e valley, my fingers never tired.'

'I am sorry for your loss,' said Aiden.

Diyafa jolted. His mouth opened and closed. Then he swallowed. 'Aye. We lost a good many. Er were eleven of us archers, ey e turned. I dinna notice e siren until she pulled Rhiffa's head off. I cunna look at my heart to give her e satisfaction. I killed her. I killed her again. I climbed through t' bodies grey, green and red. She would not die. Why for God Rhiffa came here. All he had to do was blow iz horn on iz hill an' shut e iron tank. He saved us in Rosh, iz mai didn't make it, Aa'la bless her flame. Iz dai, my mai, we become family. Tis a blessing he is dead dead. I saw your silver arrows strike her, bless ye.'

Aiden wondered if he should mention it. 'The battle was won by bravado shown equally by Ithfirians and Darians.'

'And my lord,' said Diyafa.

'I killed only three,' said Aiden. 'A jade killed two. I understand sirens fly in packs of six.'

The green rings swung back to him, with puzzlement.

Aiden sighed. 'Your friend ran far to reach you from his steel bunker.'

'He was a fool.'

'Fool to leave his safety to come to your aid?' asked Aiden.

'I dinna need help.'

'Your position was strategic over the mouth of the valley.'

'Aye.'

'You were surrounded.'

'Aye.'

'Rhiffa raced to defend you with only his sword. He killed her with only yards to spare, that's why they turned on him. I turned my aim. It was too late. I am sorry for your loss,' said Aiden, softly.

His shoulders slumped. In the stillness of the night, Diyafa wept for his best friend Rhiffa.

25

Matthew:

With his fingers squeezing the hilt of his sword, Matthew watched the vampire.

'Rivers were dried by the blood of Abaddon. Yet here you drink it.' Roundface circled them, still stinking worse than a gutter on a hot day. 'Did you think I would not smell the White Fire?'

He hadn't made a move, was he deciding if it was worth risking Gaunty's wrath?

'I warned him,' growled Roundface. 'No seed or Hellsblood from the traitor's pet!'

'Plenty in my blood. Want a bite?' dared Matthew, twirling the sword.

'You fool. I only have to wait. Or perhaps my underlings can speed the process, by tearing your limbs apart,' sneered Roundface.

'You scared of me?' dared Matthew. He leaned the sword as Rose unscrewed the cap.

'I am Grakh, Destroyer of the North. You are no lieutenant,' spat Roundface.

'I'm your mercy,' said Matthew, leaning the sword under spilling water.

Grakh froze. Then fangs grew out of tarry saliva.

Rose took a step back. 'Kill it,' she shouted.

Matthew swiped swiftly.

From eye to neck, fur and flesh caved in, melting. The snout fell off. Grakh howled, stumbling backwards. His form returned to a two-legged trembling shape. He grasped at the black crystal dangling around his neck. The hole in his face repaired quickly.

Matthew struck again, slicing the side of his abdomen.

Grakh's jaws stretched to bite him.

Matthew fell backwards, he heard Rose call his name with fear in her voice.

Grakh was growing, limbs became hairy trunks. He was a hell-sized beast, hobbling towards her on stumps before the claws took shape.

Suddenly, Grakh retreated, hissing.

Rose had splashed water onto the sword. She closed the cap and re-opened it, then spilled the entire content onto the floor. She repeated the process. He knew what she was doing. She was creating a puddle. Possibly a boundary to stop Grakh crossing. Did she really think it could stop him? Matthew wasn't so sure.

The pillars trembled. From the shadows, a sword flew. It embedded into the beast, just as it turned. Feios flew sideways, grabbing the hilt and dragging his sword through the flesh. He landed on his feet at the other side.

Matthew inhaled, his brain catching up.

Grakh was wounded, tearing fur and flesh, trying to retreat.

Matthew charged, driving the sword into the head.

Rose tossed water from the carrier.

Matthew yanked the sword. Rose wet it again.

He wasn't sure he would need it.

Deep within the tower, creatures screamed. For some reason, they were not coming to get them. Matthew wondered why. The beast was wilting before their eyes. Parts of it had transformed back to the grey-skinned vampire, but the rest was unable to do so. Grakh choked quite horribly.

Feios stretched his hand for his sword. Matthew watched him drive it deep into the back of the beast's head. Grakh howled. Bits of his body hardened and fell off, crumbling.

'I told you, I will show you mercy,' said Matthew. He took the vessel from Rose and poured water onto Grakh's wounds. The wounds healed, so he poured onto the black crystals. One shattered, the other turned green.

Grakh crumbled quickly.

Feios stepped back, his glance showed he was gobsmacked that a liquid could have such a devastating impact.

The tower shook. Matthew grabbed Rose's hand just in time as two pillars collapsed, scattering a plume of dust.

'The pillars are shells, not stone nor steel,' said Feios. 'This place was built by dark magic, possibly by the crystals you destroyed. This tower may not hold.'

Matthew wasn't sure what he meant. Grakh's second crystal was right there.

Rose lifted his sword from the remains and washed it with water from the carrier.

Matthew reached down, the crystal glowed at his touch, it was a lighter shade to Rose's emeralds. Dad had told him to take this crystal. He tucked it inside his pocket.

'I still hear them,' gasped Rose.

Feios unhooked a pouch from his belt and undid the top.

Matthew held the back of her head with one hand and lifted the pouch to her lips. She drank aylarhiyssa quickly. He felt her shiver. He kissed her. Her lips were soft, and her breath was warm on his neck. That's all he needed to know.

The rumbling and shaking were intensifying.

'Matthew!' she whispered.

He kissed her again.

Floor and pillars wobbled, he held her until it settled. Behind him, something moaned and crashed.

They turned. Pillars had collapsed.

'Sh-i-i-t,' he gasped.

'We need to go,' she said.

Matthew draped the cloak over her shoulders.

Feios led the way back to the way he came but they found the long stone staircase was covered in rubble. Their way down was blocked. Just as well, they heard frantic growls of something trying to make its way upwards.

'What do we do?' said Matthew. He was sure he could squeeze through the gap but with the devil's spawn below it was not a sound choice.

'There's only one other way,' said Feios, staring at the opening at the far end of the room.

Matthew grabbed her hand and followed Feios. The creatures had fled in this direction when Greva got angry, surely it was a way out. He passed the spot where the Charrelle dragged him.

Rose froze.

Feios backed away.

Matthew didn't like the sound of the shrieks coming upwards.

'The window,' said Rose, pulling away.

Matthew followed her to the ledge. Burning torches were like grains of sand. Feios pointed to jagged rocks that could lead to lower levels.

Rose shook her head. 'We have to jump.'

'What-?' Matthew yanked her back. 'That's a heck of a drop and we don't have wings,' he shouted, over the rumble. Dust swept over the edge.

Behind him, more pillars crumbled. 'Feios, can we climb down?'

'Trust me,' said Aroosa. She held out her other hand.

Feios hurried back to take the hand offered.

'On the count of three,' shouted Aroosa, 'We run forward. Don't let go of my hand. Remember, there's two of you that I've got to hold on to.'

Matthew wasn't sure what she planned on doing. Yes, she had flown before, but-no! Was there a ledge that he couldn't see?

The ceiling crashed.

He trusted her.

'One....'

A crack appeared below his feet. It spread rapidly across the ledge.

'...two...'

Chunks of the ledge fell away.

'...three!'

Matthew ran with her and jumped. The weight of them pulled him. But he wasn't sinking. He was sailing on air. Cold air. Behind him, something huge swept the air. Crashed and snuffed the burning torches. The rest scattered in different directions. Screams from charrelles were mournful. Yet, they weren't attacking. Why was that? Her grip tightened on his hand. He felt her pull. They were changing direction, how was that possible?

For a moment, they watched the dark monolith of a tower drop like a giant in prostration, straight onto the yellow torches. Rose was guiding them past it, to something he couldn't see. Warm air rushed towards him. He heard her say something on the wind. Their fall slowed abruptly; cold wind swept over them. His foot touched the ground.

He was speechless.

On dry grass, they breathed in the dusty air, but they were safe. Free from the tower.

Feios' shoulders relaxed when he caught sight of Loosh and the white mithrin.

The crashing of rocks continued. The dust was mainly sweeping to the far side of the wide shallow valley.

'Aya Loosh!' laughed Matthew.

Feios signalled quiet.

Matthew froze.

'We need to leave quickly. The baarda are not defeated, only their dwelling,' said Feios, quietly. 'What's that in your clothing?'

Matthew smiled, when he caught sight of the green glowing through his shirt pocket. 'Oh, this -' he pulled the chain out, '- It was on Grakh's neck.'

Loosh stepped back, horrified. 'Y-you-destroy it!'

'What? No.'

'Kildaan, dark crystals were created by the Dark King with the blood of Iblis. You will not be able to use it without surrendering your soul to the devil,' said Feios.

They looked serious. They were serious.

'That's mental,' he said.

'You are fooled by its green glow,' said Feios placing a hand on his shoulder, 'it will let you see that which makes you comfortable. Within each stone is imprisoned all the goodness that the bearer has fought with the will of the Dark King... including what nature gives us. You saw the colours of the Jade, so you let your guard down. Its darkness will seep into you, letting you see and feel what you want to feel. Slowly replacing your will with that of the Dark King...'

'My dad told me to take it. I heard him,' he said.

Rose looked sharply.

'You heard a siren, she manipulated your thoughts,' tutted Feios.

'No, that's where you're wrong. My dad told me hours before it even happened. Take the crystal, he said. I poured water, one shattered. This one didn't. This is the crystal he asked me to take. It's alright.'

'Mattie, do you hear yourself?' said Rose, taking his face in her warm soft hands. 'It was tragic. Remember? You cried with your mum and the vicar holding you. His army friends gave a beautiful honourable service. Your dad died in Syria, remember?'

Matthew felt faint. 'I heard my dad.'

'Don't you think it is odd Greva wasn't around at the end?' said Rose.

'I heard him. I-I did. I did.'

'Then let it prove it is good. Place it on the ground,' said Rose.

Don't listen to her. Keep it safe.

'Who said that?' asked Matthew, stepping back.

The Jades looked around.

'Matthew... you took it. So, you have to destroy it!' pleaded Rose.

Matthew closed his eyes to block the crystal's beauty. What was wrong with him? Why was he shaking? With all his effort, he opened his fingers and let it drop to the ground. Grass withered.

A shudder ran through him. Raising his leg, he stamped the ground. The crystal broke in three. The glow stopped.

Something screamed.

More screams erupted.

The ground shook. Gravel shifted. Suddenly, the dark night was lit up by bright light, this time coming from where the dark tower stood.

Matthew followed them quickly to the hilltop.

The land had cracked. A third earthquake was gentler. The Grim tried to hold onto the rocks, but the fort's remnants were sinking sideways with a chunk of the hill. White light blasted upwards from a crack. Then more. Showering down upon the flatland, where it pooled and began to move like water.

'Aylarhiyssa!' laughed Loosh.

'The Shaara,' exclaimed Feios.

Matthew was dumbstruck. Rose wrapped an arm around him. He pulled her close.

The still bodies of the draconi looked at peace as they swept past. On every hillside, plants came alive with illuminating colours, some grew so fast, they became trees. Nature was waking up from a deep slumber, with reds, blues, greens, and whites.

The river gave life.

26

Arif:

Tefaan's light hooves caught up with the line of green torches heading to a narrow gulley carved by molten lava aeons ago. Tefaan veered North, keeping to the straight lands which curved around the foothills of the Great Venn Varda. When they reached the next narrow valley, a column of torches was already there. Green meeting blue, but all marched silently.

The wind was so cold his lips were chafing. Arif was relieved the water inside the carrier wasn't as sharp, he gulped regularly, keeping his throat wet. The soldiers had their own thirst quenchers, one offered to Liyoot.

After the gully, Tefaan climbed the rocky terrain at pace with the soldiers.

Teiaar had left so suddenly. Had she planned to jump on another ride, or did he do something to annoy her? What is it with girls, he kept getting so wrong? No. Hang on. She was making it hard, she said as much, didn't she? She invited him to dance and told him it will be the only dance. So, she liked him. If only he knew what she wanted him to do. To be a telepath must be so cool. You could just read anybody. Any girl.

The crystal shone when he pulled it from his jacket. Strange glowing grass stretched towards it, the tips turning green making the walking soldiers gasp.

Arif waved the crystal towards them, all plants illuminated causing them to momentarily falter. They saluted with hands on their hearts and joyful grins. They were not allowed to laugh, out here. That made him feel lonely.

Liyoot, grinned. Something must have amused him.

They were at the top of the fourth hill when Arif noticed that the crystal grew ever brighter. And hotter. He fumbled in his saddle for any cloth he could use to hold it. He was about to ask Liyoot to stop, so he could ask the soldiers, when he caught sight of a large, crooked silhouette.

'What is that?' he asked Liyoot, pointing to the shadow.

'It's called Nafarinus. It is an old ruin from ancient times.'

'What kind of ruin?'

'Jade Mai said it was a place of worship. The mage say it was a very large tower where the Dark King sought revenge on the place dearest to Leybo's Counsel. Some believe it is where the Heart of Ethyrus was destroyed and will again be restored.'

'Can I look?'

'It is just rocks and stones.'

'Take me there,' said Arif.

'We will divert from our route,' said Liyoot.

'Take me there please,' Arif said, more assertively.

Liyoot pulled on the reins. Tefaan cut through the large throng of soldiers. Heading down the slope and across a rocky path, Arif watched the large boulders pass by. As they passed a rock face and a ditch, the crystal cooled down, still lighting their way, but giving relief to his hand.

The ground ascended, sometimes gently then abruptly. Tefaan kept to the embedded flagstones, which quickly changed to supporting stones used for an ancient building. The higher they climbed, the bigger the eroded stones. Tefaan had to stop when one was just too big to pass over. Liyoot helped him climb over it. Finally, they were on the dusty top. The light from the crystal shone brighter again, heating his hand very quickly. It was so bright that Arif could see the grains of the dust on the ground, as well as what lay at the bottom of the hill.

What purpose did this old ruin have? What secrets did it have? Who were the people who used it? The floor was slippery and curved around the edges. Arif walked to the small circular wall. It was a stone mantle of some kind. As he reached it, the crystal throbbed. Light pulsated.

'Liyoot, why is this happening?' asked Arif excitedly.

'I do not know, My Lord. Perhaps it needs charging?' said Liyoot.

'No? It's hot, do you want to feel it?' he said.

'No, My Lord. It is better in your hands.'

Arif walked round the small structure baffled by its purpose. He climbed on top of it, when he noticed in the centre there was another small structure carefully constructed. There were markings on the top of the stones and carvings all around it. 'Liyoot, are you able to read this?'

Liyoot climbed onto the structure and bent down to study the scribing and the illustrated markings. 'The writing belongs to an ancient dialect. I believe it says something about a power crystal.'

'Power crystal?'

'Power crystals are what makes our Jade City light when it is night. Refined magic and the minerals of Ethyrus are used for every power crystal for light and energy. If this home needed this much light, it may have been built after the Day of Calamity. Not exactly the Heart of Ethyrus,' said Liyoot sighing.

'What is the hole for?' asked Arif.

'A cradle for where the power crystal would have sat,' said Liyoot without even bothering to look.

Arif placed the crystal into the hole. It would not fit. He turned it, still it would not fit. 'Why isn't it working?' he shouted exasperated.

'Quiet, My Lord. We do not want to attract sirens. This place was destroyed a long time ago. We must go,' Liyoot urged quietly.

Arif sighed throwing his arms in the air. 'You know I was really hoping that this was the Heart, and we could fix it.'

Liyoot placed a hand on his shoulder. 'It is unclear whether Lucius Virage spoke the truth. He is the source of the story. Scribes question what the Heart refers to. Ethyrus was in no need of such an enormous source of power, it flourished and was prosperous and the suns gave all that was required. Stories give hope to people at bad times and worse. Stories may be lies to deceive us. That is all.'

Arif withdrew the crystal and followed Liyoot back to the mithrin.

They made their way out of the ruins and down the slope to the flatlands where the soldiers still marched in their thousands heading for the Valley of Three Points and to the inevitable war that waited.

27

Aroosa:

The garrison of warriors were waiting in silence. Aifa had told her the people just needed one memory for her to share, a place where she felt at peace. She was a queen now. This is what queen's do. Aroosa closed her eyes and recalled a moment from a trip two years ago. She was sat on a beach with her parents. Stephanie had been laughing that day, sitting beside Matthew, who kept stealing glances. Aroosa had been happy too. Her little brother had been right. She said what was on her mind, or rather, croaked it, or did she whisper? Anyway, it worked. It caught his full attention. He backed towards to his mother then walked back. This was the hour that Matthew had told her he couldn't stop thinking about her. Quite loudly. Proudly. She had stopped breathing. She heard their gasps, first with awe, then with confusion. He should have waited until Dad came back.

'On Earth, they only have one sun. It is yellow,' said Aifa.

The warriors were filled with admiration and, bewilderment.

'Is that your world?' asked Edric, breaking away from his garrison. His eyes were blue and green.

His friends followed him.

'Yes. This is Scarborough,' she said.

'Scabor,' he said.

'Edricus is a son to both cities,' said Aifa, smiling.

'Scarborough is a town close to where I live on Earth,' said Aroosa.

'What be that?' he asked.

'It is the sea?' she said.

'See?'

'Salt and water. What you call Ayla's Tears. On Earth, we have five oceans. Animals live on land and in the oceans, which we call the sea,' she said, watching Edric's friend nudge him. All three boys didn't look much older than Aiden, but Aifa said they were born a waking ago. She found that hard to believe.

'Is it true? Do you drink Ayla's tears?' asked Edric.

His friends were both horrified and fascinated.

Aroosa felt for the water vessel on her shoulder. 'Yes, I do. I drink water like you drink aylarhiyssa,' she said.

'And you drink aylarhiyssa,' said his friend.

'That's why you be our queen,' said Edric.

She smiled. If all else failed, she could use the water like Dorothy of Oz.

Aroosa heard a crackle, then the dark night sky turned turquoise. General Daash turned on his mithrin and signalled they were moving.

28

Aiden:

'I seek refuge with Allah's perfect words from every Shaytaan,' whispered Aiden.

On the giant flat rock, Aiden didn't need to look to know they were talking about him. He heard their voices as he prayed the evening prayer. And ignored it. It didn't help that his saliva was turning bitter and upsetting his stomach. The facemask the Ithfirian archer gave him couldn't mask the smell of putrefaction wafting in from the valley, even though it had been sprayed with Ithfirian scents, and incense lollies were burning around him slowly. The stink bothered him less than their gossip. They couldn't believe a boy of his size could kill a beast. He was nearly as tall as Arif. The second tallest in class. The smallest in his year was Javed, who happened to be the smartest repairing phones and laptops.

'Idiots exist in every tribe,' whispered Misfa, tightening the goggle's straps for him.

His heart thumped. Misfa had noticed his body language knowing he was the outsider. He hadn't read his mind. And wasn't referring to what they had just seen.

'Yes,' he croaked. The generals were due a swap. Ithrandir should do that already!

Misfa taped an end to his neck. 'Nightlighters draw power from our bodies. The Jades have magic, but we have better gadgets. Can you see?'

'It's zooming in automatically,' said Aiden. 'Wow. It's like a red day. The view is stunning. Oh! Obelisks. Rows of… obelisks… surrounding our hill. I say, that's clever. Controlling the flow of Grim. Gosh. Everything is so clear.'

'We quell the damned, like our forebears did many times. We have two generals on the battlefield. General Ingoliff in reserve,' said Misfa.

'Daraan envy Ithfirian blood, because we never run from a fight,' said Ebosh, unstrapping a roll of arrows, before dumping it into a barrel.

'What about Lemoff. Are they good fighters?' asked Aiden.

'Ere, the Clayborn asks how be Liyoomot'inians?' shouted Ebosh.

The archers guffawed.

Misfa stepped onto his rock. 'Eruh! Eyes on our mage. Strike fast if they get infected.'

The guts and rotting flesh forced him to fix his scented mask tightly. Ithfirians were defending each other with swords and machetes. One of them stood back nervously, like Arif had been.

How was Arif coping? This was not his war. If he'd only found the right door to Earth, they'd be dealing with university applications and Matthew would be looking after Aunt Stephanie.

This is your fault, George.

Draconi slammed their shoulders into the obelisks. They cracked as they toppled. Giant clubs smashed the Ithfirian machinery meant to chew the Grim. Sirens swept from the air to cut them. Shaking bodies and elongated jaws showed transformations were happening too quickly.

Ithfirian lady warriors worked together to slay a Draconi. An hour ago, he might have enjoyed it. But ever since Ithrandir had beheaded his own commander, his stomach wasn't the same.

'We cannot save infected souls on the battlefield,' Misfa had said, when he vomited. 'It comes from high up, we slay.'

He meant Eliza. As if that wasn't weird enough, Ithrandir had continued fighting like nothing had happened. Not a frown, not a sigh. Slaying monsters with Wayne had been one thing, but this was a grand scale of monster-bashing. George said he was meant to be doing torch-bearing stuff. What does a torchbearer do where guts are spilled, and heads fall off? Aiden turned, his eyes searching for the Cave. Poor Herionus, out there alone.

Whoosh.

The red arrows flew North. Ithfirian archers held their breath. Magic didn't guide the arrows, just skill and fear and hope. Most hit their targets, but only a third killed. Jade arrows flew West, striking and killing the damned as they came into view. Even these arrows could not slow giants. Misfa said a draconi could kill a whole battalion if ignored. His ice arrows felled them on first strike.

He was admiring Ithfirian and Jade commanders working together when he felt it. The icy chill he felt at the back of his neck wasn't the breeze. It wouldn't surprise him if he was being watched. A vinx. Teiaar had noticed her die. He'd kept silent in the cave for a reason. She was the weakest if he could believe the power David talked about. No job done until his job was done. It wasn't over until it was over. No celebration until all feet touched Earth. She wasn't the one that threatened every living thing in the universe.

Focus on the present.

Bodies piled high at the mouth of the valley, which suited the Damned. They stomped over their dead with their grey rotting feet. The Ithfirian army were swamped. General Ithrandir fought harder with his sword.

He paused suddenly to yell at his soldiers, who immediately scattered. Hooves thundered down the hill. Rotating blades tied by rope between each two mithrin drove into Draconi and Grim. The front riders steered, while the rear riders swept their swords. Arrows forged from Jade magic struck the escaping Grim.

Ithrandir had reached his rock. A commander offered him a Krill pouch.

A mithrin's shriek caused everyone to gasp. One of the dead soldiers was now biting mithrin and rider. Bones cracked. Their cries were hideous. Their pain he could not bear to watch.

'Message from General Ithrandir,' said a commander, tapping his shoulder, 'Lord Aiden, take them out.'

Ithrandir nodded once, to acknowledge these were his words. Aiden wondered if Ithrandir had telepathic abilities, he felt he did, so why did he not send the words to his mind? Maybe he thought he couldn't handle it. Aiden took aim. His neck tingled as he gripped the calligraphy tightly to pull on the silver bowstring. Ice arrows struck the hellspawn.

The soldiers rushed to behead the infected mithrin.

Aiden took off his mask to hurl.

'Drink this,' said Misfa, unscrewing a Krill pouch.

'I'm okay,' he said, but then allowed the pouch to reach his mouth. The krill was good, but it couldn't get rid of the foul smell from the battlefield.

'Is it finished?' asked an archer of his friend who wore a Nightlighter.

'I can't see any,' said the friend.

'The battle has only begun,' came a solemn reply from behind them. A general disembarked from a battle-clad mithrin, which had a red mane.

Aiden watched as soldiers suddenly came to attention, saluting with their hands on their hearts.

Ithrandir's mithrin trotted to him. He climbed onto it, nodded to Izan, then departed. Izan came onto their rock for a better view. 'It is too quiet.'

Aiden placed the goggles back on. The flowers had stopped glowing on the hills, but he couldn't see any deadhearts.

Suddenly a cry from above caused them to turn. Ithrandir, looked panicked, pointing at a stretch of hills beyond their scope. Light from vegetation was snuffing out.

Aiden's heart sank.

'It's Greva!' gasped Izan. 'MOVE! DO YOU WANT HELL TO ENSLAVE YOU? FALL BACK!'

'George,' whispered Aiden, 'I know you can hear me. I want to kill that thing. Tell me how.'

The hill was alive with shouting, running feet and galloping hooves. Aiden covered the general, swinging his arrow from the sounds in the sky. He fired. A siren fell. The soldiers hacked her immediately. Izan galloped to shepherd everyone into a rapid retreat. He stopped for two injured soldiers who were struggling to run. They climbed onto his rear saddle. 'Hold tight!' he yelled.

'Angels conceal the joy of death, so clayborns can respect the fragility of their bodies and embrace life,' said George. 'That thing is not happiness. Hellsborn enslave you with a drop of blood. And where might I be, should you wander eternity eating flesh?'

'Has it got a dark crystal?' whispered Aiden.

'It goes by another name,' said George, folding his arms. 'That one is but half the size of Draje, yet sly as the serpent that fed the apple. Turn around, return to the Jade City. Fulfil your promise. Let djinn upon djinn.'

A snort blew the back of his neck.

Aiden turned.

General Izan had returned. The battle-clad mithrin rubbed his nose on Aiden's face and neck, causing him to giggle. Aiden took a handful of sweet rocks from the bag he was given. He opened his palm, letting the creature take them.

'Misfa, ride as fast as you can to the Jades and request two battalions to join us immediately. The hellsborn lords have arrived sooner than expected,' said Izan.

Misfa nodded curtly. A small mithrin trotted to Misfa before he even turned. Aiden wondered if the mithrin were like Herionus, could they understand language? They seemed exceptionally calm.

Misfa galloped away.

Turning, he gasped. Talons closed on Izan's shoulders and lifted him.

Aiden fired.

The siren shrieked. She dodged red and green arrows as she tried to escape.

Izan hit the ground.

Aiden focused on her fleeing figure, aware that siren eyes will be watching him, they would know if he saw clearly through the dark. The bow was magic, let them believe it had a mind of its own. He jolted as she turned. Then let go of the heavenly bowstring. Ice arrows struck her neck and chest. She crashed onto a draconi. Aiden pulled on the bowstring, adjusting the light to the notch where it split in two, then he let go. Two ice arrows slammed into the giant. It crumbled before it toppled.

Aiden sank down with relief.

A Darian held Izan's distressed animal by the head, firmly, and spoke to calm it.

Soldiers and archers gathered quickly. Izan shivered. A jade warrior knelt to inspect his wounds. Aiden watched as he poured Aylarhiyssa and recited something in a whisper.

'By Ayla's grace, all is well,' said the warrior.

Izan drank the Aylarhiyssa and Krill that was offered. 'Thank you Lihun, Son of Dezra.' He got up and straightened his coat. 'Ready your swords. This is the hour. We do not tire. War is not won without the swift strike.'

The commanders withdrew.

Aiden wondered why everyone had helped the general, but not their comrades.

'Stop there.' Izan's eyebrows were creased together, but his voice was measured, 'War strengthens the weak and whittles the strongest. We will be tremendous. If not already. I hear you killed a beast, yet no master of minds can penetrate your clayborn head. Are you troubled? Or are you trouble?'

'I don't know,' said Aiden.

'Good,' laughed Izan. 'Get to higher rocks, Child.'

Aiden's face flushed. 'Yes General,' he said hoarsely.

The general climbed back onto his mithrin. 'Fades of Echira and Deelya,' he yelled, raising a broad sword. 'Our blood is red. We defy the curse. We see the night. We conquer its terror!'

Aiden suddenly got a weird feeling his mithrin was looking at him. The glowing eyes were shaped like Herionus. Would things have turned out differently if he had mounted Herionus? He could have fought off the siren's attack, he was sure of it.

'When did they choose to deny Elissa?' asked George. 'The white sun was used to bind Iblis. And again, for Abaddon and his vinx, Ilgra the Drooj.'

Aiden glared. 'Where've you been?'

'The old fool repeats the ill of his forefathers,' said George, folding his arms.

'Do you know what I've been thinking?' said Aiden hotly, 'How odd you arrive, each time. I'm thinking our time together is not linear. The George before is not the George after. And this is pointless natter!' Aiden followed the archers up the hill.

George floated to his side. 'What do you know of the Fallen?'

'Which one?' asked Aiden, regretting it as soon as the words left his mouth. He didn't want any answer. He never liked the stories.

Four mithrin towed a giant cutter, the wheels crushed gravel and stone, forcing soldiers to step away hastily as it rolled by.

George blocked his path. 'The devil.'

Aiden waited for three soldiers to pass out of earshot. 'High Djinn Iblis was commanded to bow to the Uncloned. He refused. Angels delivered an ultimatum. Djinns fought djinns, Iblis used dark fire, which no djinn had seen before. The good won. He lost. Ya-de-ya.' Aiden passed him.

Another cutter rolled by.

'Halt Torchbearer. You asked a question and I deliver an answer without an answer, it is the best I can do,' said George.

'Do better,' said Aiden.

George popped in front of him again. 'Your aarta… be in trouble.'

'What?'

'A nefarious siren is heading towards her,' said George. 'They need her. A vinx for the vinx.'

'Heading from where?'

'Not from the caves. She is cloaked by the vinx. You have but three hundred ticks to save your sister,' said George.

Aiden walked down the slope until he was hidden. He leaned against a rock and closed his eyes. He hoped anyone watching would think he was stressed. The sight was all he could use.

He was there. In the sky, right beside Aroosa and a turquoise lady, casting fireballs at sirens at the mouth of a cave.

'One cannot cast a spell for she will see you,' whispered George.

'I know.'

'You cannot speak to your aarta. She will hear. You have seventy ticks,' said George.

Aiden looked round for the siren. But saw only those already engaged with the Aruzans. When he saw the dying Jade, lying below the caves, he remembered a very important lesson that David had taught him.

Anything and everyone are your weapons.

'You see him?' asked George.

'Yes.'

'We will bond. He may see me, and the vinx may see him. Elahi, pray you will appreciate my haunt,' said George.

'I will.'

'Breathe in,' whispered George.

Aiden woke inside the Jade, pulling the pain from a broken spine inside his own and filling the Jade's lungs immediately. The Jade opened his eyes. He groped for the spear. But he struggled to move his legs.

Aiden gasped. He had to take all his pain. If he could just breathe.

George whispered in his ear. 'Elahi. I hold you, you hold him. Breathe in. Breathe out. You have but thirty ticks.'

Aiden breathed deeply for the Jade.

Hear me, I am your fire, I take your pain. I give you breath. Get up, Son of Deelya.

The Jade pushed his weight on the rock to get to his feet. For a moment, he paused, watching the resurrected queen fighting sirens alongside Lady Aifa. Ayla had not forsaken them. Blessed be the Jade-Azuran bond. What a sight it was, bringing tears to his eyes. The Jade Queen had returned to them, in a Clayborn.

Aiden inhaled. And exhaled.

The Jade closed his eyes.

And felt her. Hurtling at speed. Evil to its core.

'Light of light!' exclaimed the Jade. He climbed the rocks at speed, sending shockwaves through Aiden's body. He closed his eyes again and felt her. His legs bent, like he had done many times before. Then he flew with the spear and dropped, striking a throat just a second before the siren had reached his queen.

The turquoise lady yanked Baji. Her eyes filled with horror.

The siren dropped.

The Jade landed on top of her and rolled. Pain hit him like a bomb.

George was gone.

Aiden opened his eyes. Tears fell quickly. He waited until George reappeared. 'Is he going to die?'

George shrugged.

There was something different about him.

Aiden wiped his face. Then marched back to his spot.

George matched his pace. 'Iblis was chained in binding magic. Quite a feat, Elahi. The High Djinn who had authority over every world in every galaxy, now bound by those he taught.'

'For a ghost who doesn't care, you care,' said Aiden.

'Made possible by dust from Elissa that weakened him,' said George.

'I'm very grateful,' said Aiden, stopping suddenly.

'Elahi! Are you paying attention? What ails you? A lesson is always important,' said George.

Aiden stepped around the boulder. 'I got a sense there was more that the writers were not saying.'

'Scrolls tell of a bliss that returned to the good folk of fire,' said George, passing through the boulder.

Aiden ached to see Herionus. 'There couldn't have been bliss if Iblis was able to poison your emperor with his blood. I understand his wife cheated.'

George broke out a wide smile. 'Behold Fioha! Have I ever mentioned how your cheeks are like the plums in my mother's garden? Our neighbours stole her plums, and all her cattle. That's why my Dai took her to Babylon Terra.'

'Your mum lived on Earth?' said Aiden, surprised.

'She had a good life there I'm told.'

'Your point being?'

'A powerful emperor reborn as Abaddon the Terrible, destroyer of worlds while his traitorous beloved was bitten for full vengeance,' said George. 'They shook worlds to the core. Every queen drew power to stop his contagion. Many fell. The vinx devoured them, increasing her might. What could our blessed do against the devil's spawn? The Jade Queen drew power from Deelya and Elissa, while the Ithfirian queen struck with Echira. Elissa has novuple the power of any star,' said George.

Aiden knew this already. 'No offence, the Jades are your people, not his. Izan Iftshifius is a steel warrior. He probably hasn't seen magic to understand it.'

George sighed. 'If this is the best from the warriors of Ithfir, we are doomed.'

Aiden rolled his eyes. 'You're already dead.'

'A mist of despair has risen from this battle to stifle the flame of my soul,' said George.

'Let me get this right, you are telling me without telling me, that there are power stones at play here. If the queens drew power from the suns, they would use precious jewels, and they were combatting the same. Are those dark crystals from…?' Aiden turned.

George had already disappeared.

'Move like the fire within you,' shouted Izan from afar. 'Slay. Step back with your wits about you, let your mage slay. My men face North. The rest hava!'

'Izan can't hear you. Gosh, what that must feel like,' said Aiden. And hurried uphill to the wall of archers.

Uphill, in ten-minute shifts, Jades worked in pairs to keep the enemy filled with arrows. But Ithfirian archers looked more like townsmen, daunted by yellow torches on surrounding hills carried by the ravenous dead. Their eyes were tilted with worry they could be enslaved to the devil.

'Ayla protect us!' prayed an archer.

A draconi trudged past the fallen obelisks. Aiden took aim. The ice arrow struck its chest, it stumbled, falling onto corpses.

'FAY NA –'

The archers raised their bows to take aim.

'- KIFF!'

A volley of red arrows fell on the yellow torches.

Siren claws grabbed the soldiers manning the machines. Dracon trampled through the speared defences, pushing obelisks aside. Panic ripped through the wall of soldiers. Izan's shouting was having negligible effect. When a siren dipped to grab him, a few broke ranks to flee. Aiden followed her flight and released the string. The ice struck her neck. Her head fell off.

Jades rushed to their aid. Red and green arrows were released to kill her sisters.

Aiden turned his attention to the draconi. Firing as they hobbled closer.

The wall of soldiers parted suddenly. Six Ithfirians were hideously transforming. Izan hurried forward to put them out of their misery. Keeping a watchful eye on him was hard work.

Aiden's arms ached. Draconi or siren, the attacks on Izan were too frequent, like they were to wear them down. Galloping hooves made him turn. Ithrandir was heading down. Why so soon? Aiden lowered his Nightlighter to see.

Izan's cavalry was hidden near the lower rocks, waiting for a command to charge West. They hadn't noticed the damned had breached from behind them.

His ice arrows barely made a difference. There were too many.

'Seeds of Satan!' Giant Eliza pointed her staff, all the rubies glowed. 'Thieves! How dare thee trespass on Ithfirian lands in the shells of my kin?'

A red beam passed over the enemy. The damned caught alight, crumbling, still trying to bite. A path had been cleared. The cavalry retreated up the slope. Shields reformed a wall.

Aiden was astonished. He wondered if Eliza was even aware of this moment. How did it work if you shared your body with several dead queens? Did she agree with all their actions, or did her POV not matter?

Misfa's friend choked suddenly, ripping off his goggles. He pointed, still unable to form his words.

A dark mithrin trotted slowly through the toppled obelisks. The caped figure's face was hidden, but from the sight of the fleeing soldiers, Aiden knew it couldn't be good.

The dark rider raised his hand. The dark crystal in his neck grew.

Eliza cried out. She staggered backwards.

Aiden ran to her.

Eliza had slumped to the ground. Her staff lay shattered.

He removed his Nightlighters and picked up the giant ruby off the grass. 'Eliza?'

'Eddie… what am I doing?' she sobbed.

'Are you hurt?' he asked, placing the ruby on her palm. He choked suddenly.

The collar squeezed on his trachea as he was hauled. The guard shoved him against a jutting rock. 'You have no permission to address our queen,' he seethed, through a mask.

Another guard joined him.

'I don't need permission. She's my sister,' said Aiden.

'Is she though?' said a raspy voice.

Aiden stepped back, glaring at the hooded djinn.

'Related by blood? Blood is how we determine kin in Ithfir.'

Matthew would have punched that glee off Thallas' face.

'Eliza, tell him to back off,' he said, his voice trembling.

'Eddie, I need to be alone for a while,' she said, accepting the guard's hand to help her to her feet.

'Get back to your post, archer,' said Thallas, blocking Eliza.

Eliza climbed back into the Royal Caravan.

Aiden retreated back to the giant rock. When this was all over, he would make sure Eliza was removed as far as possible from that guy, he made his skin crawl.

Ithrandir repeated an order to a commander, he sounded stressed.

Behind the rider came a new wave of Grim and Draconi.

The sudden chill to his neck made him turn. He couldn't see the face for the hood.

Aiden plucked his bow, each time a rotten hand swiped the air. The arrows flew wide.

'Greva is mocking you,' said Misfa's friend.

You know better than to be angry. What do we do in these situations?

Be a rock.

Be a rock.

Be a rock.

Izan lifted his gaze to Ithrandir. Ithrandir was clearly troubled that the Royal Caravan was departing with Ingoliff's soldiers. The tent was gone. 'We are all we have,' he said to a commander. The commander ran for Izan.

Aiden felt their dismay. Ingoliff had fled the battle. So much for Ithfirian courage!

To his horror, Izan jumped from his white mithrin to hack at the Grim. Had he not seen the archers were busy trying to quell those infected? The Red Army was shrinking fast.

Mithrin riders surrounded Izan, using all manners of steel to clear a path for him.

Aiden's quick hand missed a siren but hit a giant. The draconi moaned, then toppled to the ground. A chill swept through him.

Where the hell was George?

Greva dismounted from his Hellsborn. His posture was straight, shoulders relaxed. He turned a deathly grin.

Izan managed to mount his gentle creature, he pulled the reins to turn towards the Hellsborn mithrin, his sword was aimed for the dark lord's heart. Greva's legs had grown monstrously. A claw lifted the white mithrin by the neck, as if Greva had done this, many times.

Hooves scraped dirt.

Neighing churned his insides.

Bones snapped. Greva held Izan up for all to see, then ate his neck.

Soldiers withdrew in terror.

Greva tossed Izan's body.

The white mithrin shook. Bodies curved and stretched, causing djinns to gasp. Hands clawed dirt.

'Mercy, my lord,' pleaded Misfa's friend.

Aiden took long breaths, then settled his fingertips between the carved calligraphy to stretch the bowstring to its limit. Ice flew four times to deliver mercy. The abominations crumbled.

'Shame about the aethon. No creature should die for a fool,' said George.

'Izan Iftshifius was brave and sweet. He fought for every beating heart without a thought for his own,' said Aiden. 'Where were you?'

'Pondering why one gives an oration on silence. Your sadness was rooted elsewhere. Were you not happy at home?' asked George, frowning.

Aiden exhaled a laugh from his sobs.

'Oh Elahi, are you weeping for a fool?' asked George.

'Careful, or I'll tell you to get lost,' heaved Aiden.

The bugle sounded retreat. Ingoliff directed his troops south over the peaks. The cavalry and Ithrandir's soldiers were confused.

'Belay that order,' yelled Ithrandir, raising his sword high. 'I am your general. You have a sworn duty to fulfil. We fight! In General Izildus Izan Iftshifius's honour and for all of Ithfir, stand your ground!'

Some ignored his orders and fled uphill, but it was heartening to see that many stayed.

'Only fools give their lives to a lost cause,' said George, appearing on the rock beside him.

'Today is a good day to die,' whispered Aiden.

'Today is barely day, barely night. Who will rescue that pathetic creature you sorely miss?' scoffed George.

'Herionus would fight,' said Aiden.

'Do you see suns in the sky?'

'Oh, but you do, don't you?' said Aiden. 'Ghosts pass through veils to haunt, which means whatever is hiding this planet in darkness, is something you can see through. So, are you saying it's cloudy up there? Because if it's one thing I know, djinns are clever with words.'

'You think I am clever with words Elahi? Can you solve this? I see rocks and I see a ball. I feel beating hearts and a waste of space.'

When George turned away, Aiden felt it. The faint tug, he should ignore. No magic was allowed. But why had George mentioned it? Aiden looked down at the ground but let his mind stretch far where the deadhearts entered a cave. It was cold and sparse, but not as chilly as the weather outside. They carried no prize but their need to obey a command to lie down.

I will not feel.

'Why-are we-?' he whispered.

'You are right to guard the words you want to utter. It is a nest. Her nest. Take one step more and they will sense you, no matter if they are sleeping. Probe them and they will know who you are,' whispered George.

They would strike from here, the best of them. Aiden turned around. In the back of the cave, deep inside the twisting chasm, a white creature slept in a furry ball.

Aiden felt for its heart and found two, beating slow and heavy. He inflated the chest to quicken the beats. Then blinked hard.

George grinned, looking quite smug.

'You're irritating,' said Aiden.

George pulled away from the rock. 'A Great Red Queen flees with a third of her army. It is unheard of. Best all fall on their swords now.'

Greva eyed Ithrandir.

'Do we give up?' asked Aiden.

'Not a chance,' said Misfa's friend, releasing an arrow. He picked up another from the bucket.

'Our Mage of Ithfir have become pitiful. Deserving of what comes to them,' said George.

'All I see are good souls,' said Aiden.

George faced him. 'Wise words if ever spoken Elahi. Izan said you will be tremendous. So be tremendous.'

Aiden was startled. For a moment, he absorbed the battle. Then climbed onto a rock and took aim at a Draconi, his fingers gripping the calligraphy. Then swung his body sharply. He let go. And again. And again.

Greva swerved out of the way, hurling his dark crystal necklace into the air. The first arrow missed him, but the second shattered the black crystals. Another struck his left arm, solidifying it. He fired again to shatter it. Greva fell.

The ground shook. The zombies collapsed. The Grim fled.

Izan's cavalrymen cheered. Then charged.

Sirens landed around Greva.

Everyone fought harder.

Aiden's ice arrows struck the lower belly of Greva's beast. The deafening shriek frightened the living mithrin. His seventh arrow threw it sideways.

Aiden fired again, but a siren dived to save Greva. Suddenly, Greva and the sirens were gone.

29

Arif:

Arif weaved through the soldiers, to reach the tent. The ones surrounding the tent talked about the last time they had killed vampires. Fond memories of people they had lost. Even the one holding the flagon had been on missions with his father.

'My Lord, Ayla blessed you with a rank no djinn can reach. If you would talk to them, remind them we are going to win the war,' suggested Liyoot's blue-haired friend, Commander Ayoshua.

'What the hell,' whispered Arif, after turning away. Was he out of his mind? He was expecting him to reassure soldiers that he had never met before, who had far more combat experience, that somehow, they were going to win a war. A war he knew nothing about.

Aside from Mr Cropper's History of Conflict, which was about historic conditions during the two wars, not actual fighting, what the hell did he know? Okay, Mr Copper did cover Sun Tzu, but did he remember anything from it? He had been too distracted by what Karen and Eliza felt about his breakup with Julie, while sat two rows behind them, inhaling her perfume. Julie. Jesus. Julie. He messed that up. Sighing, he walked into the tent. The one with cloak must be the general, he looked the smallest and oldest. Yet still near seven feet and ripped with muscles. Fuckup reporting for duty he should be saying. 'Hello,' he said, nodding.

The general looked to the commander in blue armour.

The commander's eyes dimmed, while the general straightened. Arif got the feeling they were talking, and he wasn't privy to what was said.

'Send him away,' said the general.

A soldier moved quickly to yank his arm and throw him out of the tent. Arif slid on the ground. He got back to his feet, ignoring his cut hand and stinging elbow. The soldier blocked the entrance with his towering figure. 'You are less than a child,' he said. 'Go back to the city.'

'Ocoyo, is this the courtesy you give in Lemoff these days,' scolded the voice from behind him.

Arif turned to see a Darian general who wasn't there a second ago. A Jade and an Azuran touched ground beside him.

'Salomalom General. The clayborn is not to re-enter, orders from General Vendriff,' said the soldier.

The general unsheathed his sword and placed it in the hands of the Jade. 'Give me a moment.'

Arif watched the general enter the tent with the Azuran Warrior. The Jade placed the sword under his armpit and took his hand. 'We must seal your wound, before Hellsborn race to temptation.'

'I don't have any glue,' he said.

'Lord, what be your designation?' he asked.

'Arif.'

'I be Leto, son of Dezra,' the Jade said . His eyes dimmed before he spoke, 'You must forgive this insult. I know Lemothinians can be crude, I cross cities to help my dai trade kumashan.'

Did someone tell him to say that?

'Oyoy, his dai bringitt egg-laying kumashan and cloth to see my aunt,' grinned Ayoshua, appearing from the dark suddenly.

Arif noticed Liyoot's eyebrows lift. 'You all look like you know each other,' he asked.

'Dezra is sister to my mai,' said Liyoot.

'Dezra would ask that I watch over you,' said Leto.

'Cool. So, you're cousins. Do you have any brothers and sisters?' he asked.

'He has four brothers and seven sisters, from different fathers and mothers,' grinned Ayoshua.

'I am here beside a miracle and Torros is fighting with Lord Matthew, so yes, House of Mithgarth is blessed,' Leto turned the chafed skin.

Arif flinched. Leto smeared a green ointment on the cut, it sealed instantly. 'Thank you. Can I ask, is that your clan?' he asked.

'It is indeed,' said Leto, rubbing the ointment off his skin. 'Though Jades belong to many.'

'Nice to meet you, Leto the Jade,' he said.

'Almost,' said Leto. His dimmed eyes showed he was listening to those in the tent. He straightened to glance at Liyoot.

'Come, they summon you,' said Liyoot.

'Er, I'm not going back inside,' laughed Arif. 'The general is right. I barely know what I'm doing.'

'Do any of us?' asked Leto.

'This is survival, Lord,' said Liyoot. 'We must give all we can to keep all of us alive. Or hell will take us.'

That was something Teiaar would say. Arif sighed. He gestured for Liyoot to lead the way.

As soon as he entered, the glaring heat from one side of the tent halted his tracks. 'I will make myself clear, you are a child. No amount of reasoning from any respectable warrior changes this, because you are a child. Your lack of abilities find you grace tonight, only because you are defended by djinn. And because you are a child. The Jades want you here. And Azurans want you here too. Thus, I am overruled. Do not get in our way. If claws rip your head from your shoulders, or if you become infected, it is of no consequence. Even if you are a child.'

'Of course,' he said, surprising himself how calm he replied.

'Krill juice, my lord?' asked the soldier Ocoyo, holding the flagon closer.

His stomach twisted, sending gases to his throat. Arif took a step back from the hot sweet smell. 'No. Thank you,' he said, exhaling half the syllables.

'Drink, Child,' said Vendriff. He walked round the table and lifted a goblet. Ocoyo poured. Vendriff shoved it into his hand. 'It is custom to down Krill before battle.'

Was this his way of saying sorry?

'Okay,' he said, forcing a smile. What was it Osimion said? First sip fire, second heavenly peace. Arif took two sips. Then closed his eyes and downed it all. He gasped. The aftertaste was like raspberry and caramel ice-cream. The energy coursed through his veins.

All eyes returned on the scout. 'Draje leads his Army of Dead with Lord Ghraum,' said the breathless scout.

Ocoyo poured again from the flagon. The scout drank to recuperate from his long run.

'Any cavalry?' asked General Vendriff, waving away the refill.

The scout paused, and panted, 'None... only Grim!' He drank more.

'How many sirens?' asked the Darian General Tipu.

'Biyosh counted twenty draconi,' recalled the scout, 'We saw no charrelles.'

The generals absorbed the information, one looking quite puzzled. 'No sirens. Can't be true, surely?' said Tipu.

'We also sense no sirens,' said the Azuran warrior beside Tipu.

'Lord Osimion is not worried,' said Leto, suddenly. His eyes undimmed.

'Osimion is not old enough to remember how we lost Kaspa,' said Vendriff.

'Aye. If we had not lost Kaspa, who is to know how we would have fared with Rosh,' said Daash.

'Okay. So, if we prepare for the worst-case scenario,' said Arif. 'What would that be?'

'We are in the worst-case scenario, boy. The deadhearts are upon us. All scenarios lead to Hell,' said Vendriff.

'Draje has never been one to predict,' informed Daash. 'Vendriff hacked his head off, but Draje recovered.'

'What?'

'I cut his neck until his head was hanging by fur,' said Vendriff. 'Draje regenerated and took Rosh. He listens to his sirens more, unlike other lords. His vulnerability was to fool us, it was a trap to lure an Azuran Priestess and an Emerald Sister. Ayla have mercy on our shortcomings.'

'S-so you're saying we can't kill him?' gulped Arif. He scowled.

'It was before the Jades shared with us, what they knew. Every deadheart has a hellstone, this contains a hellspirit, the source of their power. Destroy the source, they cannot regenerate,' said Vendriff.

'Yandraago had one,' recalled Arif.

'The worst case,' said Tipu, thoughtfully, 'Sirens may already be attacking Lemoff. Though Draje would want us to be there to witness its fall. He hates Greva, so he will use a strategy that will not cost him any of his loyal vampires.'

There was silence at the table. Vendriff supped from his flagon. 'Draje could have reached Lemoff without any of this spectacle. Passing through here is to feed Ghraum, his sixth born, who feeds on fear. Ghraum will split his army in an aim to tire us. This is how we left our posts at Rosh. If Ghraum has no sirens, then he will have tainted arrows, all with his blood. Infect us, we must defend ourselves from ourselves. Our fear is heightened. He will strengthen while we weaken. He has no need for speed to get to Lemoff.'

Arif considered his words. 'What if we attacked them?'

Their eyes turned to him.

'You said Draje will let Ghraum split his army. What if we do the same – attack Draje at the same time as his son is engaging with us at the pass here... would he expect this?' asked Arif.

'For what purpose?' asked Tipu.

'To kill Draje?' he said.

'You expect to kill Draje with so few Jades and Azurans?' asked Tipu.

Arif swallowed. Eliza always warned him about his gob. 'I-er-why are we here?'

'We are here to halt the Dead Army,' said Vendriff. 'We can't kill deadheart lords. The lords are unkillable.'

'My brother killed a lord when we arrived. With Ayla's Tears,' he said, opening the water carrier. He dropped water onto the grass, so they could see it wilt before their own eyes. Then he gulped it down and closed the cap. 'I have a sword. I need a chance to use it proper.'

'Do you always say what you are not thinking?' asked Vendriff.

'Oh, you mean like stating the obvious. If your citizens are tanned when this world has no sun, it begs the question, is the sun really gone, or is it that we can't see it?' said Arif.

'This is why you shouldn't be here. You're scared,' said Vendriff.

'I'm not scared to speak my mind, General,' said Arif.

Vendriff walked around the table, bringing his giant armed presence into his personal space. 'What would you do if the dark lord was this close?'

'You know it's weird how you call a vampire a lord, it's a monster, but no evil should be given a rank above yourselves. I know you're telepathic, so I'm just going to say it. My brother and sister both have an up on me, they each killed a beast. Matthew went to God-Knows-Where and destroyed a tower. Like any sportsman, I will not be outdone. I want my own kills before I leave your planet, otherwise I'm never going to live it down. And that, is motivation enough to overcome anything that comes my way.'

'Are all Clayborns this… simple?' exhaled Vendriff.

'Why are there no sirens with Draje?' asked Liyoot, suddenly. 'Assuming, they have been diverted to Lemoff, surely some would stay with him?'

'We have not sighted any,' said the scout.

Vendriff returned to the table. 'It is not beyond reason to believe a lord could have eaten them. Though Draje eating sirens, is highly doubtful. But then, sirens leaving Draje for Greva, is even more baffling.'

'It is why he heads to Lemoff,' said Tipu.

'Come again?' said Vendriff.

'To recruit,' said Liyoot.

'He asks for death,' said Vendriff.

'I am for the motion,' Tipu said, thoughtfully. 'Draje would never expect the audacity of being attacked, he knows we fear him. If we force him to the front at the same time as Ghraum, both beasts on top of Grim causing chaos, our archers will have to work harder, but it solves the issue of dark riders against our cavalry. Let's give the clayborn a chance. If he should maim even Ghraum, Draje will retreat.'

'Beasts? Like two..?' The image of Yandraago returned in all it's terrifying ordeal. Arif suddenly wondered why he opened his gob.

Tipu chuckled. 'Defeat is inevitable, let's dance with fate. I will update General Daash.'

'What if there are sirens, just hiding?' he said, hoping for another solution.

'Our archers and the warriors from both tribes will come to your aid,' laughed Tipu.

30

Aroosa:

They came to a standstill.

Aroosa was captivated. Thousands of djinn eyes glowed behind her, all of them connected to Aifa. Should they not be wearing goggles to be inconspicuous? Or did the Shield-shell do everything? It was impressive to think they had travelled so far without discovery. 'Sirens surely fly, yet our spell works,' Aifa had whispered.

She was meant to ride with Daash on his mithrin, but the thought of letting him decide whether she sat in front or behind him, didn't appeal to her in the slightest. She told him she didn't mind walking with the Jades, who were skilled in spells and magic archery. The Shield-shell matched their pace and allowed her to see the surroundings as visible as looking through tinted glass on a cloudy Earth day. The gulley was wide enough for the armies to pass through without trampling flowers. The walls on both sides were high. Height was no hindrance for the dead.

Did the shield-shell hide everything? How wonderful it would be to explore this alien world without the dark. Could deadhearts see the green flowers in her dress? The threads glistened every time the emeralds glowed. 'It's beautiful,' Arif had said, before departing with a Lemothinian battalion. The soldiers had surprised her with 'safe hunting aarta' and their smiles made her blush. No boy of that pedigree had ever paid attention to her before.

Wait a minute. If she can see through it, what guarantee is there that Hellsborn can't see her?

Someone scraped gravel.

Aifa cocked her head.

General Daash signalled to halt.

Everyone stopped.

Aroosa rested her feet without disturbing gravel.

They were crammed in a gulley, a precarious position. Were they expecting her to pull a miracle to protect 2000 Jades and seven garrisons of Lemothinian soldiers pulling strange machinery? The emeralds gave her power. How did they work? What kind of science was it? Suddenly, she felt stupid. The British Army never used weapons without understanding them.

'It takes many years of weaving spells to complete an Azuran bow,' Aifa told her telepathically.

Aroosa tightened her grip on the bow. 'I don't have any arrows?'

She could feel Aifa smiling. 'In conflict, time is the greatest foe. Every split-second is life or hell. Azuran weapons draw on power the eye can't see.'

The whispers made her turn.

Behind the white stalks, were tall yellow stems with orange or lilac petals. Over every flower, strange bees hovered over pollen light. Even butterflies had woken up from an eon of hibernation. 'Nature survives in the cities,' Matthew had told her. Here it was waking up.

Aifa's command went straight to their telepathic minds. It was silent again.

Eliza did what? Guess it sounds sensible. Must have been trying to keep them safe, taking them off the battlefield, surely? Wait... Aiden wounded Greva? Gosh. How did Aiden get from being the boy upset by Dad-not-hugging-him to... a hero complex? His way of coping with... Yes. He didn't care to be seen, he just needed to feel valued. Oh Aydie. How on Earth could I not know what you've been going through? Embarrassing, them saying all that after dinner. Of course, I should have said something. Aydie. Talk to me when you're ready, we love you.

General Daash raised his hand. All stop. Ahead, the gulley joined the Vedaffy Pass.

Soldiers scattered to their given positions, allowing the machinery to roll forward. It stretched into a crane hauling a giant ball with chained teeth. Archers climbed up the gulley to position themselves between the rock mouth.

The neckless giants with bone-grinding teeth were enough to give nightmares in normal circumstances. They stood unnaturally still, as if waiting to be activated. Below, the lower category vampires – the Grim - hurried to serve the occupants of the tents. A chill ran through her bones. Aroosa found herself backing away. No heart should be pounding, they could hear it. They already know! Slow breaths. Slow breaths. Slow. All these people putting themselves in danger. Eliza is doing it. Matthew went all the way to Dozukh. What's the worst these bitches can do? Infect me– been there, done that. God is closer than my jugular vein. Right?

From the tent, charrelles crawled out and stared in her direction. They were struck by Jade arrows.

The crane squeaked.

The sky was lit up by streaks of blue. Azuran arrows dropped, setting fire to beast and tents. Vampires attacked through the shield, biting soldiers even before the tents burned down. Behind her, siren claws grabbed soldiers of both armies tossing them into the air. The Azurans defended brothers with shield spells and hurried to give Rhyissa to the infected. Jade firepower was swift and precise, killing charrelles.

The sirens were bigger and deadly, taking position to infect Daash's commanders just to taunt him. One siren shrieked, pointing at Lemothinian machinery.

'Kiff re farr!' shouted General Daash.

The archers only killed four charrelles. Aifa flew, her skin glowed as she chanted a spell in her native tongue. Archers defended her rear. Darians defended the archers with only their swords against charrelle claws. Draconi clubs swept with devastation. Aifa's eyes blazed as she tapped into her inner power. Fireballs appeared from her palms, cerulean hot. Aifa threw them at the Draconi. Burning giants were pushed aside by more Draconi. The crane moaned. The chewing ball swung. Heads fell.

This was too easy.

Aroosa hurried to climb a rock for a better look. In their thousands, the grim were running past the gulley and not into it. Sirens had distracted Azuran Sisters. The archers were trying their best to kill as many as they could, but it looked like their mission was in jeopardy. These grim were heading to kill her brothers.

Her neck tingled. She turned. Perched on the rocks above the cave, charrelles were staring at the hovering sister. Directly underneath Aifa, dead hands sprung from the soil. Did Aifa know about the six heads below her? She was busy fending off sirens.

Aroosa supported her bow on her knee and pulled gently on the string. A tremor rippled through her arm; an arrow appeared surging with Azuran power. Slowly, she adjusted her aim to the charrelles. And released.

The arrow hit one in the neck. The charrelle choked, trying to yank it out. Aroosa pulled on the string again. And released. 'No,' she gasped. The arrow flew off course.

Sirens broke through the dirt, one pulled the choking charrelle's arrow, tearing out neckbone and oesophagus. Her disintegration caused them to shriek. Aroosa drew again. The arrows dropped. The charrelles glared, their decayed lips were moving. Shava shoont, kiff ri tar came a whisper. Aroosa felt dizzy.

Whum.

Aifa's fireball had set them ablaze. Soldiers hacked at one body.

Sirens chanted spells to put out the blue fire. Aifa flew to retreat. Then turned with speed, releasing fireballs.

Put down the bow, trust your instincts, they will serve you better.

Aroosa looked round sharply. She could've sworn the voice came from far.

Sharp pain jolted her. She turned. Only rocks behind. She felt her shoulder where she could have sworn something hit her. Her fingers found blood. Cold spread down her side. Her arm felt heavy. How was this possible? Numbness spread down her arm. She dropped the bow.

Not again.

Crap.

She bent down to pick the bow up with her other hand. As she raised herself, her eyes connected with a floating lady. The chill from the Hellspawn spread to her insides. Aroosa closed her eyes and turned her head, trying to prop the bow with her trembling hands. There was no way the Azurans would let her near them… she had aylarhiyssa! Course she did!

She unscrewed it and took two gulps.

A hand struck her face, the pouch flew along with a mouthful.

She ran.

Her lungs felt heavy.

White eyes came to stare into hers. 'I know you,' it said. A chill ran through her. The second had grey in her red eyes. Aroosa's feet didn't respond. The next were full red. She was caught by devil snakes. The sixth blew into her eyes.

She could not see.

'Aa-aarta!' they whispered.

Sounds of battle faded.

Her heartbeat slowed. She couldn't breathe.

'Aa-aarta.'

She felt the ground moving away. She was floating to their lair, where Matthew would never find her. Hellspawn would find him. And kill him.

Why haven't they bit you?

Again, that voice. Her hearing returned. She was floating away from the battle. They hadn't bit her because she was already infected. That's it. They were buying time to nurture the Hellspawn inside her!

One of them stroked her hair.

She recoiled. Her hand touched the power stone.

Why resist, said Hellspawn.

'Aa-aarta,' whispered the sirens.

This is the end, said Hellspawn.

Aroosa inhaled deep breaths. Below the whispers, she heard another.

You are not alone.

I am not alone.

'Come to us-ssss!'

'I beseech thee, Allah,' she whispered, 'Unlock my body to the queens of the past.'

The grey-faced sirens hissed. It suddenly occurred to Aroosa, that they had retreated. And the sharp pain in her spine had dropped to the pit of her stomach. Hang on. Did that mean the words were working? The lonely whisper came again. 'No darkness too dark, no light too bright,' she repeated. With every pulse of the emeralds, her bones grew. Aroosa surrendered to the powerful surge rippling through her body. Her voice was deeper now, 'We are Children of the Green Star, Deelya shields all beating hearts.' Her eyes burned with emerald rage. Deelya's cosmic fire formed in her palms. She tossed them swiftly, striking siren and beast.

Bloodthirsty devils came with jaws wide.

She was the weapon.

'Spawn of Shaytan, begone to Jahannam!' she bellowed. 'For I am Jade Queen, eternal shield! Binder at the ruin of Iblis.'

Barely had the cheer from the Jades and Lemothinians erupted, when claws pounced. The tide of

Hellsborn kept smashing machinery sending soldiers to scatter, where the charrelles could infect them. Azuran archers and warrior sisters got busy saving the army. Jades fought to quell the stampede of Draconi. Steel clashed bone. Arrows struck faster. Aroosa spun to release enough fireballs. The valley was rocked by explosions. Charrelles fought harder, trying to grab her arms or scratch her, but she was faster. All six burned with merciful emerald fire.

Aifa looked pleased. 'Jade Queen,' she said.

'Jade Queen,' her friend echoed, laughing.

Shock filled their faces suddenly. At the same time, she heard from behind the sound of a spear striking bone.

Her hands formed another fireball quickly. But the siren was plummeting to the ground with a spear in her neck. The way the Jade fell was all wrong, his body didn't bounce.

Aifa set the siren's corpse on fire. Aroosa dropped to the ground and ran to the Jade. She probed for a heartbeat. 'Aifa!'

'Alas. His spine is broken,' said Aifa.

Aroosa took off her cloak and placed it over him. 'I don't know if my cloak can fix bones. His pulse is slow. Is there a bone-fixing spell? We have to do something!'

'Bone-fixing of this magnitude requires meditation and the careful hands of a practitioner who knows which bones we need fixing. We can divert the break instead to one of his limbs, it will be painful, but he will live. We need a third sister,' said Aifa, looking upwards.

Azuran fireballs exploded on the mountains on each side.

Izmilla dropped to the ground. 'We have to be quick. There are too many.'

Mages surrounded them.

Aroosa knelt to join hands with Izmilla and Aifa. Aifa led a chant, then touched his arm. The Jade's inhale was long and desperate. His beautiful glowing eyes filled with awe, then shame, 'Thank you, Jade Queen.'

'You haven't told me your name,' asked Aroosa.

'Ispen,' he said.

'Thank you for saving my life, Ispen.'

'I was his vessel, my queen,' said the Jade. 'The charrelle threw my body to the rocks. I lay with overwhelming pain. Then an angel I saw, bringing warmth to my soul. He said, hear me, I have all your pain. I give you your breath. I am your legs. Then I saw you. And I felt her chill. Coming in very fast. I don't know how I climbed the rocks, my flame had dimmed, and it was still dim when I speared her. I am truly blessed.'

Aroosa looked to Aifa.

Aifa didn't seem to know what to make of it either. 'You saw an angel? What did this angel look like?'

'Light of light,' said Ispen, cheerfully.

'I think you are still recovering from the fall,' said Aifa.

Aroosa sighed. 'Ispen, maybe you should not mention angels to anyone else,' she said. 'Right now, we need to be focused.'

'Yes, my queen,' said Ispen.

A haunting wail echoed over the mountains.

An Azura called with urgency. Tumbling rocks cascaded dirt behind them. Aifa took to the sky and fired on the mountains. The avalanche sealed off the valley. Draconi were met by rocks and a wall of long shields.

Slowly, Aroosa brought both her hands together. The energy release hurled her a hundred feet back, but she managed to regain control, concentrating the beam further until the archers were forced to run to the rocks and the cave to shield their eyes. She stopped only when the valley bed had turned to green lava.

Rocks hissed. He feet touched the hillside to stand beside the astonished.

An army from hell had been reduced to ash.

31

Eliza:

It felt like she had been here before, in this moment, on this hill. Steadfast against the horrors of the night, the giant towers cast a green glow in every direction. It was built with sophisticated shielding. It did not threaten the likes of them. There were people inside. The general seemed to be nattering about all things but the question she had asked why they were doing this.

'We are not doing this,' said Eliza.

The rubies shone. The queen seized control of her breathing, it felt like she shared her concern. Thyjiswyn trotted closer to the hill's edge. She waited for the creep to ride up beside her.

'Thallas, tell me again,' said the Great Red Queen. She ached to look inside it, though under better circumstances than Thallas had intended.

'There are three million Grim heading to the Venn Varda, far more than we anticipated. The Hellsborn are already inside Lemoff. Azurans will become hosts. And Jades will crumble. We will not survive the purge from the Dark Lords. The Hellsborn lords promise clemency, it is stated in the treaty.'

The queen felt he was right.

Something didn't seem right, but the queen had accepted the true horror of the situation she now faced. The risk of losing everything, unless she took drastic action to save her people.

Thallas spoke again, his words grinding the reality causing her disquiet.

'It is the right thing to do. Though, only if you command, Great Red Queen. We can save the Jade City if we claim it. Under the treaty, we can prevent the Hellsborn from entering. Saving the Jades and Daraan. My Queen... please... give the order. You have seen Greva for yourself, it is only a matter of time that he will approach from the hills. They only want the clayborn world, our treaty will ensure peace for djinns. Look below, your people wait. What will become of them if we are swept aside? With the Jade City, we have power to barter for Lemoff and Aran Daran. We will negotiate the release of your friends from the Hellsborn Lords.'

The rubies stopped glowing. Eliza gasped for air. The grey mithrin was still beside her and the crone was still talking. What had been agreed? Red torches lit up the flatland. Thousands of solemn Ithfirians ready to do her bidding, those poor djinns! They would never want to attack that peaceful city, surely? Though they would give their duty regardless.

... Teiaar's home. The city that gave home to the boys.

No... she could not allow it... NO!

She glared at Thallas. The Deceitful. How she hated him now...

Then her eyes burned with red again and her features tightened as the Great Red Queen emerged, sitting erect and regal. She was resolute in her decision now; she would protect her people at all costs, regardless. Her affiliation was to the Red City and all Ithfiria, this pre-ceded and super-ceded all alliances.

To Eliza's horror, she gave the order.

The grey mithrin galloped to the soldiers, Ingoliff barked commands. A bugle sounded. Some of the soldiers at the front charged towards the gates. A flurry of red arrows flew high over the walls of the green city. The attack on the Jade City had begun.

The Great Red Queen raised her new ruby staff before pointing it at the gates.

'Ela mon Kiff!' she cried, her voice resonating deeply.

A red fireball shot out of her giant ruby and hit the gates head on, blasting shards of wood everywhere. The gates rocked but the splinters returned back to the gate. Magic protected the gates, but a very small hole had been created.

She sensed them. Behind the gates, Darian Guards rushed to strategic positions, to watch the Red Army from the small peek holes in the walls. And Jade Sisters rushed out on to the tower balconies to launch their counter offensive. Wyfzira appeared on the roof of highest white tower.

Her soldiers pushed hard against the gates, but they stood steadfast in their place. The Great Red Queen pointed her staff again, this time at the right of the gates where the gigantic hinges held the gates in their positions.

'Ela mon Kiff!' she cried, her voice echoing deeply.

Another fireball shot out. The gates rocked again. The blast created another hole in the Thidrassen Oakenstone wood, but the hinges held firm.

Ingoliff shouted commands for soldiers to climb the walls. They would breach and open the gates from inside. The soldiers that ran were young and did not know they were the first to ever try. She would reward them for their courage.

Thallas smiled, looking pleased.

The attack was going well, and the gates would open to let her forces in. She would march right up to Wyfzira's Hall and demand a peaceful surrender of the Jade City. She would sack his position and declare herself First Ruler of Aran Daran, in accordance with Thallas's advice. No one would be harmed. She would negotiate with the Jade Council the terms of their peaceful existence. After all, she is the Great Red Queen!

A wave of green arrows hurled towards them, hitting the advancing Ithfirian soldiers. Another wave followed within seconds, and another. Soon, the sky was filled with green blazing arrows that hit with precision. Her soldiers were dying.

Eliza felt her tense.

Ithfirians raised their large shields as crouched on the ground.

'Ela don Kiff!' bellowed the Great Red Queen, pointing her staff at the walls of the Jade City.

Two fireballs slammed into the upper section of the wall. Bits of large green stones tumbled to the ground. There were bodies scattered amongst the debris on both sides of the wall.

'Ela don Kiff!' boomed the Queen again, pointing towards the lower section of the wall.

Two fireballs shot out of the staff.

Stop it! Stop it! Stop it!

The queen felt Eliza's panic. Her rubies dimmed. The fireballs dispersed as sparks before they touched the city's walls.

She stared at her ruby bracelet. Eliza felt her regain control.

'Ela don Kiff!' she cried again. The fireball shot out dispersing again into red sparks.

This time her powers were being countered by Jade magic.

It was the Jade Sisters! Thallas looked stunned. The queen admired them for responding to the attack so quickly.

She summoned her powers from within.

'EFFI TAR FER RENN...' but her words were cut short by a hail of green fireballs exploding all around her. Over the city heights, seven Jade Sisters spun and hurled their green bombs. She saw General Ingoliff's mithrin topple, crushing him as it fell.

Green explosions tore limbs of the Red Army.

Surviving soldiers fled for their lives. Running, as fast as their feet could carry them. Her fearless Red Army that had been led all the way from the southern hills, disintegrated before her eyes. Those at the gates were quickly surrounded by the Darian Guards, who rushed from secret passages and jumped from the wall heights, pointing spears in their faces.

She met the eyes of Wyfzira, filled with sadness. She felt all their hopes fade away.

She felt no betrayal from Eliza. For seizing her powers. They both felt a weight unlike no other, in the bottom of her stomach.

The Jade bombs stopped falling.

Eliza felt relief.

'Great Queen, why have you stopped? We need to get inside the city,' said the grinding crone. 'Continue your strike!' This crone had led her here, though she blamed herself more for relenting.

'It's over,' she said firmly.

'Continue your strike!' shouted the crone.

The queen steered the gentle Thyjiswyn to head South.

32

Aiden:

On the Southern hill facing a Venn Varda valley, archers were relieved for replenishment. Misfa wasn't back yet, so Aiden continued firing from the rock until he heard Misfa's friend shouting. He took the advice to have a break. Somewhere on Earth, it will be first light, he hoped it would be England. He placed Misfa's shawl neatly on the ground for his head. Just as he finished the morning prayer, a battalion from the Daraan arrived and immediately ran down the hill. The air of despondency was gone, Ithfirians settled on the rocks and were eating and drinking fast so they could return to fight. Their replacements seemed to be working a plan, the Daraan were busy coordinating systematic manoeuvres to repair the barricades and defend Ithfirian commanders from the Grim. It was strange for the archers to watch Darians putting all their effort into protecting their kin. They had never seen Ithfirian and Daraan fighting side-by-side. Stories be damned, this was a new brotherhood, solidarity was their best weapon.

Aiden didn't see the arrow until it fell next to his foot. He turned to step down from the rock. Hair prickling too late, a second arrow grazed his left arm. He missed the step. A rock scraped his knee. He hit the ground hard. For a moment he lay there, feeling quite shaken.

No one came to his aid.

Why would they?

He sat up to inspect his cuts. He could head to the first aid tent. Maybe not. He didn't feel like idle chatter. He got up, just as hooves passed by. A Darian cavalry headed down the hill.

A ranger with shoulder-length green hair stepped down from a gentle creature with a purple mane. Nethrin's new grey coat reached below his knees. He looked smart beside General Turc. The green eyes went brighter when he saw him.

'Salomalom, is it a welcome reprieve you bring with you?' said Ithrandir, cheerily.

They hugged courteously. Nethrin hung back.

'Mage, khar orders are te 'bandon khese hills,' said Turc, gravely.

Ithrandir listened.

'Daraan will ensure your safe withdrawal. Head to Vinx Fell. Deadhearts will be hot on our feet.'

Ithrandir nodded. 'Any news from the East?' he asked, looking down at the ground.

Turc inhaled. The topic was difficult for both. 'Aran Daran… is safe,' he said. 'Your queen is on her way to Ithfir.'

'What of the two?' asked Ithrandir.

'Ingoliff is no more. Thallas still accompanies her.'

Ithrandir was quiet. Aiden wondered how he would manage the matter on his return.

'Ana se occurred, Ithrandir, ich no bearing on mage here. Khere is no ill will between Daraan and Ithfir. Khis matter we resolve judicially. We punish ke responsible. My condolences to General Ingoliff's family.'

Ithrandir looked up. 'Amesedjinn.'

Turc steered his mithrin around him to head to the tent. 'Ready your men to pull out.'

Aiden was relieved. Greva was gone, he hoped. The Hellsborn were easing off. Not that he didn't enjoy being at the frontline, it was time to find the others. Ithrandir told the commanders to order their djinn to retreat uphill with their wits about them. Nethrin headed downhill. Aiden lowered his bow, the graze in his arm was hurting all the way to his shoulder.

It was suddenly quiet in the Venn Varda valleys. No damned attacking, yet it was odd, he felt he was being watched. Where was he when he was needed? Archers headed for the mithrins, he wondered how far they were pulling back. Turc's men took flank, as Ithrandir's soldiers withdrew uphill. Jades had already disappeared, but Aiden knew they couldn't have gone far if Turc's men were still here. Should he wait for Nethrin to hitch a ride? Nethrin could be on an assignment. If Wyfzira used him, then surely his time was precious. Asking to hitch a ride might hamper whatever Nethrin had to do.

Aiden walked over to an archer, who was picking up his leather satchels to sling them onto his back. 'Kaas, can I ride with you?' he asked.

Kaas straightened. 'I have orders to carry the injured, My Lord. Ask Deffi for a ride.'

'Where is he?'

Kaas nodded to the two soldiers strapping shields and vessels to a saddle.

Aiden sighed. Avoiding the dirt path, he trudged uphill from rock to rock. Suddenly, a cold chill shot down his spine. His limbs were numb, he couldn't move. The second came with pain and he tumbled. As he lay behind the giant rock, feeling déjà vu and confusion, his heart started pounding.

Cursed you are. Cursed will serve. She binds you. Iblis made us. Abaddon owns us.

Oh God.

He reached for the pouch clipped to his belt. Finger and thumb unscrewed the cap. Halfway to his mouth, his hand froze. The pouch flew, landing some feet away. Aylarhiyssa glowed. Then absorbed into the ground. Plants grew quickly.

The vinx we serve.

Aiden used rocks to raise himself to his feet, but again he lost all feeling and fell. The pouch still had aylarhiyssa inside, not a lot, but enough.

Let us in.

'No,' he said, but it came out as a growl.

If only Clayborn hands could reach.

The thing was taunting him.

You are cursed. You talk to a ghost. We talk to a ghost, Hell make you a host.

It would learn everything.

He tried to stand up. His legs froze.

They will see us.

He was infected.

Infected.

Infected.

They will chop our heads.

No. They were friends!

Selwa protects us.

His fingertips dug into the dirt to haul him closer to the pouch. His stomach slid, but the leather tunic sounded like it was ripping. He pushed the ground with his toes. As he grabbed a jutting rock, he saw his hand turn grey.

Dark King we serve.

His bones thickened, sending waves of pain to his lungs. Saliva fell onto dirt. The pouch was only two metres away. It may as well be a mile.

'What's your name?' gasped Aiden.

Clayborn scared. We bite him... We drink him!

'You're already inside me. I'm not scared. I just want your name,' said Aiden.

Eshkinivsten bite Feroshan.

It would use him to infect Ithrandir! Aiden concentrated on his hand, willing his fingers to move. They twitched. He grabbed the rock to pull the weight of his body. His body slid three times on dead grass before his hand stopped.

What does you hide?

'Show me her,' he said.

What does you know?

'Only what you show me,' he said, grimacing from the pain.

There she was. Tall and deadly. Her slim face would have been beautiful if blood pumped through her veins. Long fingers plucked a strand of the dark hair wrapping round her body. She used the strand to prick herself, six vampires were enthralled as they watched. Dark blood rolled down her arm, she held her hand over an arrowhead. 'Infect them all. Bring the ice archer to me,' she hissed.

We bring you to her.

His heart rolled. 'Shaytan Eshkinivsten, is she your family?'

Who does you hide?

Aiden concentrated on taking longer breaths. 'Give me back my hand and I'll look in my pocket for their names.'

One you may save.

'Nethrin,' said Aiden.

You lie.

'Nethrin.'

Cold and numbness reached his throat. His jaw felt heavier, migraine pounded between his eyes. He moaned and heard a snarl.

We feast on the last. Ice bow to hellfire she casts. Opens the ring. Beating blood and flesh, we sing. Hell on Earth... Abaddon feasts. Iblis wins. All hail a cursed clayborn gave birth... to me.

Cold fog crept over his vision. Conversations in his journey, in the Red City, the Jade City and the Beast flashed before him. Eshkinivsten was opening his memories, pausing on his parents, Aunt Sophia, the weddings he had attended and the friend he had made at the start of the school... it wanted to infect them all.

A growl left his throat.

They were close. Eshkinivsten heard the beating heart before hands came down to turn him. Fresh blood was here. Sustenance to quicken his stay. His jaw stretched.

The djinn withdrew with his sword outstretched.

With burning torches, shadows came closer, wafting flowers, mithrin, magic and steel. Riders of the Jades... wearing face masks. Fear rose inside Eshkinivsten.

'Hold him down,' said the one with green fire in his eyes.

The boy knew this one. From the journey.

Boots weighed on his new shoulders.

'Don't hurt me Nethrin?' said Eshkinivsten, mimicking the boy.

Greenfire did not flinch. Not an eyebrow, not a muscle, but his heartbeat had quickened. All that blood inside him. Drain him and make him. Eshkinivsten's growl grew louder.

'Hold his legs Diyafa!' said a deep voice quickly.

'Easy Deffi, be gentle with our kildaan,' said Greenfire.

Eshkinivsten kicked as one took hold of his ankles. This body was too tiny and light for large heavy hands.

'His eyes are gone. Are we sure we can save him?' asked Deepvoice.

'Give me your aylarhiyssa,' commanded Greenfire.

'This shouldn't have happened,' said Deepvoice. 'A guardian kildana should have had.'

'Stay with us now, Lord Aiden,' said Greenfire. He brought the vessel to his lips. Eshkinivsten spat. To his dismay, the venom landed on Greenfire's faceguard. Eshkinivsten stretched to bite, not seeing the quick of the hand. Something rammed between the jaws. It tasted like stone. Eshkinivsten bit hard, but it wouldn't break.

Eshkinivsten howled as Greenfire gripped his chin and poured from a vessel. He wanted to spit it out but could not. He struggled wildly as white fire rolled down his throat. A thousand volts surged through his body. The heart pumped faster. In his last gurgle, sorrow filled him with what could have been.

Aiden grabbed hold of the vessel and gulped down the White Fire Water until his jaws stopped aching. The left side of his body was on fire, the monstrous nails broke off. 'More,' he gasped. Ithrandir's commander opened a pouch and gave it to Nethrin. Aiden took three gulps. And three more. His skin was changing back. The cold was leaving him.

He felt Nethrin's fingers press on his wrist, listening for a heartbeat. Soldiers shouted. Arms tightened around him. He was lifted. His arms jolted as Nethrin ran. They levelled off. They must have reached the top of the hill, past the tents to the ridge facing the moors.

'How is he?' Ithrandir sounded close.

They slowed. 'My lord has a heartbeat. His eyes recovered,' said Nethrin.

'Aeloof. Save for Jades accompanying General Turc, we are e last. Kildana was targeted. Sirens will not be far. You know where you need to be,' said Ithrandir. 'Godspeed.'

'Godspeed,' replied Nethrin.

Footsteps receded; hooves approached softly.

'Pouch of Krill f'when he rouses,' said Diyafa's cousin, Deffi. 'I found no blanket, but I have a robe.'

'Shall I place 'im on ay mithrin, Nethrin?' asked a familiar voice.

Feena snorted as she bent down to her equine carpus.

'No, Diyafa. The siren will know her attempt failed, we will be hunted, I will ride hard,' said Nethrin, wrapping a blanket around him.

Aiden felt the lift and jolt. Nethrin fastened him to Feena's saddle and covered him inside his robe, twisting his hand until the reins were wrapped around his hand.

33

Arif:

In ancient armour, the Army of Grim stood in eery silence, carrying everything they had died with. Liyoot said they had fought the devil's creed, now they served it. The breeze carried the stench. Bile rushed to his throat, forcing him to lean over and vomit. Leto had given him a sweet to suck, which tasted like mint and honey.

It was a gut reaction. He wasn't soft. No.

Arif inhaled softly. He was sure they could hear his heart hammering.

The yellow torches only illuminated the vampire riders, the true horror greeted him once he put on the goggles. There were so many. He was here. And they were out there. How could he have let this happen? If they were in danger, he wouldn't know. Why had he let this happen? Eliza leaving them had stopped him thinking clearly. He should have taken charge, making Aiden, Matthew and Aroosa stay close until they worked out how to get back. Aroosa was probably with Matthew. Aiden was probably alone. If anything happened…

Arif tugged at the goggles to rub his eye, Liyoot had tied it tight and told him the goggles and the mask were his lifeline. 'The air will be contaminated with droplets of Hellsborn blood, you do not want to be infected. Should you be, Azurans will gladly chop your head. You are too small for their comfort.'

That wasn't spoken in jest.

Arif felt for the water carrier along his saddle, dreading he'd misplaced it. The mithrin shifted its position as another rider came up beside him. This was Liyoot's friend, an Azuran commander. Was he the one who offered to chop his head? Suddenly, the hair on his neck alerted him to the fact the strap hung from it. The vessel was tucked behind his left arm.

'May Ayla keep you,' whispered the commander.

A vision of Teiaar turning to smile at him came as if to dampen the terror of this night. Her eyes had stretched, glowing differently than when he first saw her. She wore that silky dress, which folded softly in his fingers. Did she like him? Like proper? Did he have a chance in hell with her? How far did telepathy work? Did she know he was thinking of her... right now?

Teiaar was probably giving useful advice. Or fighting valiantly.

The mithrin neighed. It responded to the name 'Zenith' and had a long white mane. Above the legs, were patches of blue and green, showing it was a crossbreed of two cities. The eyes glowed blue on green and it responded to the Azuran's nearby, giving him the impression that it may have been domesticated within the City of Lemoff.

A vampire pointed his sword at him, causing Azurans to look at him. Arif ached for it all to be over. The attack should have started by now, surely?

'Be patient,' came a voice from behind. Arif watched the mithrin halt beside him. 'They wait for their Lord to give the signal,' said General Vendriff, relaxing his hold on the reins.

'Can you hear my thoughts? Are you telepathic?' asked Arif.

'You send your mind everywhere. Hellsborn will have seen your connection with Teiaar. If one vampire points to you, know that he will be competing with many, you are a new prize to please their masters,' Vendriff said.

The general seemed calm considering the circumstances.

A hand touched his back.

Arif turned. 'Place this inside your ear,' said Leto. 'It shields your thoughts.'

Arif took the dot.

'They have launched the attack,' said the general, quietly. His eyes dimmed. 'Give the order, Commander.'

A rider galloped up the hill to shout commands to the archers.

'What will Draje do?' asked Arif curiously, thinking it would be better to be prepared for his next move.

Vendriff's eyes were still dimmed. It was weird to watch telepathy. How different were djinn brains to his own? 'Draje is pushing this way. It is too early to say if it is working. Nevertheless, we need to rob him of calm,' Vendriff said, eventually.

Careful not to spill water onto the mithrin, Arif got down from the saddle and opened the water carrier. He twisted the sword under the spilling water and soaked the sheath.

The calm was arrested with a roll of drums and a thump to release shrieking arrows. The battalion was lit up by green then blue. The arrows soared on the whisper of spells.

Lines of Grim dropped. Another volley was fired, again with Azuran spells. Grim riders howled and shrieked.

The Jades aimed.

The riders fled.

Suddenly, Leto's friend Cobin fell off his mithrin. Leto jumped down.

Arif heard bones crack. Cobin's eyes were empty of life. Leto had unhooked his aylarhiyssa pouch when Liyoot's sword impaled Cobin's neck. Liyoot twisted the sword and the head fell off. 'He was gone,' said Liyoot.

Leto barely blinked as he climbed back on his saddle.

Jades and Azurans stared at Leto, whose eyes never dimmed. Arif wondered what was going through his mind. Were they eavesdropping? What was the appropriate response in their culture?

A distance away, Jades chanted a shield.

'INCOMING!' shouted General Vendriff, with all the power of his lungs.

Another chant arose from the Azuran Warriors behind him. Arif couldn't hear what they were saying. But it worked. Arrows froze, one just inches from him. Zenith trotted back from the arrowhead dripping with dark blood.

Soldiers forced the arrows to ground, with their swords. Ayoshua swiped his.

Arif looked at the General. 'Where did they come from? I can't see anyone.'

'Hellsborn archers are positioned behind Draconi,' said Vendriff.

'If spells can stop arrows, can we not use spells to stop Draje?' he asked.

The general laughed. 'Azurans have had magic since the Age of Cataclysmos Perversion. Djinns had to ally with Angels over commands from the Fallen. Spinmasters taught us then. Now we learn from Jades. And Jades learn from Azurans. We are two and the same. Alas, not even the best magic can match the devil's knights.'

The Azurans repeated their chant.

It was not English.

'What are they saying?' said Arif straining to hear their words.

'Bismilla natafeenasan! Ef-ffyleed. Kindayeeshytan efliffalood. By the All-Powerful! No harm shall come us. Evil heed, we are a shield. The words alone have little effect, it is what they conceive with their thoughts that gives the words power,' said the general. 'Tipu is worried. He asked why there are no sirens countering our spells?'

Poisoned arrows tumbled ineffectively to the ground again.

Suddenly, Vendriff straightened on his saddle. His head tilted, listening to the breeze.

Liyoot glanced with alarm.

Vendriff raised his sword high in the air. 'DARK LORD!'

Arif grabbed the reins just in time. The mithrin sped up, as if it heard a command that his own ears could not. Arif leaned into the roaring wind, wishing Liyoot was riding with him, at least he would feel reassured someone was controlling the animal. Every three seconds, the Jade spell cleansed his goggles from spatter. Hooves gathered pace beside him. He didn't want to risk turning his head to see who was riding beside him, the speed was intense now.

Over muffled battle cries, he saw the Hellsborn close the gap with spears. Blue arrows struck them hard and fast. Zethrin slowed over the burning carcases.

The blow of a horn sounded familiar. Where had he heard it? Yes. From the cave. The Army of Dead had split, or had it? Yellow torches burned on three sides. It occurred to him as he came to a stop beside Vendriff, that they might have galloped into a trap.

And then he saw the juggernaut of darkness emerging at speed from between the swell. So many dark riders, with vicious beasts, led by their lord and master, whose sword was aimed at the general.

Christ.

'Protect the general!' screamed a commander.

Arif urged Zenith forward. He would strike the hand that held the sword. Suddenly, a beast and a Hellsborn leaped over him, causing Zenith to shriek. She turned, jumping, with her front four legs raised to defend herself. She shuddered, despite his calming words. Before he could turn his head, Draje had disappeared.

He had failed to prevent an exit of the Vendaffy Pass.

The near miss had shaken the cavalry. Mithrin twisted their rear halves to one side, to force an abrupt stop. Some raised their front four legs out of fear, allowing vampires to overwhelm the riders.

Extended jaws and tainted swords struck Vendriff's best djinn.

The Lemothinians were turning faster than they could defend themselves. Soldiers were now fighting their own.

The smaller beast bit djinn and gentle creatures.

'KIFF RE FAR!'

Arrows struck the beast's neck and hide, but clearly missed the Hellstone. A mithrin galloped towards it, the commander leaped with both hands ready to drive his sword into the back of Ghraum's neck.

Fangs snatched him mid-flight and tossed him. The commander crashed into a mithrin, toppling a soldier. To his horror, the commander bit the soldier. Darkness flooded the soldier's blue eyes. Jades tried desperately to reach them, but the beast bit their mithrin, dragging one to ground by its neck. The Jades were saved by Liyoot and Leto, who quickly became surrounded.

Ghraum was constructing a new army.

When the beast cut Liyoot from escaping, Vendriff galloped quickly through the infected and drove his sword into Ghraum. Ghraum twisted, throwing Vendriff off his mithrin. To Arif's relief, the gentle creature bolted.

Ghraum transformed back into a giant vampire. A hellsborn mithrin with bone-crunching fangs appeared suddenly. Ghraum grabbed Vendriff and hauled him onto the hellsborn mithrin. From the saddle, he held Vendriff by his throat for all to see. Ghraum was in no hurry to infect Vendriff. It was working, soldiers were retreating.

'Have no fear!' shouted Leto. 'Do not feed this Hellsborn!'

Of course! Ghraum fed off fear.

Arif jumped off Zenith and ran. He threw the sword. To his dismay, the sword was deflected. Arif ran to grab it and used his momentum to leap and strike Ghraum's chest. He felt the snapping of bones and the squelch of a heart, before dropping onto his feet. He turned to see Vendriff had fallen. Ghraum yanked out his sword, the spilling of hellsblood had no effect.

The hellsborn mithrin tried to bite him. The jaws grew wide, showing a monstrosity of fangs.

Hooves thudded. Suddenly, two white legs slammed into its neck. The second hit threw the Hellsborn's front in the air, the rear four legs re-adjusted to balance itself. Ghraum tried to steer it round, but Zenith's hooves were faster. The third hit caused something to crack and the Hellsborn pet shuddered and hissed. When it toppled, it crumbled to dust.

Ghraum landed on his feet. The look of vehemence passed over his face quickly. Dragging his large black sword, he lifted his other palm.

Zenith was thrown by an unseen force.

He watched her get up, hoping she wouldn't return. All around him, the two armies fought Hellsborn, severing with all the speed they had trained for.

Ghraum waved vampires away. 'This one is mine.'

Arif stretched his hand to summon the sword to return.

Ghraum caught an arrow and tossed it. 'It is your fault, your brother is Hellsborn.'

'What?'

'Whose secret you spilled on the Feast of Eid, Aiden becomes Eshkinivsten, son of the vinx,' sneered Ghraum.

He's reading your mind.

'Get lost,' he said.

'You have lost your kin because you betrayed and abandoned him. You shall serve me well,' sneered Ghraum. When he raised his long grey palm, Arif felt a wave of tiredness wash over him.

Arif backed into a zombie and swerved to face both.

On seeing Ghraum, the zombie fled.

'Gosh. You're not very popular, are you?' said Arif.

'Bow Clayborn.'

'Humans don't bow to djinn. Didn't God send you a memo?' said Arif.

'I am your master,' hissed Ghraum.

Arif straightened. 'I am my own master,' he said.

'Yet you wish for Father to save you,' sneered Ghraum.

'No.' He twisted the cap.

'Such a deadly poison in your hands. Hurl it if you can.'

Ghraum had become two. No four. Five. Six.

Shit.

Sound of battle faded.

What in hell?

'None can save you, Are-eef. None but me,' whispered all Ghraums.

The soldiers and the Hellsborn were not moving. It was like time itself had become stuck.

Arif wasn't sure which Ghraum was Ghraum.

'I see her round plump body. Does blood taste sweeter in Mother?' said all Ghraums.

'Gosh, did that line ever work?' said Arif.

'You have one you can save. Who will it be?' asked Ghraum2.

'That's very kind of you. Are you sure you're meant to be merciful, aren't you from Hell?' Arif watched each of the Ghraum's for clues.

'I will not spare,' said Ghraum5.

'You think of one, and love another,' said Ghraum6.

'Your kin are vessels for harvest,' said Ghraum4.

'So essentially, you are backtracking on your offer?' he said. He tilted the vessel, water splashed onto his sword.

'Save one by a curse as old as Iblis,' said all Ghraums.

'This is hardly a fair fight,' said Arif.

'Your father will feast on your mother. Your mother will eat her brother. So, ending the line of Zeinab Sehroz, mother to Colonel Shukker. Unless you beg from me,' said Ghraum3. 'Perhaps I spare she to spare he.'

Arif steadied his voice. 'I'm gonna kill you, let's get that straight.'

The crystal emanated darkness, draining the air from his lungs. It occurred to him then, from which crystal he had felt the weakness first.

Holding the vessel tightly, Arif thrust his arm, water flew.

The illusion faded to one Ghraum, whose face was melting from one side. Dark eyes turned white. The lord staggered back, while trying to hold his face together.

Arif closed and unclosed the cap and threw water.

The black crystal shattered.

The sound of battle returned.

Ghraum howled with rage. Then attacked him.

Arif didn't even think about reacting, the sword just struck Ghraum in the same place Vendriff had. Arif felt a shudder from the deadheart. The wet sword kept thrusting.

Scarpering to a rock, Ghraum hissed, then his body shook and skin shredded.

For a second, he felt relief.

Ghraum flew, claws outstretched.

Arif ducked. A claw yanked his leg. He was dragged a few meters. Arif reached for the water vessel and twisted the cap into place. Cold claw gripped his neck, he jolted the vessel. Water landed on the hellsborn's fangs.

Ghraum choked. As the deafening shriek left the hellsborn's throat, every djinn jolted. The ground shook. Arif found himself surrounded by djinns wanting to watch the dark lord crumble.

Hooves trotted softly towards him.

'Zenith, you saved my life!' he said, his voice shaking. Tearfully, he hugged the mithrin's neck.

'Well done, Lord,' whispered Liyoot.

Zethrin neighed.

Arif suddenly remembered, 'I-I need Aylarhiyssa. Quickly!'

'Alas, my pouch is empty,' said Liyoot.

'Have mine,' said Leto.

Arif thanked him and set out to find him. The General was behind the rock. His eyes had lost colour, his skin was greying.

'Stay away!' he rasped.

Liyoot walked to the other side.

Vendriff snarled, wildly.

'General Vendriff... it's only me,' said Arif. 'The child you hate, right?'

Liyoot grabbed his arms, the general struggled, but Liyoot's grip was solid from experience. He bent Vendriff down. Leto parted his jaws and wedged a rock, 'Now,' he urged.

Arif knew from Matthew's account that he needed to protect himself from spitting and scratching. He checked his mask and goggles. Then he unscrewed the pouch and poured aylarhiyssa into Vendriff's mouth.

A long moan arose from his throat.

'More,' urged Liyoot.

Arif poured slowly until the pouch was empty, Vendriff tried to cough it out, but spasms made him gulp down what was in his mouth. With every gulp, his skin changed. Colour returned to his eyes. The Jades let him go slowly. Arif lay Ghraum's black sword at Vendriff's feet. The sight of it caused him to gasp for deep breaths. Vendriff crumpled to the floor.

Ayoshua knelt with Krill.

Arif took a deep breath. 'Liyoot, Ghraum said-er-is Aiden, my brother okay?'

'Lord Aiden and Nethrin are on mission. Everything is as it should be,' said Liyoot, after his eyes dimmed.

They were interrupted by Lemothinians who wanted to make sure that Vendriff was recovering. Arif looked on with tiredness, gladly taking the Krill when Leto offered. The commanders reeled out their reports of casualties, and soldiers unaccounted for, as well as any intelligence they had gathered by those who had been cleansed of infection. Vendriff barked his commands to try and disguise his own trauma. Liyoot announced he was going to return to Osimion. Then grabbed the hand of the last commander, to gasp, 'Ibb, take the Child of the Chosen. You must reach Lemoff.'

34

Aiden:

'Darling Fiori. Open your eyes,' whispered the voice. George.

Aiden stirred from his sleep, barely opening his eyes. He sensed George had gone but he was safe. The blanket moist from his fever did not enter his thoughts. A Jade was telling a wrinkled healer with long purple hair that they needed to put all patients into carriages. A silky voice wasn't inside the healing tent, it was out there. Far from this hill. Past the bubbling brook and a battle raging with blue fire. Beyond the mountain with the dipped nose, lay an insidious encampment. A chill spread from his neck, jolting his eyes wide. He knew that voice. The creature is likely to sense him and know he could hear her. All his training had led him to this moment. Aiden stopped his heartbeat. And drifted on the breeze inside the tent held by bones of creatures long extinct. He was numb to the fear stifling an Emerald Sister's lungs. The fear was justified.

For a moment, his body lay lifeless on the straw and blankets.

Then his head turned. 'Fire in clay and clay in fire,' he whispered, 'See her.'

The whisper would carry through the valleys, coded to one set of ears. It will be received, but will he be heard in the midst of battle?

Alarmed cries drifted by his tent. He sensed a healer freeze.

'Breach,' yelled a soldier.

The Jade told her companion to grab the pile of blankets. She lifted an old djinn over her shoulder and left the tent. Darian soldiers entered to take the injured.

Strong hands lifted him off the straw.

'Sleep, Little One. Deadhearts will not find you, not while Nethrinus breathes.'

35

Aroosa:

Aroosa had a feeling she was being watched. Floating to the ground, the wind blew her dress. Her feet touched land softly.

'Do you feel that?' asked Aifa, glancing.

'I do,' she said, sadly.

Flowing through crevices underneath them, hope hadn't arrived fast enough. The Shaara will help the wounded, but not the dead.

Daash spoke gently to a wounded archer who sat trembling. There were too many wounded, with severed limbs. She hurried to attend to the infected. Aifa had organised the Azurans to triage, Jades delivered treatment. Broken limbs temporarily fixed with spells. The infected were fed aylarhiyssa. Those that died had a prayer read upon them before their heads were separated from their necks. Bile rushed to her throat, but she swallowed it out of respect. Immortal sons and daughters had been lost forever.

Aside from the glowing eyes, her tingling neck made her feel something dangerous was nearby. But the hills were silent. Nothing moved from the landslip.

The breeze lifted her hair.

Fire in clay and clay in fire…

Aroosa looked up sharply. The whisper sounded like it was hers the second time. Sweeping sensations gripped her body.

See her…

Her body turned. Suddenly, her mind had joined with another. Far North, overlooking the side of a mountain, an encampment of tents was surrounded by dormant giants on their feet. She was floating softly to the ground in someone else's body, with an urgency to confront a siren knowing well it may take her life to save many brethren. Aroosa wasn't sure if Ophelia was aware that she was there, only that she had entered the deadheart territory too deep, past the point of no return.

Ophelia closed her eyes, 'Arbana!' she whispered to slow her heartbeat as she touched the ground. Her appearance was turned translucent to camouflage her presence. She waited a moment behind the large boulders for any movement from the biggest tent. If the demon knew she was here, she would be too cunning to let her know. The tent was large enough for a dozen mithrin to be fed. Where were the Charrelles known for tearing into each other for a siren's favour? Why was it so quiet?

'It takes great courage to be an Emerald Sister,' Mai said. 'What purpose do you envisage for yourself, Ophelia?'

'The Emerald Path is my destiny, Mai,' she had replied, gently. 'In the name of Ayla, I take oath to be a daughter of Deelya, to bring back the moons and the three suns. I will preserve all beating hearts.'

Mai sighed. 'Your heart is set. Do you not understand that you will outlive the Daraan... all your friends, your associates... do you want this life knowing the possibility that an extended life may be spent in solitude?'

Why was she having flashbacks?

Swallowing the dryness in her throat, she crept into the wall of the tent. The folds would take her closer to the table. At the far side, a tall figure in black was scouring over a large map. The ground within the tent was covered by black and red leathers, carefully bound, and patched together to soften the ground for her bare feet. A soft bed had been laid with cushions. Since when did Hellsborn have comforts? The Damned were devoid of any civilised behaviour. She was no ordinary siren, this was made for her, a rank that explained what she had sensed.

She stilled her breathing.

The vinx's long hair indicated she had once lived an influential position. How strange it was, that she was now alone. Neither Siren, nor Grim on guard. None waited for orders at her side. The opportunity was too convenient for Ophelia's liking.

'You came to kill me,' croaked the Siren Queen.

Ophelia stilled her panicked heartbeat. She crouched down to the ground, between layers of the tent.

'Be careful Vinx!'

Greva!

Confirmation. Not that she needed it. Should she look?

'You feasted on Lord Bussa and Grishan,' croaked the Vinx. 'A moment of desperation has strengthened you like nothing before... now you believe with your wound you can repeat your recovery.'

Ophelia edged silently to peer through the gap.

The skinny vampire was missing an arm. He was glaring and grinding his jaw.

The vinx didn't even turn to face him.

'Draje should never have allowed your abomination,' hissed Greva, edging closer.

'Though I admire your audacity, Greva,' croaked the vinx, 'It would be wise to take heed of your instincts.'

'You are weak. You have not fed,' growled Greva.

The Siren Queen spun to him. She grew until she towered high above him. Her voice deepened with anger. 'Shall I feed on you?'

Greva recoiled. Her dark crystal grew, sucking power from his own.

He dropped to his knees. 'Restore me!' he said. Then he lowered his head all the way to the ground and pleaded, 'Restore me!'

Ophelia was in awe.

Aroosa was baffled. Why would a vampire lord bow to a siren?

The vinx calmed, returning to her size, 'I shall restore you. I see a purpose that will serve the Dark King well...' she paused, to watch him '... on his arrival.'

Greva stood up sharply. 'Abaddon is... coming?'

'Dark King will have use for the power of three.' She spat on his stump where Greva's arm used to be, then her eyes widened and darkened. Her whisper echoed, 'Niffa lyanta kinda kand ehud. Ffiyaffa! Feena kinda lyanta maaghl ka.'

'The clayborns,' he growled, 'fight with deadly weapons.'

Vinx rolled the dark crystal in her fingers. 'The outcome of this war...' she croaked finally, '... has no bearing on the King's arrival.'

Vinx turned back to her table as Greva turned and left the tent.

Aroosa wanted Ophelia to leave.

'You needn't hide yourself,' said a gentle voice, 'I know you're there -'

Ophelia froze.

'Off-eel-iya... my forlorn...'

Her heart skipped a beat. It was different. She knew that voice.

Her lips were charcoal. She was taller and stronger looking than her previous life. Her pupils had lost their emerald glow and mutated to a lifeless grey. The black crystal hanging from her neck, had once been an emerald, inherited from their father, a remnant of a world lost with the stars. The warrior's armlet, which had once stretched to her elbow with Deelya's colour, was contaminated too. Despite this, she still looked elegant.

'How is Feios?' she asked.

Was that sorrow in her eyes?

The question resonated like the day she had walked towards her old mother and placed her hands in her palms, speaking softly with the love from her heart, 'Why are you lonely, Mai? Are you not happy with the city's love?' she had said, tenderly.

Mai turned away. 'What is happiness if it lacks those I love?'

'You have me,' she said, softly.

'I fought the Dark King. I fought battles and considered myself victorious... but how foolish I was to not notice that I had lost my war.'

'You have the Daraan. Everyone loves you.'

'To be loved again and again, and to lose again and again. No achievement fills the void.' Mai wiped her eyes, then forced a smile, 'I do not wish your life to be as mine.'

'Get out of my head,' said Ophelia.

'I miss her too,' said her sister. 'Mai had the wisdom we all wanted, but her loneliness concerned us.'

'Did it? Is that why you stayed away?' she asked.

'Feios is your fourth husband, I don't think you have ever loved anyone as much. Does it not strike you that you are foolishly following the same path as Mai?'

Ophelia's task suddenly looked arduous and more difficult. The Siren Queen was Fenn. She thought like Fenn and spoke like Fenn.

Fenn smiled sadly. 'Look at you -' She advanced with her arms outstretched, but Ophelia withdrew just as quick.

Fenn halted. 'I was only going to hug you.'

'You're a vampire,' said Ophelia.

'Hmm. Who is more dangerous here? You came to kill me...' she said coolly, turning. She walked to the bed and sat down.

Was there a chance of saving Fenn?

Your sister is dead, Aroosa whispered.

'You were right, I stayed away. You needed each other. I missed my dai,' said Fenn.

'We needed you too,' said Ophelia, edging closer.

'You were always better than I. The knowledge you had of the seventy-seven tongues, the skill you had in taming the flame, the patience you had with mother. I was a thorn. Though I loved you,' said Fenn.

'Yes, you did,' said Ophelia, her eyes filling with tears.

'You took care of Mai. I was grateful. How I missed you,' said Fenn.

Ophelia stepped into the tent. 'Fenn, I can help you.'

'Did the green witches not send you to do their dirty work? Kill your own sister? The one who loved you more than the missing suns?' asked Fenn.

'Let me give you aylarhiyssa,' said Ophelia. 'If there is any way I can save you, it's through White Fire.'

'You've brought aylarhiyssa?' asked Fenn, softly.

'Yes.'

'Your efforts are foolish. You know that to be true, Sister-Emerald of the Jades' said Fenn, with an uncanny smile, the resemblance to her sister gradually fading.

'Fenn -'

'My name is Selwa!' she snapped, leaping to her feet. Darkness filled her eye sockets. 'Fenn was betrayed by the Sisters of the Flame. She died...' she paused to watch her words cut deep into Ophelia, 'as her world around her crumbled. No one came to her aid. Do you remember, Ophelia?'

Aroosa felt Ophelia's blood turn cold. Overwhelming sadness filled her. Memories flashed before her, of feeling helpless as others decided for her. A decision she had regretted many times over the years. A question she had asked herself time and time again, if she had gone to her aid, would Fenn have survived?

'We received the news too late,' Ophelia said eventually finding her voice.

'Is that what you tell yourself... you an Emerald?'

'It is the truth,' she choked. Tears streamed down her cheeks, 'when we heard... Draje had already taken the High Counsel of Rosh... we could only save the refugees... it was decided against...'

'Aaaa-aah!' Selwa's eyes widened. She rolled her hand in the air, '...it was decided! Naa-w we come to the truth... someone told you it was not worthwhile saving your own sister.' Vinx floated, her mouth came to Ophelia's ear. 'Your own... flesh... and bl-lood.'

Aroosa's heart thumped for the both of them.

'We were not prepared for Draje,' said Ophelia.

'The Jades frightened?' Selwa the Vinx cackled with laughter. The whiteness of her eyes darkened. 'Not likely! Ophelia the fool.' She returned to the bed. 'It was a calculated decision by the Mage, listening to ladies too old for magic.' She softened her voice with relish, 'Did you know that your sister survived for nine days, hidden among the passageways of the White Building of Rosh?' Selwa watched for her response.

Ophelia's whole body tingled with shock.

'Oh, you didn't know?' gasped Selwa delightfully.

'No.'

'I distinctly remember waiting... and praying... for salvation from my most loved and respected. Salvation at least for my son... all alone... gnawing my finger to stop himself crying. I could not comfort him... when Drafus ate him.'

Ophelia inhaled sharply, sobbing.

Vinx stood up in rage, 'You never came! I cursed the air she breathed!'

The rage passed. Then she smiled, her black lips exposing white jagged teeth. 'Did you promise our Dai, on his final breaths that you would keep your sister close and protect her with your life? Did you?'

'I'm sorry Fenn,' whispered Ophelia. 'I-you had a son?'

The darkness faded to Fenn. 'Ofias.'

385

'Ofias,' repeated Ophelia.

'Yes. I named him after the third moon painted in our sanctum. Do you remember, you once told me you loved it because the scrolls said it offered the light of every sun, despite the seasons, despite the weather and despite it being the smallest.'

'Yes.'

'Ofias went quiet before the beast broke the doors. Do you think he knew what was to happen? They say the best of us are aware at birth,' said Fenn, mournfully.

Ophelia saw the baby. Her sob turned into a wail.

Fingers snapped.

Aroosa jolted.

Aifa was staring into her face with power-filled eyes. 'You stopped breathing. Where were you?'

The fighting was at a lull. Azurans watched with curiosity.

Aroosa dropped to her knees. 'We have to help her,' she gasped.

'Etienne, bring me the aylarhiyssa,' shouted Aifa.

Aroosa drank God's Fire Tears and took the flower pellet on her tongue that was offered to her.

'What did you see?' asked Aifa.

'Ophelia has walked into a trap. The Vinx is Fenn,' said Aroosa.

Aifa froze. 'You saw Fenn?'

'We have a Vinx?' gasped Izmilla.

'Tell me again, how you saw Fenn?' asked Aifa.

'I don't know how,' recalled Aroosa. 'I heard a voice. Then I was looking through Ophelia's eyes. I don't think she can kill her sister.'

'We should summon the Emeralds,' said Izmilla.

'For what end?' asked Aifa.

'A vinx is a god killing demon,' said Izmilla, quite petrified. 'The scrolls literally state that she targeted those who captured the Fallen. She ate them to take their power. Then she ate their babies. If Fenn is a vinx, then this is truly bad, a vinx cannot exist without another host.'

'Precisely. We will not play into her hands by delivering our powerful. Did you get a sense of how far she was?' asked Aifa.

'Past our armies, old ruins, mountains. I think seventy miles,' guessed Aroosa.

Aifa's head turned as if she was absorbing her words. 'We won't get there in time. It is just Izmilla and me, Jade Queen. We will bond.'

Aroosa let their hands join, palm to palm. Then closed her eyes.

She was back again in the cold tent. Ophelia was on her knees, feeling quite drained. The gentle stroke from the Vinx was soothing to her. 'I need you,' whispered the Vinx.

'Fenn?'

'That's right.'

'You said your name is Selwa,' whispered Ophelia.

'We are one.'

'We are one,' repeated Ophelia.

'You expect me to kill you… You came to me, Aarta.'

'Yes. I did.'

'Finally, my dearest is by my side. I need you,' whispered Fenn.

'I need you.'

'Two sisters avenging Ofias.'

'Ofias,' whispered Ophelia.

'No longer alone. Reshaping all worlds in our image. A vinx you will be.'

'Ophelia,' whispered Aroosa. 'Selwa is not your sister.'

'Fenn was selfless,' whispered Aifa. 'Benevolent, Fenn would never want her sister in harm's way.'

Aroosa repeated the words.

Ophelia pulled away from Selwa and stood up, 'If you are my sister - Fenn, then you would never have spoken of revenge. Fenn was not like that - she earned her place in the Emerald Elite with dedication and kindness.'

The Queen of Sirens looked startled. 'Who is with you?'

'Your crystal has grown. You were biding time, weren't you?' said Ophelia.

'Would you turn your back on Fenn for a green witch?' she growled.

'Fenn would want to drink the aylarhiyssa,' said Ophelia.

'JOIN ME,' Selwa's voice echoed, deranged and distorted.

Ophelia noticed that her eyes were darkening, suddenly that her mission had fallen into jeopardy.

'You are not alone,' whispered Aroosa.

'Draw strength from us,' whispered Aifa.

Ophelia lifted herself into the air with emerald fire in her fingertips. 'Am liffay-l aagl ush yee!' she cried, holding her right palm towards the Vinx. A green beam hit Selwa throwing her backwards. She fired again.

The Siren Queen fell on her back again. Then suddenly she leaped into the air, hovering with evil vehemence, bringing long talons, sharp and deadly; ready to tear her to pieces. Her teeth could crush her skull.

The black crystal sucked power from her beating heart. Ophelia let gravity free her from the dark beam. The impact shook all her insides. She grimaced as pain spread down her spine. Her sigil had protected her. She was weaker now, but she had no choice but to fight.

'She has uttered a submission spell,' said Aifa.

Aroosa whispered back to Ophelia, that Selwa had uttered a submission spell. Aifa and Ophelia both whispered the same protective spell around her.

'Maak aal ka!' screamed the Vinx, firing dark beams from her hands.

Ophelia dodged it, but the second one hit her shoulder. Immediately spreading numbness down her arm.

The vinx moved so fast, grabbing her neck and lifting her high.

Ophelia struggled to breathe.

'I said I need you, Green Witch. It is not a want. It is a need. I would sooner drain you dry, turning you into a brainless spawn,' growled Selwa.

'A need,' she choked. 'You mean for Fenn?'

The Siren Queen stretched to an enormous length. And shrieked.

Charrelles echoed her call.

Ophelia felt the chill on her skin. 'Fenn please,' she sobbed.

The fangs stopped at her neck. 'You will return to me and submit.'

'Ilana!' cried Ophelia with the intention to altercate her position. She disappeared and reappeared floating behind the Queen.

'Effi ta far renn!' she cried, bringing both her palms together. A dark green beam hit Selwa squarely on the chest throwing to the next mountain. Ophelia flew towards her and saw the Vinx lift herself to her feet, staggering briefly before steadying herself. The Emerald Sister spun faster than the eye could see, firing green bolts. The Vinx was ablaze in green fire, her skin welted with the intensity. But then the fire turned black. And her skin was restored. Ophelia continued firing, but the Queen of Sirens leapt from the mountain.

Ophelia pursued her through the Grim encampment, the vampires threw their bodies to shield their queen. The Vinx soared, rotating. Ophelia didn't see the dark beam, but it missed her neck. The Emerald Sister flew around the encampment trying to shake off Selwa, but she was too fast. Dark fire threw her body into a tent.

Charrelles crawled towards her, growling.

Ophelia hurled herself upwards, a claw missed her. Dark fire hit her thigh. Numbness spread down her leg.

'Leave, Ophelia!' whispered Aroosa.

She sensed danger behind her.

She turned.

The monstrous-winged Vinx hurtled so fast... no time to move...

The Emerald Sister threw a fireball too late. Claws ripped into her shoulders and a lung. The yank gave unbreathable pain. Ophelia cried out. The chill told her they were reaching great heights. Selwa carried her into the thinning of the atmosphere. Droplets of blood trailing beneath her. The Siren Queen dug deeper into her body.

Selwa was giving her a message.

Ophelia was dizzy. She closed her eyes.

'I've lost her,' gasped Aroosa.

'We must hurry,' said Aifa.

36

Matthew:

Matthew ignored them. And pressed on his sword, until blood from the headless corpse oozed over the tip. The more it spilled, the more the ground hissed its contempt.

Why was it tarry black? Is this congealed blood, or is this all part of one parasite? It was paint thick. And it stank summat rotten. Can't be blood, surely. What would it look like under a microscope? No. He would not risk taking a sample home. Not a chance.

'It is dead now, My Lord. You can toss it,' repeated Deffi, much to the delight of his friends.

Fine.

He used his boot to nudge it down the steep hill. The stench was at the back of his throat. He took off his mask so he could vomit.

'Put your mask back on or return to the tent!' shouted an Ithfirian commander.

Matthew spat on dirt. And put back on his mask. He had to be doing something to not have to worry about Rose.

'Matthew, I can't explain it, I have this strong feeling I have to help,' she'd said.

'Are you for real? I-we-just got you back,' he'd said.

She'd kissed him then. Not a peck. A proper kiss with all her body leaning into him, it was the first time she'd kissed him in front of her brother. And it was her best. He was taken completely off guard, that he didn't even think to question what she'd said until she'd left.

A woman had grabbed her hand and helped her kill her first parasite. Now she was connected, and she felt she could trust her. A million questions should have popped into his head, to say to her in that moment. 'She's beaten parasites twice,' Arif had said.

Matthew forgot he was there. 'So, what are you saying? We just… let her go because she's hearing voices?' he'd asked, hotly.

'Just saying, Aroosa's… different now.' The way that Arif was watching him was another surprise.

Arif now knew. And he wasn't a total dickhead. This… was… a new world.

Would you believe it? Rose, making other people's problems her own?

A zombie reached his side of the hill.

Deffi glanced.

Focus.

How on Hell could they defend Valley of the Two Tongues with so few soldiers? He couldn't see any soldiers other than Deffi's battalion. Maybe that was the point. Not be seen. But if vampires were creatures from hell, surely… they could see them in the dark better than they wanted to believe?

Matthew drove his sword into the eye socket, he hated the squelchy sound of it being snagged on brain and snagging on skull. His boot nudged it down the embankment.

'Are you okay?' asked Deffi.

'Yeah. They're coming in small numbers.'

Deffi's friend told him how to thrust into the neckbone and twist until the head fell off. At first, Matthew ignored him and stabbed the zombies, but they kept getting back up.

The new way didn't squelch so bad, and the quick end was satisfying.

Deffi shouted for everyone to keep their masks on.

Rocks were thrown in their direction. At first, they could only run to dodge them. When giant boulders smashed through the spikes, Soahn took a spear and hurled it. They heard the moan of a giant tumbling into the gorge. When the next wave was sighted, Soahn ordered everyone to evacuate to the Jade stronghold. The Jades were going to set a trap.

Matthew ran to the tents, but they were empty. On the way up the hill, Torros struck any zombies that got close to him. What an amazing dude! 'You're super-fast,' he laughed.

'I am Daraan,' boasted Torros.

Dark spatter covered the goggles Soahn had given him. Matthew tried wiping it off, but only managed to smear it with his hand. The zombie blood chilled his skin. 'I can't see,' he yelled.

Torros hurried back and wiped his goggles with cloth. 'The goggles are old. You should ask a Jade for new ones, with the Vision Spell,' said Torros. 'You will never have to clean your goggles again.'

Explosions lit the night. Green flames spread fast through the valley. He saw the vampire rider at the same time Deffi saw the zombies climbing behind the rockpiles.

'We have to stop them if we are to escape,' said Deffi.

Torros, Deffi and Diyafa were showing him how to kill without getting too close, and with as little contact as possible. He moved his whole body to get as good as them. Swift strikes, felling each zombie with merciful severance. Matthew didn't care who asked them to watch over him, the fact that they were here protecting his blindside meant they were decent.

On his instruction, Diyafa's arrow hit the vampire's dangling hellstone, the rider fell off his hellsborn beast.

Matthew ran to the top of the hill, Deffi hauled him onto the mithrin.

37

Aiden:

Herionus…

Herionus. You know its name.

I know his name.

What did it call you?

I am Aiden.

Does it call you Aiden?

No.

Show us.

Herionus… asleep.

Call to it. Where does it sleep?

On the hill.

Which hill?

Sullen.

Take us to its light.

Who are you?

Whiz.

Aiden opened one eye after the third whiz of an arrow. The rider was standing on his stirrups, firing while Feena picked up speed. Nethrin was defending him. Nethrin the Jade… Such a nice fellow.

The icily presence jolted Aiden awake. Deadly eyes in the sky, ascending and descending. Aiden couldn't move his head to see. But his neck tingled. Not from the vampire riders. From above. He closed his eyes and focused. Two of them were struck by Nethrin's arrows. He guessed another had been killed earlier, for now there were three. And they were faltering in flight to glare at the largest. The large one turned. The others turned. Why were they retreating? Had they probed his mind? While he slept?

'Nethrin-Nethrin! Stop. We need to kill all the sirens. Quickly,' he gasped.

'Eloha Feena,' said Nethrin.

Feena picked up pace.

'Eloha,' said Nethrin, pulling harder on the reins.

Words spoken would safely allow him to conduct this manoeuvre, but no spell nor powers could be used by him.

Only training will save you.

Aiden lifted his bow from the saddle and undid the hooks pinning his body to the saddle seat, and twisted his arm, until the strap was wrapped around his elbow. He slid onto the stirrups. Feena began to turn, pushing his weight against her hide.

Aiden fired quickly. An ice arrow missed the leader. A charrelle disintegrated before she hit the ground.

The second was enraged.

Feena faltered on a dry riverbed.

Nethrin drew his sword and leapt off the mithrin.

On solid ground, Aiden plucked the bow as the teachers had taught him.

The charrelle dodged his ice arrow and swiped two more. His fourth grazed her side, causing her to falter.

The fifth struck her neck. The sixth shattered her chest. The seventh ensured her body crumbled.

The large one was enraged. She dropped to the ground. Dark beasts surrounded them. Vampires leapt off.

Swords clashed. Nethrin fought three of them.

Aiden primed his bow. A dead hand knocked it aside.

Nethrin stabbed it, but the vampire was impervious to blood oozing from its neck.

Aiden was unhooking his pouch of aylarhiyssa when a flash of green blinded him. The blast tossed a dark beast onto one of the vampires. The second vampire ran.

Nethrin's sword beheaded it with one strike.

A dead hand grabbed hold of Aiden's shirt, dragging him to a dark beast. Aiden dropped his weight. The vampire was strong enough to haul him in the air. Aiden tossed the aylarhiyssa into its face.

Jaws stretched when it roared. Darkness in its eyes melted away. He coughed.

A sword came out of his neck. Nethrin twisted it until the head fell off.

'Why would you do that? He swallowed aylarhiyssa, he could have been saved,' yelled Aiden.

'No, my Lord. Your pouch was small. He is a deadheart longer than he was a djinn. At the most, we would have had three unpredictable minutes. The siren has fled,' said Nethrin.

'No. She's here. Watching us,' said Aiden.

'Hellsborn seize a vessel. Hellsborn feed on soul,' it whispered.

Rocks tumbled from the hillside.

George appeared beside Nethrin.

She landed heavily. Twice as big as the others.

Aiden primed his bow.

'Come closer. I'll show you how Jades behead your kind,' said Nethrin.

'Spoken like a fool. Be warned, Elahi. She is faster than an arrow, she can knock your weapons and crush both your spines before you blink,' said George.

'Eshkinivsten,' it whispered.

Aiden stepped back.

'One should wonder why she landed over there. And not here,' said George.

'Eshkinivsten,' it whispered.

'No,' exhaled Aiden.

'Eshkinivsten, come with us,' it whispered.

'Eshkinivsten is dead,' yelled Aiden.

'I smell our kind,' it howled.

'My Lord. Do not listen to it,' said Nethrin. 'She is trying to trick you. Dark blood-'

'-stains a vessel,' it whispered, matching Nethrin's voice. 'Stains deliver a soul. Why do vessels think they are pure?'

'Go away!' yelled Aiden.

'I smell you, darling Eshkinivsten. She aimed. She stained.'

Aiden released an ice arrow. But she was too fast, lifting Nethrin's neck in her long talons. 'Come Eshkinivsten. Feed!'

A chill passed through his body. His heart stopped. His hands swung sharply. Two arrows left the bow. Time slowed, but the arrow did not. It struck the siren with precision, shattering the shell protecting its parasitic heart. The siren's head swung to bite Nethrin. The second arrow shattered her jaw, crumbling the crucial feeding glands it needed to heal itself.

It shrieked.

The third arrow shattered the hellstone. She crumbled.

Nethrin fell to the ground.

George stepped out of Aiden's body.

Hot tremors rippled through him. Aiden dropped to his knees and vomited. 'Yuk! Yuk! What the hell did you do that for?'

'Darling Fioha, wish for life, not hell,' tutted George.

'A ghost possessed my body,' choked Aiden.

'I declared we are bound together for the entire duration of your life. One is permitted to ensure one's treaty,' said George.

'You can't invade my body without my permission,' scolded Aiden.

'I have done so before,' said George.

Aiden straightened. 'Y-you did?'

'A ghost does not need permission to save a life,' said George.

Aiden felt sick. 'You taste something rotten.'

'It will pass,' said George.

'Ugh. It's disgusting,' Aiden wretched again.

'A ghost has no physical matter. A ghost is merely a ghost, lighter than light.'

'A ghost is dead. Dead polluted my body!' spat Aiden.

'You are experiencing signals sent by your brain to flood enzymes in your body. I harmed you not. Unlike the hellspawn,' said George.

He remembered how she looked. Was she looking directly at him? Or at Eshkinivsten? Could she see him if it was a Hellsborn memory?

He vomited again. 'You can't invade my body!' wheezed Aiden.

'I assure you I can,' shrugged George.

'Your ghost? Is it here?' asked Nethrin, his forehead was filled with creases, as he looked around.

Aiden straightened. 'Nethrin. Dear God. Are you okay?'

'Unharmed, my lord. You saved my life,' said Nethrin, softly.

'George saved your life. Is she dead, like proper?' asked Aiden, craning his neck.

'It is dead,' said Nethrin.

'Dead as dust,' said George.

Nethrin walked closer and kneeled to inspect him. 'Is this the same ghost you mentioned in the White City?'

'Yes. You might ask, how can anyone be stupid enough to be haunted for the rest of their lives? And you would not be wrong. I am… Every-world-stupid. And I have not got a clue how to undo it,' groaned Aiden. 'Are you freaking out?'

Nethrin's eyelids widened, 'What is this word, freaking?'

'Are you scared and mortified?' asked Aiden.

'Not presently,' said Nethrin.

'Is she right?' asked Aiden, softly, 'About reverting?'

Nethrin frowned. 'Some sought the scourge after they were healed. Mistakes we made, which we learned from.' He unhooked a pouch and unscrewed the top, drinking Krill to replenish. He brought the pouch to Aiden's lips.

Aiden became aware George was watching him flood his throat with krill. He clicked his tongue from the burning bitterness, glad to be free of the foul taste.

Nethrin fastened the pouch to his belt. Aiden wanted to depart already, but all green glowing eyes expected a question from him. 'Am I – by any chance – still carrying a hellsborn?' asked Aiden.

'No.'

Aiden's face heated and his nostrils inflated. 'She said she smelled it.'

'Deceit from a siren, nothing more,' said Nethrin softly. 'My Lord, we caught it in time. We cleansed it from your body. Perhaps the hellsborn smells what has departed, or perhaps it feared your strike and spoke for distraction. We shall never know.'

George gave no clue of what he was thinking.

Aiden swallowed. 'Can you take me to Sullen Hill by Leybo's Cave?'

Nethrin froze. 'Sullen Hill is off our path,' he said, questioningly.

Aiden cleared his throat, 'It's important.'

'A dark lord was sighted near Ithfir. While that may not be confirmed by our own, riding that way is treacherous.'

'I know. Please, Nethrin.'

For a moment Nethrin stared. Then his chin jolted. 'Deadhearts followed us ten gildard. Could have struck us. Instead, they turned back. My Lord, what could hellsborn have learned?'

'Don't ask me, Nethrin. And I will not tell you lies,' said Aiden, fiercely.

Nethrin straightened. His chest rose. 'We must climb onto Feena. We ride swiftly, and we do not stop.'

Aiden accepted the lift back onto the large creature, this time, Nethrin placed him at the front. Feena seemed relieved they were setting off, for she galloped quickly.

38

Arif:

They were passing over land with no glowing vegetation. Arif couldn't see anything for the dust flying into his eyes, but tilts and jolts told him he was crossing hills. He wondered what the others were doing. Liyoot said Aiden was on mission, so why had Ghraum lied? Poor Aiden, this place made him grow up too fast. As soon as this was over, he would tell Aiden he was sorry. It wasn't right what he did. Dad only got mad because he humiliated 'the family'. Eddie's secret was Eddie's to tell. It wasn't fair, not that it really mattered. Aiden took the whole wide world in his quiet little mind, and just... read a book.

And he would tell Matthew, it was okay for him to announce his relationship with Sis. He would stand up to anyone who said otherwise. Then he could tell Teiaar he was cool. And it would be true.

She probably already knows he can't stop thinking about her. Do people get married on this world? Wow. Yep. Not going to fuck this up. Okay, djinns are naturally... that much taller than humans. But if she could make him grow, surely, she can shrink? Or just do that spell Ffelidio-whatever, he didn't mind having magic inside him. Tingling light-headedness, he could get used to that. And if they did go home... Aroosa... he could tell her he was staying. Matthew might stay if Sis is staying. Eddie would have to go home, obviously. Eliza? Eliza would be relieved he found someone.

'Be honest, we're not a good fit, are we?' Eliza said, when he told her he didn't want to break up. 'Eddie's right. We've known each other so long, I'm like a sister. I know you adore me. I'm just not girlfriend material for you. And you know it.'

That day had crushed him. Eddie the knobhead.

It was time he stopped blaming him.

That donkey rock, he'd seen it before. He was sure he had passed here before, was it the place before or after Nafarinus? He lifted the crystal higher, the light had little effect on the ground. Had plants been stifled by a Hellsborn?

Commander Ibb pulled on the reins. Dethrin trotted closer to Zethrin, Ibb's eyes glowed the same blue as the city's lights. 'There lies Lemoff.'

Flashes of light showed chaos ensuing within its walls. An explosion caused part of a tower to collapse. A dust cloud arose, smudging the blue lit buildings. A beam of light swirled through the gates.

Then Arif saw him. By the broken gates, Lord Draje sat on his Hellsborn mithrin.

'He hasn't gone in,' whispered Arif pointing towards him.

'No. Why? The gates are broken, so the Grim have penetrated, so why not Draje?' Ibb sounded confused.

'He's mine!' said Arif.

'But the General said -'

'The General does not know what we know,' he said, looking at Commander Ibb. 'This could be Lemoff's only chance at surviving.'

'He is powerful,' said Commander Ibb staring at the black figure.

'Yet mine!' replied Arif. 'I'll force him away. Give your people a chance.' He undid the water carrier's cap and drew his sword slowly, the water dribbled down the sword into the sheath. 'Gellana!' he said to Zethrin suddenly. The white mithrin jolted forward. Down the slope they descended. The light of the crystal causing a cascade of colour to flow down the valley.

'Approach from his right!' he heard Commander Ibb shout.

The two mithrin sped silently towards the blue City of Lemoff, at equal pace, but the distance between them grew.

39

Matthew:

New barricades were built swiftly. Long, thick metal spikes were driven into the ground by Darian soldiers. Nethrin's group of Jades chanted until the spikes multiplied to form teeth that no flesh could pass. Bags of dirt and rocks were placed meticulously to reinforce the long spikes. Barrels of thick green slimy substance were spilt on the enemy's side. Forty drums blocked the gap at the end, with three archers ordered to defend it.

Large Darian machinery were wheeled to face the west. Huge drums containing arrows laced with green powder were placed into the central vessel, ready to be emptied and fired at a moment's notice.

Matthew took position between the Ithfirians and the Daraan.

With his heartbeat pounding in his ears, he closed his eyes and breathed long and slow.

A Jade lifted his hand, a signal that the enemy were within range, three Jade arrows were fired at the spilled tar-like substance. It burst into flames spreading across the barricades.

Dark green flames caused a dense green smoke that first headed towards the Daraan, but when Teiaar closed her eyes and whispered, it reversed direction and covered the valley for quite some distance obscuring and hiding everything from the enemy's approach. They would not be able to see the hidden spikes, the Darian armies, the Jades, or the Darian cavalry waiting for them.

Matthew watched a scout rush from the top of the hill to his comrades. Seconds later a flare lit up the sky from the East. He felt a tap on his shoulder.

Matthew turned.

Liyoot beckoned.

Matthew followed him to the mithrin.

A bugle sounded.

Matthew climbed onto the gentle creature and lifted the shield from the saddle.

Ithrandir had a new helmet and face guard, as he weaved through the ranks towards the gap.

The Jades closed their eyes.

Silence fell.

The soldiers closed their eyes too. Matthew realised it was so the dark lord could not tap into their senses. The Jades were most likely probing the darkness with their skills.

A heavy rumble moved gradually towards them. Hooves grew louder from the other side.

The enemy was slowing.

Matthew and Liyoot waited behind the gap for the signal. The snarling grew closer. Ithrandir raised his arm slowly.

Something growled.

Matthew's heartbeat quickened. He flexed his fingers around the sword and closed them tighter.

Hooves moved towards them very fast.

Suddenly, there was a thud and a neigh and then a cry. Another thud and a neigh. It happened again, and again. Snarls erupted. Shrieks from beasts.

Matthew smiled, as the spikes impaled the hellsborn. He counted twenty-six, before a silence ensued.

Ithrandir was listening, Matthew couldn't tell if his eyes were closed, for the helmet he was wearing.

Liyoot held his sword higher. Matthew watched as the other cavalrymen did the same, even though their eyes were still closed. He followed suit.

'Head South,' snarled one of the shadows in the green fog.

There was a shuffle of hooves and a rumble. More shrieks from dark beasts.

The enemy had found more spikes in that direction.

Shrieks came from further along the hill's edge. More spikes met their snarls. Matthew counted at least thirty different howls.

Suddenly it went quiet. Matthew heard his heartbeat once more.

A lone set of hooves began moving upwards along the perimeter towards them.

Something was searching for a way in.

A hail of green arrows flew suddenly.

Matthew watched them fall into the fog.

The Jades around him had their eyes closed and were whispering under their breath.

Matthew nudged Liyoot. 'What're they doing?' he whispered.

Liyoot signalled quiet with his finger. 'Deadhearts have cold energy, unique hellsfire. We guide our own arrows to their hellsfire,' came Liyoot's whisper into his head.

A head appeared above the fog. A green arrow struck the eye. A shriek left its throat, a second arrow struck it's hellstone, shattering it. The vampire burst into flames. And toppled backwards.

The fog was dispersing. Burning torches showed the bodies of hellsborn beasts and vampires impaled on the spikes. The one who was searching suddenly saw the gap between the spikes. His eyes were red, and his face was missing flesh, probably torn by a spike.

Ithrandir saw the arrow just in time and swerved to avoid it.

The Grim Leader looked alarmed.

The cavalry charged through the gap to meet the hellsborn. Jade archers targeted the vampires before the swords came to behead them. The Grim Cavalry had a bigger number. Dark beasts got their legs trapped into the smaller spikes, leaving their riders at the mercy of the charging allied cavalry. Some were thrust onto the larger spikes, they squirmed until green flames found them.

Matthew was ordered to wait until the dead cavalry retreated. One tried to cut off Ithrandir. Matthew leapt off and ran quickly, catching the dark blade with his sword. He struck back, slicing deadheart fingers. The Grim Rider shrieked.

'Hellstone,' came a whisper in his head.

Matthew saw it on the finger. He stamped it with his boot. It did not break. The Grim Rider was growing new fingers. Matthew spat on the ring. The dark crystal cracked.

The Grim Rider howled.

Matthew stabbed its heart.

He pulled back.

Scales disappeared. The vampire fell to his knees. Colour returned to his eyes. It almost looked like the vampire had been cured. But then the face crumbled and all that was left was an old, battered uniform.

Ithrandir grabbed his shoulder and pushed him. 'Fight from safety.' He turned when they had left the gap. 'Well done.'

40

Arif:

I can do this.

The Three Points lay on his right. He hoped to God he would have an element of surprise. Draje was still transfixed on Lemoff. Eight hooves, however light, would be familiar to anyone who lived thousands of years and had many battles. Draje obviously can sense him. Should he lift the shield from the saddle? Suddenly he felt foolish having rushed into a manoeuvre without planning it properly with Commander Ibb.

Draje was fifty yards away from the gates. No Grim.

Commander Ibb changed direction for a collision course.

Arif knew immediately why. Ibb was trying to draw Draje, giving him a moment to get closer to wound him. How an accomplished commander had faith his little hands could do more damage to a monster than himself, he just didn't understand.

The giant sword swiped downwards, beheading the white mithrin, throwing Ibb twenty feet. With momentum, the mithrin's body crumpled, its four back legs lifted high into a somersault before it slid sideways.

Arif's blood ran cold. Zethrin neighed, swerving from her path. They galloped away from the black beast towards the shuddering heap. Arif pulled on the reins to stop beside the fallen friend. Rage filled his eyes.

Draje was terrifyingly huge.

Arif pointed his sword, keeping his eyes locked, knowing full well the beast would win.

Draje mocked him with laughter.

The pouch flew from his other hand, hitting his face.

Startled, the Hellsborn mithrin retreated six steps. But the white fire water was already upon his skin. Stinging. Causing the dark lord to rub his eyes.

Ibb leaped to strike.

The sword beheaded the animal, like for like. Draje was thrown off.

He scrambled to his feet, growling, changing into a beast. Zethrin's hooves hit him first. Arif stepped sideways, cutting the dark lord with his sword. He could see the pain was hitting Draje like a bomb. How odd that a monster could die from a few drops of water.

He stabbed the monster in the throat.

Draje grasped at the hole where infection spurted out. He choked. The monster was shuddering, just like he had caused all his victims to shudder. The deep moan that arose so loudly, caused both Arif and Ibb to step back. A haunting howl echoed over the city walls. Draje shook, then fell forward.

All was silent.

And still.

'Is he dead?' gasped Commander Ibb.

'In the movies, they drive a stake into the vampire's heart. Or we could do what he did to your mithrin and chop his head off,' said Arif fiercely.

Suddenly, Draje was a beast, running on all four legs away from the city. Arif watched in shock as the beast disappeared.

Sounds from the city changed. The Grim returned to the gates. Seeing Arif beside the Dark Lord's dead animal, they tried to flee. Explosions erupted. Warriors charged upon the Grim. From the walls, archers mobilised weaponry to strike those fleeing the city. They had the upper hand now. Draje was gone. And his power.

'Are you alright?' asked Arif, kneeling to look at his leg.

'Dethrin is not,' said Ibb.

'Sorry about your pet. said Arif, gloomily. 'That was just… awful.'

Commander Ibb stared with loss.

'Your leg looks wonky,' he said.

'I feel it. Dethrin does not,' said Ibb, his lip quivered.

'I think it's broken,' said Arif.

'I saw… Draje is resistant to swords and magic. What did you throw?'

'Aylarhiyssa! I'm afraid I've exhausted my supply. I'll get help. Do you have any to drink?'

'Wa, just a little,' Commander Ibb said, reaching for his pouch from his belt.

Suddenly, there was a loud bang and a lot of commotion just inside the gates. Arif and the Commander stared towards the noise and saw a battalion of Grim fighting to escape from the city. The Ithfirians blocked their retreat, but then the Grim charged together pushing and slashing their way through. They lost a dozen in the process. Scrambling through the gates, they rushed down the slope pursued by Lemothinian soldiers. Arif tightened his grip on his sword to rise to his feet, though he need not have bothered. Azuran Warriors appeared on the city walls, firing their blazing blue arrows. All the Grim fell. Hordes of Lemothinian soldiers and city guards rushed to set them on fire.

'We lose many, but Lemoff lives,' said Ibb.

The city had survived, strangely because the Dark Lord had not ventured inside, for what reason, puzzled Commander Ibb and Arif when one of the Azuran Warriors strode forward to meet them.

'Hello! Can we have some help here?' yelled Arif.

'Is he wounded?' shouted the Azuran.

'He's broken his leg,' said Arif aloud.

The Azuran drew nearer and yelled to his comrades, before quickening his pace towards them. Lemothinians had arrived for their aid.

'Oh, it's Ibb!' said one of the Lemothinian soldiers.

'Aya Ibb!'

'Aya Elias!'

'Aya Ibb!'

'Aya Dood!'

'Aya Ibb!'

'Aya Pakius!'

'Aya Ibb,' said the Azuran Warrior kneeling down beside him. 'We'll need to take you inside the city and then we can fix your leg.'

'Thank you, Mafius,' said Commander Ibb allowing him to hold the pouch to his lips. He drank the aylarhiyssa until it finished. Then the Azuran reached for a smaller pouch on his belt and made him drink it.

'Dethrin is dead,' said Commander Ibb gripping his arm.

Sadness filled his eyes.

'I know. I'm sorry for your loss,' he replied softly, 'We shall ensure he is properly taken care of.'

Commander Ibb's head lolled back, woozy from the elixir he just drank. His eyes closed and gradually he fell into a deep slumber. The Lemothinian soldiers lifted him onto a stretcher and slowly made their way back to the city.

Mafius bowed his head, his hair slipped off his shoulders. It was darker than the other Lemothinian soldiers, but still his city's colours. 'It is an honour to meet you, Chosen One. It would be a pleasure if you accompanied us back to the city. Lord Kimbaroff has requested your counsel,' he said. But his piercing eyes conveyed he had no choice.

'He-Oh – okay.'

41

Aroosa:

Aroosa had never flown so far. Ten accompanied her through the chilly atmosphere. A spell had been whispered around them, but every time she swerved, Aroosa felt the sharpness of the icy polar wind. They had left the Venn Varda Mountains and passed over another. This mountain range stretched all the way to the polar region. And yet, she felt the surge even here, deep within the crust, a power was pushing its way through every crack and hole.

She wondered if Eliza could feel it too. Would she be thrilled? What would she do to get a better view?

Aifa pointed to an impact crater. Izmilla saw another. Ispen beckoned to them.

On the flat mountain, emerald fire had torn through this encampment of the damned. Bodies and apparatus burned. Even giants. The yellow torches showed charrelles had been here, with a lord, or a Vinx.

They landed, Ispen ever so watchful for her safety. Aifa had cautioned him about his arm, but he had been determined to stay with them.

'It's abandoned,' said Izmilla.

'This was the Siren Queen's camp,' said Aifa.

'How far would she have taken her?'

'Join hands, we are stronger together,' said Aifa.

They made a circle of three. Aroosa closed her eyes and let her emeralds take her there. She remembered the sound of Ophelia, and what she had felt when she saw her sister.

'Do you feel it?' whispered Aifa, in her thoughts.

'Yes.' It was a faint breath from behind the next mountain. She waited for it to get close. A breeze lifted hair from her neck. She opened her eyes, to find they were dropping gently over the ice mountain. They floated over a strange formation of stones. The pyramid head had an inscription. It must have been a dwelling of some sort. A faint heartbeat echoed in her ear. They all heard it.

'It's weak, but steady,' said Aifa.

'She's alive,' smiled Izmilla.

The Warriors overtook them now. The Jades tossed torch balls to illuminate the frozen terrain. The Azurans passed over the ground, scanning for any sign of the Vinx.

Aifa whispered something. Then the heartbeats quickened. It grew louder in their ears as they neared her.

They landed when they saw her lying with a crooked leg.

'Ophelia, our Emerald Sister - oh, how the Jades will welcome you home!' said Aifa.

'How the streets will rejoice with songs to honour you. Stories will be told in all Ethyrus of how you faced this night alone, against the Mighty Queen of Charrelles,' said Izmilla.

Aroosa covered her with the cloak. The healing began immediately. Colour returned to her slim long face. The roots of her hair showed her emerald hair had once been darker. Ophelia was more beautiful than she imagined. Her hands were long. Feios was a suited spouse. Once she was revived, Aroosa brought aylarhiyssa to her lips. Ophelia took deep breaths, then she groaned, and her hand dropped.

'Her chest is rising strongly now,' said Aifa.

'The cloak is healing her,' smiled Aroosa.

'Fenn,' gasped Ophelia, 'The Vinx!'

'There is no sign of the Siren Queen,' said Aifa. 'We are still looking.'

Ophelia closed her eyes. Then she smiled, raising her palm to touch Aroosa's face.

'I'll join the search,' said Aroosa.

'No, we can't risk you. Not while you are still learning,' said Aifa, getting up. She floated away.

As she straightened, Izmilla grabbed her wrist. 'We have no idea what kind of trap the Vinx will ensnare. Aifa is best suited.'

'My Queen, Etienne and I can carry Lady Ophelia to Lemoff,' said Ispen.

It was nice to see so much enthusiasm from such a lovely boy, his long-toothed smile was heart-warming. Two souls from different planets, yet he had saved her life, by risking his own. His friend was shy, but she had seen him fight. From their thoughts, she had learned they were skilled with their weapons, learning from the age of four. Were Jades her people now? Her new family? So different to the world back home. Or were they? How did she know? She'd never been telepathic on Earth. Surely, most people will be nice in their own minds. It was nice to feel loved. No wonder Eliza chose to stay. How could their world have become so dark?

It was a while, waiting in the bitter cold before Aifa returned. Aroosa felt the switch instantly when she started telling Ispen how to carry Ophelia. Something started troubling Aifa, and it wasn't the news of her find. Aifa had circled the mountain ridge and flew over the valley, but there was no sign of the Vinx. Eventually she found a pool of dark blood soaked deeply in the ground. It gave the impression of a severe wound. Droplets led to a cave in the mountain. She had returned for Izmilla, together they would seal the cave.

'No!' gasped Ophelia. She got to her feet, by squeezing her weight into Aifa's and Izmilla's hands.

'Take me there, Aifa.'

At the sullen cave, no amount of Jade flames could make this place look inviting. The rocks were treacherous, the cave openings gave her the creeps. Aifa warned them to form a circle. Aroosa waited for the sisters and Ispen to come closer, she had a bad feeling about what might lie deep down. No sooner than her feet had touched dirt, than the vampire rats spilled from the six caves heading towards her.

'Ildiro!' gasped Izmilla.

Aifa created a wall of cerulean fire around their circle. The rats pushed their burning bodies through it. Ophelia blasted them back.

Aifa returned them to the air.

'Is this not too easy? A vinx would want us to believe it is her lair,' said Aifa.

'You call this easy?' shrieked Aroosa.

'The Ildiro are guarding a body,' said Ophelia, pointing.

Aroosa could just make out the shape. Then the smell hit her. It was in the back of her throat, seeping into every part of her body. More repugnant than the tower, she would never be able to wash it out. 'Is she alive?' she gasped.

'It's a lot of blood,' said Ophelia, moving closer to blood-soaked ground. 'She has retreated here to die.'

'Are you sure, Ophelia?' asked Aifa.

Aroosa flew closer to look. In the biggest cave, Ispen tossed a Lemothinian flare. A body sat up. The Ildiro formed a wall around it. The creature wailed hauntingly. The second scream pressed into her eardrums. Selwa's eyes were monstrously dark as she clucked, spurting dark saliva from her throat.

'She is chanting.' Ophelia faltered. 'Do not let her near!'

Aroosa realised her magic wasn't working when the fireball failed to materialise from her hand. Aifa was chanting a shielding spell, but her magic wasn't working either.

Ispen hurled a spear, but Selwa dodged it. She stood up, talons grew from her hands and feet. It was then that Aroosa saw the bodies. All around her. Dead faces turned.

'This is her nest,' said Ophelia.

'Retreat!' shouted Aifa.

They flew as fast as they could through. It was only after the cold air hit her face again, that Aroosa realised she had let fear get the best of her. She turned to see Selwa crawling with her head tilted and her body extending.

'We missed the chance to kill her!'

'She's drawing on their powers,' said Aifa.

Selwa hissed. Then took long strides on her monstrous sized limbs. The entrance crumbled as she pushed her way through it. Screams erupted behind her.

Aroosa suddenly became aware that the others were looking to her. 'How do we kill her,' she asked.

'We combine our powers,' said Aifa.

The screams were hideously loud. How could they possibly kill that thing?

'She's huge!' gasped Aroosa.

'She will devastate our brothers,' said Izmilla, fearfully.

'We cannot let her leave,' said Ophelia.

'We are Jades and Azurans. Our ancestors have faced this demon and prevailed. We will defeat her,' said Aifa, her voice strangely deep.

Aroosa wasn't sure. With her heart beating fast, she stood with their wall.

When Selwa emerged, she staggered into the open on all fours. Aroosa felt Aifa's relief. Selwa had not been able to transform into whatever Aifa feared she could become. Ispen's rock smashed into her head. She growled.

Suddenly, two white furry arms grabbed Selwa's leg and dragged her into the adjoining cave. Selwa struggled and managed to break free. The white furry giant's third and fourth claws grabbed her neck and torso, then smashed her against a rock. It smashed her into the ground back and forth. It roared with both of its jaws. Then backing into the cave, Selwa's body disappeared in two long drags.

'What was that?' gasped Aroosa.

'An agriscylla,' said Ophelia. 'I've read about them, but no one has seen one since the curse began.'

'An agriscylla,' laughed Izmilla.

'They eat the living. And they eat the dead. I have a feeling the resident of this terrain may not have been happy to wake up to find someone had claimed it.'

'My Queen is she dead?' asked Ispen.

'I don't feel anything,' said Aroosa, frowning.

'We must not be fooled,' warned Ophelia. 'We felt nothing until we entered her nest.'

'If any of the sirens have survived the agriscylla, we should make sure they cannot help her,' said Aifa.

'Seal the caves so she cannot escape,' said Ophelia, sadly.

Aifa created a cerulean fireball, and then nodded. Izmilla bound it with a spell she had yet to learn. Aroosa closed her eyes and recited what Ophelia whispered, then she brought both her palms to face each other. Feeling the vibrations surging through her arms, she asked the queens of the past to seal the Queen of Charrelles.

From within the cerulean fireball, an emerald core expanded, sucking all its power and the bind before shooting towards the cave. It split. All was quiet. Then six caves illuminated like the daylight Ethyrus had been denied. The mountain shook. From a great height, rocks and dirt slipped to cover the entire cliff ledge.

'Will we survive the night?' whispered Izmilla, sadly.

They watched the dirt turn to glass.

'We have to,' said Aroosa. 'Give everything we have to stop the Army of Dead. We need to save each other. In any way we can.'

'You are beautiful.'

Aroosa turned.

'Our Jade queen returns in a Clayborn, has there ever been such a blessing?' said Ophelia.

'Not since Feios found you,' teased Aifa.

Izmilla roared with laughter. 'Feios gathered all the Jades to declare his love and turned and she wasn't there! Ophelia had gone to hunt a charrelle. Poor Feios, went pale with fright.'

'Don't make me start with your stories, Izmilla!' said Ophelia.

'Quiet!' hushed Aifa.

Aroosa watched Etienne standing on a rock, listening to the wind. He shook his head.

'I don't like this place,' whispered Izmilla, looking around.

'I have to find my life stone,' said Ophelia. 'She tore it off. And I kicked it from her hand. I can feel it, it is nearby.'

'Ophelia's life stone is old, from the Second Tribe,' said Aifa.

'Let's find your life stone and go. I have something to do,' said Aroosa.

42

Arif:

Dead bodies were being carted to a giant bonfire. City Guards were already hard at work trying to repair the gates. There was rubble from a few collapsed buildings. Wide streets illuminated by white lamps, narrow streets with blue fire. Arif followed the Azuran warrior, even though he wanted to get back to his brother. He couldn't see any electrical wiring that made the stones glow, they just glowed. Small buildings were hexagonal, built in a different shade of blue stone. The large buildings were round and imposing. The fortified blue towers looked magnificent. He couldn't help admiring the fact that the citizens had created high walls within the city, should they need to seal off a district. Though he didn't quite understand how, didn't sirens fly? They reached the top of the slope, catching first glimpse of the Keeper's Residence through broken gates.

To Mafius and Ibb's surprise, Draje's Hellsborn had only managed to get this far. Draje brought no sirens, Mafius said. That statement troubled him more than it gave relief.

A tall man dressed in a white robe and a dark blue sash hurried across the huge courtyard.

'It is Lord Kimbaroff,' said Mafius, as the white figure neared them. He seemed surprised that he was coming to them. It must be urgent, he thought to himself.

'He is the Keeper of the City.'

'Lord Arif!' called the white robed man, panting. He bowed quickly and said, 'Pleasure to meet you, blessings from Lemoff. I have an urgent communication from Lord Wyfzira.'

'Wyfzira?'

'Ya, Lord Select of Aran Daran. Shortly before the attack from Draje... which I must say was quite admirable on how you distracted him before launching your own. I was in the tower and saw your genius, I was overwhelmed with glee I must say. What was in the pouch that you threw at him?'

'Aylarhiyssa!'

Mafius raised his eyebrows. 'You threw Aylarhiyssa at Draje?'

'Well – yes! Only as a distraction – I wasn't sure if I could get close enough to him with my sword. The aylarhiyssa went in his eye -'

'- and blinded him!' Mafius nodded. 'Ingenious.'

'Yeah–it gave me a chance to use my sword.'

'Well done indeed. Although, Draje will recuperate, and I'm not sure aylarhiyssa will be as effective the next time you have an encounter, Hellsborn magic will weave resistance into his crystal,' said Lord Kimbaroff.

'Saved our beloved Blue City,' said Mafius grinning.

'I'm not sure I can be thanked for all of it,' replied Arif truthfully. 'Commander Ibb bought me the time to consider my move. A whisper suggested the aylarhiyssa.'

'Whisper?'

Arif thought about it. 'Sounded like Teiaar?'

'Teiaar the Jade?' said Lord Kimbaroff pondering. 'Her skills must have improved considerably. Then again, she is a fast learner of the Jade Path. She'll make a good Emerald Sister one day; I can assure you of that.'

'So - I really did hear her whisper?' said Arif,

'Yaya. An old Jade trick - connecting to your mind at times of danger! You must be quite close – er- both of you – relatively - for it to happen.'

Arif went red.

'Anyway – er - what was the message?' he said changing the subject.

'Yaya - the message! Strange that it came via a messenger and not a Jade, though who am I to question Lord Wyfzira's use of carriers. Shortly before the attack from Draje, I received communication from Wyfzira - brought to me by none other than Boosh the Brave, the finest scout that our two cities can offer.'

Kimbaroff's lips pulled in opposite directions. 'Though, it seems strange to me... he has requested that you go to the White City.'

Mafius said astounded, 'For what purpose?'

'To enlist the Eli.'

'For what? Prayer?' said Mafius, with disgust.

'We ask not,' said Kimbaroff.

'Eli have pledged their lives to folly. How can we depend on those who sacrifice their brethren so they can sit in worship? They have never helped us,' said Mafius, glaring.

'Lord Wyfzira has requested so... and I have promised that you will accompany Lord Arif on this task,

Mafius Mefiticus, Eleventh of Olocon,' said Kimbaroff, watching his reaction.

Mafius scowled. When he turned his head, his eyes dimmed. 'I am grateful to be a descendant of Lady Olocon. I will be honoured to accompany Lord Arif to seek the counsel of the Eli, although I cannot see a fruitful end. Lord Wyfzira has better sight than I, it is wise for me to follow.'

'Aptly said Mafius!' said Lord Kimbaroff grinning. He slapped him gently on the shoulder. 'I bet your Jade friend said the same in your head, did she?'

'It was my mother,' he replied.

Kimbaroff laughed. 'Of course, it was!'

'First, we will renew our stocks of aylarhiyssa, and then we will go,' said the Azuran Warrior walking off to the other side of the courtyard. Arif saw him converse with another soldier.

'You must excuse Mafius for his display of scorn. He has been through trauma, with the loss of his mother and maternal kin when the City of Rosh fell to the Damned,' said Kimbaroff sighing.

'I'm sorry to hear that,' said Arif courteously.

'He has a good heart for his people, but sometimes he regards our decisions with a little cynicism.'

'Oh, that's normal in our world. I wouldn't worry about it,' said Arif, shrugging. He was about to say he liked Mafius better for being sarcastic but stopped short when he remembered that they were not human at all. And might regard his comment rather strange. It then occurred to him that he was in the presence of people that were not human! How awesome was that? All those great people looking at the stars in search of life on other worlds, dedicating their whole lives debating and researching their science to prove that alien life possibility existed. And here he was. Wow!

Lemothinians were semi giants. Empathetic, gracious and protective. Most skilled in the art of magical warfare. They had only one enemy – the Hellsborn! What would they be like if the Hellsborn were suddenly vanquished? They probably would not have wars with each other. Or would they? Would everything change?

It's a shame they lived in darkness.

From behind him, came a dozen soldiers pulling a large corpse on a trailer covered in a long blue sheet. They passed him, chanting a prayer for the deceased. As they turned ahead, Arif saw the tail from underneath the sheets.

Arif sighed. 'Poor Dethrin! It seemed so gentle.'

'Wa!' agreed Lord Kimbaroff with sadness in his voice. 'I have seen many moments, such as this in my very long life, but it never gets easier. Dethrin will get a special service and a prayer for his servitude. May Ayla grant him peace.'

'That's nice,' said Arif.

'It's the least we can do. The mithrin are very special to us Lemothinians, more so than the Jade. Dethrin has saved many in his nine hundred years. He deserves more but we live in troubled times.'

'Nine hundred years?' said Arif aghast.

'Wa! I know... he could have lived for another ten. Couldn't be helped, I'm afraid.'

Not only did the djinn live for thousands of years, but their animals did too!

'Wow!' he mimed to himself.

Standing under a white flame lamp Mafius was deep in conversation with his soldier friends. There seemed to be five of them now and one of them held the reins of a mithrin feeding on something from his hands. One walked away in a hurry.

Arif suddenly remembered what he wanted to ask. 'Lord Kimbaroff... Ibb thought it was strange that the dark lord did not enter your city,' he said, questioningly.

'Commander Ibb was right in his assumption,' said Lord Kimbaroff sadly. 'Unfortunately, it took the fall of City of Rosh before our people learned we had to devise a better method of stopping Lord Draje. Hardly a hundred years now, but the wound is still so deep. Azurans have been hard at work with the Jades to create a definitive answer to Draje and the Northern Lords.'

He smiled meekly. 'Strange, isn't it? It takes the massacre of our neighbours before we really pull together and try to find a solution. Could we not have tried before? Would we have saved the City of Rosh, do you think?' he sighed. 'Thankfully, it was Draje that came, and it was Draje that our shield spell was cast against. Had it been the Western Lords, then Ayla help us! We would not have been so lucky.'

'Did anyone survive from Rosh?' Arif asked with concern.

'Over thirty thousand Jenn there were and five thousand Eli, but not even seven thousand survived. Even then, it was thanks to the Emerald Sisters having the foresight to create tunnels, that they managed to get away with their lives. We had to disperse the refugees to both cities. Eli continued praying to the end. We had to force a hibernation spell and carry them out, we lost many doing this. So many perished! Ayla have mercy.' Kimbaroff shook his head.

Arif imagined the depressing image of the city being evacuated and wondered what the City of Rosh was like. Did they have their own unique colour? he wondered.

He looked up at the city towers and noticed the beautiful, decorated stone used at the tower heights. There were carvings all along the roof edges and curious markings that seemed to him, to indicate the identity of the families that resided within each building.

'How old is your city then, if you don't mind me asking?' said Arif with intrigue at the tall blue buildings which cast a colourful mood on the city below.

Lord Kimbaroff was impressed by his interest in his city.

'Oh, the city is very old. It is written that Lemoff was built even before General Leybo's days and the Great Revolt of the King. Our people are very proud of our humble habitat and have always protected it from the threat from the Damned. I guess, you could say it is near a hundred thousand years, according to our records, though I may be wrong. It might be more.'

'A hundred thousand years?' said Arif incredulously. He shot a funny look at the Keeper of the City.

'You doubt my claim with cynicism,' chuckled Kimbaroff. 'I don't blame you Kildaan, I would too. I would advise, under better circumstances, when you visit again, I shall show you around the city better and you can take your time exploring all that there is to see.'

'Thank you, Lord Kimbaroff. That is a very generous offer,' said Arif smiling.

Mafius and his soldiers laughed heartily.

'What exactly am I going to say to the Eli, that's gonna make a difference?' he asked, mystified.

Ahead of him, Mafius accepted a bundle from the returning soldier. He bade farewell respectfully to each of his friends. Then turned to the soldier holding the reins and thanked him.

'I would not know, Lord Arif,' said Kimbaroff. 'Wyfzira thinks highly of you, I am sure something will come to mind.'

'Are we ready then,' asked Arif when Mafius joined them.

'I have two additional supplies of aylarhiyssa for each of us,' replied the Azuran Warrior, throwing two pouches from four at Arif, who caught them and placed them on his belt.

'Keep a vigilant eye. May Ayla deliver you safely,' said Kimbaroff.'

'Thank you,' smiled Arif.

'Fetasha!' urged Mafius.

43

Aiden:

Nethrin steered wide from the Ithfirian city, trusting the dried riverbeds that led upwards to an ancient derelict town, where the statues of forgotten kings lay broken by a gateless wall. Glowing flowers marked a boundary where no evil could cross. Feena kept to the slope, well away from the road and the giant dark stems that grew around the town's walls. The hill levelled off before a deep gorge. An old bridge was lit with green and blue lanterns. Nethrin's arms relaxed, releasing his grip around Aiden. Aiden was relieved he could move freely. 'This bridge is protected by old magic. Not even the dark lords can cross it. We are safe here,' whispered Nethrin.

Feena seemed at peace with the bridge, taking her time crossing it. They arrived on Sullen Hill surprising Aiden, because he had not seen the bridge the last time he was here. They crossed the moor filled with illuminated red and blue flowers, the white forest to their left and Leybo's cave to the right. When they reached the white light of the long trumpet flowers, Nethrin started humming. Aiden didn't think there were any hellsborn nearby either. The sky though... would they know? Aiden wasn't sure.

A circle of violet forlorn flowers marked the place where the vinx fell.

'We're here,' whispered Aiden.

Nethrin held his elbow as he disembarked.

Aiden ran to the stone unicorn. He stroked the face. It was cold solid stone. 'I don't understand,' he said. 'I thought he would waken.'

'Why is this creature so important?' asked Nethrin.

George turned and looked up.

'We are out of our defensible perimeter. What do you intend to do with it once it is awake?' asked Nethrin.

'He is my friend,' said Aiden. 'He called me here.'

'Did you hear a voice?' asked Nethrin.

'I have a strong feeling,' said Aiden.

'That could be due to us,' said Nethrin.

Aiden froze. 'Us?' he asked.

'You are a puzzle, my lord. The Jades cannot read you. And if the Jades cannot read you, that makes your vulnerability quite unique, harder to detect.'

'What?'

'Possession. While the Daraan and Azurans have strong discipline to prevent manipulation, there are some who have mastered mischief. The Red City homes plenty who are unruly,' said Nethrin.

'Yeah. I learned that' said Aiden. 'Again Nethrin, what did you mean due to us?'

'Some of our protection spells can affect your instincts.'

'What-no. This is not magic. I- why are you looking up?'

Nethrin smiled. 'He comes.'

'What?'

'Indeed. I, too, am at loss for words,' grinned Nethrin.

Aiden inhaled. 'You're not making any sense. Do you need a sip of Aylarhiyssa? I need our brains working at full capacity to work out how to wake him.

'I sought advice from our fair lady,' said Nethrin.

'Good. Can you do your mind-talking thing and ask Teiaar how to do the restoration spell?'

'The city forgets he lives. He is not one to stray from hibernation pods,' said Nethrin. 'Yet he wakes. He left the city for you.'

Aiden glared at him. 'What're you talking about?'

'She said we must wait,' said Nethrin.

'For what?'

'For me,' said a deep croaky voice.

It came from the direction that George was staring at.

Two pairs of feet landed on the luminous silver grass. Euthalia unwrapped her arm from a frail djinn, who hobbled towards them using a cane. 'I am Odana,' he panted, 'former keeper of Aran Daran. Let me look at you boy.'

The closer he got, the taller he got.

'Clayborns on our wretched world mastering our tools.' The old djinn kneeled. His green fiery eyes seemed as if they were about to fall out of their wrinkled sockets. The shape of his face looked familiar. Especially the insignia on his robe. His fingers were bent, but soft when they touched his forehead to move his hair. 'Such a slight boy, yet he masters a bow like a warrior,' wheezed Odana. 'The dead army rises, yet our world breathes. And have you ever seen… such vibrant colours?'

Aiden didn't know what to make of his words. 'It's phenomenal,' he said, glancing at the glowing moors.

'What is your designation, boy?' He could tell by the dimming of his eyes, that the old djinn was trying to read him.

'Aiden.'

'Huh,' wheezed the old djinn, 'Like the prophet?'

'I don't know,' said Aiden, trying not to breath his breath.

'How long has it been since you first caught sight of your ghost?'

George frowned.

'Feels like forever,' he replied.

'To be haunted is to be cursed. The cursed spook the dead just as the dead reek to the living.'

'Really?' Aiden didn't know what to make of that.

'There's a story of one girl who faced an army to give our ancestors time to repair shields. Even the beast king retreated,' said Odana, polishing his monocle with his sleeve.

'Right. So. You think I can halt the dead army?' asked Aiden, incredulously.

'You killed a lord. You were spawned. And cured. You were followed,' panted the old djinn.

To Aiden, that sounded like a question.

'Okay?'

'When hellspawn fails, vengeance is… assured. From a siren.'

That sounded like another question.

'Meaning?'

'When you arrived, we placed protection spells in your clothing. We know sirens seed more hellspawn than all the lords and the dark king put together,' said the old djinn, slowly.

'Wow.'

'Failed in your case,' said the old djinn.

'Thank God.'

'Perhaps it has something to do with your haunting,' said the old djinn, sounding sarcastic. 'Or due to your friend. After all, a unicorn is rare.'

'She… wanted to know where Herionus was,' said Aiden.

'In dark magic, there are many uses for blood and bones from heavenly creatures. Narthrins can easily escape this world, but it stayed to save you time and again.'

'Yes, he did.'

'We cannot allow hellsborn to gain its power. I was jolted from hibernation by this conundrum, boy,' wheezed the old djinn, gesturing to Nethrin.

Nethrin went to his saddle.

It occurred to Aiden that the old djinn was trying to put his mind at ease. Yet he knew more about Herionus than they had said. Which of the Jades had read their minds and reported to him? 'You hibernate?' he asked, watching Nethrin take a leather case from the saddle.

'We all hibernate on this world. The dead army retreats after it culls enough to feed. We survive and procreate, preserving a supply of blood,' said the old djinn, waiting for Nethrin to remove the leather casing. 'Then we hibernate to beat the long dark.' Nethrin extended the pipe with a pull. The old man took the pipe and uttered something under his breath. The pipe end lit up. He took two long puffs and blew out rings. Suddenly, his voice sounded calmer and younger. 'Some go mad, some die sad. Those that survive are smarter.'

'Sounds awful,' said Aiden.

'They had you both. Why would sirens retreat?' He was looking at him, but his eyes had dimmed again. A tell-tale sign for a djinn probing him.

Aiden spoke with alarm, 'You think I was targeted?'

'Blood feasts lie at the three city gates and our defences. Not chasing a little morsel like yourself. Frightened our young apprentice, Nethrinus here. This in turn frightened Euthalia. Anything that frightens Euthalia, frightens the rest of us,' said the old djinn, putting the monocle on his eye.

Aiden's eyes burned. 'I'm sorry.'

'Ugh. Well. You are breathing,' he moved closer to peer. 'No corruption in pupils or irises. No discolour of skin. A single heart beating. You look and smell pathetic. Human.'

Nethrin turned to hide laughter.

Aiden grinned.

'I say again, Odana. That is my designation,' said the old djinn, smiling.

'Nice to meet you… Odana,' said Aiden.

'What is your ghost doing?' asked Odana.

Aiden blinked, 'Watching you.'

'What does that tell us Euthalia?'

'We should hurry,' said Euthalia, straightening.

Odana turned his head to a hill where the flora had plunged in darkness. 'The Army of Dead arrives. The Emerald Elite are skilled in accomplishing a cleanse, but not experienced with your particular delicate friend.'

Aiden spoke quickly, 'I-I can't leave him here. If you help me revive Herionus, I will give you something which belongs to your city.'

Odana stepped away. 'No barter.'

'Please,' he said.

'What is his word?' asked Odana, looking to Nethrin.

'I beseech you,' said Aiden, quickly.

'There is no need for that, kildana,' said Odana.

'Jades are sworn to help those who ask,' said Euthalia.

Odana sighed. 'Aside from pains and aches of a body worn down, age blesses one with experience and wisdom. I have lived one such instance to know what can be recited. There is enough aylarhiyssa under the cave, which we will summon. Hasten, surround the narthrin.'

When instructed, Aiden closed his eyes. Then pictured the soft thuds from hooves and a hot sloppy tongue when Herionus licked his face. He remembered how Herionus faced the giant beast in battle, how he blasted the beast with the energy in his body to protect them all. He recited the old words from Odana, syllable by syllable. He felt the heat from the old djinn pass through his body.

Stone cracked.

Silky hot droplets rained on his face.

Aiden opened his eyes to find he was spinning with rocks around Herionus, with his wrists firmly held by Euthalia and Nethrin. Emerald fire left their bodies in long strands to pass into the cracking ground. White Fire water gushed from the cracks, spraying over the stone unicorn. Odana and Euthalia recited the mantra louder. The shell broke.

The eight-legged narthrin bolted forward.

'Herionus!' gasped Aiden.

The white unicorn turned half circle towards the cave, raising four legs into the air, energy pulsed in its stomach.

The hills were flooded by a blast of light.

Aiden's toes touched ground.

He ran to his friend.

44

Matthew:

The zombie kept coming at him with half a neck. He had to do it. But the sight of it filled him with disgust. He kicked it down the hill, hoping to catch his breath. It returned too soon. Matthew drove the sword and twisted with both hands until he heard bones snap. The head fell off. Finally. He stepped away to vomit before the torso tumbled.

The mask needed replacing. He tossed it and put on the clean one. The goggles readjusted again.

This was the last stand. There could be no retreating, Ithrandir had said. The battle to defend the hills seemed never to end. He had lost count of how many he had turned to ash. It was odd that he still had energy. How come no one was tired? The Jades must have spiked the beer, he wouldn't put it past them.

Boom.

Boom.

Boom.

Dirt rained. Cries were drowned out by the constant ringing in his ears. Ithrandir was in a panic to save infected soldiers. Aylarhiyssa was fed quickly, swords were used against brothers. A soldier used his own sword to commit suicide.

Who threw the bombs? The Jades searched the night sky.

No siren in sight.

Matthew couldn't help staring at the poor suicider. No one paid any attention. Were they betrayed by their own? Why wasn't anyone else thinking that?

The ground was covered in rocks and body parts. The ringing grew louder. He felt nauseated and dizzy. Sidra was nowhere to be found. He didn't blame her. He needed to sit down. Matthew staggered towards the gap. Suddenly, a hand shoved him. He fell to his knees. Matthew got up quickly, just in time to see a Grim's head fall sideways as a silver blade pulled back.

The Grim could have had him.

Christ.

'Thank you!' he said, though he could not hear his own words.

Diyafa turned, saying something. Matthew didn't have time to look! Hands heaved him onto a mithrin's saddle. The animal quickened towards safety. Facing the wrong way, Matthew stared in dismay as the battle raged on without him.

The ringing was fading.

Hands hauled him down from the mithrin. The Jade was saying something to his face, but he too had a mask on.

'I can't hear you,' he said, making a gesture to his ear.

A bolt of green sped over their heads, causing a flash on the battlefield.

Everyone turned to look up.

Three luminous bodies were closing in fast. The Jades looked relieved, if not pleased to see they wore green.

The air was lit again by bolts of green. The hills were on fire.

Matthew exhaled when he recognised one of them.

Rose looked confident now with her new role, she looked mighty, like her new friends. Did her hands make the fireballs, or did they come from the emeralds she wore? How did her powers work exactly? The dress was new, though she was always elegant. A dress is only cosmetic, she would say. Her friend got respect from the Jades. Who was she? And what was Rose staring at? Her eyes suddenly glowed. Gosh, he was still getting used to that.

She was safe and well.

Thank God.

Her lips were moving. Her eyes were glowing. Was she chanting?

A hand grabbed his wrist. This Jade was a woman, no older than Teiaar.

Matthew looked back to steal another glance at the battle from the sky, only to be yanked inside the large tent.

The Jade said something to the older purple-haired sitting companion, who reached into a pot and poured into a cup a brown gooey liquid. They floated the cup toward him.

'No thank you!' he said. From the look on their faces, he must have yelled. 'Can you give me something for my _'

The Jade grabbed his wrist again and gestured to a sleeping wounded soldier with a finger on her lips.

Matthew tried to whisper, '- hearing, please? I need to be out there.'

The companion thrust the cup in his hands, guiding them to his lips. He grimaced, as the gooey soup entered his mouth.

Immediately, he felt something unfold in his ear canal. With each mouthful more of his hearing returned.

'... finish it all before we pour some more. Eh aarta, isn't he brave for a kildaan.'

'Aye he ith.'

'You have to drink three cups, before we can let you go,' said the Jade sternly, 'Otherwise, you may experience long term damage to your hearing. The remedy is the finest we have brewed for injuries like yours.'

'Three Cups?' he said making a horrible face. The liquid was sour and left a nasty aftertaste.

The Jades laughed.

'Hearty concoction it is,' said the companion with an accent he had not yet heard. "T'll gav ye strength t'you never tho't you had, my brave Metava Vastari Kildaan. Y' can oos t'at for where y're goin' Daffari lyanta kinda Kand Ehud. Drink no' f'r y'r wits t' be with ye.'

It was odd how she said that, and he felt like Mum was talking. Her language didn't sound anything like Mum's. Matthew stared at her gentle features. He emptied his second cup ignoring the taste and the look of the liquid and stifled his gut reaction to vomit the liquid straight back out.

He took deep breaths after he'd finished.

To his dismay, the Jade took the cup from his hand and held it out as the companion poured the third helping.

The Jade placed her other hand on his shoulder as she handed him the cup. 'Will do you good, My Lord. Drink quickly, as you did just then.'

Matthew felt his guts churn. He took the third helping only because he didn't want any permanent damage to his hearing. He swallowed saliva nervously, before lifting the cup and drinking the liquid fast. He almost wrenched it out but managed to swallow before it left his throat. He dropped the empty cup from his trembling hand.

The Jade offered him a sweet.

'Sweeten ye buds with' t'finest honey butter. No biting now. Suck slow,' said the companion.

Matthew was glad of the salty sweet taste.

'Ayr ye go, see,' said the companion cheerfully smiling, her rounded cheeks beaming rosily. 'Aldun no'. Ye tek ker no' meh Brave Likkle Kildaan.'

'You speak... differently,' said Matthew, smiling.

'Oh, don't worry about Shasta. She's from the north,' explained the Jade. 'Shastas kind ruled the polar regions before the dark descended. Many wakings ago, her people retreated to the magic in Rosh,' she shook her head, 'Draje ransacked Rosh a waking ago. Shasta's kind were almost wiped out, if it had not been for our mothers. Shasta kept her colours. Long may she live, and may Ayla keep her as she is.'

'Bless 'e, Aarta,' said Shasta softly.

Matthew felt saddened. To both their surprise, he leaned over and kissed her cheek, before realising what he had done.

Shasta touched her cheek in amazement. 'Well'll be!'

Matthew left the tent in a hurry.

The commotion was welcome to Matthew's ears. Soldiers hurrying to their duties. Glowing arrows soaring to hit an enemy unseen in the distance. The Jade archers were taller and slimmer than their Darian brethren, he wondered how their diet was any different for their training. As he turned the corner of the encampment, he caught sight of Rose hovering above the hill's edge with the lady in the dark dress. He stepped aside to let two Jades pass him.

'Who is she?' he asked quickly.

They stopped in surprise.

'Ophelia is an Emerald Sister, My Lord,' said the other Jade Warrior. 'She has fought and succumbed a Siren Queen. Long may she live.'

'Long may she live,' he replied. This seemed to please them, and they continued walking to the Krill Tent.

An Emerald Sister? Probably a high-ranking position to be an emerald anybody, he supposed.

'EFFI TAR FER RENN,' echoed deep voices from above.

Matthew watched Rose spinning with Ophelia, releasing streaks of green fire at the distant enemy. The faster she spun, the thinner and brighter the fire became. How on hell did she do it? How did she get the bracelets to work? Would they work for him? Nah. He preferred the weight of his sword. Realising they needed him to fight, he moved quickly in the direction of the battle.

'Lord Matthew!'

Matthew turned. A familiar djinn was holding the reins of a mithrin, whilst guiding his own mithrin towards him.

'Feios, you've got Sidra!' he said, grinning.

'You heard me. How are you ears?' asked Feios.

'Perfect. Did you know they have a concoction that just un-popped-'

Feios didn't seem to want an explanation.

'Sidra is better now from her injuries,' said Feios. 'A relief to see you are too. I know you miss your mother, but you must silence your memories. She will want you to return alive. Sirens heard you last time and they will trick you. A million Hellsborn are heading this way. Magic needs every hand in battle, for even Jades cannot contain such a number.'

'A million-' Matthew drew breath. What is left to not to believe? He sighed, then climbed onto the saddle. Feios passed him a shield, which he had dropped on the second wave. Matthew eased his arm into the shield's handles, then lifted his arm a few times until his shoulder was comfortable with the weight. He reached inside the saddle strap and lifted the sword.

Sidra followed Feios towards the battlefield. Dark plants dimmed from their shimmering colours.

Suddenly, there was panic on higher ground.

'THE DARK LORD!' yelled a lookout.

'DRAFUS!' yelled another.

Hooves sped, taking Feios to his position.

'Beware the Epiradium,' said Teiaar, in his head.

Matthew glanced, but she'd gone. He urged Sidra to follow Feios. He had almost caught up when the sound overtook him.

Whuee-eee! Crack! Weeeee-eee!

Matthew turned his head. Osimion was in the air, spinning a whip around him. The faster he spun, the louder it whistled and the brighter it glowed. His two friends had whips too.

Coming down from the next hill, on Hellsborn mithrin, the Grim Leaders were alarmed. They backed away.

Crack!

Three heads flew with dark spatter.

Matthew was glad of his mask.

Osimion and his epiradium friends targeted Grim Cavalry. Vampires arrived to save one of the Grim Leaders. Osimion almost had him. Sirens attacked Osimion. Jades took to the sky to defend him.

Fighting was fierce. Matthew didn't want to risk Sidra in the thick of the Hellsborn. On his right, plant life snuffed out. Something was coming down the mountainside.

Matthew urged Sidra to turn. She was a good girl, heading towards it. Charrelles flew by, they were ignoring him.

'Stay where you are!' a whisper commanded in his thoughts.

Sidra sensed it, for she stopped.

He saw the streaking green glows before arrows struck sirens. He heard cries as charrelles claimed their own prizes.

Teiaar opened her arms wide.

'Effi tar fer renn nata nesh yee chass!' her whisper carried. The Charrelles were suddenly yanked together into a cluster over the spiked ground.

Aroosa and Ophelia fired together. Charrelles were ablaze. They fell, impaling on the spikes. There they burned, creating torches for the defenders to see more clearly.

Matthew focused his attention to the darkness. Somehow, he could tell Osimion was watching him. He didn't care for their concern. He will kill a deadheart lord. No doubt about it.

Hooves approached him. He rode faster towards the coming beast. Just before the edge of the dead vegetation, he ordered Sidra to stop. Dismounting, he turned Sidra and pushed her to go back.

Lord Drafus roared.

Mathew ran wide and swept down so his sword could cut the beast. Drafus didn't even flinch.

The moment is here, my dear Jades. You know what needs to be done!

Was that Osimion? What did he want?

Drafus was growing. Skin split for new fur. Bones snapped for bigger claws.

Matthew charged to behead it, slicing at the metamorphosing neck. The blade met no bone. The flesh closed. He thrust his sword again. Again, no effect.

Eyes of the Beast turned upon him.

'Can't you face me on two feet? Coward are you, Drafus? Coward Drafus. Coward Drafus.'

The roar nearly popped his ears. The stench was awful. Matthew was glad of his faceguard.

It came towards him. Matthew staggered backwards, toppling underneath Sidra. Sidra jumped, almost trampling him with her middle legs.

'I told you to go!' said Matthew, scrambling to his feet.

Sidra neighed, then hurried away.

The beast's growl was deeper now, the transmutation was almost complete. Large black fangs protruded from every angle of its mouth. They were not as big as Yandraago's, deadly all the same

The Beast jumped. Matthew dodged out of the way, then returned the sword at the creature. Drafus was ready to pounce. Something hit him, causing fur to burn in a green fire. Another green arrow slammed into its neck, jolting the beast, and saving Matthew from its jaw.

The Beast shook off the arrows.

Matthew charged. Ice struck his blade, as he delivered a blow to the beast's neck at the same wound. Dark blood gushed out.

Drafus staggered, clearly shaken.

Another ice arrow struck his hind, Beast Drafus roared again.

Hands grabbed hold of his arms and pulled him onto a mithrin. Loosh was steering. Osimion fired three times to allow some distance to come between him and the beast.

'Let me off. I had him,' shouted Matthew.

'Look again,' shouted Osimion.

Matthew turned his head to see Draconi and Grim surround the beast. Okay, so perhaps he hadn't seen that. They stopped behind the spikes.

Matthew dismounted to watch.

Osimion spun his finger in the air.

Rose hovered over the barricades in view of all to see. She raised her hand and released a dark green fireball.

The fireball hit the beast's neck, pushing it back. Evil crystals emanated darkly, absorbing her green fire into Drafus' own power. Still, he looked weakened.

Rose's voice echoed through the valley.

'HELLSBORN, WE'LL GIVE YOU MERCY. BEHOLD OUR LIGHT.' She raised her hands, '... AM ZIDD ZIDAAN YEE FIYO JADE FAR ETONA...'

A fireball threw Drafus.

The three armies cheered. Then charged with renewed energy. They tore the arriving Grim with sharp steel, clubs and battering shields.

Drafus was smaller now. And losing form. Each hit increased his transmutation. Suddenly, new horns grew to surround his dark crystals.

Rose's voice echoed louder, '... LAAGUSH NATA PELONA...'

Matthew ran to the vampire lord. Osimion cut him off.

Matthew tried to go round him. Osimion grabbed his arm. 'Lord Matthew, your beloved, Aroosa must do this for our people. She is queen now!'

Queen.

Rose was a queen. What on hell did that even mean?

The soldiers watched with bated breath.

'I want one of your epiradiums,' he said.

Osimion laughed. 'Training first.'

Matthew pulled a face, 'What training?'

Drafus was scrambling to his feet, the long black cloak disguised his injuries. The Draconi shuffled to shield him.

'EYANA AMINA... ELWEE NASS...'

The fourth bolt of fire shattered a horn. The fifth threw the lord against a Draconi.

'... FER AM FIM JADE FERANI!''

The Dark Lord's body jolted with the sixth blow. The seventh shattered his other horn.

Rose spun until her body turned hot. Green fire erupted like a raging tongue to engulf the Dark Lord. The fire grew brighter, setting vampires and zombies alight. When it went darker, only the dark lord still moved. The

Grim and Draconi were no more. The lord struggled. Dark crystals cracked. Fangs exploded. Dark eyes sank, leaving only a green void.

Drafus shrieked.

A bright green flash was followed by a white one, incinerating the newly arrived hellsborn.

All was quiet on the Venn Varda.

Everyone stared. Something changed in their eyes.

Matthew followed Osimion and Sidra through the gap, 'Let me make this clear,' he said, 'Rose is going home with me.'

'The war is far from over,' said Osimion, through his mask.

'You know what my mum said to me once? War never ends, it sleeps. In sleep, it mutates and possesses brainless minds, until hell breaks loose. What do I know about hell? Sure, this is literally hell-breaking-loose. A lot is at stake, I get it. Course, we'll help. We'll help your people become safe. Just as long as we all remember, when all this is done, Rose goes home with me,' said Matthew.

Osimion stopped and bowed quickly. All the Jades did, when Rose touched ground.

'Ophelia,' said Rose. 'Do you feel it? Draje is coming. His numbers are too great...'

Ophelia's eyes dimmed. They touched their palms. 'Yes,' said Ophelia, opening her eyes, 'Will it work?'

Rose frowned. 'I hope so. It calls to me through every bone in my body.'

'Then you must heed it,' said Ophelia, 'may Ayla keep you.'

'Wait a minute. You just got here. What calls you?' he asked quickly.

'Matthew, you shouldn't ask. They may be listening,' said Rose.

'Who?' asked Matthew.

'Sirens,' said her other friend.

How many bloody hell were there? Where could they be hiding?

Hooves drew near. Tefaan came to a halt. Sidra neighed, then licked Tefaan's face.

'Mount quickly, we join Ithrandir's cavalry,' said Osimion climbing behind Loosh. 'Draje is coming.'

'This nightmare is still going on!' moaned Matthew.

'Are you hoping for a quick end? The Army of Dead numbered six million. At the most, a million Hellsborn were expelled by our ancestors' hands. With the Red Army reduced to a battalion, it is only us and the Lemothinian Army that must stop millions of Hellsborn.'

'I hope your million is less than my million,' said Matthew, feeling exasperated. He veered Sidra to follow Tefaan.

Osimion waited for him to pull up by his side. 'We die to save the living.'

45

Eliza:

After entering the Imperial gates, Thyjiswyn galloped all the way to the Imperial Dome. Citizens of Ithfir had been scared, watching her pass by as she made her way through the city. It was over. Being a queen was done. Yep. This was an alien world. Alien people. Take from it the experience… and go home.

Home.

Tears fell.

Eliza hugged Thyjiswyn's neck, then hurried inside, the ruby lighting did nothing to stir the Bodysnatcher this time. Through the domed hall, her long red dress floated over smooth stoned floor. She was aware of the footsteps behind her as she headed towards her private chambers at the rear of the building.

The ladies put down their scrolls and followed her to her room, leaving Thallas standing alone in the hall. A maid and a servant bowed. They had cleaned the room in her absence.

'Athena, there will be many wounded coming home. See that the best practitioners are available, no expenses spared,' said Eliza.

The podgy lady nodded.

'Don't… let the crone here,' she said, tearfully angry.

The ladies glanced at the podgy one. She nodded again.

Eliza spotted the large poster bed in the centre of her grand bedroom. It was draped in a thin red veil from the tops of the bed posts. One side was tied back to expose the welcoming decor on the mattress.

Eliza sighed.

She would miss this. The ensuite was the best she had ever seen, with soap that squeezed from fake fruit. And so many jets that covered all of her body. The bed had layers upon layers of frilled silk and velvet pillows, some with embroidered patterns and some elegant with prints. Each a different shade of red that coordinated with a sheet or a blanket. The fluffy rug on the floor were real furs, which had appalled her when she was told, but then the nun had promised her it was from an animal that died naturally. It was an honour for the animal to serve the Imperial bedroom. She could live with that. It was so soft and cosy to her feet. On the wall, small, recessed crystals scattered little images of an ancient time on the ceiling. Eddie would have loved this. It was a luxury like no other! She imagined that none other than Her Majesty the Queen of England would have anything else as extravagant, or maybe Hollywood, the White House, or the kings of the Middle East - then again maybe not!

She caught sight of her reflection. She looked ill. Her eyes were sunken. Her face was as pale as the Ithfirians themselves, yellow with worry. Was it her remorse that weakened the queen's powers? Or was it the queen draining both? Maybe it was a good thing. Let that horrible woman withdraw deep inside, never to reappear!

Would they give her something for a migraine?

How could she face them? Will they even want to? Oh! Those poor soldiers.

'This is why science is so much better than politics,' she exhaled. 'Safe and reliable. No lying, no backstabbing-oh God. What have I done? I should never have come here.'

Eliza kicked off her comfortable heeled boots and dropped herself face forward on the bed. The delightful softness folded itself around her shape. She let her hand slide over the cool silk, then gripped the sheets, pulling one to cover her face.

'My Queen.'

Eliza waited for the servant to leave.

'Would you drink some wine, My Queen?' asked the Maid.

'No.'

'I would not ask, but I see our mother in you. It is fermented with our best fruit and… from a very old recipe from my mother,' said the maid, nervously.

Eliza sighed. She took the glass.

The maid waited until she drank it all.

'My Queen, would you like nourishment prepared for you?' croaked the maid shyly.

'No – thank you. Just… see to those coming home,' she said, hoarsely.

Double doors closed softly.

46

Arif:

Arif felt safe now. He didn't know why. Since they were still exposed between the cities. They had taken a path to the East, moving upwards as the ground ascended into a long steep climb. Sometime later, the ground levelled off for a short while before descending. A crimson glow seemed to lighten the sky. Mafius turned his head to glance at him, he seemed surprised. As they drew near, a dust plume lifted into the air. Arif was glad for the mask, but the goggles needed wiping.

As he did, Mafius urged Zenith to slow. Zenith stopped altogether. Mafius was silent, probably overwhelmed by the scenery.

'Are they not meant to be here?' asked Arif.

'No, my lord.'

'What are they?' he asked.

'Drahoot!' gasped Mafius. 'I have seen these in scrolls. They are meant to be extinct. How can this be?'

The giant trunked flowers were closed, standing proudly against a dark sky, as if waiting for the moment Spring would appear. There were millions, lighting the land better than streetlights at home in dear England. Underneath, smaller flowers seemed to be basking in the light, their own colours shimmering in reds, purples, whites, and blues.

'If we should fail, we die knowing Ayla displayed splendour to give us hope in the eternal night,' said Mafius.

The mithrin slowly descended beneath the jungle of flowers.

'It's beautiful!' laughed Arif.

'Lord Arif, I know I want to stay and look upon this beauty forever smitten. We should take advantage of Nature's light, which may have been placed for our benefit. We should ride fast to the White City, so that we may fulfil our mission as soon as possible. We are needed on the frontline. The sooner we can get this over with, the sooner we can focus on the Army of Dead,' said Mafius.

Arif didn't mind the speed anymore. This was mithrin magic! The finest beasts on all Ethyrus! When the hill climbed, the Drahoot continued with them. Arif was sure it excited Zenith. She sped over an ancient riverbed, leaping over ditches, until at last they sighted the tall towers and grand walls of the Great White City. At the foot of the city, Drahoot plants gave the gates a wide berth.

Zenith slowed after climbing the hill. Arif stared at the magnanimous beauty of the White City. The White Towers were not as high as the Jade City, but they warned all who approached of the power that lay within its walls.

'Ayana Gelada!' shouted a voice.

Arif followed Mafius's gaze and saw a spy hole, small and square placed strategically into the white stone and just meters above them. How could anyone see who was behind it?

'Mafius Azura!' shouted Mafius.

'Aya Mafius! Sabur,' replied the guard with relief.

They heard shouts and a shuffle of feet from within the walls, a grinding noise grew louder until the gates opened wide.

Zenith trotted in. Two guards came running towards them and blocked their path. One primed his bow, pointing it at him.

'Ana multana yeea nozlurkinda Ilfa Taffy?' said the bowman.

Arif guessed he was asking what brought them to the White City. He was picking up words quite quickly now. Was he one of Leto's brothers? Should he ask? Would it be rude? 'I need a lesson in your culture,' he would say to Teiaar. She wouldn't say no to that, would she?

Would you learn anything?

'Arif, you're not going to remember this, because you never do. You didn't embarrass Mum and Dad because it was funny, you did it because you want to see me suffer. Nothing you ever do will make me suffer. There's nastier shit out there. I'm me, I can't change me. You're you, so be you. My brother. And when you're not stupid, you'll remember people love you.'

Arif's eyes burned. Had Eddie said that? How come he didn't remember? Hang on. Did someone hack his head? Did they pluck a memory he didn't know he had? Who did that?

He opened his water carrier and drank quickly. His throat ached.

I'm sorry Eddie. I'm going to make it up to you, I promise.

Arif wiped tears with his sleeve.

'What business have you in this city?' asked the guard Phiran quietly.

'Our business is our own,' Mafius said coldly.

'That's him. I recognise that tone like the missus on a good day. Very well Mafius! Be quick on your quest, for I shall be returning to Lemoff shortly. I hear it has survived Draje. This is great news! I must ensure my missus is okay,' he laughed jovially and moved out of the way to let them pass.

'Hallowed are the Eli!' he called after them.

'Hallowed are the lazy bones,' replied Mafius.

Mafius led the way over a gentle sloping road, cobbled with white stones that shone like they were newly laid. The city seemed proudly cared for by its visiting caretakers, with a list of names scrawled on each street. Arif couldn't help admiring the spotless buildings and clean roads. Like Aran Daran and the other two cities in Ethyrus, all the stones of the buildings radiated in the true colours of the city. Stone light made it feel like the sun was in the sky. Wide roads took them all the way up to the Grand Oval Building.

How come there were no signs of any Hellsborn in this city? Were they afraid to come this far? Or was it heavily protected?

No lights in any window. The white towers seemed eerily quiet. If no one lived up there, who repaired them? They seemed well preserved.

Zenith neighed gently as they arrived at an Oval Building. A guard came running down the stairs from the entrance and helped Arif down from Zethrin with his gentle hands. He took hold of Zethrin's reins.

'Where are you taking her?' he asked. Another guard took hold of the reins from Mafius.

'To be fed and cared for, My Lord,' replied the Ithfirian guard softly, lowering his head as if a king had spoken. 'They will be here upon your return.'

The Ithfirians led the two animals towards the end of the courtyard where Arif saw for the first time a dozen stables were already occupied by mithrin and labourers. They were obviously doing a very thorough job here in the White City!

As they neared the top of the stairs, two guards tilted their spears blocking their path.

'Ayana Gelada?' asked the Guard gruffly, on the right. 'What business have you with the Eli?'

'Our business is our own,' replied Mafius curtly, and the two guards stepped aside to let them pass.

It's a password, thought Arif to himself. He ran up the remaining steps through the thick entrance doors.

'Hallowed are the Eli!' he heard the guards mutter as he passed.

'Hallowed are the lazy bones,' replied Mafius.

The doors were shut behind them. The passageway dimmed as the outside light was shut out. Wall torches burned strongly to compensate, though it must have been designed this way.

Mafius led Arif upwards, until they both arrived at a wide T-junction where steel barriers cut both sides. He peered into the depths. And was amazed to see that the lower level was densely occupied by slim giants in hooded white gowns. The giants were either reading something he couldn't see or were sat meditating. The silence was so deafening, that Arif would never have guessed anyone was in the building if he closed his eyes, let alone hundreds of giants.

Mafius pulled him closer towards him.

'I don't know if you are already aware, but the Eli have to be addressed altogether by yourself,' he whispered in his ear. 'They are a collective and make decisions in this manner. There are no singular leaders, or privy councils and there haven't been any since the Great Revolt. I would advise you to take the staircase on the right, it is better perceived by the Eli if you address them directly from their right.

'I don't know what advice to give you, considering the circumstances, My Lord, for what you aspire to achieve has not been done since the ancient times. I wish you well regardless. Speak from your heart Lord Arif, they will hearten when you are honest and sincere.'

'Right then... er thank you Mafius,' said Arif. He was very nervous now.

His heart pounded at the thought of addressing all the Eli together at one time, as he reluctantly walked to the descending staircase on the right. To his surprise, the stairs were made from emerald coloured glass and there did not seem to be anything for him to hold. There wasn't even anything to hold the staircase in the air – it just hung there!

He stopped at the top, frowning and bewildered. He wasn't comfortable that the stairs were made of glass. He never liked the ones in the Mall either, he imagined the glass breaking and ripping through his skin as he plummeted. This glass seemed stronger somehow, but it was a long way down!

Mafius laughed. 'It is safe, Lord Arif. The steps are not unworthy of their maker. If it may please you, keep yourself positioned in the centre as you make your descent. I shall follow closely behind.'

'Thanks, Mafius,' he said.

He did exactly that. Shuffling to the centre of the stairs, he took his first step. The gaps between each step had looked too large, but it seemed to have adjusted for him. He gathered speed until he had passed the curve and came face to face with Eli.

They stopped their prayers and turned to face him in unison. Then they bowed in one sweeping move before raising their heads again, looking down at his small figure. The great hall suddenly felt short of oxygen. He took long breaths to slow his heartbeat. Just as he was about to say something, they spoke as one resonating voice:

'Welcome to Thespa, the White City on Ethyrus. Take from our gardens our best. Arif make your rest. Join us and be blessed. Forget the Hellsborn King, betrayal of djinn upon djinn, calamity from sin. We lose to win.'

Okay. They knew his name. Of course, they knew his name. This was not going to be easy. Speak from your heart, Mafius had said. Was it even worthwhile giving a speech? They weren't bothered about the fact that their whole planet was sitting in absolute darkness, ruled by bloodsuckers. If the Damned won, there would be no White City. He remembered the Draconi, the distorted and deformed images of their former selves. They had once been the Eli, now they were the walking slaves to the dark lords. He could not let that happen to these people.

'Citizens of Thespa… may I compliment you on such a fine city. The years must have been kind, if you hadn't noticed, your arses seem to have rubbed the stone into lumps, don't tell me it's comfortable. Your world does seem slightly neglected. But it must have been fabulous one time. That tells me you must have been a great people. And now you've shut yourselves in here, like the world doesn't matter. But it does matter, because the world is still revolving around you, and your impact on it is still happening even if you are not contributing. I have a feeling you struggle to forgive yourselves... for something. I don't know. You must have done something bad. Maybe lots of things bad. And now you're full of guilt. Maybe, this is all your fault. Maybe, it isn't. I mean, where I come from, we believe things happen to teach us a lesson, you know. Once the lesson is learned, we adapt and apply the lesson to our lives. Mostly it is to show people kindness, and sometimes it is to build a better home, or a better family. I respect your commitment to asking God to forgive you... noble. Isn't it stupid though? Don't you think you've taken it a bit too far? Can't you just do a fast or something? We have Ramadan, maybe you just need a holy month? I mean, I don't understand why you can't end this whole nightmare. My friends and I have travelled from Earth – we've seen shit no one would ever believe. Hell shit. Evil shit. My brother is tiny compared to you. It's not easy being a human. But we fight. Matthew's mum has cancer, he's here, fighting for you. I got my sisters and my brothers out there doing crazy shit. I am asking you as an Adam – I mean Adam's descendant...   to implore you, to make right for yourselves and everyone – giants, and djinn. Because this is - kind of - spilling into my world now, don't get me wrong we want to help and we are helping, but we also want to go home. So come and save Ethyrus. At least, help us do that if you can't be asked getting off the lumps up your arses. Say it. Let my ears and the ears of Ethyrus bear witness to… the depth of your suicidal insanity. So, what's it going to be?'

Complete silence.

'What about Rosh?' he asked.

Heads turned. It felt creepy. But creepy good! He had their attention.

'I'm told the Eli were praying when Draje ransacked the city. Though YOU might think this is honourable… It's a bloody travesty! Only 7000 Jenn SURVIVED from a population of 30,000! Did you even think about that? Don't they matter to you? Please do take the time from your important prayers to remember how your people had to be carried out… because they couldn't be bothered to lift a finger? I mean I couldn't believe it when I heard them talking. That is just downright disgraceful. How -'

'Lord Arif!'

'…YOU'D JUST BOTHERED…'

'LORD ARIF!'

'…eh?'

Mafius straightened away from his ear. 'Ears of Ethyrus!' He was grinning. 'They have begun their deliberations, My Lord.'

'They are? Wha-? But they're not speaking,' he said.

'Eli have mastered telepathy to inhibit eavesdropping on their deliberations. We are extremely fortunate that they are deliberating at all. Normally they fall asleep. But Ears of Ethyrus must have heard,' Mafius said with a laugh.

The silence was boring. Giants who barely blink were of no use to anyone, he was sure. Where were their weapons? What was Wyfzira expecting from them? Arif sat down on the steps. Mafius joined him, digging out a dry bread biscuit from a parcel in his pocket. He broke it in half and offered a piece. Arif took it and thanked him.

It melted in his mouth. The weird hot sweetness hit his taste buds. His tongue became sore from the heat. He wished he had Hathor's Tree with him now. A nice meal would help the time pass by, something like a chicken fillet burger and chips. Some juicy fresh strawberries and ice cream would be excellent as a dessert... or would he rather have a banana...

The Eli turned as one.

Arif stood up with Mafius.

Lights dimmed, making their creepy eyes even more creepy. Arif wondered if he had carried his father's laser measurement and was brave enough to use it on the Eli, he could prove that they were almost four and a half times the size of a human! Yet the tall figures of the Eli, were not bulky like the Draconi. No, their figures made them appear as if they had been stretched somehow.

They moved, creating a small circle between them.

Suddenly, their words echoed in unison more resolutely this time.

'Come forth Mafius, son of Leficus and Lemithicana, We respect the coming of the Metava and the words of the kildana, we hear the awakening of the elder. Though we fear only Aa'la, we agree not to disagree. We see what you have seen. We hear what we chose not to hear. And the loss of the City of Rosh, still tender with regret, a tragedy we should not forget. Come forth Little Braves, we ascend. We go to war!'

Relief washed over him. Arif hurried to follow Mafius down the stairs and into the circle. A gentle grinding noise accompanied the rumble. Arif looked up and saw the domed roof had begun to rotate to one side. The shape of the night sky changed from the picture of a moon to a complete dark circle.

When the rumbling finally stopped, a long arm hauled his body under an armpit. The gentle hum became a deep chorus resonating louder.

'Aaaaaaaaaaa - yyy – ll – aaAAAAAAAAA!'

The white marbled floor was slipping away. Further and further, they climbed, leaving the safety of the brightly lit hall. When it was no bigger than his fingertip and the air was thin, he felt the knot in his stomach tighten. The Eli changed direction, forcing him to swallow nausea.

He saw Mafius being held by another Eli, as they changed from vertical to horizontal position, Eli passed him fleetingly. How strange they must look now, the mighty blue warrior who was taller, was now petit in comparison to the Eli holding him.

The Eli shifted his position as if to show the wondrous sight unfolding around him. To his amazement, he spotted many other domes all along the Great White City opening and releasing giant white beings into the pitch-black sky.

47

Matthew:

Matthew tried hard to avert his eyes from the dying Darian. He could tell from the look in their eyes, it was heart-breaking for Loosh and Osimion. So, not just a comrade. These people were meant to live for a Millenia, according to this solar system's measurements, whatever that was. To have such a long bond and then to experience death – especially as immortals - it must be harder than a human death, he was sure.

It was extraordinary to see them recite for him. Exactly how many light years was this world from Earth? On an alien world, he had witnessed aliens giving last rites to their dying.

A Jade confirmed to an Ithfirian commander that 'many sirens were killed' by the queen and Aifa. Who was Aifa? Rose seemed to have made a full recovery since Dozukh Fort. Dozukh Fort still gave him shivers.

Matthew waited until Sidra was ready to move. He passed through the spiked barricades and weaved his way out, avoiding anything that could harm her.

From this vantage point, Matthew could see down Death Valley to the Venn Varda. Yellow torches were coming slowly, dotting every hill. Millions, Osimion had said. This was now believable. Zombies led by Grim Leaders. Every Grim Leader had a vampire master, and the masters served the lords. How did sirens fit into this hierarchy? Thankfully, he couldn't see Draconi. There could be a few out there in the dark.

Why would deadhearts need drums? He was thinking this, when Feios came closer and told him the vampires use drums to control the zombies.

'Why?' he asked.

'Lesser demons are controlled by hellsborn sound,' said Feios. 'We hear a drumbeat. They hear commands.'

'So...' Matthew thought about it, 'Is there any way we can change these... I mean... Militarily, we should use all means... Can we... control it?'

Feios chortled. 'Lord Matthew, the things we have tried.'

Right. This wasn't the first war, for them. But if drums control zombies, surely knowing how hellsborn hearing works might help them to learn how to turn it to their benefit? Right? Makes sense. These people depend on magic, maybe they need a completely different view? Elly would say so. Queen of Ithfir. Yep. Ask Elly first chance he gets. This shit can't reach Earth. Just... can't.

'Mage of Daraan, Lemoff, Ithfir and Clayborn,' called Osimion loudly from somewhere along his right, 'Wear your masks and goggles, do not remove them for any reason. We are all that there is between our beloved cities and the impending doom that threatens ALL LIFE. I need not ask you to fight very hard... for I know that all of you have already done so and that you will continue to do so... but I ASK THAT YOU FIGHT WITH THE LOVE OF YOUR LORD AND KIN; YOUR BELOVED CITIES HELD FIRMLY IN YOUR HEARTS... so that you may survive this night. Abaddon cannot return to our world. The outcast king - and the master he serves - will have no hellsborn from us!'

There was a cheer of agreement from the cavalry and the soldiers amassed behind them.

Howls arose from the Damned.

A bugle was sounded to drown it out. Front lines moved into the valley. Their purpose was to win the next hill and hold it. A high-ranking vampire was there, one they could probe when captured. Then they would kill it. Senior Jades were forbidden to go in case it was a siren trap.

The Damned were spilling down from the hills.

Osimion raised his hand.

Streaks of green soared to reach the target, giving quick illumination to the dangers rushing towards him. Explosions rocked the adjoining hills, still the hellsborn eyes came.

Matthew waited for the wobbler and the one with jaw in jaw.

Ice arrows hit both at the same time.

Matthew watched them crumble, then glanced backwards. Somewhere behind the spiked barricades was Aiden firing relentlessly, having perfected archery skills. That kid was something else since he stepped foot on this planet. He smiled.

Osimion lowered his arm and the cavalry charged forward, with microwire tied from saddle to saddle, it couldn't be seen, but it could slice through anybody that came in its way. Matthew hoped they stayed away from him.

Sidra was surrounded. Matthew gripped his sword tightly and thrashed their hellsborn jaws to stop Sidra getting bitten. Sidra kicked two behind him, she kept jostling her position to ensure he could face them.

A green arrow caught one he missed. 'Fetasha!' he ordered. Sidra charged down the slope at speed. Mowing the dead was satisfying. Behind him, Torros and his soldiers were more than capable of beheading the flattened Grim.

The rolling hum from Darian machinery was above him now. The manufactured arrows somehow incinerated zombies, what was in the steel? Was it magic, or just a chemical reaction? Why did Jade arrows illuminate deep green and Ithfirian arrows glow red? Jade arrows had more luck incinerating vampires. No. If there was someone counting the statistical probabilities of Eddie's bow, they'd know he had more success with his arrows. Gosh. Why didn't he pick a bow back in the Diadromos?

The roar drew his attention.

Matthew raced to defend Loosh. He liked the look of Loosh's scythe, he was using it like an extended golf club, smashing Grim heads before they got close. His own sword was great, it seemed to have a life of its own. But having a bow, now that would be awesome.

The humming stopped. The next volleys were hand pulled; red, blue, green and ice rained down on the throats of the walking dead.

They were on the next hill now. Matthew's job was to ensure the Damned didn't cut them off in the valleys. He paused only to look in marvel of the Jades spinning their bodies in the air, using epiradiums to behead hundreds at a time. And Azurans releasing fireballs at the hilltops they hoped to capture.

When Osimion froze, so did the Jade commanders. Matthew turned to see what they were looking at. Even though it was dark, he heard the rumble coming from the distant mountains.

'It's Draje,' said Teiaar, landing momentarily. 'Order everyone to pull back.'

'Quickly now!' shouted Osimion, as he landed.

The commanders of the Four Armies hurried to shout the retreat.

As he swung the scythe into the throat of another Grim, Matthew saw him.

The large black shape amongst the yellow torches was unmistakably a dark lord. Osimion had unsheathed his sword, trying to buy time for the retreating fighters moving their way through the spikes. Feios went to aid those fixing the barricades. Liyoot and Loosh kept the Grim away.

Matthew steered Sidra to charge towards Draje, ramming and trampling the Damned. Matthew kicked the occasional one, to avoid their jaws. It was reckless, he knew, but the sooner these demons died, the sooner he would get home. He had covered quite some distance when Sidra slowed.

Sidra came to a complete stop at a small ditch. Matthew egged her on, but she neighed protest. She sensed overwhelming danger from the Dark Lord, if not the glaring Grim Leaders by his side. Suddenly, he realised he'd made a mistake. Aiden may not be able to fire as far, and Sidra having stopped may have been a good thing. 'Come here, you scumbag,' he whispered.

It was odd to see the Grim pass by, no longer paying any attention to him. Draje had seen him now.

Matthew raised his left index finger to his throat and mimed slicing it.

Draje sneered, leaping from his hells-born mithrin.

'Back Sidra,' shouted Matthew, Sidra turned and galloped like her life depended on it.

Heavy thuds behind him told him Draje was now a beast.

Sidra took him through the scattered Grim not caring if any were trampled. When he caught sight of the green torches, he urged Sidra to slow. And stood up, balancing on the saddle. 'Eddie... I need your arrows now!' he yelled.

The beast Draje knocked two Darian riders and trampled a zombie.

Hellsborn came charging. Liyoot and Nethrin cut them down.

Matthew jumped down. 'Fetasha Sidra! Fetasha!' he said, pushing her away.

Sidra galloped to safety.

Matthew raised his sword. Ice arrows caught his blade. The chill passed through to the hilt.

Bless our kid!

An ice arrow slammed into beast's upper back. Draje howled but managed to shake it off. Matthew thrust his sword into the beast's neck. The beast lifted.

Matthew didn't see the claw. He fell to the ground hard.

The claw nearly landed on him, Matthew rolled and got to his feet. He was unarmed. He watched the Beast stomp, trying to shake off his sword. It looked like the beast was losing shape, but the fur grew again. The hide stretched, bones cracked, muscles thickened, the head grew and grew.

Hands hooked his arm and knee, hauling him onto a saddle. Hooves hammered dirt. Diyafa held him tightly, whilst Deffi steered the mithrin through a gap to safety.

When they reached Teiaar, there was no denying the epiradium Jades were weakened from Draje's proximity.

They shouted with urgency now, telling all to fortify their breached defences.

Osimion's raspy breathing was showing it was taking all of his effort to compose himself.

'It's the dark crystals, isn't it?' asked Matthew.

'Draje has picked off strategic fireborns who gave power to his dark flame. We lost Jades, Azurans and Rozinians. Draje is strong, but we are together.'

'Can we really hold this hill?' asked Matthew.

'We have no choice,' said Deffi.

'Though Draje is not making sense. Why attack before using your best?' asked Osimion of Teiaar.

'His best? What do you mean his best?' asked Matthew.

'He means. where are his sirens?' said Teiaar.

'Matthew, did you see his hellstone?' asked the kid.

'Left chest. He moved and I missed it,' gasped Matthew. 'When he's on fours, it moves underneath him. He's covered it with fur now, I doubt you'll see it.'

'I'll get him,' the kid said.

Matthew was sure he believed that. 'The Jades say he's stronger than Yandraago,' he said. 'Yandraago was a nightmare. Draje has weakened everyone.'

'Draje feeds on the powerful,' said the kid.

'Well, there's plenty around,' said Matthew. 'Just look. You want me to tell them to get back? They're holding the barricades. We need them. Eddie, look at me. You read a lot. You know a lot. I reckon you might have an idea what weakens that zombie fuckface. Just tell me how to kill it.'

'You sure you saw only one under his shoulder, how far down was it?' asked the kid.

'Armpit. Why, what are you thinking?' asked Matthew.

'I was thinking the hellstone might have some significance of being there,' said the kid.

'Posterior and middle cerebral arteries,' said Matthew.

'He has another hellstone,' said the kid.

'Crap,' breathed Matthew.

The Darian machinery pumped the skies again with arrows. Arrows felled Grim but had no effect on the giant nightmare.

With Matthew's sword still protruding from his body, the beast Draje charged to the spiked barricades, bending the little ones with the weight of his claws. Bigger spikes drove into his body, Draje pressed on, bending the spikes until they were uprooted.

Feios yelled to say Draje was clearing a path for his minions!

'AARTA! MAGE! DRAFF E KAND EHUD! ALWA KIFF! ALWA KIFF!' Teiaar shouted at the top of her voice, running behind the archers.

Magic arrows hit Draje from all directions. Draje was unhindered. Senior Jades spun in the air, launching fire from their bodies. Green fireballs ripped into his neck, but the North Lord was determined.

Another row of spikes was uprooted.

A green shield rose to the sky. Osimion and the senior jades had their eyes closed, they were chanting a spell.

Draje charged, ramming his head into the wall of green fire. The crackling was deafening.

Panicked cries spread through the defenders.

Matthew faced his rage, determined to end his thirst for blood. Draje pressed slowly the monstrous head against the green shield. The crackling grew intense, Draje withdrew when his fur caught on fire. For a moment, it seemed like Draje was in intense pain, Matthew hoped he would transform back so he could kill him. But then Draje straightened, bringing his whole body to the green firewall, slowly his monstrous head began to sink inside the shield.

Everyone held their breath. When they saw his neck, soldiers and Jades ran out of fear.

'Yee-eassss!' hissed Draje.

Matthew picked up a spear and drove it straight through its tongue.

It would buy them a minute.

No honourable vow to preserve the sanctity of life could be asked of Draje, he was here to kill all. Hell's lord hellbent on their destruction.

'He draws strength from our fear,' Matthew shouted. No sooner had he spoken, did the head return through the shield.

The green shield collapsed.

Grim were charging.

Jade arrows struck fast. Darian soldiers lined up to protect the archers.

Ice arrows slammed into Draje's neck. Flesh crumbled off. Another hit his forehead.

Good on you, Eddie.

Ophelia took to the air with the Jade Sister Fellowship. Her beam of energy was joined by Teiaar's and Aifa's.

Matthew put his mask and goggles back on and hurried to help the defenders. Someone tossed himself a sword. He found himself fighting with Ithfirian soldiers. He aimed for necks, just like the Ithfirians were doing. The Grim were slipping past them.

Matthew kicked one to land on a spike. There it writhed until he chopped its neck.

Suddenly, the soldiers were retreating. Matthew turned to look, the beam from the Jades had turned darker. The Beast Draje was stretching, like he was enjoying it. Osimion looked panicked. He threw a shield into the beam.

Teiaar and Ophelia fell. Jades took to the sky to catch them.

An ice arrow struck a dark crystal.

Draje roared, but the loss of a crystal transformed that part of his body. Draje staggered, he picked up a dark crystal shard and swallowed it.

Getting it to stretch, that's what they needed to do. Matthew wanted to see if Teiaar was okay, but the zombies kept coming. An Ithfirian soldier shouted to stay close. He was working a routine with Torros, getting the damned towards the spikes, where he could impale it and let Torros do the beheading.

Holding his armpit, Draje headed to the Darians. Matthew watched the poor soldier's head being lifted. Draje bit down on another's neck, causing panic among the Darians. The infected trembled. More violently.

His new hellspawn set fire to the Darian machinery.

Draje wanted more.

'Teiaar, tell me you're okay,' he whispered.

'Matthew, we can't hold him. He is too powerful. Get back,' she whispered in his thoughts.

Oh crap.

Where was Rose?

Draje was the beast again, advancing through their defences. Defeat was facing them all now. The Ithfirians were fighting to the end.

Then he saw it. The kid frozen. Draje heading towards him.

'Eddie!' yelled Matthew. He ran through the spikes.

Herionus landed beside the kid. He stretched onto his hind legs. A pulse of bright light burst from his chest.

'Herionus!' he laughed. How the-? He looked well.

The Grim were running.

Matthew couldn't believe it.

Draje seemed shaken, taking steps back.

Then he roared.

Matthew covered his ears.

Herionus sent another pulse of light. It was brighter than the first.

The dead and their cavalry retreated again.

Herionus pulsed again.

A poisoned arrow hurtled towards Herionus.

The kid struck it down with his own.

Draje shrieked. Six riders charged to surround their lord.

Behind the kid, light grew as something passed over them. They were fast. Lots of them.

Grim panicked. The dark mithrins turned to flee.

Matthew withdrew to higher ground. The scene was extraordinary! Glowing giants flew to hearten everyone's soul. Was that Arif with the blue haired guy, he looked so tiny. An army flew over the battlefield. Were these what made the Draconi? They were not hunched monsters. They were slim and graceful.

Draje was shrinking. What weakened him, was it Herionus or the giants? Why? How was this possible?

'The Eli -here?' gasped a soldier.

'Praise be to Ayla!' exclaimed another.

Wind howled as they flew faster over the barricades. Eli dodged poisoned arrows. Two vampires took to the sky in rage, but they were touched by the Eli, and they fell. One only a few feet from Matthew. No eyes remained in its sockets. Its skin had shrivelled. He watched it turn to stone.

When he looked up, he saw the Eli taking their light to a neighbouring hill, to the fleeing vampires.

The four armies were chanting now. 'Night to light, gentle to might, hallowed the Eli!'

But the flying giants stopped there. And turned back. The Eli carrying Arif landed. Another lowered his friend. 'That was cool Mafius,' Arif said. 'Matthew! Is that Draje?'

'You have no idea,' laughed Matthew.

'Is that Herionus? I thought he was sick?' said Arif.

'Jades must have fixed him. Why aren't the Eli killing the lot of them? If you have a death touch, you've got to kill them all,' groaned Matthew.

Arif shrugged. 'We have to be grateful. We get a breather.'

Matthew followed Arif to the wounded Dark Lord, Arif opened his vessel, splashing water over his sword.

Teiaar drew close. Mafius came to stand beside him.

The senior Jades stayed at a distance, on order from Ophelia, who watched grimly beside Osimion.

Draje gave no sense of what he was planning. Or did he know this was the end? His drool-covered fangs were grinding inside his mouth.

'Keep back, Aiden,' warned Arif.

'We hear you. We smell you. Would we not anticipate this moment?' sneered Draje.

Matthew became aware of his heart pounding. 'What did he mean by that?'

'Back!' commanded Teiaar.

Jade commanders hastily obeyed.

'He is coming,' sneered Draje. 'You will wish you had offered your necks to me.'

'Bring it,' said Arif, driving his sword into Draje. On withdrawal, the wound sealed immediately.

Draje rose to his feet.

Everyone stepped back. Matthew yanked Arif quickly when he saw Draje spit.

A large spear impaled Draje into the ground. A second and a third spear pinned him tightly, soaking the ground with his poisonous blood.

Draje suddenly looked exhausted.

'Do not be deceived. This demon has escaped before,' called Osimion, to the soldiers who wanted to harm him.

'Arif, it's not our debt that must be paid today,' said Matthew quickly.

Arif seemed to get it. 'Yeah. We shouldn't deny our friends justice to their tormentor.'

Draje tilted with a sneer.

The spears wobbled. Chains rattled.

The Jades were whispering their spells with their eyes closed.

Ithrandir turned to say something to Osimion.

'Arif. Can I have any water, I must have dropped mine?' said the Kid.

'Think I've lost mine too,' said Matthew.

Arif lifted the carrier off his shoulder and passed it to his brother. 'Eddie, I'm glad he's better. But where's Herionus gone?'

Eddie seemed surprised his brother asked. He looked round, 'It's too dangerous here,' he said.

The poor kid's lips were dry, but he still offered him a drink first.

Matthew gulped it down quickly, then passed it back. 'Okay. So, they kill him, but we chop his head off. I'll do it. He's got to be dead dead. That last vampire killed six soldiers.'

'I agree. Who gets to kill him… General Ithrandir?' asked Arif.

Ithrandir turned from Osimion, 'Alas, this one, has blood debt to our emerald friends, and those from the North.'

'Teiaar-?' said Arif, turning around.

'Ophelia,' she suggested.

Everyone turned to look at Ophelia. She was mortified. 'Ask not. He is waiting for an elder to venture close. One feed will be catastrophic.'

'Kildana!' bellowed Osimion.

Matthew turned.

The kid was talking to the kneeling lord. He hadn't seen the spikes were no longer in the ground. Draje had broken free.

'No-Eddie!' bellowed Arif.

Matthew ran. And yanked the kid by his arm.

'Are you out of your mind?' shouted Arif. 'What the hell goes through-?'

'Arif,' gasped Matthew. He couldn't believe it. Draje was drinking from his water vessel.

The Jades froze watching his mouth and throat melt. His skin was rosey, his eyes no longer dark, but an incandescent shadow of an existence long ago. His eyes never left the kid as his body crumbled into dust.

'Ayla's beard!' whispered Loosh.

'The bane of Ethyrus is no more?' gasped Teiaar.

'Bane of Ethyrus no more!' shouted a commander. His shout was copied by many who came running to check for themselves.

'What did you do?' gasped Ophelia.

'I gave him water,' said the kid.

'You gave him Ayla's tears. And he drank it-Draje the North Lord, Ransacker of Rosh, Tirris, Arcadeon… the Soul-Snatching Demon of Ethyrus?'

'He said his name was Graco,' said Kid.

'Who?' he asked.

'Him,' said Kid.

'Why would that… thing… tell you anything?' asked Arif.

'He asked me to ask him,' said Kid.

'Who?'

'George,' said the kid.

'Who is George?' yelled Arif.

'My friend,' said the kid.

'We have a George on this planet?' asked Matthew, studying the faces of those around him. They all had glowing eyes.

'I wasn't in danger,' said Eddy.

'That was a killing machine. From Hell! Course you were in danger. Every single one of us is in danger,' yelled Arif.

'He wanted a drink,' said Kid.

'Okay Red Riding Hood-the-wolf-is-not-a-wolf-idiot. You are no longer allowed one thousand yards of any deadheart. Give Matthew your bow.'

'No.'

'Now!'

Aiden took off his bow.

'He's lost it completely,' said Arif, shaking his head.

'Eddie, what did you do to get Draje to kill himself?' asked Rose.

'Nowt,' shrugged the kid.

'Did he force you to give him a drink?' asked Teiaar.

'No.'

'Draje was weakened, yes. But he was not one to end his own life,' said Teiaar.

'George said to ask if his name was Graco, Lord Keeper of the Scimitaff,' said the kid. 'So, I did. Draje didn't answer. But his eyes turned white and pink. I asked Graco, are you thirsty? No. George told me to say, will you take a mouthful of mercy? That's it-that's what I said. Graco grabbed it and drank really fast.'

Ophelia's chest rose with disbelief. Then growing alarm, but Matthew couldn't tell what they were talking about in their heads, even Teiaar seemed to be part of their conversation. Senior Jades surrounded them in a tight circle.

Suddenly, the ground shook. The rumbling drew closer.

Teiaar shouted for everyone to get to higher ground.

The soldiers ran up the slopes just in time. Waves crashed as they turned the corner. Glowing water pushed it's through the valley depths, rolling and tossing rocks as it passed. Matthew watched the bodies float by, so many of them. The Grim were silenced forever.

'Woah,' exclaimed Arif.

'Over gullies and dusty plains, the Army of Dead will be carried. Bringing an end to fear we endured,' said Eddy, quietly.

The kid had read it somewhere.

Matthew couldn't believe it. Rose must have done this. Rose. He whooped with joy, shaking Nethrin and Feios to laugh with him.

The Jades did rejoice, hugging each other with tears. Ithrandir laughed once his trusted lieutenant confirmed what Matthew already knew. Then all his soldiers celebrated with Ithfirian beer.

'Is this the end?' gasped Teiaar.

'No! This is not the end. We have a vinx,' said Aifa. 'And if she is not ended, this will all be for nothing.'

'Tell me, how does a child control a Narthrin?' asked Osimion, turning quickly.

'I don't control Herionus,' said the kid, with surprise.

'He doesn't. Herionus helped us all against Yandraago,' said Matthew.

'Where is it?' asked Osimion.

Kid shrugged.

'Child, you stood an inch from the Hellsborn lord… with no fear. How long have you been seeing this ghost?' asked Osimion.

'A while,' said the kid.

'Since you were infected?' asked Osimion.

'No.'

'Since Vinx Fell? How long is your while?'

'Since… around… I arrived?' said the kid, his face turning red.

'Since…' Osimion was startled. He looked to Teiaar.

Teiaar swallowed. 'Lord Aiden talked to himself quite often. Wyfzira thought it insignificant.'

Rose touched the ground. Matthew went to her but was blocked by Izmilla and Aifa. They were speaking to her without their mouths.

'Mage of the Jade,' said Osimion.

Matthew turned to see him glaring at Nethrin.

'It is true, he is cursed since before the White City. The Eli gave no indication this to be an infiltration, or any dark spells,' said Nethrin.

'Is that good?' asked Matthew.

Osimion gasped. 'Have the cogs of our elite lost sense? Eli are not without flaw. We have a Narthrin, when no creature survives in the wild.'

'Eli have never allowed shadows past their gates,' said Feios.

'Feios, Disciple of the Emerald Flame, do you stake your honour on this claim?' shouted Osimion.

Rose moved into the circle.

Feios' chest rose.

'George is not a shadow,' said the kid, staring at the ground.

'What seems to be the problem?' asked Matthew.

'The problem, Mage, is that the kildana has been to three cities and who knows how that has exposed us? The cursed are designs of higher demons.'

'Now hold on a minute,' said Arif. 'Don't talk about my brother like that. He's not cursed, he's just stupid.'

'A dark lord does not deplete the entire Emerald Elite one minute, to drink death the next,' said Osimion.

'What're you on about?' asked Matthew.

'Yeah. What are you implying?' asked Arif.

'Arif, no one is saying Eddie is possessed,' said Rose quickly. 'We have to make sure Eddie is not in danger. A vinx has been confirmed. She is far more deadly than Draje.'

'You're suggesting… he's being controlled by sirens?' Arif pulled a face. 'Sis, do you even hear yourself?'

'Look where we are. You see that glow, that's the Jade City. Aside from the fact, Draje was within sight of Aran Daran, he made it clear Hellsborn want to reach Earth,' said Rose. 'A Hellsborn most powerful lord commits suicide after smashing our defences and depleting all of us? Tell me how that makes sense?'

'It doesn't,' admitted Arif.

'You will be guarded at all times,' said Osimion. 'You will wear an All Seer. For your protection.'

The Jades placed a jewelled band on the kid's forehead. The metal sunk into his flesh, causing Eddie to cry out.

'Get it off!' shouted Matthew.

'I'll give him something for the pain. He won't feel any discomfort,' said Rose.

'This isn't right, Rose!' said Matthew.

'This isn't right, my queen!' she yelled, growing. 'Do not think for one minute, the dead are gone. We are all that stands between extinction of all species. We saved only today! Jades had armoury more advanced than Earth will have in 1000 years. It failed. They use magic to save their species. Look at this world. Earth is not this lucky.'

Three giants broke away from the Eli crowd and approached them. They knelt on one knee.

'Childlord Aa-riff,' said the Eli. 'We have tasted, and we have tested. We were hands that extirpated humans. Then we were hands that saved your species. We make errors and we do them well. Eli do not mourn the weight of the past. Eli do not break for mortal plight. Eli do not fear the end, nor the devil's blight. We remembered Rosh and voted. Luck saved the hour.'

He stood up to leave, then faltered. 'Childlord, Eli resent humankind. You are surprisingly tongued for such a fragile being. No doubt, the one who sent you knew it would intrigue. We had no wish to permit your return. Words you imparted for your ghost and Narthrin gave sway. You thrust yourself into Hell's breath and offer mercy. That grants you and your kin sanctuary at our gates.'

Teiaar spoke quickly, 'Mage of Light, will you not help us defeat the Damned? You know our struggles are not over.'

Eli were lifting off the ground.

'Children of Echira, Elissa and Delius, we removed the dire circumstances overwhelming you,' said the Eli.

The soldiers cheered.

'You are fools to rejoice.'

All fell quiet.

'The war you fear is upon you. Devils have sworn to take you. You have amnesty in each other until he awakens. Giving light to see your beloved, is the pitiful dice tossed by a vain soul with a sick mind. We have lived this war. It will not end until it ends. Seek light and darkness comes. And it comes. And it comes.'

'Seek we will,' promised Osimion, to cheers from the Daraan.

The Eli floated upwards to his kind.

Matthew watched the white-hooded giants disappear over the dark peak of the mountain. They were heading North-East, maybe to stop at Lemoff?

When they disappeared, the horn sounded loud with alarm.

Another Dead Army.

48

Eliza:

Eliza closed her eyes, seeing an image of the Darian City, the Jades staring down at her with those glowing green eyes.

She moaned.

How stupid was this queen? How could she have let herself get suckered by Thallas? The crone. Oh, God. Day one should have warned her. That crone had lied before her very eyes, and she stuck up for him.

Eliza sat up.

So, this is all her fault. She should have sacked him. Humiliated Thallas first, then she wouldn't have been in this mess. So, what if she had been knocked down by a vampire. Eliza is not one to be knocked down. Eliza gets up and punches Denise Rafferty and knocks her to the floor. That's what Eliza should have done. Got up and found a way to kill that monster.

Why didn't she think this at the time? How did she get here? She remembered attacking the Dark Lord and seeing him deflect her fire. The rest of it seemed to be a blur. She could not remember how she got to Aran Daran. The image of Thallas asking her to give the order to attack the City of Aran Daran came flooding back. How could a mighty queen thousands of years old have allowed this to happen?

The Great Red Queen had been respected and feared! Izan had given his life for Ithfiria, to protect the Jenn from the Damned - to protect Ithfir! Such a brave and courageous man, such a noble and respected man, his would be the highest honour. Hers would be the greatest shame. Now... no one will care for her. Not the soldiers she betrayed, nor the soldiers injured. Everyone had given her so much honour and love. All gone. Even the newfound allies in the Jade City. One minute she was glorious, next minute she was after their blood!

Oh God. How could she be so stupid?

Could she not just say this is all just a super-big-might-as-well-curl-up-and-die kind of mistake! She will leave without setting foot in the Jade City. Would they drag her there to face trial? Oh, why couldn't she take these stupid rubies off?

It was like the bracelet was somehow fixed to her bone. The skin slid down, but the device wouldn't budge. Mum could take it off.

Tears rolled down the side of her face.

Izan had been nice, such a nice fellow. She had disrespected him, she was sure. Never mind anything else – so many anything elses – this was so bad to stomach.

Izan.

She wept uncontrollably.

A fist hammered on the door.

She was about to shout for the person to go away, when the knock came again.

Who could this be? It wouldn't be any servants; they would not be so brash.

It could be Ithrandir!

What would she say to General Ithrandir? How could she show her face now? Those gentle eyes would avoid her gaze.

She wiped her face quickly with a sheet. She stood up and glanced in the dresser mirror, straightening her hair and her clothes. Her makeup was skewed around the eyes. She wiped off the smear with a hand towel and spit. The eyes still looked puffy but presentable.

She sighed deeply.

The knock came again.

'Come in!' she said loudly, firming her cheeks.

The double doors opened and in came the commander.

'Oh, it's you-'

Eliza tried to hide her disappointment. She softened her voice.

'-come in! It's Commander Soahn – isn't it?'

'Yes, My Queen...' his voice wavered as he looked down on the ground.

He seemed troubled.

'Commander-?'

He glanced and seemed hesitant. Then looked sideways. Eliza saw the reflection of Thallas staring from the corridor.

She stepped back until his reflection was gone.

'Lord Thallas has requested your presence in the Imperial Hall, My Queen,' he said loudly. Then to Eliza's surprise, he turned sideways and whispered: 'Beware My Queen!' with his head still facing the ground.

He withdrew backwards through the double doors, taking hold of both door handles.

Eliza was shocked.

The commander lingered for his orders.

'T-t-tell him, I'll be there shortly,' she stammered.

The commander closed the doors.

Eliza paced the floor in panic. She fingered the red rubies from her necklace trying desperately to think of what Commander Soahn was trying to tell her. He had warned her. Her life was in danger! From what? From whom? The Darians could have killed her at their city; they had already rendered her powers useless. The Lemothinians she didn't know that well, besides they seemed harmless to her. Could it be General Ithrandir? Had he heard? No, he couldn't possibly kill her. They liked each other's company. Besides, he didn't seem the type... or, could he? She hadn't sensed anything untoward from him, but then again - would she have sensed anything? No, Ithrandir would never threaten her. Could it be that awful General Ingoliff? No, she distinctly remembered him tumbling over from his horse-thingy. He couldn't possibly have survived when it fell on him... even if he had, he'd be wounded.

It must be Thallas! He must be behind this. Thallas the Deceitful! The commander had been scared of saying something in his presence. Scared of Thallas? Thallas? No. No. Think. Think. He was the one who originally made her the Queen. It didn't make sense!

What have you got yourself into, Eliza? Why could you not have stayed with the others?

She breathed in long. And breathed out long. And again.

The rubies shone brighter and brighter. Her muscles thickened. She was growing. She kicked off her shoes and grabbed her staff. Eliza caught a glimpse of the Great Red Queen in the mirror, she seemed older than before.

She swung both doors wide with hardly any effort. And strode towards the Imperial Dome, fierce and regal.

On the right side of the hall, Ithfirians bowed down respectively. They seemed to be traders, all fifty of them. The left side remained empty, dark, and haunted by recent events.

Thallas lowered his head as their eyes connected. The commander came to stand by her.

No servants. She walked to her throne and sat down.

'Why have you summoned me, Thallas,' she asked.

'We have a visitor that requests your counsel, My Queen,' he said, snidely.

He was hiding his discomfort. Why would Thallas of all djinns, not want to be in her court. Could he be scared of her justice? The visitor… have the Jades already sent someone?

'My counsel? Who?'

In the far corner of the vast hall, emerging from the pillared corridor, she caught sight of the black figure entering her hall. Her neck turned cold, and her heart pounded.

'Soahn, take my staff and go to the Royal Tombs and lock the door. Do not let anyone in, unless he bleeds Feroshan,' she said, quietly.

'No, my queen.'

She turned her head, 'Go!'

Soahn ran. The crowd fell on the floor, their faces touching the ground and trembling with fear.

Thallas joined them.

His long strides came at speed, silently drawing power away from all crystals in the large domed hall, including those buried underneath. Lights flickered and went out. One light returned by the lifting of his hand. Footprints had stained the sanctified marbled floor.

Lord Greva stopped and tilted his head.

'YOU HAVE THE NERVE TO COME HERE!' her voice shook the building.

She summoned the power from underneath her feet and tossed her rage, the fireballs knocked Greva backwards, but his crystal only grew. Was this how the sisters of Rozina had died? Betrayed by their own who desecrated holy ground, robbing them of the strength to defend sanctuaries where generations of mothers and mage had joined, giving thanks to the Almighty for the benevolence from their queen? This could only be the work of a vinx. Where was she? She fired again and he fell to the floor, yet she knew it was already too late. She had not sensed her. The hellspawn were in her city. Greva got to his feet, his eyes as dark as the devil she had faced an eon ago.

Ithfir was doomed.

Not by a long shot!

'Effi tar fer renn daffari yee!' she bellowed. The walls shook. Dark Lord continued towards her.

The next fireball threw to the bottom of the hall. Greva got up, unscathed. The queen continued firing. The fireballs sank into him and had no effect. The last time she had engaged a leader of a coven, her fire had been so intense it had consumed him.

He was closer now.

'Devil, nothing will save you. Not you, not the vinx, nor Dark King himself. STOP WHERE YOU ARE! I

AM THE GREAT RED QUEEN, I COMMAND YOU!'

His face filled with insidious fascination. 'Who is it that you think you are Thilgrid Eftienherr to command me?' he hissed.

The Great Red Queen stepped back.

'We know all of your names, and all of your hosts, all your power is undone,' he gestured with his hand towards the people lying on the floor, trembling, 'by your own.'

'True Ithfirians do not betray their own,' she said.

'In your eleventh host, you surrendered your throne for your sister Lecilvi and came to this colony world, to build a clone city, for cloned subjects. How wonderful it must have been under your reign, had the Dark King not come.'

'Bring your worst, Devil,' said the G.R.Q., glaring.

'Hell is in your home,' sneered Greva. 'You will be my vinx and devour their defences.'

'There it is. You want to be Dark King,' spat the queen. 'Adwa the Halfborn, I told him then as I tell you now, you will never kill him. I am no pet!'

'Many wakings ago, I tried entering this city. Angelfire was too strong. In your absence.' He tapped the floor with his foot. 'And now nothing. Could I remain unscathed if your powers had not been un…picked? Which of these foul-tasting morsels undermined your armies, and the cradle of all your power? Shall we ask your subjects?'

He floated to them.

They trembled and cried, still face down.

'O Ithfiria… who is greater… the Great Red Queen… or Me?' he said, smiling with glee.

'You are!' they whimpered. A moan erupted from the crouched.

'Who?'

'Lord Greva,' they said.

'Who is Lord Greva?'

'Lord and master!' they said.

'What shall I do with the queen?'

'We have no queen!' they cried. One began wailing.

Eliza felt the overwhelming dismay wash away the queen's remaining strength. She fell back on the throne, her staff falling from her hand. Her ears ringing with betrayal.

'Renounced by your own people.' His shape drifted towards her. 'One you can save,' he sneered.

Eliza looked into his pitch-black eyes and lifted her chin, 'You shall not have the pleasure. They will hunt you down and rid your curse. Lord no more, master of none.' She kicked Greva down the step and stood up. 'I do not submit to you! I shall NEVER! Heed my words, I will be your undoing. By Echira, YOO-OU shall diminish!'

Eliza heard the roar, before she was thrown over the throne, into a corner. Greva's nails bit into her chest, she grabbed his throat and grew until he was lifted off the ground. It took all the queen's strength to snap his neck.

She staggered back to her throne. Gasping. She had minutes, at the most.

'Ithfir, my kin, a disease has infected you and it is not hellsborn blood. It is a curse as long as time. You are condemned if you take no action.'

She felt the cold steel stab into her. She gasped, feeling her size shrink rapidly as the sword again pushed through her organs and slid out of her rib cage. She crushed the hellsborn's neck before she fell. She felt her fire retreating to the rubies. Deep inside her mind, Eliza grasped the fading powers of the Great Red Queen and reached outwards spanning the lands for the one who would understand. *Arif, restore the heart. You have the eye. You know you can. Hurry. Save me. Near the crystal … ruby.*

'I wanted to take my time with you,' he snarled, cracking his bones in place.

He would feed until she died. It was odd that she felt so calm.

She felt the tug as the fangs sunk into her neck, spreading numbness through her whole body. Eliza was slowly being drained by a devil spawn. The devil pulled her blood faster, flooding her body with hellseed.

Her heartbeat slowed.

And then it stopped.

49

Arif:

They had been fighting for an hour. Arif had just thrust his sword into the chest of a large deformed Grim, when it happened.

He felt a tingle and his heart slowed, making him weaker.

'Arif... hear me...'

The whisper sent a cold shiver through his bones.

Then he saw her. Eliza staring at him with that same look when they rushed to the hospital for her aunt's collapse. Except, she was dragging her body to a pillar. Struggling to breathe. Bleeding from her stomach. A vampire lord grabbed her head and bit into her neck. Her eyes glowed red and then he was looking through her eyes.

Djinns crouched forward, with their hands clasped behind their necks.

Thallas was kneeling, he felt her pity for him.

A snarling whisper echoed inside her mind; Do you really think I could enter the Imperial Hall... and remain unscathed... Who undermined you before your powers peaked?

He was looking at Eliza again. '... save me...' she whispered, '...restore heart... they fear... You have the eye... you know you can... bring crystal... ruby-'

Her eyes flickered. He felt her cold. Her heartbeat slowed.

'Eliza! Eliza!' he shouted.

Their footsteps came running.

'Arif!' he heard Matthew yell. Swords struck bone as they defended him from the Grim around him.

He was with her again. Eliza closed her eyes.

The last beat caused his own to pound harder.

No.

No.

He gasped.

The sudden chill shocked him to his body. He dropped his shield.

'Arif! What the hell?'

His friend's face was clueless.

Oh God.

He felt hands lifting him away. They carried him behind the barricades.

'It's Eliza...' he sobbed. Turning, he grabbed Matthew's sleeve to pull him closer. He drank from his flask to untighten his throat.

'What the hell?' his friend said. 'Do you want to sit this out? There's a tent back there, the ladies are nice. They'll give you soup.'

He managed to utter it, 'Matthew, she-she's... gone!'

Matthew looked at him pitifully, 'Yeah. We lost loads. Look, Teiaar's around. I've seen the way you look at her. You're not falling for someone else, now are you?'

They placed him on his feet.

'No. Matthew. Eliza is gone. Eliza!' he said tearfully.

Matthew stared as if he'd gone mad.

Arif took deep breaths.

Feios hurried over. 'You saw an apparition-'

'I have something to do...' Arif said. He ran towards the senior Jades.

He heard Matthew following. He heard him panting. Maybe he shouldn't have said it before it was verified. He hoped it wasn't true. He shouldn't believe it.

But he felt it. Oh God he felt it.

Arif reached the Jade Sisters who were conversing with an older djinn. 'Teiaar, it's Eliza... you've got to help us. My best friend... she's-she's been killed... by Greva.'

There was a moments silence as they absorbed his words.

Teiaar looked horrified.

The Emerald friend straightened, inhaling, 'I see this image in your mind... Are you sure of the source?'

'Yes. I don't know,' he choked.

Aroosa landed. Poor sis, with all her powers she looked confused.

'Lord Arif saw an apparition,' said Feios. 'I felt it. It came not from darkness, but darkness was stifling.'

Arif remembered suddenly the urgency in Eliza's message. 'I saw him... coming towards her. She said his name was Greva... Greva said Thallas undermined the Great Red Queen's powers before they peaked. Eliza fought him. Then she was on the floor. Greva.... I felt her heartbeat stop...' Arif watched his friend.

'Ithfirian Queens are renowned for projecting apparitions,' said Teiaar.

'Get lost,' said Matthew.

Ithrandir hurried towards them.

Osimion turned. 'Mage Feroshan. The joy you had at seeing the Shaara, I would deprive you not. Yet here we are. The Mage of the Jade express our deepest sorrow.'

'Our queen is... slain? When?' he said aghast.

'She reached out to the boy with her final breaths... history has recorded this occurrence by an ancient predecessor. Also, we have... tested the south with our collective thoughts,' said Osimion.

'And what did you find?'

Osimion cleared his throat, 'Only... grieving.'

Ithrandir fell to his knees, wide eyed with shock.

He wished he had known about them.

'Atrocious,' said the old man scowling. 'Tell me child, did you see where this struggle took place?'

'The giant hall in the Red City... Teiaar called it the Imperial Hall?' said Arif straightening his position.

Teiaar's eyes dimmed, as she faced due South.

'Impossible!' Osimion said, turning to the old man. 'The Imperial Hall is protected by angel shields. Odana, a dark lord couldn't have-?'

'I have no doubt... Lord Arif has indeed seen a tragedy,' said the one called Ophelia, frowning.

Odana's jaw parted, he suddenly looked pale. 'Nothing would surprise me with Thallas,' he uttered.

'Fuck off Arif, tell me it's not true?' sobbed Matthew.

Arif pulled him into a hug, he held him until Matthew's breath returned. Then led him to sit down on the ground.

'Breathe,' said Teiaar.

Aroosa brought water to his lips. 'Drink this Matthew,' she pleaded.

Drinking didn't stop him crying, 'It's stupid. No! I haven't even seen it with my own eyes. We're not going to believe it until it's proven. We can't…'

Arif nodded, 'Yeah.'

'What did Elly say exactly?' said Matthew, sniffling.

'We're going to get him, I promise,' Arif told him.

'Apparitions heed warning of some great importance,' said Odana.

'Focus on the now,' Eliza used to tell him.

Arif straightened quickly. 'Eliza said… warned me about a heart… of Ethyrus! I have to get going. Feios, you take me back… there's this place… I can't remember… called… Naf-Naf-something that me-and-Liyoot visited on our way here… a mantle made of stones. You have to take me there now!'

'Nafarinus?' asked Feios. He shot a look to Ophelia.

Arif clicked his fingers. 'Yes! Nafarinus – we need to be there like yesterday!'

'You must go with them,' said Ophelia.

Matthew got up quickly. 'If Greva is there, he's mine. I'm going to kill that bastard.'

'If I recall correctly, Greva was blessed with two sets of parents, incredibly wealthy,' said Feios. 'He was no child out of wedlock. A bastard would be insulted.'

They climbed onto Sidra.

Sidra galloped at speed up the rugged terrain, leaving the bright lit camp to absolute darkness, then to a hill covered in glowing purple and pink flowers. When they reached the ruins, glowing white flowers dominated nature and the forgotten dwellings. The higher they climbed, the bigger the ruins, the rockier it became with scattered stones. The top of the hill was surrounded by an ancient stone wall.

Feios pulled on Sidra's reins. She halted.

Arif slid off the saddle. Feios turned his head listening to see if they were followed.

'What is it?' asked Matthew.

'Eliza wanted me to restore the Heart of Ethyrus,' he said, leaping from stone to stone, to climb the hill of stones. When a stone slipped, he reached out and Matthew grabbed him, steadying his balance. They moved upwards as fast as they could.

'What is this Heart of Ethyrus?' asked Matthew.

Feios flew past them, landing on a ledge. He turned again to stare at the darkness, then at the lower hills covered with glowing red plants.

'Don't know -' Arif leaned forward again as the stones under his feet began to slide, '-watch yourself!' he shouted.

'I'm here,' said Matthew, from a big stone. 'How're you going to restore it?'

Arif straightened at the top. 'Eliza thinks it's important. She told us to hurry. So, obviously that Greva doesn't want us to. So, we're going to do it.'

Matthew frowned, placing his hand on a large stone, he pulled himself upwards. He straightened on top of the old wall. 'Must've been giants who built this, have you seen size of these stones?'

Arif smiled, watching his friend. 'We have Egypt,' he said.

'Stonehenge,' said Matthew.

Arif laughed.

'Quiet!' urged Feios.

They followed his gaze.

Below in the flatland, colourful plants were snuffed of light. A dark path was extending towards them at great speed, bringing a rumbling louder.

'We have company!' shouted Feios, drawing his sword.

Arif gripped Matthew's sleeve. Matthew turned and spoke quickly: 'Do what you have to do and do it quickly! Have you got the water carrier?'

'It's in my saddle.'

Matthew slipped and slid off the stones to reach the bottom. He grabbed his sword from the saddle and pulled out his own water carrier. He opened the cap with a hurry and washed his blade.

'Feios, your sword!' he cried.

They could hear the rumbling getting louder by the second.

Feios held out his sword and Matthew splashed it in a hurry. The rumbling was deafening. The beast leaping at great strides, seemed smaller and had thinner legs, yet it still brought death upon nature as it passed.

Feios and Matthew ran to block its path. Matthew pointed his sword and shouted.

It leaped over him, onto the stone filled slope.

Feios threw his sword.

Arif hurried to the platform of stones.

The round ledge was covered in strange scribing. He placed the crystal into the groove. It stayed. The sound of their cries made him feel desperate. What and how was he meant to make this happen? He lifted the crystal and turned it upside down. It wouldn't sit in the groove. Arif turned it round again, fully conscious that danger was ever close, threatening the life of his dear friend.

'Truth be spoken with the eye,' he whispered.

The beast roared. Matthew cried out.

Arif turned and ran back to the slope.

The beast was half-way up. With Matthew's sword sticking out of its hind leg, the beast roared, trying to shake it out. It was imbedded too deep. For a moment, Arif thought it might buy him some time. But the beast used its chin and claws to hoist itself up.

Matthew and Feios clambered after it.

The Beast sent a landslide of stones towards its pursuers. Feios stabbed at its other leg. It roared again. Then kicked another landslide.

Feios slipped all the way to the bottom.

'Arif! What're you doing? He's coming!' yelled Matthew.

Arif ran back to the mantle of stones.

What truth? What truth? What truth? He uttered many things. Bringing his face closer to the crystal, he tried to study the stone engraving, but he couldn't see much in the dark. Maybe just find a clue, any clue.

'What did you do to my cousin?' he heard Matthew yell.

The beast growled.

Then he remembered.

Arif leaned closer to the crystal. And whispered.

The crystal came alive again. The grooves illuminated one by one, spreading faster until all the scribing on the hilltop were illuminated. The humming made Arif step back with surprise. Something vibrated underneath his feet.

'IT'S WORKING!' he shouted over the din. What was working, he didn't know.

The ground shook.

Arif backed away. The mantle lifted, awakening something deep inside the hill.

'I stabbed Greva's head,' shouted Matthew, reaching the top of the stones. 'But he's scarpered.'

'Where?' shouted Arif.

'My Lords, Greva heard this noise and was frightened. Perhaps we should also retreat,' said Feios.

Cracks in the ground grew bigger around them. Vibrations were disturbing the ruins. Arif followed Feios and Matthew, leaping down from stone to stone. It was odd, but it seemed like the stones were rearranging themselves around him. Arif almost missed a ledge, but Feios grabbed his elbow, preventing his fall.

The air was getting lighter. A white beam shot up from behind them. Arif felt the vibrations in his eardrums. The blinding white light came from a green casing rising from the platform. The crystal at the top, pulsing like a growing beacon.

Who knew?

The rumbling was too loud, Sidra was neighing with fright. The earthquakes were getting longer, like a mountain was lifting off the planet.

Arif hurried to Sidra. Feios reached down and lifted him up into the middle saddle.

They galloped until they had reached some distance from the growing hill. Then they stopped to look back at the sliding dirt. Large pillars rose to a tremendous height replacing the hill with a strange giant temple.

Arif stared in awe. The green casing had been the tip of a dome. The humming grew louder. The pulses of the crystal swept the sky until it was a constant beam, so bright that even when he looked at the ground, he had to shield his eyes.

Then everything went dark.

Still.

Quiet.

'It hasn't worked?' muttered Matthew.

'I think it has!' said Arif excitedly, staring upwards. 'Look!'

The sky had cracked! The giant cracks were white edged and spreading.

'Ayla have mercy!' exclaimed Feios.

It was a little scary, watching cracks push out dark fragments, like a lake sweeping sheets of ice. The white dissolved too. Tarry droplets were followed by heavy glowing rain.

Feios jumped off his saddle. Arif followed Matthew. They stood on the slope, watching the rainfall dwindle.

Suddenly, stars twinkled. Three moons cast wondrous light.

Feios gasped, wide eyed. Tears brimmed at his large green eyes.

They had a sky!

A sky!

'You did it, Arif,' said Matthew, with disbelief.

'Flippinora!' laughed Arif.

50

Aiden:

'Our Lord, complete our light for us. Indeed, you have power over all things,' whispered Aiden.

The city's towers seemed to have brightened in the past hour, though he knew they were empty.

Aiden drank from the water vessel. Then breathed deeply for relief, as he pondered those words. 'They resent humankind,' he said, quietly.

'Could they end this? Is that the question in your mind? Do you think the Jades have not already tried?' asked George.

'You tell me,' he said, hoarsely.

'A story for another time,' said George.

'Why would they tell me?' asked Aiden.

'Who knows? The Eli are a strange tribe. They have a long memory of that day when they lost their rank to a clayborn, but a very short one for their own shortcomings,' said George.

The sound of cheers rose from the courtyard. George peered through the arched window. 'Only fools celebrate when we are in jeopardy. Taking down the

Great Red Queen was her first strike. Now she may grow with no balance to measure. The vinx plays the long game, steeped in treachery.'

'They have a right to celebrate,' heaved Aiden.

'Perhaps what we offered him was mercy after all.' George turned. His face stretched with pity. 'Is this not barbaric?'

His head had throbbed from the moment they bound the seer to his head. Pain throbbed down his spine. With each pulse, it took the breath from him. It now hurt his lungs and his legs at the same time. He picked up the leather sheath A wave of exhaustion swept through him. He was aware George was watching as he fastened it to his waist.

'The Jades of my day would not have done that to you,' said George.

'It's not their fault,' he whispered.

'You helped each one of them and tipped the balance weighed against all. And they will never know.'

'As it should be,' he whispered.

'Elahi, sit down before you fall,' said George.

'I have to be somewhere,' said Aiden.

'If one could end the inevitable with one swift strike. Temptation is a knife to cut a throat, be it a beast… or your own,' said George.

'What're you talking about?' said Aiden, picking up the bow.

'Oh come! This look I have seen in many. One strives to cheat an enemy. To end it all. A need to feed a beast weighing your heart,' said George.

'You can't read me, so you know squat,' said Aiden.

'I read you plenty of times. I do not need to read the history in your mind to pluck your strings. You woke the agriscylla because I teased you.'

Aiden thought about it. 'How did you know she'd be there?'

'History,' smiled George.

'So, it's from your time,' wheezed Aiden.

'An agriscylla hibernates to join its partner on another plane. You may wake it, but it is only truly awake when it has no course but to descend to this plane. Good thing it took its time,' said George.

'She's not dead,' said Aiden.

'Oh, she is dead, as are all Hellsborn. Chances are, it ate part of her. Then went to shut its eyes. She resurrected herself and ate the agriscylla.'

Aiden looked sharply. 'Is that possible?'

'Pray Elahi! Didn't you know? Slain by hand the hellsborn body dies. And her darkness would have transferred to another siren, who would have taken months to learn of her powers. But eaten by beast, no! Selwa returns. She will be more powerful now,' said George.

'All the more reason,' said Aiden.

'Let Jades do what Jades do. You will not find her,' said George, glaring.

'I don't need anyone,' said Aiden.

'Elahi!' scolded George. 'You cannot possess a djinn to kill the queen of hell.'

'I'm not listening to you,' said Aiden, straightening the bow's strap over his shoulder.

A ghostly hand wrapped over his wrist, sending a chill through his arm.

'You cannot,' pleaded George.

'Why?' Aiden inhaled the sob.

'Never mind the vinx, her sirens will see you as clear as day,' said George.

Another wave of exhaustion forced him to sit on the bed. 'You don't know that.'

'Why are you not afraid of her?' asked George.

'I fear only Allah,' he whispered.

'Don't run, don't hide should be the whisper in your mind. She is the Fallen's revenge. You must open as slow as an Elyssian Raimundii flower, otherwise she will eat you. Literally, eat you. And your entire planet. Even the Dark King and the mighty armies of the gods struggled to contain her first incarnation. She is the most evil, treacherous thing to walk on any world. Do not hurry blindly.'

Aiden shrugged. 'Okay.'

'Devoid of fear is no doubt your master's doing. Yet I heard him warn you not to confront the vinx.'

Aiden looked sharply.

'Malachi's skills were forged before your galaxy was born,' said George. 'A high djinn and a secretive Fianehedrin who body hop, tame monsters, create empires and destroy entire civilisations, all without breaking a covenant with People of Light harvesting your Clayborn souls. There is no greater tongue-smith. No greater fire than his hands. This Hellsborn contagion, Malachi fought. And lost.'

'Meaning?' he said.

'Malachi is there, and you are here. Has it never occurred to you to question why he sends you? Are you as expendable as a legionnaire without a garrison? Do you not think the dark king would have turned to ash by now, if a blade could end it all?'

The nerve of him!

'I think you died older. You're missing your own memories, did you know that?' wheezed Aiden, hotly.

'Pray Elahi, what were you thinking risking everything to allow strangers to resurrect a unicorn? To perform such a ritual, you let them into your mind.'

'I know what you are doing, George. You're annoying me to keep me awake. It's working. I'm annoyed,' chuckled Aiden.

'Malachi may have shielded you to the best of his ability, but who is to say what they learned?' said George.

'Are you saying I can't trust your nephew?' asked Aiden.

'Odana is my nephew. Yes, we are in the safest place in all Ethyrus. But the night was long. So long! What horrors have rooted here? What horrors have moulded my nephew of today?' asked George.

Aiden couldn't believe what he was hearing. 'So, you're saying I can't trust anyone?'

'Not a soul,' replied George.

'In your memory, there was a day when you were in pain. Your servant took off your shoes. You told him the Dark King with all his lords could not enter the Great Red City.' Aiden's eyes heated, 'Greva did.'

George shrugged. 'Most likely the vinx is behind it.'

Aiden passed a hand through his hair. 'I believed it. It's… my fault,' he whispered. If they found out, they would not speak to him. 'I shouldn't-I shouldn't have left her there,' whispered Aiden.

'I have said this before, a torchbearer's moulding will have come at a price. Lives have given… time and sacrifice,' said George.

'I didn't want it.' Air was crushing his lungs. Aiden got up and headed for the door.

'Victory demands patience to unwrap what one is taught. If the vinx learns that the Archdjinn trained you, sooner than he has prepared for. All deaths will be for nothing,' said George.

Aiden turned slowly. 'I don't want anyone... to die.'

'You are worthy. I see it now,' said George.

Aiden closed his eyes. 'Draje said Abaddon is coming,' he whispered. 'Teiaar said technology failed. You've seen magic fail. So many died. What will any of us do?'

'You are doing something by doing nothing,' said George. 'Conceal thyself. The opportunity will present itself.'

'If I stay, they'll stay,' whispered Aiden. 'This fight has to be... won... without needless loss of life.'

'As it should be.'

Aiden's throat tightened. 'I can't lose them, George.'

'I know.'

'It's my burden. If I survive, I would like to see you again. If I don't, then this is goodbye,' he whispered.

'Am I not a ghost who witnessed the suns in the sky? The miracles of mercy from a Clayborn soul? You put others before thyself, passing tests ancients designed. Let me help you,' said George.

'You won't even tell me your name,' said Aiden, sadly.

'I am committed,' replied George.

'To what?' he asked.

'To your will,' replied George.

Aiden opened his eyes. 'You're just saying that George.'

'Your cause is my cause. Your life is my Deathlife,' said George.

Aiden felt relief wash through him. 'Eliza deserves... justice,' he said.

'Part no shields when evil surrounds you, swift your blade as they blink,' said George.

Tears rolled down his cheek, 'I need a good friend. That's all.'

'Knights we are. All demons are anchored. Find anchors and break their moor. That is our focus. Not this moment. Not while you are softened by loss.' George sat down on the chair by the door. 'You march with light. We'll hold it high.'

It was strange to hear George speak like this, he sounded older, but looked the same.

'I'm meant to not show emotions, all I can think about is the what ifs,' he said, sniffling.

'Is every mission not a series of trials?' asked George.

Aiden felt the floor spinning. 'It hurts George,' he whispered.

George stood up. 'To the hall. Hold the walls, Elahi,' he commanded softly. 'One foot in her memory. And another. You are not alone. Did I not say I am with you until you die?'

Aiden focused on his breathing. He let the walls guide him, sometimes with both hands. The throbbing was followed by stronger pulsing pain. It felt like an age, passing over Oakenstone and marble floors, each step taking strength from his body. The doors flew open. He didn't think he used magic. Or maybe... There were no walls to hold. He saw the bench underneath the floating crystal birds.

Halfway there, Aiden collapsed.

51

Matthew:

Matthew was glad to step inside the Oval Dome. The air was cooler than outside, where the suns had conquered all, bringing Earth-like green to all the land. But when he saw Feios falter, he ran to reach the figure lying on the floor. 'Eddie!' he said.

The kid's eyes were closed. Matthew knelt to listen for breathing. The kid's breath sounded raspy.

'Eddie?' he said.

Her feet stopped beside him.

The kid opened his yes. 'Matthew, it hurts,' he whispered.

'Aiden, I gave you something for the pain,' said Rose, kneeling beside him.

Eddie closed his eyes.

'He's cold,' gasped Matthew.

Feios felt for his pulse. 'Fifty beats, his breathing is shallow. What is the normal heartbeat for a human child?'

'That's low. It should be seventy-seven at least,' said Matthew. 'Rose, what the hell is that thing?'

Rose straightened. 'Matthew, I-I didn't know.'

'Tell me how to get it off,' he told her.

'They whispered a spell. I can ask,' said Rose.

'Who put a seer on this child?' boomed a voice from behind.

Matthew turned.

The giant hurried quickly from the stairs.

'Lord Wyfzira. The Emerald Mage ordered it for his protection,' said Feios.

'Protection? A Seerlock? Come moments like this, Feios of Fenn, one wonders what is it that we suffer!' scolded Wyfzira. 'Where is he?'

'What is the matter, Lord Keeper?' said Osimion, coming in from the courtyard.

'Yes, pray tell, what is the matter, Emerald Mage?' said Wyfzira. One of his shoulders was higher than the other. 'A seer on a child?'

'For his protection. There are certain things we need to investigate,' said Osimion.

'I offer my deepest regret.' Wyfzira bent down to lift Eddie's eyelid.

Matthew could tell Rose was appalled, but he didn't want to look at her.

'A Seerlock protects one from a hostile mind,' said Osimion.

'Osimion is a young Emerald, by Jade standards. If he was not, perhaps he might have learned that a Seerlock was originally devised to limit telepathic connections by a hostile mind! Which this child is not, by any means. A Seerlock can be released by pressing thumb and finger on the green dots on the side, like this,' the seer hissed and released Eddie. Wyfzira lifted Eddie, 'I will carry him to the infirmary.'

Matthew picked up the contraption and followed.

52

Matthew didn't feel like talking. He must have nodded off, because the topic had changed and now shouting filled the streets. He couldn't see musical instruments, but it sounded mostly strings. He welcomed the drums when they started beating. Aran Daran was celebrating. He followed the boys to show his face, for the ones who he knew were okay. They were giving out food and drinks without any currency or barter. Storekeepers were too happy for Matthew's liking. The city guards were having dancing contests. As the day wore on, more of them came into Euthalia's chamber.

The third sun was in the sky. Every Jade and Daraan was either outside or standing on their balconies, waiting for the white sun to set. That part of the sky would turn violet, not deep red like the first one. When it disappeared, the blue sun would look green, this was the moment they wanted to celebrate. They had scrolls and books in their hands, to check if it was really like what the historians had written. In one of them towers, was the knobhead. He'd vacated the Oval Hall because he was asked to by the Senior Jades.

'Is this because Matthew had a go at him in the hospital?' asked Arif, chewing a cheeseburger.

'Yes, it was,' said Rose.

'Don't blame me,' retorted Matthew. 'You're the one mixed up in the Jades. I have no say in their matters.'

'You don't? Are you for real? First of all, you are Clayborn. Your biological composition gives you rank above all djinns. It's part of their belief systems. Just because you don't see it that way, doesn't mean all djinns don't. You have been splendidly heroic. Everyone is telling stories about you. Then you are related to the G.R.Q., which automatically propels you to the High Council of Jades. So, when you shouted that you didn't want Osimion within a mile of Aiden, of course they were going to take that seriously. They asked me how many miligildard is a mile, so I told them. Now Osimion is living in a tower one mile from here.'

'I never meant for him to move out,' said Matthew.

'I know that. Matthew, what did you think was going to happen?' asked Rose.

'I'll have a chat with Eddie. Then we'll sort it,' he promised.

It all made sense now. Why there were cities, aligned to different stars. There was something about this sun that was soothing. Or maybe it was a spell. Matthew wouldn't put it past them. The Jades had left them in peace, after the kid had woken up and cried in the infirmary.

Elly loved him. Elly loved everyone. Oh crap. How was he going to tell Tom? What would he say? A vampire walked in and killed her?

Matthew wished it had been him.

Tom, I am so so sorry. I left her there.

Mathew took deep breaths, listening to Wyfzira talk about the funeral process. The Jades had trooped in to listen, Matthew smiled for them. All was forgiven. He wished it was that easy. But the more he listened, the more his throat began to tighten. And then he couldn't look at any of them. Not even Arif. She was everyone's fault. Every one of them. Or maybe all his.

Elly.

Poor Elly.

Rose stared. Was she listening to his thoughts now? Maybe that contraption should be on her? No one should be in his head. No one.

Eddie came and sat beside him.

Ophelia sat too.

What the hell.

'Kildaan,' said Wyfzira, 'how are you feeling at this time?'

'Bromana japyasa Ehud Wyfzira,' said Aiden. 'Amra yee fer hyata.'

Ophelia laughed.

'You spoke Jenn with perfection,' said Wyfzira. He sighed. 'I have some news which may or may not comfort– depending on how you feel right now – Thallas was found. And had been chained. Why he was heading West, is strange.'

'Had?' asked Arif.

'He said they found him heading west,' said Matthew.

'No – I know that. He said – Wyfzira… you said had. Why?'

Wyfzira stared, then sighed. 'Ithfirians tracked the treacherous advisor. He surrendered. They dealt justice in the manner they saw fit. And interrogated him in the Ruins of the Old Scimitaff. The ancient senate. Thallas probably realised Ithrandir offered a kinder fate to that which waited for him in Ithfir, had the people decided. Ironic isn't it... Thallas wanted to die in an old Ithfirian relic, watching the setting of the crimson sun... the very sun that he tried his best to deny us all.'

'Thank God for that!' said Aroosa.

'I should have been there,' said Matthew.

'Would you have watched him die?' asked Ophelia.

'I don't know. The fact is, he was responsible for my cousin dying and no one bothered to ask me, so I'll never know, will I?' he said.

'No Darians were asked, we had no sway on the matter, Lord Matthew' said Ophelia.

'Did they tell you what Thallas said in the interrogation?' asked Arif.

Wyfzira sighed. 'Thallas confessed he undermined the Great Red Queen's powers from the onset, under instruction from Greva. His allegiance has spanned some years... he invited a siren into his grandparent's home, where she learned of a tunnel that passed the tombs to the Imperial Hall. He has been bleeding his people every time the drums thumped. And used their blood to weaken a path through the Angel Seals. From eleven descendants from the eleven queens preceding the Dark King. For this reason, Greva was able to enter. We are working with the Azurans on how to reverse this violation.'

'Where did Greva go?' asked Matthew.

'The North,' said Ophelia.

'No disrespect to you, I was asking Wyfzira,' said Matthew.

Aroosa leaned back in her chair.

'Reports say the North,' said Wyfzira.

'But you don't believe that do you?' asked Matthew. 'I saw you flinch. And I don't care what the official line is, I just want the truth. Where is the most-likeliest place Greva will go. Because I faced him once and he killed my cousin. I have a right to know.'

'Yes, you do,' said Wyfzira. 'Greva would go where the suns are the weakest. The furthest reach of Echira, Deelya and Elissa is the South Pole, knowing well that we do not yet have the resources to pursue him there. We do not. Patience, Lord Matthew. He will resurface, or we will build those resources to hunt him.'

'The reason why we said the North,' said Aroosa, 'is because we found a vinx nestled in the Venn Varda. Greva was seen before the attack on Ithfir, in her tent. The vinx has fled North.'

'So, you assumed Greva would follow. Instead of verifying it properly,' said Matthew.

'We are still verifying,' said Ophelia. 'But you are correct, we cannot reveal our true efforts while they are still in motion.'

'Thank you. That's all you had to say,' said Matthew.

53

Arif:

Aiden's bed in the Infirmary overlooked the Eastern side of the city. Arif couldn't stop staring out of the long windows. No more than a million, Wyfzira had said. Leaving three million zombies the vinx could use. He shouldn't be thinking about it. It was a glorious morning -a morning Eliza would never see. A tall tower reflected the green sun onto others and then received the reflection of the red and white suns. What a sight to see. Pity it was too hot to stay out too long.

The strange long-necked bird on the sill, sang like it had always lived with mornings.

'Sweet Elly, Clever Elly, Darling Elly, you left me too soon,' he whispered to the bird.

The bird took one look at him and flew away.

Eddie was better. Eliza would have chewed their ears for letting Osimion do that to him. He had to step up. Be better, she would say.

'I will be better,' he whispered, feeling his nostrils heat up.

After getting dressed, he had returned to the Infirmary. There seemed to be less distressed soldiers now, the Jades had been working hard all night. To his relief, Eddie was sitting up, talking to Matthew, who needed every kind word anyone could say to him. Wyfzira's doctor had wheeled in a contraption that showed an image like an X-Ray machine, but when he flicked the switch, it showed organs, and when he flicked it again, it showed poor circulation of energy inside Aiden's body. The doctor hooked up an 'infusion' to the sides of his head and over his heart, until he was satisfied the lines were moving upwards on his contraption.

They stayed up, all dusk, listening to the sounds from the ward, some quite heart-breaking. He had insisted Matthew take a walk to get a drink. There were no long nights, much to the delight of the people in the city, who kept thrusting strange drinks in flagons into his hands, every time he went outside for air. He became lightheaded and couldn't help thinking Mummyjaan would be annoyed, even though he knew she was on another planet. So, he politely declined any more. Matthew knocked them back and didn't seem any better for it. Poor thing would be a sorry state for a long time.

Getting Matthew home to his Mum, had seemed important yesterday, before he realised what state he was in. What if his Mum wasn't recovering? What would another loss do to him? Eddie woke up and Matthew cried with him.

Arif found himself walking as fast as he could away from the Infirmary, ignoring bodyguards who just attached themselves to him. He wandered through the hot city. When he returned, they were all gathered around Eddie's bed. Aroosa finished talking with the Jade Sisters.

521

Her eyebrows were tilted the same when Naneejee died.

A prayer was read by Odana in gratitude for a new morning. Then they ate pancakes provided by Hathor's Tree. The Daraan also wheeled in a trolley filled with triangle toast, bellclover honey, Shaimanni tea and marmalade porridge.

The old djinn, seemed quite fond of Eddie, passing him food to try. 'Nethrin found this Gogoplum growing outside the gates of the White City. It appears there were many blessings that we could not see while the world was dark. The veil is lifted, what a blessing it is. Don't you think it is huge?'

'Massive,' said Arif.

'It's almost like a fig, soft and very sweet,' said Eddie. 'You want to try some?'

Arif took a bite of the melon-sized fig. 'Tastes like mango,' he said, causing Eddie to giggle.

'That wasn't even a joke,' he said.

That brought a smile to Matthew's face.

'I thought I would let you know that Ithrandir has been elected last night as new Keeper of Ithfir,' said Odana.

'Who gives a shit?' said Matthew.

'Well, it makes sense,' said Arif. 'There's sure to be uncertainty after what happened. People need him to fill the vacuum, and who better to do the job? I like Ithrandir, he's noble. He knows his business.'

'Does he? Why didn't he know his own people would betray him? Betray Eliza?' asked Matthew.

He had a point.

'Ithrandir is probably asking the same questions,' said Aiden.

Arif nodded. 'It's hard not to judge people around us.'

'We shouldn't blame Ithrandir for what others did,' said Aiden.

'You're right. Yeah,' said Matthew. 'My head hurts just thinking about it.'

'So, who's made general then, to take his place?' asked Arif.

'A very fine young man called Soahn,' said Odana thoughtfully; 'two other commanders whose names escape me at this point. We shall be going there today.'

'We are?' said Sis, coming to attention.

Was she still listening to the banter of Darian folk with her new telepathic powers, or was she fully here because she felt bad about letting that knobhead hurt Eddie?

'Ithrandir has declared a week of mourning for the Great Red Queen. Her funeral procession will take place before she is laid to rest. The Jade Council will send their most influential dignitaries to pay their respects. Wyfzira will be there, as well as Teiaar, Ophelia, Feios and I suppose... yourselves. You will go won't you – good! The Jade Council regard you as our own. Before you leave us... you should know you are Friends of the Jades. May Ayla return you safely.'

Arif almost stopped breathing.

'Thank you, Odana,' said Sis, smiling.

Odana left the room after bowing to each of them.

'What does he mean before you leave us?' asked Aiden.

'He's expecting us to go home,' said Arif.

'When?' asked Matthew.

Arif swallowed for his dry throat, 'We should probably check if the door has opened. Ethyrus is restored.'

'I don't know if I want to go home,' sighed Aroosa. 'I like it here.'

Arif's eyes burned.

'Come now,' said Wyfzira cheerily beckoning with his arm pointing to the door, 'your hearts are deep in sorrow. It will be a while whence any recover. Be healed by any kind words we offer. May our memories forge eternal. That this day your dearly beloved bled for us.'

Ophelia led the way to a lower hall. They received applause from a tightly packed audience.

Teiaar looked busy, surrounded by Jades. How could she still be thinking about Hellsborn on a day like this? He crossed the floor and asked permission to speak to her. He guessed she was reading his mind, when her eyes dimmed. A smile grew slowly. He followed her to another table. There was no dancing this time, and he couldn't ask anything he wanted to ask because Matthew joined them. Then Aiden. Then everyone else. But she stayed with him, and her words were measured. He knew what she meant. She was probably wondering the same things he was.

And so, the evening passed into a celebratory atmosphere. Matthew drank Krill with his friends. Aiden mentioned that he felt hot and Deffi overheard. Minutes later, he brought them a jug filled with a strange green luminous drink.

'Is that slush?' he asked, blocking Aiden's hand from reaching it.

'This is Bimi,' said Deffi, grinning. 'It cools.'

'So, it is slush. Okay Eddie.' He let him take a glass.

Deffi poured eight glasses, since Teiaar, Nethrin and Diyafa were seated with them.

Aiden took a sip. 'It's not icy, it's fruity.' Aiden drank it fast.

Nethrin reached across the table. 'Don't -' but it was too late. Aiden had emptied the whole glass in one go!

Numpty's lips went blue.

Arif laughed.

'Eddie, you nutter!' laughed Aroosa.

'Deffi, you should know better!' scolded Teiaar.

She signalled to someone passing who gave her the shawl she was carrying. She wrapped the shawl around Aiden.

'Bimi is a powerful concoction which cools you one sip at a time,' said Teiaar, placing her arms around Aiden and squeezing to keep him warm. 'Diyafa, a glass of Olikuss juice. Add a few drops of Krill and bring it here swiftly.'

She was sharing her body heat.

Diyafa left in a hurry.

Matthew felt his forehead. 'He's cold. His skin feels clammy.'

Numpty was trembling.

'Does it feel cold?' asked Sis.

'J-j-just a l-l-litt-ttle,' stammered Aiden.

Diyafa returned with two glasses. He poured a few drops from the taller glass into the smaller one.

Her eyes wanted him to do it.

Arif took the glass and brought it to his brother's lips.

'This one you must drink fast, Lord Aiden,' urged Nethrin.

Aiden downed it fast. Seconds, later the glass was empty. His rigor had stopped.

Colour returned to his cheeks.

'Do you feel warm?' asked Teiaar.

'Yes. Your body is hot,' he said.

They laughed.

'Well,' he said. 'It looked like you were becoming an Azuran.'

They didn't laugh.

54

Aiden:

Arif was giddy comparing the white sun and the green sun to anyone who would listen as they climbed the hill for Ithfir. Aiden couldn't help feeling a sense of déjà vu every time he glanced at the sky. A green butterfly landed on his finger. When he peered closely, the fur was also purple. He whispered, 'Peace be upon you,' before lifting his hand, but it did not fly off. It landed on his knee and was quite content travelling with him to the Red City. He missed Herionus, he would return, he was sure. The one whose stomach was empty followed from a distance to his caravan. He was ignoring everyone. Matthew was entering the city responsible for betraying Eliza. It was tempting to lower his protection spell to tap into Matthew's thoughts, but that would risk everyone. There were eyes and ears everywhere. Ithfir could not be trusted. To his relief, Matthew didn't mind Feios walking up the cobbled road beside him. Feios probably heard everything Matthew was thinking about. Matthew was okay. He should be worrying about George, where was

527

he? It felt like he was close, like the corner of his eyes close, but so far, he hadn't seen him.

Ithfirians were determined to work outdoors and eat outdoors, just so they could watch Echira from crimson dawn to devil's dusk. Traders cut glasses and were fitting them to customers at the request of the new Keeper. 'Days are long on Ethyrus,' said the street trader, determined to sell him a pair of shades. 'Not so for Ithfirians. We count the time of Elissa before Echira as 'Shahar'. And when Echira sets, Daraan believe it is day, for Deelya has risen. Not so for Ithfir. We call the period of Deelya as 'gassac', meaning dusk. Wear this, witness the three sisters as Elissa sets. And rejoice for Echira!'

'Thank you, George,' he whispered.

The City of Ithfir looked less creepy in daylight. Shops and homes were no longer boarded. Homes needed rendering, and a fresh coat of paint. No dancing or singing, or welcoming traders, or returning fighters receiving the city's blessings. It was customary for a city in mourning to not speak, the trader had said. Aiden couldn't help wondering how much guilt they carried.

Feios seemed worried. The Emerald Elite had a meeting with Wyfzira behind closed doors. Everyone came out looking bruised, even Euthalia. 'We are at fault. Thallas's treachery ran deeper than we had believed. We should have acted,' Gisthenia had said to his sister. 'This is a huge setback, should Abaddon return.'

Aiden climbed the steps of the Imperial Hall and stepped into the cool hallway. People bowed and curtsied as they passed. Under the dome, the crowd parted down the middle respectfully, to allow them to reach their chairs. Somewhere, on the balcony, someone was weeping.

Aroosa took her place beside Ithrandir. Ithrandir waited for the Daraan and Lemothinian to be seated, then took a deep breath. 'Welcome Mage and Aarta of Echira, Elissa and Deelya, welcome Chosen Ones. There is sadness in Ethyrus. Though, our crimson sun can be seen like a dream, and Abaddon's curse has been lifted, our people weep for the fallen, and the sleeping eyes of our Great Red Queen. Eliza came to us on a wing of a prayer, salvation from Heaven. But we failed her in every way.' His voice broke. He took a sip of aylarhiyssa and continued, 'Ravaged her powers before she bloomed. Yet here we are beneath crimson skies, clouds above and blossom and spring, red birds returned, look up and see. Our hearts are burdened. For Eliza prevailed and delivered us free.'

When he heard the weeping, Aiden sobbed.

The old Aroosa would have needed to write a speech and question everyone beforehand how she sounded. Watching her, made Arif nervous, because he inhaled then sucked his lip.

'Ithfiria… what sorrow fills your hearts today,' began Aroosa. She raised her voice, 'We may feel we did not know Eliza Hughes, but Eliza knew us in her actions. For those deprived, let me tell you now, of who she was. Eliza was strong, reliable, filled with promise, joy and life… who cared and appreciated the natural world. This is why, she fought on the battlefield at Leybo's Cave. She was a friend and a sister… to everyone that caught her eye. Her kindness knew no bounds. Eliza came from a world with blue skies and a yellow sun, where trees waved in the breeze and the birds sang their song… to a world plagued by Hellsborn, where a terrifying beast launched upon us.'

Some gasped. Some moaned.

'Eliza was not perturbed,' continued Sis. 'She ensured the generals had an effective strategy to protect Lemoff. Though her powers were undone by insidious treachery, Eliza's vision guided us to end the curse plaguing Ethyrus. Now suns protect you and moons watch over you. We are eternally grateful to have known Eliza, host for the Great Mother Thilgrid Eftienherr. May they rest in peace.'

'Ameen,' said the crowd.

'That was nice,' he heard Matthew say.

'Do you want to speak?' she asked.

Matthew shook his head.

Ithrandir glanced. Wyfzira moved forward. The Jades stood up. Aiden followed them through the Royal Chambers, through a long courtyard leading to a vast mausoleum, where servants bowed respectfully.

Aroosa sobbed when she caught sight of Eliza.

Wearing her regalia, Eliza lay on a red sheet in a glass coffin. White petals were scattered over Eliza ó hAodha, the Great Red Queen.

The Jades knelt, while Arif and Matthew cried.

When the Ithfirian preacher led a sermon, Aiden no longer felt like crying. He couldn't unsee what he had just seen. Though he dabbed his eyes for their benefit.

Asif couldn't stop staring. He was speaking to her in his mind.

They weren't looking. Aiden retreated to the city traders. Still no sign of George. Not even a whisper of cynicism. When the crimson sun set, he saw them coming down the cobbles.

'Come Kildana, we have a place to visit,' said Wyfzira, overtaking him with a stride.

55

Aiden ran through the giant golden gates and was disappointed but not surprised that George had disappeared. 'You're going to have to slow down. I can't keep up with giants.'

'An extraordinary person, like yourself?' said Wyfzira.

Aiden laughed, running up the grassy hill. Wyfzira led the way to the rocks, where Aiden had given his friend a name. The stone path exposed itself under thick moss.

Aiden took a shortcut to head him off. 'Why are we going to Leybo's cave?' he asked.

'You'll see,' said Wyfzira.

Inside the cavern, the time it took to get to the giant monoliths, seemed quicker than the first time he passed through. Wyfzira pulled him behind the long monument dedicated to a general and his sister.

'You are an Eli, aren't you?' asked Aiden. 'The original Nephilim.'

Wyfzira turned and smiled, his eyes glowed ever brighter. 'Indeed.'

'How is that possible?' he asked. 'How are you separated? I thought the Eli were a collective. The book said, when God created the First Tribe, they bonded as one. The bond was so strong, arrogance was born.'

'You are in fact correct,' laughed Wyfzira, 'Like you said... one mustn't turn his back on his kin... Djinnkind is my kin. Humankind is my kin. All God's creatures are my kin.'

Aiden felt the warmth. 'Cool.'

Wyfzira's hand sliced air vertically.

The shield was different to the ones he was used to. They were inside a green cuboid.

The others passed him quickly. They stopped by the monoliths to hug the Jades. Then went through a doorway that suddenly appeared.

'Time is passing quickly out there,' gasped Aiden.

Wyfzira squeezed his arm. 'Not many know about this particular story of the first jade queen, but the statue you touched was created for a singular purpose. After the Fallen was chained and taken to Hell, Alfina decided she would surrender her immortality and pass her powers to an heir. Except she had many daughters and many sons. She created the statue to test who was worthy of inheriting her powers. They all touched the statue. Nothing happened. So Alfina put her fire into her stones and created bracelets that could choose a person worthy of leading the Jades. That method was successful and scribed. Everyone forgot about the statue.'

The Jades departed.

The door was gone.

Aiden stepped back, with alarm and puzzlement.

'Come,' said Wyfzira.

With every stride, their green cuboid followed. When they reached the monoliths, the door appeared again. This time it was white.

The djinn, who arrived, walked straight into their cuboid.

Aiden gasped. 'How is this possible?'

'Malachi is Archdjinn, master of chains, master of doors,' said Wyfzira.

'Wyfzira is one I trust on this world,' said David.

Aiden frowned. 'Won't she see us?'

'Not through this shield,' said David, his head turning. 'Bless my eyes. You found it?'

Aiden let him inspect the bow. 'You gave it to me.'

An image popped into his head. David was remembering gifting the bow to a young Hoplite, 'This was created by the brother of the djinn who created the bow Gandiva, and what a battle that was. A lot has happened, Aiden.'

'Still happening. One is becoming,' said Aiden.

'And what do we do when one is becoming?' asked David.

'We don't assume. We allow her to resist,' said Aiden, watching the Archdjinn.

'If we took action today, what are the outcomes?' asked David.

'She wouldn't become the vinx. Hell Queen has the upper hand with a version we have not found. And we lose a good sister.'

'History repeats itself,' said Wyfzira, sadly.

David sighed. 'Now tell me about the ghost. What did we learn?'

'He's my… fireborn father, isn't he?' asked Aiden, quietly.

They straightened, though they hid shock from their faces. 'What makes you say that?' asked David.

'At first, I had this feeling he knew my dad,' said Aiden.

'We were careful to exclude your parents, for their safety,' said David.

'The emptiness inside of me…. Feels like the loss I had when you wouldn't let me use my powers in school. When you said I couldn't go on Wayne's mission. All Father, I know my powers are bound. It is to protect me, I get it. I did not acknowledge it because you taught me. But it's obvious. I have powers that can only be inherited... from… a djinn. My mother is human. Don't get me wrong, I love my dad. But I have always felt there was something missing. It feels like such a long time I have been waiting. George showed me how to save my sister, still it never occurred to me that he was the clue. Every time he spoke, it had meaning. Every time he looked at me, it had meaning. I remembered thinking, I found him. In all the improbabilities, my dead dad came looking for me.'

'When did you realise?' asked David.

Relief washed through him, Aiden laughed. 'When I was poisoned by the Seerlock.' He rubbed his temple. 'It was heavy and stifling, like it was sucking all my strength. George kept me going. I sensed he was scared. For me. At the same time, I felt this incredible warmth wrap around me, probably slowing the poison. How was it possible that we were linked this way? Only blood and love are this strong. I woke up in the hospital, remembering his teasing. George has been protecting me all along. I remember thinking, this is what a dad would do.'

'Too soon,' said Wyfzira.

David reached for his face. He felt Wyfzira's heat. Aiden remembered David plucked memories like strands of hair, but then he was standing in cold.

The air whistled through the roof of the cavern.

'Aiden.'

He looked up.

'Behind you.'

Aiden turned. The two elders were seated on a rock, looking puzzled by his wandering off. 'Sorry. I thought you said it was safe?' he asked.

'We should always side with caution,' said David. 'Stay in the bubble.'

'Yes, All Father.'

'Tell me about the ghost,' said David.

Aiden shrugged, 'He was annoying. But useful. Doesn't remember who he is. I named him George.'

'Tell me what you saw,' said David.

Aiden straightened, 'When Arif walked to Eliza, the guard asked him to step back. No one was allowed near her coffin. But in that moment, her rubies glowed.'

'What does that tell us?' asked David.

'Stones of Echira glowed when Thilgrid Eftienherr inhabits her host. Thilgrid cannot power her stones if the host has no beating heart. It was a precaution that Thespilla asked of Thilgrid, during the First Rebellion, Thespilla knew she may not survive Iblis. It means, Eliza is breathing,' grinned Aiden.

David didn't grin.

'What will you do?' asked Wyfzira.

Aiden thought quickly. 'We need to bring Arif back, or at least the Eye of Ethyrus. It will boost the rubies with enough power to complete her healing. We need her.'

'Yes, we do,' said David.

The smile gave it away. David was hiding something.

'How bad is it?' he asked before he could think.

'Aiden,' David exhaled. 'Petra and Wayne were chasing a lead. They discovered our Great Council Scimitaff was infiltrated. Imam Shafi dissolved it. There was a struggle in the library. Rabbi was hurt. We could not hold the insidious. Imam Shafi gave his life.'

'Oh no. He was so nice. I still have his books,' he said.

'Wayne is missing,' said David.

Aiden straightened. 'What?'

'Eloyhin found a vinx,' replied the Archdjinn softly. 'She is the source.'

He remembered to breathe. 'Okay. Sounds like… Wayne. Too big for his boots. That's why he's not here, isn't he? What can I do?'

'Leave Earth to Earth,' said David.

'What? He-He's my… brother,' he gasped.

'We do not feel. Remember your training,' said David, kindly. The look from the top of his eyelids told him it was a scold.

'Nine become one for Ilgra's Doom,' recalled Aiden. 'One killed by ice arrow. One killed by white fury. One on Earth. One survives Ethyrus. Where there is one, there is always another nearby, so two are becoming. Three to uncover.'

'Stay on mission,' said David.

'Here?' he asked, his eyes burning.

'I had a vision about your parents, it is not one to ignore. You will tell your brothers what you saw. Let them find reason to return,' said David.

'Do I tell Matthew about his dad?' asked Aiden.

'I already have,' said David.

He tried his best to smile. 'All Father… find… Áine,' he said, hoarsely.

David placed a hand on his shoulder and turned him to face the door. 'We enter each battle, son of sons and father to fathers. Their courage, our courage. Do you see what I see?'

'I do,' said Aiden.

'Walk faster.' David stepped inside. The heavenly scent of the Hallway of Worlds spilled into the cavern.

It was obvious now why George was missing. He turned quickly. 'You will watch Eliza, won't you?' he said.

'With all my fire,' said Wyfzira.

'Dark King is coming,' whispered Aiden.

Aiden Deen and the Lost

Preview:
The Second Coming, Aiden Deen And The Lost.

Matthew entered to find everyone had already gathered around the long table. Three sizes of people looked strange, but not unusual for one who was accustomed to counsels in the Jade City. Aifa, Mafius, and an armed Azuran Warrior by the name of Limma, stood beside Ithrandir. Wyfzira and General Soahn were on opposite sides. Dad stood between the Jades and the kid, not realising he was also blocking the kid's dad. But he seemed quite content talking to Arif. It was weird seeing Dad there, it was even weirder seeing Mum standing there, no sickness, no worries. Course, it was the end of all worlds happening right now, but she looked happy. She was trying to ask Rose about her jewels, but Rose seemed to be talking inside her head again. At least they were there. Aunt Sophia was sat in the chair, she had made up her mind to stay clear and do some knitting.

A three-dimensional map of the territories lay from edge to edge on the table. The Venn Varda and the ruins of Rosh seemed to have been constructed with matchsticks, though Matthew hadn't seen anyone use matchsticks on this planet.

Eddie flashed a joyous smile at Ithrandir, who returned it warmly.

'Now we are all here, we can start today's proceedings,' said Wyfzira. 'As some of you are aware,

Selwa, the new Siren Queen, has been sighted. She has begun to test our strength on our own defences, though this does not concern us as much as the possibility of having one of our Emerald mage or aarta fall prey. The latest attack almost achieved this on a routine visit to Ithfir, and close to the ancient trading town of the Daraan. Needless to say, we were very lucky that Selwa did not succeed. No one was taken, and the harm was limited. However, from what we have learned recently, the vinx is strengthening her numbers, as well as her strategy. She opened a roongorwan, allowing the Barda to invade our world, most likely from Keffi. We believe she can send sirens to Earth. If this continues, then everything we have worked so hard to achieve will be for nothing.'

'It is time for decisive action to rid ourselves of the vermin, once and for all,' said Ithrandir.

'She has proven evasive,' said Teiaar.

'We have to keep hunting her,' said Matthew.

'And play right into her hands?' asked Osimion.

'So, we're gonna play chicken, are we?' he replied smartly.

'Lord Matthew, we have many questions that our elite are unable to answer, such as why the seas are not rising fast enough. Why the birds are not migrating. And why our herds are nervous and afraid. The curse is broken, so everything should have returned to how it used to be. Something is not right,' said Osimion.

Dad was scowling, but Matthew had already let Osimion off. 'My concern is valid. Our kid -Eddie- said the vinx is a devourer of all life. You leave her alone, she's going to get stronger,' he said, turning back to the map.

'He's right. A hell queen is treacherous,' said Aifa, 'But may I remind you I have two Azuran warriors unaccounted for. We can't confirm if they have fallen or are just lost.'

'We assume the worst,' said Teiaar.

'I get what you're all saying, but Matthew's right, we need to put her down,' said Arif.

Matthew wondered if he really meant it.

'You can't put her down until we locate the other,' said Dad.

'There's another?' he asked.

'A vinx can't exist without another host. You kill her, her powers will be absorbed by the other one, who I gather, we haven't found yet,' said Dad.

'So, we find the other one,' he said.

'We have strength in unity. Until recently, we were only patrolling near our cities, now we have the entire continent and not enough fit to give service. It is too risky until we have intelligence of her movements.,' said Ophelia. 'We should rebuild our defences and restrict the territories of the Damned until we are ready to deal with the vinx. I can direct our sisters to keep looking.'

Wyfzira sighed. 'Perhaps it would be wise for our esteemed Mage to share with us what vile rant was uttered from Selwa's grey lips, for the benefit of our cousins.'

Osimion looked across the table at Dad. 'She called your name. Richard. She said, you cannot stop… the king. Ethyrus is already mine. I find it intriguing that she is concerned about your capabilities, considering you've just arrived. How… does she know you?'

'They had an encounter with sirens on Earth,' said Teiaar.

'Words from a deranged siren,' said Ophelia.

'I'm not so sure,' said Osimion.

'We should assume she has other hosts,' said Teiaar.

That sounded like she knew something. Why was she looking down. Was she mind-talking?

'If that monstrous, evil annihilator returns, no city is safe,' said Wyfzira.

Rose and her Jade friends swapped glances.

So far, Dad hadn't talked much about his time here. Mum didn't want him to ask, but how else could they learn what he knew? How did counsellors get soldiers to talk?

'You are not suggesting the dark king Abaddon is returning are you?' gasped Mafius, looking quite pale.

'Is he a bad one?' asked Mum.

Matthew laughed.

Dad couldn't help smiling. He stared at her until she grinned, 'What?'

'The dark king is the source of the contagion,' said Eddie, inhaling long. 'He drank the devil's blood.'

The kid seemed different with his parents around, he looked happy.

'It's not possible,' said Limma.

'Yeah, my brother was saying that certain events have to take place before the king's banishment can be lifted, didn't you read them in the scrolls, Eddie?' asked Arif, leaning over the table make eye contact.

'Who's Eddie?' asked Mr Deen.

'Arif behtey, can we call your brother by his real name. Aiden is such a lovely name. It loses its meaning you know,' said Aunty Sophia.

'Jee Mummyjaan,' replied Arif, his face turning red.

Aunt Sophia turned her eyes back to her knitting.

Eddie was incredibly quiet.

Maybe the parents shouldn't be in this room. The Jades hadn't said owt. Maybe they won't. Hospitality has a limit.

'Wa. Sure, another vinx has risen. But she is nowhere near the capacity of Ilgra the Evil One,' said Limma.

'We will destroy her long before she can even contemplate that event,' said Aifa.

Was she reassuring herself?

'I am afraid that moment has come and passed,' said Wyfzira.

The giant was hiding too many secrets.

'What do you mean?' asked Ithrandir, frowning.

Wyfzira inhaled deeply. 'This is going to come as shocking news. I believe the scrolls mention that the new hell queen will rise to take on the mantle left vacant by Ilgra, within nine incarnations. We are not sure if all nine versions will be concurrent, certainly there were two versions of Ilgra when Keffi fell. That's nine times we have to kill her. Nine chances she gets to invade Earth. She will set in motion the return of the Ancient Visitor, who stood boldly by General Leybo's side as he faced Abaddon the Terrible at the Great Battle of the Three Points. The scrolls are perfectly clear in the prophecy, stating that when the visitor returns with the mark of Oleena the Magnificent, then the banishment spell would cease to exist. It warns us to find the one weakness that Abaddon the Terrible carries on his person, so that we may either kill or banish him again. If we banish the Hellsborn king, we diminish her power and we can defeat the Hell Queen.'

'Yes, precisely,' said Limma. 'I have studied the scrolls for years. It says with the mark of Oleena the

Magnificent, his grief-stricken words will hearten Ethyrus free from the Damned.'

'Lord Wyfzira, why do I detect something is unravelling more than you are telling us?' asked Osimion.

'He's protecting their minds since they got here. Wyfzira, you are blocking my link. Teiaar cannot read you either. What is going on here?' asked Aifa, scowling.

Uhoh. The giant was in for it. Now here was a woman he didn't mind. Aifa was alright. She might not be a sharpshooting warrior like Teiaar, but she certainly knew her stuff.

Rose shot a glance.

Matthew inhaled a grin.

Wyfzira's tone deepened. 'Selwa the Vinx has been meddling in the affairs on Earth,' he said intensely. 'We believe she has sent sirens to release the Dark Ones that had been imprisoned by the holy prophets. The political landscape is in turmoil. Humans are being harvested. Earth's guardians are fighting for their lives. It is only a matter of time until the People of Light intervene, and we will not be able to stop the End of Time. We must address the danger closer to home. Selwa set in motion his return. He returned. Were you aware that the Elemma Idreen is from the Clayborns?'

Everyone straightened.

This was getting interesting.

'Perhaps I'd better explain,' said Dad, coughing and swallowing to clear his throat. Dad opened the buttons of his shirt and pulled his collar to expose a scar on his upper chest.

'As you can see, my skin has been burned,' said Dad. 'From there, I guess you can't see it so well. But from here, it's upside down, so I can always see it. The original seven prongs are the seasons of this world and the holy order. And this little star is actually a tiny image of a handshake… my handshake. It was incorporated into the family crest belonging to Oleena.'

Teiaar's hand lifted to her heart.

'Ayla have mercy,' gasped Osimion.

'Matthew, your dad and I were going to talk to you about this,' said Mum.

'They meant well, Matthew,' whispered Rose.

'I don't get it. Who's Oleena?' asked Matthew.

'I am the Elemma Idreen,' said Dad, with a stricken look, his voice trembling. 'Oleena was...'

[Shukriya with buttercups for getting this far. I reckon it's time to put kettle on. Going to have a long cup of tea. x AB]

Printed in Great Britain
by Amazon

37175421R00310